Killerbyte

Cat Connor

All names, characters, places, and incidents in this publication are fictitious or are used fictitiously. Any resemblance to real persons, living or dead, or events or locales is entirely coincidental.

First published by Rebel ePublishers 2009
Edited by Jayne Southern
Formatting: 9mm Press
Publisher: 9mm Press, New Zealand 2024
Original Publication date: 2009
Country of first publication: South Africa

ISBN: 978-0-9814256-2-7
ISBN: 978-0-9814256-9-6
ISBN:978-1-7386219-6-5

With Thanks

Cat would like to thank the following people:

Caleb, Rebekah, Patricia, Josephine, Joshua, Caoilfhionn, Brianna, for being amazingly supportive and for understanding that writing is my thing.

Chrissy Gordon, for being my greatest fan and for total impartiality at all times.

My parents, for instilling in me a belief that I could do anything I wanted to do. So I did.

Galileo, (aka Chadd Michael), for teaching me the value of never saying 'never' and for letting me model Mac on him. Thanks for the dance.

Simon Burnett (author) who has been incredibly generous with his time and is always willing to read and offer suggestions.

Graeme Johns, (author), who knows exactly what to say when the shit hits the fan and who is an all round good guy. I owe you a couple of bottles of wine!

Dave Bean (swear blogger) for his brilliance when it comes to mascara.

Kane Griffin for being the first non-writer, non-biased reader, and exceptionally tolerant neighbor, who doesn't mind being filmed or stalked!

My awesome editor, Jayne Southern, and my equally awesome first publishers.

Much love to you all,

Cat

For the dead who haunt and amuse,

more power to you!

Chapter One

Jaded

You're gonna die, you bitch!

I looked at the words sitting alone on the expanse of white. A ridiculous thought occurred to me. The words were innocent. They had no volition. Just photons squirted out by a display system.

"Uh huh," I said to myself. It was a shame this moron couldn't see my eyes rolling. Woo-hoo, someone else wants me dead. I held the cursor poised over his idiotic nickname, Addictedtolove, waiting. Sunday nights bring out the miscreants; the later it is, the worse the behavior. It was almost Monday.

I'm serious. *You are gonna die.*

I typed a reply, *I'm sure you are, bye-bye*. Then hit the twenty-four-hour ban and watched him disappear. The chat room went quiet; to enjoy the moment I clicked off Real Player and with it the latest Grange album I'd been listening to. The room plunged into deep silence. I stretched my legs out under my desk and tapped away at the keyboard. *What's that now, Stormy? Twelve death threats?* I looked up to see her answer on the screen.

Yup, she replied.

I'd set a new record, the most death threats received in one night. Excellent.

I typed: *Well, that's me for the night then, best check*

my doors and windows.

Stormy replied: *LOL. Talk tomorrow.*

I shut down the computer, not tired, but not interested in sitting at my desk all night either. The house creaked and grumbled like an old man settling into a rocking chair.

I prowled around the house, both upstairs and down, checking every window, door and deadbolt. It wasn't fear that motivated me. It was boredom. Funny really, boredom wasn't something I tended to suffer from. Perhaps I was wrong about the boredom. Maybe it was me being just a little sick of my own company. It sure as hell wasn't empty threats from chat room weirdos. I mean, what were they really going to do? Turn up on my doorstep and shoot me? I think not.

I live outside a very small town, west of Lexington, in Rockbridge County, Virginia; more an old village than a town. It's a long way from anywhere and not the type of place where one has unexpected visitors.

I stopped thinking about chat room weirdos and made a firm decision.

In the morning, I would drive north and visit Mac. What I needed was fun and he was the perfect person for the job. Mac was fun with a capital F. It didn't hurt that he was drop-dead yummy either.

Halfway up the stairs, I heard a car door slam followed by heavy footsteps moving in the direction of my back door. The chat room screen flashed in my mind. People I know would not be visiting at this hour of the night. I scurried up the remaining stairs to my office, snatched my gun from the desk and crept back down. The kitchen light was out, but from the glow of the security lights outside, I could see the silhouette of a head through the back door's frosted glass window. A stupid rhyme popped into my head, 'One two, they're coming for you; three four, don't open that door'. I slipped through the darkened room and stood on the hinge side of the door. It took conscious effort to keep my breathing calm and mind centered. My body was willing to react without the go-ahead from my brain and controlling the twitch in my trigger finger wasn't going to be easy; it didn't like being disturbed in the middle of the night.

The door handle moved, keys rattled. The door handle moved again, this time twisting back and forth. The frame groaned under applied force to the door. Keys rattled once more and the handle now moved freely, unrestrained by the lock, but the secondary deadbolt kept the door from opening and seemed to annoy the person outside the door. It was almost ghostly as the handle twisted back and forth, even if mortal cursing emanated from the dark silhouette. My cell phone rang in the other room.

I backed into the living room and answered the call as I kept my gun trained on the door. I had to wonder how and why someone had keys to my house, as I thanked God for the extra deadbolts that this person didn't expect to find.

"Are you home?"

I detected an angry tone and stifled the urge to reply in

kind. Instead, I returned to the kitchen. The silhouette appeared to be talking into something.

"Yes, I am home."

"Then open the goddamn door." Yep, I was getting tone, not something I appreciated at this time of night. I recognized the voice but still had no idea how he came by keys to my home.

"Why are you out here?"

"Ellie, open the fucking door."

"How about 'No'? How about you fuck off and *never* come back?" My mind groaned: Way to be a grown-up, Ellie! My heart rate was climbing and my trigger finger itchy. He was the last person on earth I would ever give a key. He was pond scum.

I disconnected the call. No point in a brain tumor from the cell phone when he was yelling on the other side of the door. While he hollered, I pressed in the panic sequence on the alarm panel. My old pal Kevin and several police officers would be along presently, admittedly *presently* when you live forty minutes from town wasn't always as quick as I'd like. Tonight, I wanted quicker than humanly possible.

I settled myself by the kitchen counter on a stool. He couldn't get in unless he broke a window because I wasn't about to open the door.

He pounded on the door. I made coffee. He kicked the door. I lit a cigarette.

He yelled at me. I ignored him. He threatened me. "I have a free lesson in manners out here for you. I won't be banned! You need to learn your lesson."

I took a deep breath.

He violently rattled the door handle. "I have something for you. You'll like it."

I remained silent. He cursed my mother. I silently agreed with him that it was all true.

I opened a drawer and found a small Dictaphone and some new microcassettes. I pushed the record button as he told me what he was going to do to me, in graphic detail, once he found a way in.

Maybe he secretly longed for life behind bars or perhaps he was drunk. Insanity was also a possibility.

My laptop sat on the kitchen table. Its sleek black case begged me to open it.

The ranting outside became boring. I grabbed the laptop and settled back on my stool. He yelled louder when I fired up the computer. I figured he'd seen the glow from the screen, and didn't like me ignoring him.

While I basked in the joy of satellite Internet, he banged something heavy against the glass in the door. It could have been his head. God knows it's thick enough.

I signed into Messenger. My pulse quickened. Galileo was online. I smiled. Galileo, AKA Mac, always made me smile and I had someone to talk to while I waited for the police.

I typed into the chat box: *Hey, call me on my landline at home.*

Galileo typed back: *You okay?*

I'm just fine and dandy. I lied to myself on a regular

basis about all sorts of things. It stopped me curling up into a little ball and sobbing like a two-year-old.

Something that sounded like a rock hit the kitchen window.

I flinched as I typed: *Yeah, I need some company is all.*

The kitchen phone rang, followed by another string of curses from outside. I answered the call and hit the speaker button.

"Hey, Mac."

"Hey, Ellie, what's up?"

"I'm having a small problem with an uninvited visitor."

There was silence on the phone as another heavy object smashed into a window. The window vibrated but withstood the blow. I wasn't sure how much it would weather, but so far so good.

"What the fuck was that?" Mac asked.

"That was the problem." I didn't want to worry him unduly and attempted to keep my voice light. "I am being entertained this evening by Carter's verbal and sometimes physical tirades."

I heard Mac sigh.

"That's not such a small problem," he said. "You're okay?"

"Oh, yeah. I'm okay. He's outside having a little fit." Yep I'm okay. If I say it enough times, it will be true.

"Police?"

"On the way, I pushed the panic button."

"Good. So what brought this on?"

"No clue, dude. He did yell something about being

banned, but why would he fly in from Chicago to pound on my door 'cos he was banned from a chat room?" The chat room weirdos entered my thoughts. "I have, however, received a recording-breaking twelve death threats today. Guess it's just my lucky night."

Mac laughed. "I know about the death threats. Stormy filled me in on the chat room activities."

"It's nice that so many morons feel so strongly about me."

"How sure are you that Carter isn't one or all of those morons?" he asked. Now that was something I didn't want to think about in any great depth. If that was true then he was a lot sicker than I'd originally thought.

Yep, I'm okay.

Another rock hit the window. A loud crack resounded throughout the room. A shard of glass flew past me.

"Well, damn, he broke my window."

"Where's your gun?" I heard the concern in his voice and felt the beginnings of dread. I pushed the feeling away with a resounding internal, I'm okay.

"In my hand." I picked my gun up from the counter and chambered a round. I pulled the base of the phone towards me and picked up the handset, the speaker turned off automatically. With my gun in one hand and the phone in the other, I slid from the stool to the relative safety of the floor. There was little chance of me actually sitting in broken glass so I leaned against the cabinets under the sink. With great resolve, I forced out emerging fear and replaced it with general annoyance.

I'm okay, dammit!

The noise outside stopped.

"He broke my window!"

His quiet calm voice came back at me, "I can fix the window."

"Thanks."

"What's going on?" Mac asked.

"He's gone quiet. I don't think that's a good thing." I couldn't hear car sounds, so he hadn't left.

"Me neither."

Something crashed. I heard the tinkle of breaking glass. There was a thud from the living room. It wasn't good. I took a breath.

"I think he's inside."

I reached up to the counter, snatched the taped evidence out of the cassette player and slipped it into my jeans' pocket.

I could hear stumbling and cursing as he floundered around in the dark.

"Get out, Ellie."

I'm getting. No need to tell me twice.

I shoved the gun into my waistband and with the phone in my hand slid the heavy bolt off the backdoor. It was good of him to unlock the door for me earlier. I ran across the driveway, past his car and down the tree line. The security lights were blazing. I ducked into a little clearing under a stand of pines. Small branches and tree limbs jabbed me as I moved further into the undergrowth and out of view. Something crunched under my feet. I knelt down and felt around in the dark. My fingers touched sharp edges and a mess of something slimy. Abigail's nest: I'd crushed her eggs. She must've been frightened from the nest by the noise and I'd stomped right in the middle of it.

I suck as a pet owner.

"Mac?" The phone crackled. Now was not the best time to test the range on a cordless phone. "Mac?"

"I'm here. I put another call through to the police. They're five minutes away."

"Thank you." I brushed my hand across my face to dislodge cobwebs.

A loud cracking sound over by the house made me wish Mac was five minutes away. Something flew past my head. Another loud crack followed, then another. I crouched down even lower, pulling fallen branches in front of me. Random thoughts associated the sound with gunfire. I don't like people shooting at me. It made my tummy feel weird, ruined my congenial disposition, and made me doubt the little voice that told me I was okay.

"What the hell is that noise?"

"I don't know." I wanted to say he's shooting at something, but that was too frightening to acknowledge over the phone. A crazy man taking potshots at shadows was not a good thing to hear about from a hundred and seventy something miles away. I'm okay.

"Ellie, is that gunfire?"

"Maybe."

"Maybe's ass. You keep your head down!"

"I'm okay."

"Let's keep it that way."

"The house will be a mess."

"I can fix the house. I can't fix you."

I pulled the phone away from my ear for a second. "I can hear traffic." I listened. I could hear at least two cars moving at speed towards my address.

"No sirens?"

"Sirens don't make you go any faster and there is no need to advertise that you're coming."

"Yeah, I guess." I still heard anxiety in his voice and it made me feel terrible thinking that I had caused him to worry so much. I didn't know which was worse: Telling him in the morning, and him being really cross with me, or sharing the whole thing from the beginning and him worried as hell. *Catch 22*.

Another crack rang out followed by a falling branch. "Ouch." I rubbed my head. Damn, it stung. It wasn't pain, but it was a hot stinging sensation.

"What ouch?"

"Nothing, just a branch I think. Something hit my damn head." Two cars turned into the driveway. "Hang on; let me talk to the police."

"Okay."

I escaped the confines of the trees and the gnarly branches that poked and scratched me. Keeping to the shadowed area of the driveway, I waved to the first police car. I still had the phone in my hand. The car stopped beside me. Kevin zapped the window down.

"You all right?"

"Yep." I pressed the phone to my shoulder, covering the receiver. "He's got a gun."

Kevin nodded. The two officers in the car with him were already wearing Kevlar. He spoke into the radio. Four officers from the car behind walked quietly past me. Two officers from Kevin's car joined them.

"Who're you talking to?" He indicated to the phone in my hand.

"Mac." I pushed my palm to my forehead in an effort to stop the stinging sensation.

"What's wrong with your head?" Kevin opened the back passenger door. "Get in."

"Nothing is wrong with my head. It just stings." Outwardly, anyway; there was something wrong with me mentally to even be in a situation like this at two-thirty in the morning.

He took the phone as I slid into the passenger seat. I rested my head on the back of the seat, and listened as he spoke to Mac. I tried to hear what he said but all I heard was the intonation of Kevin's deep voice. Even closing my eyes didn't make the words any clearer.

Another loud crack rang out. There was a pause, then an announcement by one of the officers, followed too quickly by another sharp crack. Kevin dropped the phone in my lap.

"Stay here," he ordered, leapt from the car, and set off at a run towards the house. I peered into the shadows created by the security lighting as I picked the phone back up.

"Mac?"

"How's your head?"

"It's fine." I lied. It wasn't exactly fine. The interior light was on, I could see a lot of blood on my palm, and I could feel it trickling down my brow. I pressed my palm hard against my forehead and thought that maybe I should keep it there. A quick succession of shots, fired somewhere near my house, caused me to cringe.

"Kevin's going to take you to Holly's." I knew then he wasn't buying the 'head's fine' line.

"There's no reason why I can't stay here."

"Ellie!" He sounded a little pissed off. "This is not the best time for your usual contrary attitude."

"Contrary?" I don't think so. I am not contrary. Wanting to sleep in my own bed is not being contrary.

Mac was breathing down the phone in a very controlled way. I reached over the front seat and pulled the visor down. Vanity mirrors have their uses.

I lifted my hand off my head and inspected the damage. A decent gash and it didn't look like a branch injury. Blood was still running down my face. I plonked the heel of my hand back over the bloodied wound and pressed hard. I didn't feel any kind of joy at seeing my blood roaming free.

Someone yelled. I heard running and scuffling.

Having some lunatic threatening to kill me in a chat room was somewhat amusing, but having some lunatic act on his impulses, scream abuse, bang on my door, break my windows and fire actual bullets at me, ruined my night.

"Okay. I'll go to Holly's."

"I'm coming down."

"You don't need to." I had plans involving Mac and a museum.

"The hell I don't! Anything you want me to pick up on the way?"

A suture kit would be handy, but it wouldn't thrill him to hear that.

"I can't think of anything."

"Stay in the police car, keep pressure on that head of yours. I'll see you in three hours."

I never said I was bleeding. Kevin! I hope my loose lips don't retaliate and accidentally tell vegan Annie at the health food store that the last vegetable Kevin ate was stuffed inside a pig's mouth!

"Thank you." Tonight was not a good night. It sucked and there were a million better reasons for Mac to drive all the way down here. None of them involved a mad man, a gun, and my blood dripping all over. I started to feel quite cross.

Why it takes so long to capture one man, I do not know. Rolling red and blue lights illuminated the car interior. Either this was a migraine coming on, or another police car had arrived. Two cops carrying shotguns hurried past me. I'll go with the police car, not the migraine. I'm sure that'll come later, brought on by rolling lights and a moron with a gun.

Mauryville had never had so much excitement. The gossip mill will be working overtime tomorrow.

Chapter Two

You Got Me Rocking

Why was my arm moving all by itself?

My arm shook and words tumbled into my sleepy head. "Hey, you asleep?"

I knew the voice and wanted very much to open my eyes. They were reluctant to follow instructions. I pried one eye open.

"Hi." Mac smiled. "How do you feel?" He pushed my hair back off my forehead.

"I'm okay." Both eyes open and semi-alert are usually good things.

He frowned a little and inspected my forehead.

"Good." He leaned down and kissed my head. "This looks quite nasty."

"It feels funny," I replied, moving my eyebrows up and down. The local doctor had glued the cut, holding the edges together with butterfly closures. The skin felt tight.

"I expect it would," he said. "Do you need anything?"

I need to stop attracting freaks. I need better judgment. I need to embrace a new life as a hermit because it might be safer that way. I need coffee. I need you to smile at me and make everything okay.

I chewed my bottom lip. "Coffee?"

"Is that a question or an answer?"

"I need coffee."

"You want to get up and have some coffee?"

I nodded. Getting out of bed proved to be a little more difficult. My body decided it didn't want to move yet. It was still tired.

"What time is it?"

"After two."

It was after two on Monday morning when I sat my sorry ass in Kevin's squad car. I gave this due consideration and reached no conclusion. Not only was my body uncooperative, but my mind had stepped out without leaving a note.

"It's Monday afternoon, babe," Mac said. His frown disappeared and his eyes lightened.

"Ohhh."

I doubled my effort to sit up and get out of bed. The comforter fought back, my legs tangled in the bedding. I threw the covers back and attempted to extradite my legs manually but the sheets were wound around one leg.

"How does a person make such a mess of a bed, while sleeping?" Mac asked.

"Interesting dreams," I replied.

My brain's vacation was almost over. A little voice in my head said, 'Be thankful you have clothes on while you're flailing about like an idiot.'

"You up yet?" Mac was grinning.

"Getting!"

He took hold of my elbow and assisted the process, then directed me to the kitchen. That was unnecessary, as my nose never failed me when coffee was around. All I had to do was follow it. Sitting on the kitchen table were two large mugs of strong black coffee.

Mac pulled out a chair and pushed me into it.

"Holly's in the store, and we can go through when we're ready." Mac rocked back in his chair.

"Okay. When did you get here?"

"About eight; had breakfast with Kevin then came on over here."

Kevin, Carter ... The night came flooding back in brilliant Technicolor.

"Where's Carter?"

"Sitting in jail." He sighed. "He hasn't been arraigned yet. Kevin told me Caine is coming out."

Well, that wasn't a surprise. Kevin would have had to inform the FBI, and they do get a little antsy when their agents dodge bullets. Of course Caine would come down. I mentally slapped my head. Caine meant well. We were partners for five years before he became my boss. My stomach churned at the thought of him arriving and the lecture that would follow.

Mac played with a pack of cigarettes on the table. He spun the pack around. I watched the red and white packaging blur.

"Kevin thinks Carter will make bail, so does the Assistant District Attorney," he said.

"That's ridiculous!" I reached for the pack of cigarettes, took one out. As I lit it, I watched my hand shake.

"Kevin said the tape you made last night shows intent. He wants Caine to hear it. Build a Federal case."

I could see from the expression on Mac's face that he had heard the tape. I tried to recall what Carter had said.

"He was ranting, that's all." I didn't remember him saying anything of real importance.

His eyes met mine. "Babe, I rant ... That wasn't a rant. That was one sick lunatic with a serious problem."

"I don't remember anything that Caine could use."

"He did say something."

"Spit it."

"He said 'I flew in from Chicago for one reason and one reason only. To teach you a lesson. No one rejects me.'"

I stared at Mac. "Okay, that shows he crossed State lines with intent."

"I hope Caine can pull this off. If Carter is freed on a bail bond ... I want you to come back with me."

My heart leapt. That sounded so good, safe, protected, alive ... Like hell! I did not need rescuing. I was quite capable of looking after myself.

Six months ago, I accepted a date with the wrong guy, but I realized he was not for me and ditched him. Any normal person would've moved on. I should not have to leave my home because Carter had freak tendencies and that was the end of that!

I looked up at Mac. His eyes spoke volumes. I saw last night reflected back at me. I heard myself speak, but I barely recognized the word when it fell from my mouth. "Okay."

He placed his cup on the table and blinked at me. His

expression changed to confusion.

"What?" I demanded.

"You're not going to argue? You'd argue black was white for eternity and then change your mind!"

"I'm making a point." I felt a smile spread across my face. "I'm not contrary."

Mac laughed. "Jesus, Ellie! For a minute there I thought there really was something wrong with your head."

He thought right. There must be something wrong with me. Each time I was the least bit involved with a man it became obvious that I shouldn't have bothered. I consoled myself with the thought that I was better off having a friend like Mac than ever dating again.

"Anyway, I was planning on calling you today and coming up to see you. I was hoping we could go to the Smithsonian butterfly garden, I'd like to see the butterflies."

"We can do that. I would love to do that with you."

Yes! "Let's do that then."

Chapter Three

I Can See Clearly Now

I wandered through the bookstore looking for Holly. As I approached the counter, she popped up like some crazed jack-in-the-box. Her blonde hair gave the impression of unkempt wilderness. It suited her perfectly. She had bright-yellow price stickers stuck half way up her arms.

"You hiding?"

"No, pricing new stock," she replied, pushing a book across the counter to me. I glanced at the cover, *Are You Psychic?* I could do with psychic powers. That would remove all of life's little surprises.

I noticed Holly was staring with intent across the store. I followed her line of sight to Mac. He had his back to us and appeared to be flicking through a book. The section title above his head read, New Age. I guessed he'd found an astrology book. It was one of the many subjects that he was interested in.

Holly pulled out a chair and attracted my attention. "Come here."

I scooted around the counter and sat. She nudged me and grinned. "Is there any angle he doesn't look good from?"

I raised an eyebrow and immediately realized my mistake. My fingers sought the cut on my head and applied pressure to stop the sting. I really needed to stop raising my eyebrows for a bit.

"Nah, as far as I know he always looks good." I picked up a shiny, almost holographic, covered book from the pile at my feet and flipped it open. Pictures of angelic beings came alive and danced off the pages. "Wow, these are beautiful."

There was no response from Holly. When I glanced over, she was still watching Mac.

"Yes, he has a nice ass," I mumbled. Her head turned towards me. Her deep-green eyes seemed to penetrate my soul.

"Question," she stated. Her eyes narrowed.

Oh God, here we go.

"How long have you two known each other?"

I bit my lip. "A little over two years." I don't know why, but I felt the need to elaborate. "You know, we only met in person four months ago."

She nodded. Her eyes hinted at her purpose. "Do you have any idea what is right in front of you?"

I frowned. Damn, that stung.

"The counter is right in front of me."

"What else?" Her tone suggested I had better not have another flippant answer ready.

"Books?" I can't be told. Keeping the smile off my face was tricky. "Shelves full of books."

"Ellie!"

Her tone caught Mac's attention. He turned to see what was going on. I smiled at him and received an inquisitive expression back.

Holly called him over.

"Problem?" he asked, still holding the book in his hand. I was right. It was an astrology book: A gold star for me.

Holly glanced at the title. "Have a look in that book and see if all Sagittarians are smartasses and impossible." She huffed and tossed her mad hair over her shoulder.

Mac chuckled. "Apparently, they are only equal to Librans in that regard."

I looked at the book in his hand again. His thumb was a place marker.

"Which bit are you reading?"

He flipped the book open so I could see a chapter on Sagittarius.

"I wouldn't believe everything you read," I mumbled, and turned my attention back to angels.

Holly and Mac pored over the chapter. What's right in front of me? My two best friends having a great time at my expense.

The bell above the door jangled. It jangled again as the door shut. I looked over and saw the stony expression on Caine's face as he strode towards us.

I tapped Holly on the shoulder. Mac moved closer to me and turned to face the approaching male.

"You don't look happy," I commented. Truth is, it took a trained eye to discern Caine's moods. He didn't give anything away, and he sure as hell never looked happy.

"Ellie, Holly," he said with a nod. "You must be Mac." He stepped forward, extended his hand, and introduced himself. "SAC Caine Grafton."

They shook.

"Pleased to meet you," Mac replied.

"You'd be the only one," Caine said, then glared in my direction. "We need to talk."

He terrified most people by what appeared to be open hostility, and yet I found it difficult to keep a smirk off my face.

"Okay if we use your kitchen?" I looked at Holly. She nodded. I flashed a quick smile at Mac. "Back in a bit."

"He comes too," Caine growled. Sometimes his teddy bear impersonation was so accurate I wanted to bend and straighten him to make him growl some more. Today, he seemed less like a gruff old teddy bear and more annoyed.

Mac and I sat at the kitchen table in silence waiting for Caine to say something. Eventually he said, "He's out on bail."

"Conditions?" My heart was pounding. I didn't want this nutcase out on bail.

"He is not allowed within one mile of your home, or within a hundred and fifty yards of your person."

"You think he'll adhere to that?" Mac asked.

"No."

Words fell from my mouth, "Fuc'n Jesus, dammit!" It made no sense. "How the hell did he make bail after firing on police and a fed?"

Caine snarled cynically, "There were 'extenuating circumstances', according to his lawyer."

"And the District Attorney just rolled over and let him walk? Did I somehow click my heels together and end up in another country?"

"Bail was set at two million dollars, he made bail," Caine said. "I want you to go to your parents."

I choked out his favorite phrase, "Not in this lifetime!"

"I want you to go to your parents," Caine repeated. "You can't stay here."

Mac spoke, "Ellie's going to stay with me."

Caine's mouth twitched. He eyed Mac and then settled his gaze on me. "All right: You are back to work next Monday."

"A week off?"

"Doc says one week. Delta has a case in Maryland: Looks as if we have a connection to three unsolved rapes in Arlington late last year. You'll join them in a week."

It could be all over by then. "Those rapes in Arlington, were they the ones in the cemetery?"

Caine nodded.

They had a lead and I was on leave. I should be on my way to Maryland. "You got another cemetery rape, huh?"

"St. Anne's in Annapolis."

Damn Carter and his idiotic behavior. The delight at having a week off was gone, replaced with a sense of frustration. I suspect my voice betrayed my feelings. "I'll contact you when I get to Mac's."

Caine's eyes narrowed as he studied my face. "You better. They'll miss your input." He inclined his head and then directed a deadpan face to Mac. "I have heard good things about you from Kevin. I hope they're true." Caine stood up. I went to stand, but he pressed my shoulders making me sit back down. "There's no need to walk me out. I know the way."

Mac and I stared at each other for several seconds after Caine had left.

"So that's the infamous Special Agent in Charge Caine Grafton. He's hard to read." Mac said.

I nodded. "He is indeed. He likes you."

"How the hell could you tell?" Mac's left eyebrow arched.

"I saw his mouth twitch. That's Caine's version of a warm smile." I looked at Mac. He appeared calm; I knew he wasn't. "Do you believe this bail shit?"

He shook his head in disgust. "No. I shouldn't be so surprised. I've never had a lot of faith in the judicial system. There are too many lawyers involved in it by half."

Moments later, a shadow fell into the room. We both looked up. I half expected to see Caine but instead my brother stood in the doorway.

I had an odd sinking feeling in my stomach as Aidan spoke, "Ellie."

I recovered and replied, "How come you're here?"

"Had a job in Lexington; I called, but you didn't answer your home phone or your cell."

I couldn't answer my cell phone. It was still lying on the kitchen floor at home.

"Must've left it behind. Sorry."

"It's okay. I came right here anyway. You didn't answer

your phone so I thought I'd visit Holly." He turned his attention to Mac. "We haven't met. Are you a friend of Holly's?"

Aidan liked Holly, and I'd known that for a long time. He was checking out the competition.

"Yes, I am," Mac replied. "But I am probably more of a friend to Ellie."

I watched the cogs turn in Aidan's head. They didn't always turn smoothly, but for some reason they did today.

"Mac," he said, striding forward and offering his hand. "I'm Aidan."

How does everyone always guess who Mac is? I don't think I have ever introduced him yet.

I observed the exchange between them.

"Are you all right?" Aidan asked, touching my arm.

"Of course, I'm always all right." My hair covered the cut on my forehead, so I was sure he couldn't see it. I'd refused to allow anyone to inform my family of the incident. I struggled with the notion that they deserved to know something but eventually dismissed it. The night's drama would just serve to worry them.

"I saw Caine on his way out. He seemed grumpier than normal."

"He always looks like that. He was in the area and dropped in for a visit." I had my fingers crossed under the table. He was in the area, and there really wasn't any need to say why. "Sit down, Aidan. You're making the place untidy."

I kicked out a chair for him. He smiled and twisted the chair around, so he could see into the store. I rolled my eyes at Mac, who grinned back at me. Could Aidan be more obvious about checking out Holly?

"Wipe your mouth. You're drooling," I said under my breath.

Aidan hit my arm. "Shut up."

I punched him back. "Make me, drool boy!"

"Sticks and stones." Aidan flipped me off without shifting his gaze from the store.

"Boy, you have it bad."

"Not like you, huh, Ellie," he retorted.

I felt heat rise in my cheeks. Embarrassed at finding myself blush I mumbled something about needing more coffee and escaped to the kitchen sink. I washed the coffee pot to within an inch of its life. I scrubbed until my color receded.

I turned to ask who wanted coffee but before I could open my mouth, Kevin and Caine stormed the room. My mind threw up images of Starsky and Hutch as they would be now. Aged, graying, but still with a hint of cool.

I stood dumbstruck as Starsky and Hutch secured the room like the wannabe superheroes that they were. The only things missing were the trademark cardigan and hair. The latter was a scarce commodity on both heads and graying rapidly.

"Just checking everyone is okay," Kevin said, shoving his gun in his holster.

"Why?" Mac rocked back in his chair and gave Kevin

his undivided attention.

"Yeah, why?" Aidan repeated.

I couldn't wait to hear the explanation.

"Turns out," Kevin started. "Carter is mighty slippery."

"How so?" I asked.

"He was under surveillance, and tailed out of Lexington to here, but he gave the boys the slip."

"Oh dear lord!" I exclaimed, "This isn't exactly a metropolis. Anyone would be lucky to come across another ten vehicles on the road out of here."

"He stopped in at Parker's and didn't come out. The boys went in and found his car, but he was nowhere to be seen."

Caine perched himself on the edge of the table.

"You think he was heading back to my place?" Without a vehicle that would be one hell of a hike from Parker's Apiary. Parker's was on the outskirts of our little town and at least a twenty-minute drive from there to my place. Mr. P was renowned in the area for his honey. I hate honey, but his was supposed to be very good. He had won all manner of awards and such for his particular honey. Why do people like bee puke so much?

"It's possible," Caine said.

"I'm going home to get a few things." My announcement fell into the room, drawing a stony stare from Starsky and a stunned expression from Hutch.

"Now?" Caine said.

"Yes, now. I need clean clothes and personal items before Mac and I head north."

“We’re coming with you.”

“No, you two *find* Carter.”

Aidan had been quiet for some time. “I’m coming.”

“Fine,” I snapped. “Can we get going?” I could have been nicer, but nice was sliding out of my reach. The whole situation seemed ridiculous. How can you lose someone in Mauryville? One main road, four side streets, and they lost him!

Mac nudged me. “Come on then.” He stopped at the door. “We’ll be back as soon as ...”

Caine interrupted him, “Utmost care required.”

Chapter Four

Seasons Of Wither

By the late afternoon light, the house didn't look too bad. There was no sign of life. This was a good thing, as I live alone. I could see boards over the broken windows in the living room.

"What's with the boarded windows?" Aidan asked.

"There was a small incident in the early hours of this morning," I replied. "I'll tell you about it later, let's just do this."

"You will need a copy of the police report for the insurance claim," Aidan said and handed me his keys.

"I'm not losing my no-claims bonus over a couple of broken windows."

I unlocked the front door.

I left both men in the living room and ran upstairs. The shower I wanted would have to wait. I brushed my teeth and washed my face, dabbing the area around the wound. I inspected it for the first time. The cut ran in a slight diagonal from my hairline to a finger's width from my right eyebrow. No wonder it pulled and stung whenever I moved my brow. It didn't look like it would scar badly.

I let my hair fall back, removing the wound from sight. I dumped my toothbrush, cleanser and other indispensable female items into a backpack. Dragged a hairbrush through my hair then tossed the brush in with everything else. I hunted for my mascara and found it in my gym bag. After careful application, my eyes came to life. Satisfied with the lashes, I dropped the mascara into my bag, and then rechecked to make sure I had everything a girl could need.

I changed into a clean, blue top and fresh jeans. I threaded a brown belt into the loops and snapped my spare holster to it. On the opposite side to my holster, I clipped my badge in its black leather cover. I grabbed clothes from my drawers. I rolled everything to fit it into the backpack. From my closet, I took a pair of brown leather cowboy boots, tugged them on, and went back to the closet for a tan leather jacket.

I still needed to get my laptop and cell phone from the kitchen.

Mac and Aidan were waiting at the foot of the stairs. Mac appeared tight-lipped and troubled.

"What?" I asked.

"Come and look at this." He took my arm and pulled. I handed Aidan my backpack as Mac tugged me some more.

"What're you doing?" I asked. He kept on pulling until I stood at the kitchen door. The room was a mess. Chairs upturned and wrecked, the table littered with broken china and splintered wood. Smashed glass glinted like fallen stars in the late afternoon sun. Blood covered almost everywhere I could see.

The knife block from the counter had tipped over. I

counted seven knives strewn across the work surface. One was missing. My eyes searched for the missing knife.

I found it by the back door, covered in blood. A splatter pattern ran partway around the walls and across the cabinets. A knot tightened in my chest.

“Oh my God,” I said. I realized the mess was recent. “It didn’t look like this last night.”

I pointed to the splatter and pooled but not congealed blood by the outside door. “Whoever bled like this is dead.” My mind raced. It was possible that someone’s life ended in my kitchen, but whose and by whose hand? Where the hell was Carter?

Mac pulled me back into his arms and whispered hoarsely into my ear, “It could’ve been you!”

“But it wasn’t,” I replied. “It wasn’t.”

“We need to get out of here,” he said.

I wanted to leave, but I couldn’t walk away from a crime scene. I could see my cell phone and my laptop, splattered with blood. Great! They were now part of a crime scene. The day had just gotten a lot worse.

“Got your cell?” I asked.

Mac released one arm and tugged his cell from his jeans pocket. I took it and punched Caine’s phone number from memory.

“Did you get prints from the kitchen last night?” I asked.

“Yes, the local police handled it.”

“Was there crime tape anywhere or did they finish processing my kitchen?”

"It was completed at first light – tape removed, windows boarded. What's going on?"

"We need a forensic team," I told him, "and I need a new laptop and cell phone."

"You're at home?"

"Yes. My kitchen is dripping in blood." I ended the call and gave Mac his phone back. "Let's go outside."

Aidan was still by the stairs, still holding my backpack. His mouth twisted in a way that I had never seen before. He leaned on the wall and stared towards the kitchen.

"Aidan. Come here," I said. He moved as if he were sleepwalking. "Snap out of it, Aid! Let's go."

He followed us outside and sat on the porch steps. He sat there staring at the ground in front of him. I motioned to Mac and we walked over to the lawn, still in sight of Aidan, but out of earshot.

"He's acting like he's never seen blood before."

Mac gave me a look, followed quickly by. "Cut him some slack that was a big mess."

"It's not like there's a body in the middle of it," I replied.

I was aware that whoever made that mess might still be around. Mac and I both scanned the trees as we waited. I looked over at Aidan. He hadn't moved.

Aidan's voice rang out. "You still worried about losing your no-claims bonus?"

"Not so much," I replied.

Mac's cell phone rang. Our shoulders touched as he answered.

“They’re ten minutes away.” Mac’s mouth was inches from my ear, his voice low.

“Good, then we can leave.”

“And ... there is still no sign of Carter.”

We waited as patiently as possible until we heard the distinctive thwokka-thwokka of helicopter rotors as a chopper came over the ridge.

I watched it hover above the tree line, black and menacing. It descended just as a black Ford Crown Victoria approached. The helicopter bumped to a landing twenty yards away. The car stopped close by us.

Caine hauled out as soon as the door flew open. He ignored us and waved to the helicopter. Three men jumped out before the rotor blades came to a stop. They wore FBI jackets and carried black bags.

Caine turned to face me. “In my car you will find a new cell phone, same number as your previous cell and another laptop.”

“Thank you.”

“I want you out of here, now.” There was no mistaking his zero-nonsense tone. Lucky for him I didn’t feel like hanging around. For once I wasn’t about to argue.

“We’ll take Aidan back to Holly’s, then go,” Mac told him.

We all turned to look at Aidan. He was sitting on the step with my bag at his feet.

“Call me later,” Caine said to me. His lip twitched. It wasn’t a smile: It was a stress twitch. I knew when he heard what I wanted next, his twitch would escalate into a major tick.

"I want my car." I waited for his twitching to stop.

Caine's expression hardened even more. "Where are the keys?"

I mentally traced events of the last few days until I remembered where I'd left them. "In my office." I hoped.

"Do something with your brother while I get them."

I removed the cell and laptop from Caine's car while Mac persuaded Aidan to come with us. I took my bag from Aidan.

He looked into my eyes. "What the fucking hell happened in your kitchen?"

"I don't know. But I think someone died."

"Is this job related? Did someone come after you because of who you are?"

"I doubt it."

"Some random stranger decided to kill someone in your kitchen?"

"Get in the truck, Aidan. I have no answers yet."

"You must have some idea."

"Not yet I don't. Try a little patience."

Aidan climbed into Mac's truck; he was not a happy camper. I waited for Caine.

Caine pulled my car up on the grass. He jumped out. "The car's clean. Get going."

"I'll follow you to Holly's," I called to Mac.

He waved in acknowledgement.

We deposited Aidan with Holly. I gave her a brief rundown of the blood bath that was once my kitchen and expected Aidan to go into greater detail once we'd left.

Mac and I drove off. This time I had the lead. I found myself watching for signs of Carter or a dead body on the roadside and in ditches. By the time we reached Lexington, I was in dire need of coffee. I could see Mac in my rear view mirror. I called his cell.

"How about dropping into a café?"

"Coffee ..." Mac replied. "... directions."

"Just stick close. I'm pretty sure my indicators work."

Minutes later, we turned into the parking lot outside an innocuous looking double-storey, red-brick building. The smell of fresh coffee floated on the autumnal breeze as did leaves from the large oak trees that flanked the building and parking lot. I counted eight cars in the lot, all late models, all tidy. We parked away from the other cars. I reached around, and put the laptop on the backseat, covering it with an old towel. No sense leaving a brand new laptop in plain view to taunt thieves. I took my bag with me. Mac and I entered the café and ordered our coffee.

He looked around the large room then back to me. "A cybercafé?"

"Yeah, so it is; I might check my email while I'm here." I smiled at Mac. "It's an illness just like gambling. Hello, my name is Ellie and I am addicted to the Internet."

"I'll check mine too, and I think they have now determined there is such a thing as Internet addiction."

We were more relaxed now. We took places next to each other at computer terminals. I surveyed the patrons for a few minutes wondering about their lives. Who did they talk to on the Internet? Which cars did they own? How many people have they killed?

Mac mumbled some thing unintelligible.

"What?"

"Glare from the window," he replied, glancing to his right. The setting sun was sending its last golden rays right through the window onto his screen.

"Switch computers." I inclined my head to my left where there was an available computer and no glare.

"Nah, it'll be okay."

We both checked our mail. I scrolled through fifty emails in my junk folder. The subject lines all urged me to grow a bigger penis. I'm a girl! I moved the two real emails hidden among the spam to my inbox.

There were fifteen other emails in my inbox. My mind stalled upon reading the subject line of the most recent.

"Jesus!" Mac exclaimed. He moved closer to his screen.

"What?" I reread the subject line for the fourth time.

"'Where, oh where, could brown-eyed Carter be?'"

I looked over, he wasn't reading off my screen.

"I have the same one." We simultaneously opened the email. There was no text. It was just a subject line. I reread the subject line again, and looked at the sender's address. I didn't recognize it or the name attached to it.

I forwarded my email to Caine with a note asking him to check it out.

"Probably Carter being a dickhead," I said, hoping I

sounded convincing, because I had a terrible feeling there was more to it than that.

"Check out the chat room?" Mac asked.

"Yeah, sure." We both entered the Cobwebs room seconds apart. I typed a quick room greeting and watched the screen as Mac did the same. I took a note of who was in the room. Twelve people, including Stormysky, Bitter_twisted, Metallurgic, Ingesting_donuts, Pebblerock, Fairywing, 4urxtc, DiedMonday, lostAdam, Dhs and us, were all regulars.

Several guests appeared in quick succession; I didn't recognize any of their nicknames. I glanced at Mac. He was frowning; his frown deepened as I watched.

He looked up. "Check this out, Ellie. Bitter_twisted copied me this instant message she received from Dhs."

I leaned over and read the message. Dhs seemed to have the hots for Bitter big time. It was just nasty.

"Dhs has always been creepy as hell," I said leaning back in my chair. Flashing red on my screen alerted me to an instant message of my own. I felt my heart sink as I saw it was from Dhs. I clicked on it and read the message. He really was creepy and more than a little scary. I wanted Mac to read it and tell me it was nothing.

"Mac, read this."

He obliged. "'Oh where, oh where, has the little cat been?'"

It sounded worse when read aloud. My blood ran cold. "Coincidence?" It seemed weird that two people would choose such similar wording. I was just in the room the previous night. I was almost certain he'd been in the room when I received at least three of the death threats. If that was the case, why did he imply with his message that I had been absent? My only answer was because he was a dickhead.

"Maybe."

I replied to Dhs with one word, *Working*.

A minute or so later, he messaged me and said, *Welcome back.*

I chose to ignore it because he was being an asshole. He knew damn well I was there the night before. I dismissed his weirdness. There were a few poems I wanted to read. All recited in text by Stormysky. Then there was a short, bloody poem posted by one of the new people in the room.

"Ack," Mac said. "Gore: Just what we don't need."

Visions of blood splatter danced across my eyes. I typed a polite suggestion to the gory poet asking that he refrain from posting such things unless warning the room first. Similar responses to such poems in the chat room had earned me many death threats. Go figure. My mind toured over the day's events. Carter used to be a regular in our chat room.

"Hey, Mac, has any one else mentioned strange emails?"

"No. They all would have sent us an instant message if they had."

"True." Lucky us, we were the chosen. Chosen because Carter was a moron. That was my most current theory and so far, it was working for me. "I'm feeling twitchy."

Macs hand covered mine. "I know. Me too."

A shadow fell. A hand clamped down on my shoulder.

I jumped almost clear out of my skin and snarled like a rabid dog. Mac hissed out a curse as we both turned to find Aidan grinning behind us.

"Moron!" I snapped at him.

"I just came in for a latte on my way home and saw you both looking awful cozy."

"I'm glad you have recovered," I said with open sarcasm. "Summoned up enough guts to ask my best friend out yet?"

"I will," he replied. "When the time is right."

"Suppose you need to wear big-boy pants and not pull-ups before you ask someone out, huh?"

"You need to get laid," Aidan whispered into my ear.

He peered over our shoulders for quite a while. We could hear the occasional slurp as he sipped at his latte. Suddenly the sipping and slurping stopped, replaced by a gasping, choking sound.

"What the hell?" I mumbled, more to myself than anyone else. I turned to face Aidan.

"You all right?" Mac asked him.

He didn't look all right. He was pale and becoming paler by the second. His finger pointed to the windowpane next to Mac. "Look."

A foggy patch had appeared on the glass. In the middle of the fog, someone had written, *Hi*.

I smiled. "Probably a kid."

At the sound of an email alert, my attention turned back to the computer screen. Life drained from me as I stared at the new mail.

Mac's voice broke the spell. "'I know where you are located. IP tracer. PS. I like your blue car. I see you. Do you see me?'"

I looked at him expecting to find him reading from my screen, but he was looking at his own.

"I have the same email."

A weird squeak came from Aidan. We both stared at the window. Numbers had appeared under the word, 208.85.487.

"What's that?" Aidan pointed.

"Oh, shit!" I reminded myself to breathe. "That's an IP address."

I pulled my new cell from my pocket and hoped that Caine had at least added his cell number to the address book on it. He had.

Mac's eyes and mine met.

I mouthed, "He's here."

Mac stood up. I watched as he went over to the counter.

It took forever for Caine to answer. When he did, I spoke first, "We need police. We're at the Interscape café on Waddell Street, Lexington. Carter may be here."

"Sit tight. Do not leave the building." That may have been a direct order, hard to know over a cell phone. Instructive tone can be confusing over distance.

"I need to have a look around."

"From the *inside* only. Local police are on the way."

"Thanks." I ended the call before he demanded to know why we were at a café and not halfway to Fairfax.

Mac came back. "They have their own servers, I just asked; that is one of the IP addresses they use."

"Ping and trace routing software," I said.

"More than likely," Mac replied.

Aidan was still staring at the window. Mac was looking at me. I saw his gaze veer as he said, "What the fuck?"

I followed his eyes to the far window, to another windowpane, another message: *C u soon.*

A chill ran down my spine. I shivered. I'm okay.

"I'm going to have a look," I announced. "You both stay put." With a degree of trepidation I dragged myself to my feet.

"No," Aidan said. A few heads turned among the patrons. He lowered his voice. "We all go together or not at all."

I considered his response. It sure sounded reasonable from where I stood. No way in hell was I going to let either of them step out the café door.

"I have a thirty-five mil camera in the glove compartment of my car. I need to get it and photograph these windows."

"Oh, man," Mac said. I knew he didn't like my plan. "Are you armed, Ellie?"

"Always." I flashed him a wink and opened my jacket to reveal my Glock 17 snug in its holster at my hip. "Can we do this before the evidence evaporates?"

They nodded. I sensed a lack of enthusiasm as they accompanied me to the door. I felt my pockets. No keys. Aidan must've lifted them. I wished I had never taught him how to do that.

"Aidan, give me the damn keys."

He grimaced and began to hand them over, then snapped his hand back.

"Come on, Aidan, time is not on our side."

"You shouldn't go out there," he protested.

I knew where this was leading and now was not the time.

"Give me the damn keys *now*."

He dropped them into my hand. "I don't like this, Gabrielle."

I gave him my best reassuring smile. The one that said, 'everything's okay'. "I'm the only one of us paid to do this shit. I'm the only one going out that door." I handed Aidan my bag.

"Maybe you should consider other employment."

I ignored his comment. It was same old refrain I had heard many, many times from him. I wanted to snap back, 'that dog won't hunt'. Instead, I told him, "I will be two minutes."

I opened the door, keys in hand, and scanned the parking lot in front of the building. I couldn't see anyone. I used caution as I hurried across the twenty yards to my car. I noted the same cars were still in the lot. No extras apart from Aidan's car and none had left.

I fumbled the keys, shoved one with much haste into

the driver's lock. It didn't fit.

"Wrong key, stupid," I mumbled to myself and tried another. Dammit, that didn't work either. I looked at the key ring. I'd already tried two out of three keys. The only one left was my house key. I scooted around to the passenger door and tried again. Neither of the keys would go into the lock; scowling at them pulled at the cut on my forehead. No matter how hard I scowled, the keys didn't magically fit the locks. I was set to cuss up a storm when something touched my leg.

My heart leapt. I glanced down. There was nothing there. Looking over the car roof, I spied a squirrel scampering up a big old tree. "Vermin," I grumbled. "Disease-ridden vermin." I had a strong inclination to shoot it.

I gave the area one last look before starting back to the café. I paused at the trunk for a last ditch effort with the keys. They didn't fit the trunk lock either.

Someone was whistling a very familiar tune. Ice-cold fear threatened as I searched the lot for the origin of the song. My mantra played for all it was worth in my head. I'm okay. I'm okay. I'm okay.

Walking towards me from the other side of the lot was a hooded figure with hands concealed in the front pockets of a dark-colored hooded sweat top. The hood was partway over the face, and shoulders hunched forward, as if braced against a cold wind.

The wind wasn't cold. There was a light autumn breeze making leaves float in a delicate dance to the ground and squirrels scamper about, frightening people half to death.

I stood motionless listening to the whistling, it was coming from the approaching form. I pressed a physical description into my mind. Gait and posture suggested the figure was male.

I looked from the car to the man to the café: Do I stay, or head back to the safety of the building? One last look at the car just in case I had the wrong dark blue Corolla. I checked the tags. It was my car.

Something felt wrong. I checked the man's position then had another look at the back bumper. I saw something on it, a dark smudged stain that looked like a drag mark. Someone had dragged something over the bumper and into the trunk. My heart pounded so hard I thought it would explode. I ran back to the café, shoved the door shut behind me, and watched through the window. I waited to see if the figure would continue past the building.

Mac spoke to Aidan from somewhere behind me, "Get your sister a coffee."

"You want one, too?" Aidan asked.

"Please," Mac said his voice was quiet. "Can you log us off those computers as well?"

Aidan touched my arm. "I'll be back."

I nodded keeping my eyes on the parking lot. Mac moved up beside me.

"What happened?"

"The keys don't work."

"Expand on that."

"I can't get the key into the lock." I was putting great

effort into not frowning as I peered into the lot beyond the windowpane.

"Epoxy in the locks? It's an old, but effective trick."

"Maybe." I couldn't shift my gaze.

"What are you watching?"

"I saw someone out there: Someone who walked very slowly, and whistled a tune." I tried to keep my voice even and calm as I said, "He was whistling, 'Where oh where has my little dog gone.' Sound familiar?"

"A little too familiar," Mac said. "What else?"

The light was dimming and the man never passed the café building. I stared at the car before answering Mac's question.

I put on my best 'it's probably nothing' voice. "I think there's something in the trunk."

Mac exhaled through his teeth. "What's in the trunk?"

"I'm not sure but I saw what could be blood smears leading up over the bumper."

"Caine checked the car out before we left?"

"He said it was clear."

We both sank into the closest chairs. An air of doom settled over us.

Aidan came back carrying a tray bearing coffee.

"Coffee," he announced as if we couldn't see, or smell it. He set the tray on the table and passed me a mug. "What's wrong?"

"The locks are jammed." I saw no need to mention the trunk and its possible contents or the nursery-rhyme-whistling stranger.

I sipped my coffee. It was sweet. “Tell me this is sweetener and not sugar.”

Aidan pulled a tube of artificial sweetener from his pocket. He showed it to me with a snappish, “How stupid do you think I am?”

“Sorry.”

“Cops are here,” Mac said. We watched two police cars turn in from the street. Their flashers lit the interior of the café, as they cruised to a stop by the front door.

I hauled myself from the comfort of the chair. “I’ll go talk to them.” I opened the door as the first two officers alighted from their vehicle. A tall blond police officer spoke as I stepped out of the building.

“Ma’am, would you be Special Agent Conway?” His voice was smooth, but not officious. He smiled and adjusted his belt. Why do men always feel the need to draw attention to their pants?

“Yes sir, that would be me,” I replied and then got straight down to business. “Did you see a male, medium build, approximately five-feet-eleven, dark hooded sweat top, indigo jeans and black sneakers, in the street or parking lot as you came in?”

“No, ma’am.”

“Will you please put out an all-points bulletin on that description? Note it, ‘Wanted for questioning.’”

“Yes, ma’am.” He spoke into the radio clipped to his epaulette. I waited and wracked my mind for the meaning of the ten codes he was spouting with great efficiency. It was like a foreign language. We used plain English at the Bureau at all times, and now I knew why; 10-23 sometimes meant, arrived at scene, but it could also mean, hit and run, or break in (in progress) depending on the County one was in. Absolutely no confusion there. I forced myself to move on before I was lost forever in my own internal ramblings.

"Do you have a camera in your car?"

The officer turned to his partner. "Alex, the cam, please."

Alex fetched the camera from the back of the car and passed it over with a new roll of film.

"Follow me," I said. I pointed to the windows and requested two photographs of each windowpane from the inside and then two of each from the outside.

"Don't suppose you have a tape measure? I'd like a scale for the outside shots if you could manage it."

"Yes, ma'am." I was enjoying the ma'am thing.

"And footprints, under the windows, if there are any."

"Sure thing, ma'am."

The officer loaded the film and began taking the shots.

"Do you have a name?" I asked.

"Yes, ma'am. I am Doug. Officer Douglas Stevens." He didn't look up from his task until he had finished. As he walked to the door with his partner, he clicked the radio on his shoulder. "Are we secure?"

The radio crackled then a voice responded, "Affirmative."

The radio call and subsequent crackling attracted the attention of several patrons more than the photographs and general police presence had to begin with. Doug became aware of the inquisitive looks and addressed the room, "Sorry to disturb your evening, folks. We have a reported prowler in the area, and are checking it out. I ask that nobody leaves until we are sure that this person is no longer around." His tone was smooth and comforting. Hell, I almost believed him.

I saw several concerned expressions on the faces of the patrons. Doug saw it too. "There is nothing to worry about. I'll let you all know when we're done." Doug exited the building with his partner in tow. The theme to *The Lone Ranger* galloped through my head. Who was that masked man?

I sat down with Aidan and Mac. We watched the other squad car cruising around the lot. They shone their spotlight into trees and under cars.

A few minutes later Doug startled me when he spoke.

"Sorry, I'm a little jumpy." My heart tried to escape from my mouth along with the words.

He just smiled serenely. "I have the pictures of the window panes and also the flower bed. We may have enough of an impression to determine size and possibly type or make of shoe."

"Great." The Lone Ranger and Tonto did good work. "There's an FBI forensic team in the area. I'll get them to come on over here when they're done with my place."

Doug raised his eyebrows. "You're not having a good day are you?"

"It's had its moments." I looked across the lot to my

car. "See that dark-blue Corolla?"

He nodded. "What about it?"

How much worse could the day get?

"It's my car. The locks have been tampered with." I lowered my voice. "And there maybe something in the trunk."

"We'll take a look. Do you have a vehicle you can use to get home?"

"Yes." Mac's truck. Mac's home, oh to be there right now, safe and warm.

"Cool."

I found myself thrown by the thought of the real Lone Ranger saying, "Cool." During my moment, Doug slipped back out the door. I stood watching as they donned latex gloves. A few minutes later, Doug signaled me through the window to go outside. He ran over to meet me at the door.

"Is your car alarmed?" he puffed. The real Lone Ranger was never breathless.

"No."

"We need to pop the trunk with a crowbar, unless you have any objections."

"Go ahead. If you find anything noteworthy we'll add it to the list for forensics."

I rejoined the boys at the window. We stood transfixed by the scene as it unfolded, overcome by a macabre curiosity that made it impossible to turn away.

Alex made two attempts on the trunk then passed the bar to Doug. The metal crunched and gave way. A metallic ring echoed against the building as the crowbar hit the asphalt. I stared, barely breathing, while Doug opened the trunk. He stepped back so fast his foot caught on the crowbar. Alex threw an arm out to steady him.

I slipped out the door unseen and edged my way between Doug and Alex. We all stared into the trunk. My eyes struggled to determine what I saw.

My brain stuttered. “What the fuck is that?”

“I’m not sure,” Doug replied. “It’s hard to tell.”

There was a mass of flesh and fabric, no obvious beginning or distinguishable end. It didn’t resemble anything in particular. I glimpsed a flash of something silvery.

“Gloves? Flashlight?”

Alex handed me a pair of latex gloves. He then took a flashlight from his belt. I lifted a piece of bloodied fabric and revealed what I thought was an arm. “Shine it here for me.”

Alex directed the beam of light over my shoulder.

“Looks like a bracelet,” Doug commented. He was right, that is what it looked like; not only that but it looked familiar.

I leaned in and read the inscription.

“Oh, man.” I gulped for air. My legs threatened to buckle. I staggered as I turned away. I managed to unload the meager contents of my stomach by the back wheel, preserving the integrity of the crime scene as much as possible. Someone pulled my hair back and had hold of my shoulders. A tissue magically appeared in my hand as

I straightened up.

"Thank you," I spluttered, wiping my mouth.

"You're welcome." Alex's voice sounded just as smooth as Doug's did. "Go on back inside. Do you want me to call someone for you?"

"Give the forensic team a hurry-along." I was facing the café and sure as hell was not going to look back at the car. I pulled my wallet from my pocket and handed over my card, "My number is on here, ask for SAC Grafton." I took a breath. "Tell him. We found Carter."

Alex frowned at me. "He'll know what that means?"

"If he asks, tell him he's in the trunk of my car."

"Will do."

I felt disjointed. The building wavered in front of me. Alex planted his hand on my elbow. "I'll escort you," he said, and handed my card to Doug.

I glanced up at Doug. I've never seen the Lone Ranger look that pale. I'm guessing I looked rough, too.

Alex gave instructions, "Make the call Doug, and get the medical examiner out here, too. Request immediate backup. We've got to interview everyone in the café."

Alex and I walked back inside. Mac met us at the door.

Alex's voice filled the quiet café. "Sorry, folks. We're going to have to keep ya'll here a bit longer. There will be four uniformed police officers arriving in the next few minutes." As if on cue, the sound of approaching sirens filtered through the air. "Thank you for your cooperation." He waited for questions. A young man stood up. Alex acknowledged him. "Can I help you?"

"Will the city pay for coffee while we're here?"

Alex grinned. "Sure," he replied. "The city gets the bill for everything consumed from now until you are released."

Now that's a generous city. Alex came back over to us.

"As soon as forensics gets here I'll see if you three can go."

"Thank you," Aidan said.

I looked up at Alex. "Can you open the back of the car for me?" I said, hoping I sounded normal and not as if it was the last thing on earth I wanted to say.

"Yes, ma'am."

He didn't ask why. Together we went back over to the car. I hung back as he picked the crowbar off the ground and pried open a back door. Metal crunched and squeaked as it gave way. These boys sure did like using crowbars. Maybe it was a man thing, something to do with the satisfying noise of metal on metal.

He popped the door then swung it open and stood back. I crawled across the seat and retrieved my new laptop. Having to replace two in one day would not have thrilled Caine at all.

"Thanks." I tucked the laptop under my arm and scurried back to the café, taking care not to look at the trunk.

'I'm okay' wasn't working too well for me anymore. I had a love-hate relationship with my job at the best of times, but tonight I truly hated it. I hated it and I was confused. It wasn't that Carter was dead that caused my dilemma: That couldn't have happened to a nicer guy. It was the way he turned up and the taunting that went on beforehand. If not Carter, then who was responsible? Was it some other freak from our chat room?

We seemed to wait forever; in reality it was only an hour and a half before Caine found us. He strode to our table looking very grim. He held a small paper bag in one hand and a pair of polystyrene tweezers in the other. I wondered what the bag contained but knew it couldn't be good.

"What's that?" I asked, indicating the baggie.

"We found this on the body in your trunk." He removed a yellow Post-it note using the tweezers and showed it to me. The writing was smeared with blood but still legible.

"'Cream of the crop, he's missing his top, no more meals à la gourmet. Breakfast of champions is not Special K.'" I read it aloud. "I don't even want to ask if that means his head was hacked off."

"It was removed from the body. We found it under his legs," Caine said. "Now get out of here," he said and dropped the Post-it back into the bag. "Stay in touch, stay safe."

I scanned his rugged and weathered face for any hint of what was happening in his head but even I couldn't determine his line of thought.

"How quickly do you want a report?" I asked him, feeling detached and very odd.

"A-sap," he replied then revised his comment. "Tomorrow, Ellie. Email it to me first thing."

"I forwarded you a couple of emails this evening before the body turned up."

"Yes, I know. What I don't know is if this related to Carter and is now over or something else entirely and just beginning."

I knew I should tell him about the death threats. I watched his eyes as I spoke, "I receive regular death threats from people in a chat room that Mac and I founded." His eyes flinched. A bad sign.

"And you never thought to mention this to me?" His tone conveyed more than a little frustration. "Jesus, woman!"

My shoulders tensed as I spat back a reply, "It's a poetry chat room for fuck's sake. What are the chances of anyone actually finding me?"

Caine's jaw squared. "I don't know Agent Conway. You tell me? We have a dismembered body and no suspects and you received email prior to discovery. And we have a poem of sorts." He still sounded frustrated. He looked from me to Mac and then back again. "This report will contain all information on this chat room."

I'd intended to provide all the information anyway but kept that to myself. No point inflaming him further.

Chapter Five

Can't You Hear Me Knocking?

I spent Tuesday hanging out at Mac's place in Fairfax trying not to think about Carter. Night snuck up on me. From where I sat on the sofa in his office, I could see Mac immersed in the glow from his monitor. The only noise in the entire house was my fingers tapping on the keyboard of the laptop on my knee. I stopped typing to read an email from Caine. It was a report of the café incident the previous day. I moved my laptop to the coffee table in front of me. My knees were getting hot.

"Hey, Mac," I called out. "They got a footprint."

"Yay," he replied.

"Size ten running shoe, male." I continued, reading the report and trying not to think about the human remains in the trunk. I was doing okay, until the report stated DNA gave a positive identification of Carter McClaren. Why should I care? I closed the file before reading the medical examiner's report.

"You online, Ellie?" Mac asked.

"Yep, satellite."

He grinned at me. "Jump into Cobwebs for a bit. I have to take a pit stop."

"Sure," I replied and signed into the chat room. "Wow, full house tonight." I watched the room and read a few poems recited by some regulars. I saw Dhs was there again. The sight of his nickname filled me with apprehension. He was in the room two days ago when we were at Interscape Café. Sure enough, he messaged me again.

Good to see you, Otherwisecat.

I replied: *Just wanted to say hello to everyone before I go to bed.*

He sent another instant message: *Let me recite a bedtime poem for you.*

A cold shiver ran down my spine as I thanked him.

I called out to Mac, "Hurry up. Dhs is going to recite a bedtime poem for me."

I watched my screen as Dhs began to type:

Dripping from the knife blade
As you surf, the edges of sleep
Longing to rest in the arms of Morpheus
Wrapped in shredded fantasy
Always watching as you dream
Bound by tattered gossamer wings
I await your dying screams
Such a sorrowful frown
Quickly erased by a delicate slice
Across a slender neck
Come sleep with Morpheus, my pet.

As the poem ended, I felt rising alarm. Mac slid behind his desk. "Am reading it."

"Oh, man," I hissed. "Could it be him?"

Mac shrugged. "He's always been freaky, sweets," he

paused. “But that doesn’t mean it is him.”

I typed into the chat room window: *Thanks Dhs, great poem.*

Images of the carnage stowed in the trunk of my car passed in front of my eyes. It took real effort to dislodge the unwelcome intrusion of the horrific scene.

I noticed Mac had left his nick on ‘away’ mode. I said goodnight to the room and followed suit by clicking on the cup icon next to my nickname. I leaned back and rested my eyes.

Less than two minutes later I received an email alert. I heard Mac’s computer chime a second or so after mine.

I opened my inbox and began to read the subject line aloud. As I did, Mac’s voice chimed in, saying the same thing.

“‘Always watching as you dream.’”

I opened the email and read aloud, “‘I await your dying scream. Such joyous imagery.’”

I forwarded the email to Caine and a copy of the room transcript. I snapped the screen shut and took a cigarette from the pack on the coffee table in front of me. I consoled myself with the thought that nobody knew where we were. I’m okay. Mac’s okay. We’re okay.

Mac frowned at his screen. “He’s got to be in here somewhere.”

I leaned back and thought about the chat room.

“The only name that stood out was Dhs,” I said.

“Ohhh,” Mac said. “I have an idea.”

I dragged myself from the comfortable sofa and joined

him at his desk. Yellow Post-it notes covered ninety percent of his desk surface, all containing small beautifully-written poems.

"What idea?"

"What if he's invisible, Ellie? Not someone we can see ..." He clicked an icon that read, *ignore all*. X's appeared next to everyone's names on the room list. Mac scrolled down and then grinned. "Lookie, babe." He pointed to an 'x' that had no name next to it. "That could be him."

"Okay. If he's invisible, how do we know when he's in the room or not?"

Mac reached for my cigarette and took a long drag before passing it back. "I've another idea," he replied, smiling some more. "We need a sentry bot in the room. A bot that will beep us every time someone enters or leaves, visible or not."

I perched on the edge of his desk. "This could be the beginnings of the break we need to find this loser."

Mac replied, "I'll get on to it tomorrow."

"Cool." I passed the cigarette back as his hand reached out for it again.

Mac's eyes cut to the screen.

"We should get some sleep, it's gone two."

I stifled a yawn. "Yeah, we should."

Mac said goodnight to the chat room and turned off his computer. He stood up, and then froze.

"Did you see David's nick in the room?"

I mentally scanned the room list: Nope, no Metallurgic. "No I didn't." My heart sank. "You don't think something happened to him, do you?"

He frowned and shrugged. "I hope not."

We had no idea if Carter's death held a connection to the chat room. All we knew was that when we appeared in the room emails came, and those emails appeared to be from the same person and possibly from a disposable email account.

Mac reached into his desk drawer and pulled out a notebook. "I have his phone number."

"You can't call him at this time of night," I told him, as his hand hovered over the phone on his desk. "What's the number? I'll call the Manassas field office and have someone check it out."

I made the call and asked that they do a backwards check on the number and send two agents out first thing in the morning to verify that David Edwards was alive and well. I quoted a case number for them to document the information and asked that they fax the report immediately to Special Agent in Charge Caine Grafton at the Hoover building.

"Okay done." I replaced the receiver in its cradle.

"Good ... bed!" Mac said. "Don't give me that look either. We both need rest so we are clear-headed tomorrow."

He turned out the office lights as we left the room. Together we checked all the door and window locks.

Mac opened the guest room door for me. The large dream catcher suspended above the bed caught my eye as it swayed gently. He kissed me on the cheek. "Sleep well, sweets."

I smiled back at him. "You too."

Mac closed the door on his way out leaving me alone. I felt tears prickle in my eyes and a lump rising in my throat. A silent waterfall of tears cascaded unchecked as I kicked off my boots and jeans.

I could barely see through my tear-filled eyes. I attempted to place my gun on the bedside cabinet. I missed and it fell onto the thick carpeting. I left it there. I tugged off my sweater and dropped it on top of my jeans and boots. I left my short tee shirt and climbed between the cool sheets.

It was a relief to turn off the lamp and plunge the room into a blanket of darkness. I rolled over and pressed my face into the pillow, hoping that the sobs that wracked my tired body would go undetected. Pent-up emotion from the previous twenty-four hours flooded from me into the soft pillow.

I gave up admonishing myself for behaving like a simpleton and let the cleansing process run its course. Eventually, I drifted into an exhausted and emotionally-drained deep sleep.

Sometime during the night, an image lodged in my mind, a knife with the blade flashing in pale light. Words appeared as if cut from newspaper headlines: Dripping, watching, slicing, dreaming, always. I rolled over to escape the images and encourage my mind to drift back into a deep, dreamless sleep. Lost in the dark, the nightmare worsened. Willing myself to wake did nothing. There was no light. Just hands grabbing and pulling. I recognized a noise: The sound of duct tape ripping off a roll. I could no longer open my mouth. I think a knee pressed on my chest. Someone pinned me down. My voice was silent as if the dream captured my words before they became audible. I breathed in hard through my nose: In the sudden intake of air I smelled a faint spicy cologne. My dreams don't have smell.

My right hand was suddenly free. I reached up and connected with warm flesh. I didn't recall dream people being touchable and warm. I wasn't asleep. A small voice in my head said, *Epithelia!* I raked my nails against the warm skin under my hand, as hard as I could. I heard a slight yelp, then something sharp and cold pressed under my jaw.

Time this ended.

I struggled to get away, kicking out at the heat coming off the body close to me and hoping to propel myself out from his grasp. He grabbed my wrists. By the way he held my wrists in one hand, I knew he was a lot bigger than me. There was a ripping sound. More duct tape! I felt it around my wrists. I kicked out some more. He sat on my legs. Again duct tape ripped. My feet no longer moved independently. I felt movement. He dragged me to the edge of the bed then picked me up then put me down a short distance later. I knew I was on carpet. A door closed very close to me. It was even darker than before. I pushed my legs out and connected with a wall.

I lay still and listened.

I heard a faint sound that I thought was a light switch and muffled footsteps. Fabric rustled. Someone moved a curtain. Footsteps again. This time accompanied by a door opening. The footsteps moved onto a tiled surface. The bathroom.

The footsteps returned coming ever closer.

"Ellie?"

It was Mac. I couldn't reply. I kicked at the wall.

A door opened. Light flooded in, chasing away the darkness and the nightmare.

"Jesus!" Mac said as he knelt down beside me.

I tried to say, "I'm okay." But I wasn't so sure and no words came out of my mouth.

He ripped something off my face.

"Ouch." I pulled my head away and saw duct tape in his hand.

"Sorry."

Mac helped me sit up. I could see a .357 magnum in his hand.

"Mac?" I was beyond caring if I sounded shaky or scared or anything else. "He might still be here."

"No one is in this room but us," he replied. "One sec."

Mac strode across the room and locked the outer door. He picked up the phone from the dresser and pressed 911. While he waited for someone to answer, he took scissors from a drawer and cut the tape from my wrists and ankles. He requested police and EMS. He gave a brief description of what he'd found and told them the person could still be in the house. Mac laid the phone on the floor.

"They're on the way," he said.

He was frowning at me but it wasn't a frown, more of a worried-concerned thing. I was fighting tears and inner terror and I desperately wanted to tell him how scared I was, but I couldn't.

"You okay?" His hand rested on the back of my head, his fingers entwined in my hair.

"I'm okay," I whispered. I wasn't okay. Somehow his gun came back into my view.

"Hey ... get rid of that. Put it away in a drawer or something."

Cops don't like to walk into a situation and find someone with a gun, it caused confusion. I wasn't prepared to take a chance that Mac could be hurt.

Mac dropped the gun into a shoebox in the closet.

"Do you get the feeling we have become playthings for a psycho?" I asked, inspecting my right hand. If it wasn't a dream then I did mark him and I had a decent amount of his skin under my nails.

"What?" Mac asked giving me a very strange look.

"Epithelia," I replied, showing him my hand. "I don't know where I scratched him, but I did, and it was deep. I made him yelp."

Mac took my hand in his and scrutinized it. "You broke a few nails in the process, babe." His smile didn't quite disguise the worry on his face or in his eyes. "I need a cigarette."

"In my bag. In the zipper pocket on the side, you'll find two packs of smokes and a lighter," I told him.

"Yay." He kissed me on the top of my head. It was affectionate, sweet, and I felt cared for. I had no idea why kissing the top of my head had such an impact on me.

"Help me up, Mac. I want one as well."

I felt a little wobbly and leaned against him for a few seconds to catch my balance. It was a relief to be out of the closet. I still wasn't a hundred percent convinced any of it was real. I tried to make sense of a dream that wasn't, or was it? I sat down on the bed with unintentional haste.

"You all right?"

"Yeah. I think sitting is safer than standing." I tested my smile, it seemed to work, and I received a smile in return. He turned his attention to my backpack.

A small drop of blood landed on my thigh. Mac sat next to me, lit two cigarettes and passed me one. My hand wasn't the steadiest. I looked down at my thigh as another drop of blood fell.

"What the hell?" I exclaimed. "Where's it coming from?"

Mac watched another drop land on my leg. "Your throat, Ellie."

My throat? No way. I touched my neck with my left hand, running my fingers up under my jaw and across my throat. I could feel something, a line that ran almost from ear to ear. I looked at my hand and found blood smeared all over my fingers.

Another drop landed on my leg.

I looked at Mac.

"It's not coming from my throat. That wouldn't drip onto my thigh. It would run onto my tee shirt." I didn't want to dwell on why my throat was bleeding.

Mac stared at me for a beat, then grabbed my hand and pulled me to my feet. We stood as far away from the bed as we could and with much trepidation looked up. Something ghastly hung from the ceiling in what looked like a piece of cheesecloth. Dark-red drops were forming and releasing, plummeting onto the exact place where we'd sat.

"Oh, euwwww." I backed away until I was leaning on the door.

"That's not the dream catcher," Mac said, before turning several shades of green and running for the bathroom.

I could hear him barfing and clamped a hand over my own mouth trying to curb the urge to vomit. Being a sympathetic vomiter is no fun especially when someone else already occupied the bathroom. I found myself looking at the ceiling trying to figure out what was wrapped in the cheesecloth. It didn't look very big. I knew all of Carter was accounted for and that knowledge didn't thrill me. It meant this was part of someone else. I hoped it wasn't Mac's cat.

A loud bang from outside the door made me jump. I settled myself with a deep breath, half expecting the police to announce their presence any second.

Mac emerged from the bathroom. I could see he was going to great effort not to look up.

"Did you hear the bang?" I asked. We made eye contact and maintained it to stop our eyes drifting to the ceiling.

"Yes."

"Hopefully it's the police?"

A flashlight beam shone into the room from outside. Several minutes later we heard a loud male voice call into the house, "Fairfax Police Officers, we're coming in."

"That bang wasn't the police," Mac said. "Different direction."

"They'd have more than one team coming in."

We waited until the booted footsteps were level with the bedroom door before Mac called out, "We're in here."

My mind ran a pre-recorded message, 'please be the cops, please be the cops!'

I heard every drip that fell from the ceiling, from the second of its release until its splashdown on the bed. All I wanted to do was get the hell out of the room.

I listened to the noise out in the hallway: Sounded like two entry teams converging.

"How did our Unsub get into the house?" I wondered aloud.

"I don't know," Mac replied. "It wasn't from the front of the house. I checked doors and windows on my way to you."

Someone knocked on the door. "Police!" A burly uniformed police officer stepped into the room. "Are you hurt?"

"No," I replied. "I'm cold. I'm pissed off. I'm in need of coffee. There's something disgusting dripping from the ceiling but I am not actually hurt."

The officer tilted my chin up with one finger. "That qualifies as hurt, ma'am. There is an ambulance out front." He turned his attention to Mac. "Sir, are you hurt?"

Mac shook his head. The cop inspected his face. "You have blood on you."

I looked at Mac. He did have blood on him, small streaks of blood on his face.

"It's not mine," Mac replied. He took a breath but his voice still trembled. "It's from up there." He pointed to the ceiling above the bed without glancing up.

"Oh," the officer said, he focused on the ceiling. "Ohhh."

Another cop appeared in the doorway. The first cop spoke to him, "Andy, escort these people out to the ambulance."

Officer Andy stepped up beside us and prepared to escort us. I addressed him, "Can I use your cell phone?"

"Why, ma'am?"

"I'm a Federal Agent. I need to call my SAC. This maybe related to a case he's working on."

He pulled his phone from his belt and handed it to me with a grin on his face. "You're her, huh?"

I tried to raise an eyebrow, but the cut on my head still pulled a little. "Her?"

"The Fed, whose ex ended up in the trunk of her car in Lexington?"

I did a mental groan, yay, now the whole state is talking about me. Guess that'll only get worse once every cop in Fairfax gets a full description of my underwear. They should get their facts straight, though. He could hardly be termed my ex when we only went on one ill-fated date.

"Yeah, that's me."

He nodded and replied, "People are scary. They're calling it the 'Chat Room Killer Case', on account of your chat room."

Oh man, how much information was released? Chat room killer indeed! A typical lack of imagination shown by all.

"Great." I called Caine. The police escorted us out to the waiting ambulance as I told Caine what had happened. He was less than impressed to find out forensics were needed again.

I chose not to tell him I had a fresh cut; it was little more than a scratch and not worth mentioning; it didn't even sting yet. Caine demanded to speak to the officer in charge. I looked around and found the officer whose phone I was using standing nearby.

I held the phone out to him. "Sorry, he wants to speak with you."

I sensed Caine was about to unleash his mean temper. The cop took the phone.

"Come on, Ellie," Mac said. Two paramedics wrapped blankets around our shoulders. I heard him mutter, "I need clothes."

"So do I," I mumbled, while being helped into the back of the ambulance.

Mac grinned. It was a little lopsided and very cheeky. "Oh no, you look just fine."

"Now how did I know you'd say that?"

He shrugged and winked at me.

It took the paramedics mere seconds to determine that I would in fact survive my current injury and that the wound was indeed superficial. The evidence I carried under my nails needed removing and preserving. The paramedics complied, and let me extract the evidence myself.

"My next request is an escort so we can get some clothes and personal belongings," I told the officer.

"Yes, ma'am, but I can't let you back into that bedroom."

I scowled. "My bag is in there and my gun."

He gave a half smile. "I'll bring your gun to you."

"Thank you." I turned to Mac. "Looks like you get your wish. My clothes are in my bag ... I'm stuck in this tee shirt and panties till I can get some spares."

"As delightful as that sounds I think it's a little too cold to be wandering around scantily clad. You had jeans in the dryer. Did you get them out?"

"No."

"Then they're still in there." He smiled and tapped his head with one finger. "Steel trap."

The officer in charge cleared his throat. "If you two are ready, I'll take you back in so you can retrieve some belongings. Agent Grafton is on his way out. His approximate ETA is thirty minutes."

We walked beside the police officer into the house. Inside, another officer told us that the upstairs was clear and Mac was free to get whatever he needed and to dress. Mac headed for the stairs. I knew he didn't want to hang around any longer than necessary.

I made my way to the basement and found a pair of my jeans in the dryer. I wished there had been a sweat top in there, too, but there wasn't. I pulled on the jeans while a police officer waited. He opened the door as I walked towards him. "Ma'am."

"Thank you. I need to go to Mac's office."

He followed behind me. I piled my wallet, credentials and cell phone on my laptop case. Mac appeared in the doorway carrying a black overnight bag and a jacket.

"You done?" he asked me.

"Yep. Is there anything you need from in here?" I gathered my belongings into my arms.

"Yeah, my wallet." He walked over to his desk and picked up his wallet and the notebook he had neglected to put away earlier. "Car keys?"

"Kitchen counter," I replied, without thinking.

He nodded. "Right, that's it let's go."

He took the jacket he'd had over his arm and draped it around my shoulders. "This will swim on you but at least you won't freeze."

"Thank you."

"You're very welcome."

The officer by the door said Caine had arrived on scene.

Mac hissed into my ear, "It's not a scene, it's my house!"

"I know. I'm sorry." I felt bad for getting Mac involved in the situation at all and even worse for bringing something so alarming into his home. I was feeling pretty low and unworthy as a friend. He placed his hand in the small of my back and walked me out the front door.

As we descended the porch steps, he said, "This isn't your fault. It's shitty as hell but it isn't your fault."

Caine was waiting for us. I read correctly his unimpressed expression. "Have either of you given statements?"

"I think they were waiting for you," I replied.

"Fine, great, good," he spluttered. "I'll get someone to take your statements." He spun around, there was an officer standing a little more than three feet away. Caine pointed at him. "Can you take a statement?"

The officer nodded.

"Then do it!" Caine demanded.

The officer stepped forward into the glow of the security lights, he acknowledged us both. I noticed something. Mac knew this person.

"Take Mac into the living room. Separate interviews. Come for Agent Conway when you're done with his statement," he told the officer.

Mac rolled his eyes at me as he led the way to his own living room. Half an hour later, he emerged and it was my turn.

After the longest, most bizarre half hour I had ever spent, I, too, emerged, wondering all the while, how insane my story sounded. I was retelling what started as a dream that wasn't. But it may have been or at least part of it may have been. Once back outside I discovered Caine barking orders left, right and center. No one was enjoying his presence.

I grabbed his elbow and commented in his ear, "This is not helping."

He glared at me, then his eyes softened and his facial muscles relaxed.

"In case you missed it ... these guys are the front line and if you piss them off they may not be so keen to help in the future!"

He twitched remarkably, his steel-gray eyes narrowed. "Gimme a sec." He disappeared into the house.

"Where's he going?" Mac asked, watching Caine stride away.

"Hopefully to apologize to the police on scene for his asshole behavior."

Mac raised his eyebrows at me. "He pissed?"

"You could say that."

Caine joined us a little while later. He appeared somewhat humbled, and his manner was more agreeable.

"You two are free to go. I want you to check into a hotel, out of this area." He handed me his own car keys. "Take my car."

Caine turned to Mac. "Sorry, Mac. We're keeping your

truck, it contains evidence."

I saw the look of horror on Mac's face. I guessed this was something else he didn't want to know.

"You're going to need clothes and such, Ellie." He gave me a long look. "Something that fits would be a start. Use the company credit cards for what ever you need, and that goes for the hotel, too. I don't want to see your actual names appearing on anything traceable to a location. Zero paper trail."

Mac looked very serious. I don't think I have ever seen him look so serious.

Caine passed Mac his gun. "Found this in a shoebox," Caine said. "Tomorrow I want you both to meet me at my office at the Hoover building. I will arrange for you to have a permit to carry and temporary credentials that say you're with us. Make sure you are always armed."

Mac's tanned complexion blanched as Caine continued with his instructions.

"Keep off the Internet; keep out of the chat room ... unless you use satellite. Use your mirrors. Be evasive. This person may be a watcher and if so, he's probably watching us now." Caine's concern was obvious in his voice, but as always, his facial expressions gave nothing away.

"Okay," I replied.

Caine studied my face. "Are you all right?" he asked, tilting my chin, and inspecting my throat. "Did you think I wouldn't find out?"

I shrugged. "I'm fine."

"Might pay to get a turtleneck sweater when you go

shopping. That's going to draw some attention."

"Good idea." I had a question burning to break forth. I just had to know. "What's in the truck?"

Caine looked set to evade the question.

"Tell me."

"We're waiting on the medical examiner. We're not sure who it is yet." He delved into his pants' pocket and pulled out a paper baggie. This time Caine read the blood-smeared yellow Post-it note to us, "'The sky is falling, screamed the martyr, my blood dripped from the ceiling, I met a fate like Carter.'"

Yay, another sick poem. So far, none of the poems triggered any familiarity in their style or lack of.

Mac and I made eye contact. I knew we were thinking the same thing: David Edwards AKA Metallurgic.

"There's a possibility it maybe someone from Cobwebs," I said. "I asked the Manassas field office to locate David Edwards when we noticed he was missing."

"I'll contact them. We're going to be here for the rest of the night and most of the day."

"How'd he get into the house?"

"We found a circular piece of glass missing from the backdoor. I'd say he cut a hole in the glass, then reached in and unlocked the door."

"It's not even an unusual skill to have." It would've been better for the investigation if he'd used some cool Special Forces way of gaining entry. At least then we could've narrowed the investigative field.

"I know. You two get going, find a hotel and get some

sleep. Meet me at my office at five tomorrow afternoon. We'll know more then."

"All right," I replied, masking a yawn. I looked around but couldn't see our belongings. "Where's our stuff?"

"I put all your things in my car. Go, Ellie, take Mac, and get out of here." Caine stepped forward and did something completely out of character. He hugged me. I wasn't a hundred percent sure how to react to that, so I didn't react at all. Somehow, a fatherly hug from my boss was enough to make me realize how dangerous the situation was. He shook Mac's hand and said something to him that I didn't hear.

We walked down the dark street and found Caine's car. I turned the ignition key and we left without looking back at the line of police vehicles or the house. The quiet suburban neighborhood transformed into a sideshow and every freak in the County attended.

Chapter Six

Tumbling Dice

We twisted and turned our way into Washington DC, doubling back several times until I was sure nobody was following us, before we found a hotel.

I took care of checking in, signing us both as out-of-town Federal employees, which was by no means unfamiliar to the staff of the Marriott. Our lack of luggage raised no eyebrows, either. It wasn't unusual for federal agents to arrive minus luggage in the early morning. I was sure agents didn't normally arrive wearing a jacket that belonged to a much bigger person and no footwear.

Twenty minutes later, I left Mac flicking through TV channels and went into the bathroom. I turned on the shower, and removed what few clothes I wore. I inspected my yellow tee shirt. There was a good deal of blood smeared on it, especially at the neck. I soaked the shirt in cold water and scrubbed the blood with soap, then hung it over the towel rail to dry. My jeans were perfectly fine so I folded them and then placed them on a shelf below a huge mirror. I stood under the hot water for a long time refusing to let my mind wander back to the events that led to us being in Washington. Despite my protests, parts of the dream managed to sneak into my conscious thoughts.

The room filled with steam until I couldn't see in the

mirror at all. I didn't want to see myself, or the latest physical wound. I didn't want a reminder.

I wrapped a thick, white hotel robe around me and began towel drying my hair as I went back out to the room.

"Come here," Mac said, holding his hand out to me. He reclined on the bed, resting on several pillows with the TV remote in one hand. Mac leaned forward and patted the bed in front of him as he moved his legs. I sat with my back to him. His legs stretched out either side of me. He took the towel from my hand and finished drying off my hair while he talked. "They mentioned the killer on the BBC. How weird is that? Even had a shot of the neighborhood."

"Pretty weird. Did they say anything much?" It just keeps getting better, now we're international news.

"Nope. Just that it appeared as though the chat room killer had struck again."

I ran my fingers through my hair trying to detangle it a little. Something tugged my hair. I caught sight of a hairbrush in Mac's hand. I smiled. "Always thinking, huh?"

"I have my moments. I scooped up your stuff from the bathroom. Girls need such things," he replied. Mac brushed my damp hair as we watched an infomercial for the Miracle Knife III.

"How's your throat?"

"My throat is fine. My forehead is fine. They both pull a bit, but it's fine." I considered that 'fine' wasn't the right word, but would do for now.

He put the brush and remote on the nightstand, and

wrapped his arms around me, pulling me close. Wednesday's sun peeked through a gap in the curtains. My eyes stung. I snuggled against Mac and closed my eyes.

Sometime later, strong sunlight dappled the room, causing me to stir. I could feel Mac's body against mine. I sighed. It wasn't so bad being rescued.

My eyes closed, blocking out the daylight. Sleep came in the safety I found within his strong arms. No dreams, no nightmares, just blissful deep sleep.

The next time I awoke, I rolled over and reached out to an empty bed. I sat up and flicked my hair back off my face. The smell of fresh coffee wafted into the room on a light breeze. I took a minute to work out where I was. A shadow fell over me. A hand reached out and brushed a stray hair from my eyes.

"Coffee, sleepy head?"

I smiled raising my eyes to see his face. "Please."

Mac was grinning at me. "You're all tousled and cute."

I felt my cheeks flush and hoped he wouldn't notice. Who was I kidding? He noticed everything.

He grinned. "You really are cute."

The blush deepened. "Shush you. Where's my coffee?"

"Get up, it's waiting." He disappeared out the door to the balcony.

I dragged myself from under the covers, rearranged the robe I was almost wearing, and joined Mac sitting at a table outside on the terrace. We drank coffee and watched people move about on the street below.

"What time is it?"

"Almost three," Mac replied.

"We should get moving. I really need clothes." I stretched my legs out in the warm sun, the robe fell away exposing my thigh. I flipped the robe back, covering my legs. I heard Mac sigh. I looked up to see what he was doing. He was grinning like a little kid with his hand caught in a cookie jar.

"Oh really?"

He laughed and said, "Uh huh."

"In your dreams!"

"We'll see."

With much effort, I ignored him. I drank my coffee while considering how the rest of the day would shape up.

A thought occurred to me. "Oh man!"

"What?"

"I'm going to have to walk about the city in socks."

Mac's head tilted back. "Oh yeah, you're bootless."

"What must people have thought when a shoeless FBI agent with no luggage and blood stains on her tee shirt arrived at the hotel at seven this morning?"

"Nothing compared with what people are going to think this afternoon. It's normal to have shoes on when you go shopping for footwear," Mac remarked. "Drink your coffee, then we'll go shop." He paused then said, "I called my Dad earlier, from your cell. I gave him your number, hope that's okay."

"Of course." I was still preoccupied with my lack of clothing. "Everything all right?"

"Yeah, Dad had already learned of last night's incident from Darren, the cop back at the house."

"Uh huh." I was right, he did know that cop.

"Darren told Dad about the killer and Mom overheard. She freaked a little. Dad said we can stay with them." He shook his head from side to side. "Not even as an absolute last resort."

"I reckon." I agreed. That was the last place on earth I would consider staying. Well, the second last place on earth: The first being my own parents' home.

"Oh, and Darren found my poor terrified cat and took her to Mom and Dad's."

"Good." I am not a cat person, but even I like Mac's cat and I was relieved it wasn't part of the cat hanging from the ceiling.

I picked up my cell phone and called Caine. "You found this prick yet?"

"No, not yet, Ellie."

I snapped, "Why the fuck not?" before wrestling back some control. "By the way, the BBC ran a short bulletin on the chat room killer early this morning."

"Not good." He groaned. "We're gathering evidence. We need a goddamn break. I have people working around the clock trying to track everyone from that chat room of yours. Do you have any idea how easy it is to create an email account with false information?"

"Well, yeah. Can't you just run a ping and trace?"

"You'd think that'd be easy, right? Ohhh no, several Internet providers are fucking us up. They're having privacy issues. I have to get warrants for people who have no names yet. Any clue how that's going down with the Deputy Attorney General?"

I took a breath. "People are dying. Not only that but dead people keep turning up near me. Any clue how that is going down with me?" I knew I was losing it. "Fuck privacy issues!"

"Settle," Caine soothed, then changed the subject. "You got clothes yet?"

"No."

"Shop, then get your ass over to my office." He was quiet for a beat, "Tell Mac I have temp credentials and a permit for him."

"Are we done?"

"See you at five," he replied.

I pressed the end button and dropped the phone onto the table. "How hard can it be?"

"They haven't found him?"

"Nope."

"Cheer up. They will. Go dress. We have to shop."

I nodded.

"I'll be ready in two minutes. It's not like I have much to put on." I may not have had many clothes to wear but thanks to Mac and his cleverness I had my mascara; it could've been worse.

Minutes later, I was dressed.

"Mac can I borrow your belt?" I asked.

He unthreaded it from his jeans and handed it to me.

"Thanks." I never did like this pair of jeans. They fit

great right from the drier but from then on in it's a case of the ass bagging out and waistband loosening almost immediately. I couldn't wait to get some that fitted properly.

We entered the elevator. I wore my short yellow tee shirt which barely met my jeans so there was little hope of concealing the gun I'd shoved in the waistband. I thought the white blood-splattered socks on my feet were a nice touch. With no hair tie to hold it back, my hair kept falling over my face. But I had a subtle coat of mascara upon my lashes and that gave me confidence.

The elevator doors opened and we stepped into the people-filled lobby. The little voice in my head told me to ignore everyone. They were just jealous of how good I looked. Yeah, right. A blond guy caught my eye then smiled. Something jerked in my memory, he was familiar. Album cover familiar. Grange's lead singer, Rowan Grange. Just my luck, one of the biggest rockers of all time sees me shoeless in DC. I looked back to see his eyes spark with amusement. Awesome: I live to amuse.

"Where shall we start?" Mac asked. His voice broke the moment wide open, I was more thankful than he could ever understand. I decided not to mention Rowan Grange.

"Brook Brothers." I glimpsed confusion on Mac's face. I could tell right off that he was trying to retrieve directional information.

"Where are we again?"

He had picked up a brochure from the front desk and

was reading a map of the area. I heard the elevator doors close, Rowan disappeared.

"Ah, the oxymoron for the day." I grinned. "Give me that map, Captain Compass. I don't want to end up in West Virginia."

"Smartass."

"I need clothes today and would like to purchase them in Washington. Not West Virginia, nor Maryland, and definitely not Kentucky!" I held out my hand for the map.

"I can do it," he retorted, clutching the map. "Just tell me where we are."

My eyes rolled. If I had a penny for every time I had heard him say 'I can do it' in relation to direction finding, I could retire tomorrow.

"12th street," I replied; part of me enjoyed his confusion.

He opened the door for me. We stepped out into shaded sunlight.

"I'm going to need sunglasses too," I muttered.

Mac again read the map. "You sure we're on 12th?"

"You're very damn lucky you don't have to fly south for the winter in order to survive."

"Are we taking the car?" he asked, ignoring my comment. He focused his field of vision up the street.

"Ah, yeah, you think I can walk like this?" I swept my arm across my body.

We stood staring at each other as a valet materialized from the sun with the car.

"You drive." I prodded Mac, who was staring at me.

"Don't look at me like that. No one knows we're here." I dropped my voice to a whisper. "There's no reason to suspect there would be body parts in the trunk."

The valet handed Mac the keys.

I wasn't as sure as I sounded about the body part thing.

"Okay," Mac said. He still clutched the map. "So we go up 12th?"

He's even more cute when he's lost. I decided it would take all day without some help.

"Yes," I said. "Then left at K St and right onto Connecticut."

"Let's do it then."

I managed to find everything I needed, though mostly not in Brook Brothers, but in the general vicinity of the store. By the time we returned to the hotel, I was a happy little camper.

The company credit cards had worked hard and fast and deserved a wee nap. We spent a few minutes in our room while I changed. I chose a pale-blue turtleneck sweater, a thigh-length black leather coat, black leather belt on faded-blue button-fly jeans, and black leather cowboy boots with a sensible inch-high solid heel. I tied my hair back in a ponytail and I sported a brand new pair of Incognito sunglasses.

We left to meet Caine. I opted to drive. It was the least stressful option for both of us. We still had guns shoved in our waistbands. A situation I intended to rectify by borrowing a couple of holsters from the armory inside the

Hoover building. I took care of the holster problem as soon as we arrived, and then we made our way to Caine's office.

Caine was pleased to see us. I sensed an odd mood. He appeared almost cheerful and complimented us on how well we looked together. I found his comments unnerving. When I cast my eye over Mac, there was no denying he looked good. His hair flopped over his forehead, falling to his eyebrows. He ran his fingers through his mane, flicking it back but it slipped forward again. I knew who he reminded me of. He had a MacGyver meets Mark Harmon thing happening and I liked it. They just needed darker hair.

"Ellie?" Fingers snapped by my face breaking the spell.

"What?" I found both men looking at me.

"Sit," Caine said. We sat in the two chairs in front of his desk. He slid a permit and a black wallet to Mac. I recognized it and wore an identical one myself.

"Carry these at all times. That leather wallet will clip on to your belt. Tuck the cover back into your waistband so it's obvious at a glance you're FBI." Caine twitched. "I have permission from the Director to grant you temporary special agent status. Don't make me regret that."

"Thank you," Mac replied. He read the card in the wallet before clipping it to his belt. He slid the permit into his own wallet and pushed it back into his pocket.

"I want you two moving again tonight, change hotels and change areas."

It wasn't an unexpected command.

"What's the chat room been like?" I asked.

Caine rocked back in his chair with his hands laced behind his head. "It's been busy. Every weirdo in creation has come out to attempt to find where the chat room killer hangs." He sighed heavily. "People are very strange."

"Stormy and Bitter?" I had asked that all members receive protection, but we had addresses for Stormy and Bitter, so they were first.

"Are in a safe house together. I have two agents in the room posing as Stormy and Bitter. Bitter was a little pissed about us moving into her home and forcing her to leave." Caine sat a little straighter in his chair and placed his hands on his desk.

"Yep, she would be," Mac commented. "But I'd rather her pissy than dead."

"So you have agents working from their homes?" I asked.

"Yes," Caine replied. "We don't want this guy to know we have moved anyone. He must be running ping and trace route software; if he decides to trace either of them again, we want him to get the same reply he has in the past."

We could both see the sense in that.

"We'll be online tonight," I told Caine. "I need a laptop for Mac."

"Take mine." He pushed a laptop across the desk towards Mac. "My sign-in is taped to the underside of the case."

"Thanks," Mac replied.

"Just be careful, keep moving and under no circumstances use a land-based server." Caine seemed to be collecting his thoughts. "We don't know how much information he has on you two. He found both your homes, for now I suggest you keep away from family and friends. Stay in neutral places with minimal contact."

"What about Aidan?" Mac asked. "He was at the Interscape Café with us."

"Aidan's fine. He's staying with your parents for now. We have increased police patrols in the area. As he was never involved in the chat room, we consider him at low risk of an attack."

I dragged my eyes up to meet Caine's. "How much do my parents know about this?"

"Your father has been apprised of the situation."

Dad, being retired military, had never overreacted to anything in his life. He would take this development in his stride. He would shield his wife from this as much as possible, due to her being highly strung. I resisted the urge to smile. Dad had often referred to Mom as highly strung, which was a polite way of saying she was fucking nuts. "I would like you to extend the same courtesy to Mac's father. He's a recently-retired police officer and is already aware of the trouble we had last night."

"Ah, word gets around cops very quickly. Give me a phone number Mac, I'll call your father." Caine had his pen poised over a piece of paper. "Where do they live?"

"Merrifield," Mac replied, and proceeded to tell Caine

the phone number. He grimaced, then looked at Caine. "My Mom makes Ellie's mother look like the most rational person on the planet. It would be a good idea to talk just to my Dad."

"What ever you think best."

Mac and I glanced at each other as my cell phone rang. I checked the display and passed the phone to him. "That's your Dad's number."

"It won't be Dad, it'll be her!" He rolled his eyes and answered the phone, "Help Desk!"

I heard his mother's voice reply, "Oh, I suppose you think that's funny?"

"Um, now is not a good time," he said, with much control.

Caine and I could both hear her yell, "This printer is a piece of shit!"

Mac held the phone away from his ear and said to us, "As I thought, printer problems again. This could take a few minutes." He stood up and walked over to the door while he spoke to his mother. Every now and then, we heard him sigh and say, "Will you just listen?"

Ten minutes later Mac handed me the phone. "Maybe you should switch it off for a bit. She's bound to call back." He sat down. A deep frown creased his brow. "If the woman would just listen ... and stop clicking the fucking print button!"

I smiled at him. He smiled back and relaxed a little.

Our families were informed. People we knew were safe. There was this single nagging feeling that not all was as simple as it seemed. FBI in the chat room would sit and trace everyone who came in. Their tasks included compiling data and storing room transcripts.

We listened to Caine's rundown from forensics.

"We have a few things so far, the assailant was at least five feet eleven inches tall, may or may not have worn a size ten running shoe, and was right-handed. We have his DNA, but no match. We have a partial fingerprint from the knife used on Carter. The cheesecloth parcel hanging from the hook above the bed, Ellie, was David Edwards' heart. Edwards was alive when his heart was removed. An incision was made under his ribs. Our medical examiner said the killer reached up into the chest and ripped out his beating heart. There were fifteen stab wounds made by an eight-inch double-edged blade; this is consistent with both bodies. I have concerns about the crime scenes: They were too clean."

I have concerns about a beating heart ripped from a person.

He paused so I took the opportunity to ask a question. "Toxicology show up anything at all?"

"Yes. I think this warrants our interest; substantial amounts of ketamine were found in both bodies."

I felt relief at that finding and hoped there was enough ketamine in his system and that David Edwards didn't feel the pain.

"Ketamine?" Mac asked.

I answered, "Special K, heard of that?"

"Cornflakes?" he replied.

"Um, I wouldn't want this shit on my frosty flakes! It's a tranquilizer used as an anesthetic but also popular on the club scene; it induces an LSD-type trip."

"How dumb are people?" Mac replied.

"They sink to new depths of dumb every day," Caine said, swiveling his chair closer to his desk.

Mac coughed. "That poem found on Carter's body: Didn't it mention Special K?"

Caine nodded.

"Is this find a coincidence, or is it possible they were recreational users?" I adjusted my posture, uncrossing and stretching my legs. "Did the Unsub know he was a user? And how?"

"That's something else we're looking into." Caine twitched. "I don't expect our Unknown Subject to remain unknown for long."

"Good to know! What about the emails?"

"Not much to go on there, but Questionable Document Analysis says there is a seventy-five percent chance they were all written by the same person, syntax and content gave us that much. I also had them compare samples with a poem and some comments made in the chat room by Dhs. They've come back with a tentative 'possible' on that. I have a warrant out for him, in the form of a Suspicious Persons Query, which is, of course, if we can find him. We don't know who he is either. They are trying to determine if the Post-it notes the poems were written on came from the same pad. I imagine that's very difficult if not impossible. The lab techs are eighty-five percent sure the Post-it poems were written by the same person; at least we have some handwriting examples."

"But again, no match," I muttered under my breath, my irritation fueled by the lack of real knowledge in the investigation so far. My good mood, ruined. My stomach rumbled, then threw in a longer complaint about the recent lack of food. I tried focusing out of the window to clear my head but found the gray fog moved into position and encroached upon my thoughts.

"Caine, we have to go," I said, standing up. I doubt whether any of them missed my stomach announcing its presence rather like a demented black bear in a campground.

"Go. Don't tell me where you move to, or any body else. I'll call you as soon as I know more."

Two thoughts stuck in my head. The crime scenes are too clean. He thinks it's a cop. "Okay." I headed out the door while Mac and Caine exchanged a few words. Mac caught me up in the hallway. I handed him the car keys.

"We didn't eat today," Mac said, and took the keys from my hand.

Once back at the hotel and in our room, Mac called room service and ordered dinner. The food was devoured with record speed and we checked out of the hotel. It struck me as amusing that I checked out with luggage when I had none when we checked in.

We sat in the car trying to decide where to go next. I pulled a map from the glove compartment and spread it out. We both closed our eyes and touched the map at the same time in the same place. I looked at our fingers.

"Damn, we even pick the same place blindfolded," Mac remarked. "Where are we going?"

We lifted our fingers and stared at the map where they had been.

"Mauryville," we said in unison. "Nooooo!"

I came up with an alternative suggestion. "How about Crystal City? We can stay at the Marriott there."

"Fine by me."

I'd bet money that the idea of more room service was involved in Mac's decision and I sure couldn't blame him for that.

Most importantly in my opinion, Crystal City was nowhere near Mauryville, or Lexington, and still a few miles from Fairfax. I really didn't want to go back to any of those places.

Within an hour, we were enjoying room service and playing on the Internet via satellite. We both peeked into the chat room. Caine was right, it was busy. We'd never seen so many new faces, or old, in Cobwebs at one time.

Mac nudged me. "Is your sound turned on?"

"Uh huh."

"I came in here today, while you were sleeping."

I watched someone leave the room and heard a beep.

"Awesome, you installed a bot, but where is it?"

"Oh, it's invisible," he said with a grin. "Hit the icon, and see how many hackers we have."

We did it. We saw one invisible guest hacker. I scrolled through the room list then back up to the top again and located the bot. It was easy to find as the words 'hacker tracker' stood out.

I had a question. "What if someone else does the ignore thingy, won't they see our bot?"

Mac smiled. "I'm way trickier than that. We're written into the program: It only shows itself to us, and it only beeps us."

I leaned over and kissed his cheek. "Damn, Mac. You're clever and tricky."

An email alert sounded. The subject line turned me cold: *Oh where oh where could the little cat be?*

I yelped as I opened the email. *Don't hide from me Otherwisecat. How can I give you gifts if you hide? I'm unhappy with you Otherwisecat. You need another lesson in manners.*

Gifts? What gifts? Oh man, was he referring to the bodies? The whole thing took another turn on the weirdness scale.

I forwarded the email to Caine.

"Do we stay in the room or go?" I asked Mac.

"Let's stay for a bit, we don't have to participate," he said.

"What do you want to do?" I asked, and scrambled off the bed with my laptop. I set the computer on the table. Mac did the same. We stood looking at each other as if we were lost. I had a thought – a bad thought – that could be lots of fun.

"We could raid the mini-bar."

Mac raised his eyebrows. "Oh, now we play with fire?"

I began lining miniature bottles up on the counter top.

"I see you have a plan," Mac commented.

I organized the bottles into two rows.

"Ah, I see a plan unfolding." He smiled. "I sense it involves mixing drinks and a horrendous hangover."

"Smartass," I replied. "No hangover, we have B-complex."

"Do we indeed?" His eyebrows rose again.

"Yep, we do. I bought a bottle from the drugstore this afternoon."

He accepted the mini bottle of tequila I handed him, opened the bottle, tilted his head back and drained the contents. I followed suit with mine, thankful there weren't any worms in it.

A moment of extreme weakness overcame me; I picked up the phone and called room service. "I would like a forty-ounce bottle of Pepe Lopaz Tequila, half a dozen fresh lemons, Tostitos, and guacamole." I held the receiver to my shoulder. "Anything you want to add?"

"Salt, and a steak sandwich; heavy on the mayo."

"Okay." I relayed the request and added an extra steak sandwich because it sounded so good.

Our order arrived. We sat on the floor in the middle of the room with the tequila, a bowl of quartered lemons, and a saltshaker in front of us while we ate our sandwiches. Four tequila shots later, we moved the computers to the floor so we could read the poems recited in the chat room. They seemed a lot more entertaining than usual. I found myself overcome by the need to comment on a poem by Dhs. Which caused the two agents in the room to reprimand me via instant message.

I couldn't remember whether it was salt-lemon-tequila, or lemon-salt-tequila, or tequila-lemon-salt. I gave up puzzling over it and slammed the tequila.

Minutes later we both received email alerts. It was him again.

There's something odd about the Cat, could it be she's missing Carter or could she be under the influence of tequila and her friend Mac?

I shoved the laptop away in disgust. "He can't know that!"

"No, he can't," Mac replied. "He's guessing."

"Tequila? Of all the things it could be. How does someone guess tequila?"

"We've talked about tequila before inside the chat room. He's probably witnessed a conversation or two."

He had a good point.

I felt myself topple backwards. Mac caught me and sat me back up. "How do you fall from a sitting position on the floor?"

"I dunno," I replied. I struggled to sit up and pour another shot. "Fuck him." I slammed the liquid and refilled my glass.

"Hey!" Mac held out his glass. The bottle wobbled in my hand as I tipped it.

"You know, Gabrielle."

I peered sideways at him. It was rare for him to use my given name. I considered he may have something astronomically important to impart.

He swallowed another drink.

He slurred. "You really are cute."

Not quite the revelation I'd expected but good to know. "Not as cute as you." I leaned sideways, resting against his shoulder.

He slipped an arm around me and kissed the top of my head. "What I was going to say before you sidetracked me, by looking like you do ... was if you need to talk about the Carter thing, I'll listen."

I held out my glass. Mac refilled it and his own.

"I met him in Chicago at his restaurant about six months ago. I was in town on a job and told him I would be there." I sucked a lemon and peered at Mac. "You know all this."

"I was thinking there might be something you've overlooked that might make more sense now."

Some days it was as if Mac could read my mind, as if he was actually in my head. I hadn't told Mac everything about Carter and me. An odd incident that occurred a few days after meeting Carter sauntered into my conscious thought.

Mac frowned at me. "What, babe?"

"When I broke my arm." I started to assemble pieces of disjointed memory together. "I don't know if it was an accident."

Mac's eyes were on mine. His brow creased. I could tell he remembered me breaking my arm six months ago. He also would have remembered me telling him it was an accident. I fell. I lied because I didn't know exactly what the truth was.

"I was out the back of Carter's restaurant in his office playing solitaire on his computer while I waited for him to finish. We were going to see a movie."

Mac was chewing his lip.

"Anyway some guy came through from the restaurant yelling and carrying on at Carter. I couldn't understand him. None of it made sense. The argument escalated into pushing and shoving then an all-out brawl. Somewhere in the middle of that, I broke my arm."

Okay. I left out a few details. The missing details were blurred, and what I did remember never felt right. I have never known why.

"Then what happened?" he asked, still chewing on his lip. His eyes darkened. He looked furious. I suspected that if Carter wasn't already dead, that he would be seriously hurting if Mac got hold of him.

I took a breath and had another drink. "I left, went back home, and never had anything to do with Carter again."

"And?"

"And ... one afternoon in the city, I overheard a name that seemed familiar ... this DEA agent mentioned someone called Xeo. The thing that struck me was that the man in Chicago had said the name Xeo."

"Who is Xeo?"

At least I knew the answer to that question. "He was DEA; it was rumored he had been undercover so long that he was using. I heard he started using ketamine then progressed to ketamine laced with heroin, and eventually heroin alone. He disappeared. Xeo became an urban legend. The agent who was talking about him didn't seem familiar at all until he rolled his sleeves up. I saw his tattoo. It was a mermaid on his inner forearm. The man in the fight had the same tattoo."

"He was an agent?"

"Yep."

"Why was he yelling at Carter?"

"I never found out."

"Did Carter know you were FBI?"

I shook my head. "No. He thought I was a journalist. He made that assumption on his own. I never corrected him."

"How many times did you see Carter face to face?"

"Five times. He had this annoying habit of turning up. Said he had business in the area and so forth. He turned up in Richmond and located my parents' home. He appeared in Washington twice. I literally bumped into him in the mall. Then he arrived on my doorstep. I have no idea how he found my house, or how he got a key."

"Chicago was the first time, and once he came to your home? That was the time he was arrested?"

"Yes."

"At a guess, I'd say he stole your keys while you were in Chicago and had them copied." Mac slammed another shot of tequila. "You think the ketamine in his system could have been the reason that agent was at his restaurant?"

"It's sure a possibility."

My head played a new tune: 'It's not always as it seems.' I had no idea what that meant, and the tequila made it so I didn't care. I wanted Mac to wrap his arms around me.

"Caine should be told," he whispered.

"I know. I'll tell him, just not tonight."

"Whatever you want, babe."

"Whatever I want? Really?" I turned my body to face him. I felt mischievous, possibly from the tequila.

Mac grinned at me. It was as if he knew my thoughts.

He appeared to have a sudden attack of sense. "We're drinking te-kill-ya, that's dangerous all by itself." His voice was low and he chewed his lip. "And yet I get the feeling you're going to do this anyway."

I pulled my laptop closer. "Let's see if he's still there first," I said. "I feel a recital coming on."

Mac leaned his head into mine as we checked. That act alone made my heart race.

"Seems he is, or someone else has hacked the room," Mac replied. "So what are you going to recite?"

"I dunno." I shrugged. I typed quickly and semi-coherently into the room to let everyone know my intention to recite. "Oh, I know." A thought occurred to me. "Remember that poem entitled 'Welcome home'?"

"Yes, with a few alterations that is the perfect choice."

"We'll change it to suit as we go," I said, and began to type the poem into the chat room:

Welcome home

The sun rose, night fell away
Revealing sadness and mental decay
Bloodstains and body fluid are all that remain
The one who did this was totally insane.
A chandelier sways in the wind
Crystal drops swirl and spin
Rainbows dance upon the walls
Falling on the bloodstained floors
Police tape glistens in the sun
A reminder, forensics aren't yet done
The body count began at one
We get the feeling there's more to come
A chandelier sways in the wind
Crystal drops swirl and spin
Rainbows dance upon the walls
Colored patterns on bloodstained floors
Don't look too closely my distant friend
The picture here is your twisted end.

I finished typing and watched as the bottom of the screen lit up with flashing red instant messages. Both FBI agents demanded to know what I thought I was doing. I ignored them. Dhs messaged me saying he liked the poem. I ignored him too. Several other people in the room sent messages or commented in the chat room. The only comment I found difficult to ignore was one from Pebblerock; he left his response in the chat room: *You and I should get together.*

I had an urge to scream 'Not in this lifetime!' Often wanting to reply resulted in me yelling like an idiot at my screen, while I typed. This time I resisted; I was chilling on tequila.

The email alert sounded, it was him. He said: *You changed it.*

I grinned at Mac. "We need to go home. I kept all the room transcripts on disk and I am sure I haven't posted that poem in months. I'm also sure I only *ever* posted it *once.*"

He nodded. "You're right. I remember you reciting it about six months ago." Mac smiled. "We have some searching to do. He may have had a nickname and a profile back then."

"Hell, yeah," I replied. "Now what were you saying about te-kill-ya?" I leaned against him.

"I was saying it's dangerous," he replied. Mac traced the knife mark on my neck with kisses.

"Really? How so?" I asked. He tugged the tie from my hair and ran his fingers through the entire length.

My cell phone jangled. I saw the name on the screen and answered it. I wondered why the theme to *Bonanza* ran through my head. Maybe it was because I couldn't remember the theme song for *Starsky and Hutch* or perhaps the Cartwright boys' penchant for trouble caused an association in my mind, turning Caine into their stern father. Or maybe I'd drunk more than enough tequila.

Caine was steaming. "What the hell have you done?"

"Nothing yet, you called too soon," I replied. I attempted to stifle a giggle as Mac turned his attention to my shoulders and kissed his way down my free arm.

"In the room! What the hell was that?"

"That was a possible break in the case. We are going home tomorrow to search computer files. He remembered that poem and he knew I had changed it. That means he's been around for at least six months." I stared at Mac as he neared my waistband. He had a boyish grin on his face as he looked up and mustered a wide-eyed innocent look.

I pressed the phone to my shoulder to muffle my voice. "Stop it," I whispered, while trying not to giggle.

Mac chuckled. He hooked a finger into my waistband and pulled me. I glared at him but it didn't work.

"I'll have some agents meet you," Caine said.

"No. Let's keep this quiet. Call it a gut feeling, but the fewer who know the better and the safer we will be."

"You know something!" Caine's tone reverberated with accusation. "This isn't the first time I've thought you know more about this than you're saying."

"No. I just think this needs careful handling. There's always a possibility that he's monitoring radio frequencies." Or that he's an agent or a cop and I really don't want to go there.

Caine grudgingly accepted my answer and told me to get some sleep.

"Oh, I will." I hung up.

Mac was laying on the floor, flat on his back, eyes closed, arms relaxed across his chest. Playing dead or asleep? I wondered. I tossed the cell phone out of reach and went to move. A hand flew out and grabbed me, pulling me on top of him. Mac opened one eye. "Going somewhere?" he slurred.

"Seems like I am already there," I replied. My lips hovered a fraction from his. I slipped into the depths of the green-flecked-with-golden hue of his eyes. My body burned with the heat from his as our lips met.

Chapter Seven

Tequila Sunrise

I woke slowly, unsure of whether it was day or night. The computer screens glowed from across the room, giving out enough light to see by. My head pounded. The B-complex would've worked better if we'd taken it instead of talking about it.

Mac groaned and then woke.

He held a pillow over his head and groaned some more. He dropped the pillow beside the bed and sat up. "Is it morning?" He swung his legs over the edge of the bed and sat with his head cradled in his hands.

"I think it's morning," I said. "What day is it?"

"Jesus, let me think," he replied. "We were at my place on Tuesday, at the Marriott on Wednesday. It's Thursday. Definitely Thursday."

My feet hit the floor. "Okay ... where are my clothes?"

I watched Mac as he peered between his fingers at the floor in front of him. Clothing was scattered everywhere. An empty tequila bottle lay between a rumpled shirt and a left shoe.

"Could be over here."

"Second question ... any clue what we did last night?"

He turned his head and looked at me. "Ummm."

I grinned. "Oh, that I remember."

"Good," he replied. His voice sounded a little croaky.

"As for what else we did. You posted a poem in the chat room."

"Oh, yeah." The events of the evening revealed themselves in my clouded mind. "We need to go home." I gathered clothes from the floor and pulled a tee shirt over my head.

"Food first, lotsa B-complex and coffee," Mac said. He straightened up gingerly, reached for the room phone and ordered breakfast.

My head throbbed as I struggled with my jeans. The simple task of dressing was torture. I sort of limped to my laptop, checked emails and dropped into the chat room. It seemed quiet. I checked to see if our phantom visitor was around. It was difficult to tell for sure but someone was invisible in the room. I left without saying anything.

Someone knocked. Mac pulled out his gun, held it behind his back, and opened the door. A porter entered, rotund, gray-faced and supercilious in his manner. He placed plates of bacon and eggs on the table and swept out.

My email alert sounded several times as we ate. I ignored everything until we had finished.

Then I checked. "Anything?" Mac asked as he poured himself another coffee.

"Uh huh. Another one from him," I said, ignoring the growing unrest in my gut.

"Read it out."

"'Sticks and stones severed his bones. He should have left you alone.'" I pushed away a more insistent feeling of unease. “No one knows where we are. We used satellite, not a land-based server. What are the chances of another body turning up here?”

“I don’t know!”

I forwarded the email to Caine. Mac and I sat in silence for a few minutes. We both knew we had to check the car.

I voiced the plan. “We’ll go down to the front desk and speak to the Concierge. They may have surveillance cameras operating in the garage.”

My cell phone rang. I checked the display. It was Caine. Who else would it be? Mac’s mother was always a possibility.

“Hey.” It was my best bright ‘hey’, it didn’t get any brighter than that.

“You got more trouble?”

I imagined his lips pressed together in a somewhat sour expression.

“Don’t know yet. We’re about to take a look at the car.”

“Where are you?”

“Crystal City Marriott.”

“You know how long it’ll take me to get there. Go check the car. If it is a false alarm, call me back.”

“We’re going to pack first, so if everything’s clear we’ll head south right away.”

I ended the call and dropped my phone into my pocket. We repacked our bags and checked we had everything. Satisfied, and with our laptops under our arms, we left the room.

“We’ll go see the concierge and check the surveillance

videos from the garage, better than hitting the garage blind," I said, as the elevator stopped on the ground floor.

"Okay, sounds good to me," Mac replied. We made our way to the front desk. About a dozen people milled about the lobby.

"Can I help?" the concierge asked, as he smoothed his satin waistcoat over his ample frame.

"I hope so," I replied. I removed my badge from my belt and flashed it at him. "We need to view surveillance camera footage from the garage."

The concierge seemed surprised and then recovered his composure. He whispered, "Is there a problem Special Agent Conway?" He indicated for us to come around the desk. He'd managed to read my name from the brief flash of the open wallet I gave him: Not bad; bet he never missed a damn thing that went on around the hotel.

"I hope not."

He ushered us through a hallway to a small room several doors down.

"In here, ma'am." He knocked then opened the door. "Justin, this is Special Agent Conway and her partner. Would you show them the garage cameras and assist them with anything else they need?"

Justin smiled a baby-faced grin. He sat in front of a bank of security monitors. Some of which were hidden behind his expansive shoulders.

"Sure Simon," Justin replied. His voice held a politeness that disguised an underlay of disgust. I didn't think Justin liked Simon.

Simon left without speaking.

The monitors all showed different locations within the hotel. Justin signaled us to pull up chairs next to him. Mac and I dumped our bags and laptops by the door and pushed two chairs to the screens.

"How many cameras in the garage?" I asked, as we stared at the screens.

"Six," Justin said. "Three on each level, one pointing into the lot from the elevator door, one from the far end, and we have a camera in the middle which is motion sensitive."

"The middle camera, can it track across the entire lot?" Mac asked.

"Yes."

"Great," I said. I knew we'd arrived around eight p.m. and it was a little after nine a.m. when we left our room. "Can you show us the footage from eight last night to ... nine this morning?"

"Which level?"

"P-1."

We skipped through the video footage. From eleven until six there was no activity at all. After that, people started moving about, but we saw nothing suspicious.

Mac thanked Justin.

Out in the hallway, I called Caine and told him the video was clear.

We waited for a few seconds before going through the glass doors that led into the garage. The walk across the lot turned my gut into a pit of turmoil. Something still didn't feel right What if the video didn't show everything? Perhaps Justin was not what he seemed to be. Maybe ... Maybe ... The closer we got to the car, the stronger the feeling became. Standing behind the car, it seemed a long way from the security of the glass doors.

Mac took the keys from my hand, unlocked the trunk and lifted the lid.

There was nothing inside.

"Thank God for small favors," I hissed.

We dumped our stuff in the trunk then peered through the car windows. The interior seemed clear. Mac pushed the remote to unlock the doors. We flung both backdoors open at the same time.

Nothing.

We settled into the car. Mac turned the key. We looked at each other and frowned. Dammit, we forgot the engine compartment. Mac turned off the ignition and hit the hood release.

He scrambled out of the car and flung the hood up.

I could barely breathe. I bet Mac heard my thumping heart. He paused for a second or two then he closed the hood and smiled. I grinned and gave the horn a tap. Mac jumped.

"Bitch!"

All I could do was smile.

Mac started the car and backed out. We felt a dull thud. Mac jumped on the brake. He shot me a questioning look.

"No idea," I said.

He resumed backing. Another thud. We stared at each other for a second. Mac backed up a little more. Then we saw it. Two legs tumbled in front of the car on the concrete. Mac braked hard. The legs bounced.

"Jesus!" Mac said. He stopped the car.

"Oh, so not good!"

We jumped out of the car and peered underneath. There were black plastic bags tied up under the car. I tried to make sense of what we found. This must be what it's like to get married in hell: Body parts bouncing like cans behind the car.

"Macabre wedding in hell," Mac said. He straightened up and looked at me over the roof.

"Jesus, you are a freak!"

I tried hard to calm my pounding heart while I dragged the phone from my pocket and called Caine back.

As soon as he picked up, I spoke, "Crime scene investigators needed."

"What have you got?"

"Body parts attached to the underneath of the car." I walked around and inspected the legs. "Looks like they're strung on aviation wire." I tried not to think of the parts as being a person, but being able to detach myself fully was as impossible as making sense out of the mind that created such horror.

"I'm nearly there. There's some crime scene tape in the trunk of the car." His voice sounded flat. I knew worry caused his voice to bottom out.

"We're in P-1."

I disconnected the call and looked for Mac. He leaned on the trunk and faced into the garage. I guessed by his expression that his thoughts lay somewhere near mine.

Disbelief at what we'd found mingled with disgust. How could anyone do that to another person? There was also a kind of morbid fascination. This Unsub was inventive and clever. How did he find us?

"Mac?"

"Yeah." He turned his head towards me.

"Open the trunk? Caine wants the area taped off."

At the very back of the trunk I saw a large black case. Mac hauled it out then crouched on the concrete and opened it up. I sensed tension but that disappeared as soon as he revealed the contents. Two rolls of FBI tape, two flashlights, four orange road markers and a first aid kit. I took the first aid kit and removed a pair of latex gloves from inside it.

"Don't think the first aid kit will do much for the jigsaw puzzle on the wire," Mac commented.

I pulled the gloves on. "I want to see who it is. Can you tape off the area, please?"

Mac nodded and took a roll of tape. I had visions of Humpty Dumpty falling from the wall and his limbs bouncing about like a marionette.

He took the end of the roll of tape and began sealing off the area.

I reached under the car for one of the closest and smallest bags. I had to lie down with my arm fully extended to undo the wire holding it to the chassis. The bag dropped with a thump. I dragged it out and untied the top. Peeling the plastic away I saw hair. I lucked out.

Mac looked around and asked, “Is that a head?”

“Yes. Male. Looks like that guy from our chat room who goes by the name Pebblerock. You ever seen his picture?”

Mac shook his head.

“Want to see him now?”

“I’ll pass.”

I closed the top of the bag. “Are you okay for a few minutes?”

“Why?” Mac asked.

“I’m going to go back and get that security guard, we’ll close this level.”

“Okay,” he said.

The whole macabre wedding-in-hell thing was more than just a little creepy. My eyes drifted back to the legs and the contents of the remaining black plastic bags edged ever closer to my conscious thoughts. I hurried over to the elevator entrance.

Two hours later, we left the hotel in a rental car Caine had arranged. Crime scene investigators were swarming through the garage as we pulled out.

I knew if the Unsub found us in Crystal City, he could find us anywhere, unless we found out how he worked. Where was the poem? The Unsub must’ve been on the surveillance footage somewhere.

I called Caine. “I looked briefly at the hotel garage surveillance tapes for the thirteen hours we were in the hotel. He's got to be on there somewhere."

"I've already sent the tapes to the lab. Of course, it would help if we knew who we were looking for."

"How about a cleaner or someone like that, someone who would be carrying trash bags and nobody would notice."

"I thought that, too. You think you missed him?"

"I know I did."

I hung up. My fingers tapped out the beat to the Bon Jovi song playing on the radio. I thought about notes, or rather the absence of a note.

"Mac, did you see a poem?"

Mac remained silent.

"Mac?" I repeated.

"Uh huh."

"You saw it?"

"Yeah, I saw it. Yellow Post-it like the last one." He didn't seem eager to share.

"And?"

"You sure?" he asked.

"Spill it!"

Mac chewed his lip, and then said, "'Hell is where I reside, toasty warm room to hide, ridding the world of those that shame. All I wanted was a friend, none of you played. Now it's my game.'"

"Jesus."

Chapter Eight

Take Me Home Country Road

After much discussion, we decided to check into a motel in Lexington. We settled on a motel one street over from the Interscape Café. An hour and a half after checking in, we were back in Mauryville having coffee with Holly.

Kevin hurried into the warm kitchen. "Hey, you two," he said, plonking his body in the closest chair.

"Hey, Kevin," Mac replied. He sounded pleased to see him.

"What are you doing back here?"

I grinned. "We have to pick up some things from home. What are you doing here?"

"About to enjoy the best coffee in the district."

I looked over at Holly. "You still pouring free coffee for the local cops?"

"Can't help myself; there's something about a man in uniform ..." Holly plonked a mug in front of Kevin. "You think Aidan will understand that?"

"No man will ever understand that; don't tell him," I replied. Mac and Kevin were watching me intently both wearing a 'chicks are weird' look.

"You want an escort to pick up your stuff?" Kevin asked.

I still wasn't over the whole Starsky and Hutch thing. "Nah."

I could see Holly from the corner of my eye. She employed hand signals to attract my attention. I rolled my eyes at her, which caused her to narrow her eyes and redouble her efforts to get me to follow her into the store.

"Hun, I think Holly wants you," Mac said.

I gave him an innocent look and followed it with. "Oh, I am silly! Be right back." I left the menfolk to their chatter and followed Holly through the door. She grabbed my arm and dragged me across the store out of earshot of the kitchen.

"Spill it!" she demanded.

"What?" I knew for sure she wouldn't buy the innocent, nothing-is-going-on routine, but I had to try.

"You and Mac, something's changed."

I bit my lip to stop the grin that was forcing its way onto my face. "What do you mean?"

"Ellie! You did it!" she squealed.

"Shush." Through the doorway, I saw Mac watching me. Damn, he made my toes tingle.

"You did. That's what's changed," she said, delighted. "This is wonderful!"

I knew the expression on her face meant she intended asking personal questions.

"Don't you dare ask me for details."

"Just one?"

"No."

"Ellie, you're no fun!"

"Oh, now that's where you are wrong, apparently I am lots of fun!" I spun on my heels and hurried back to the kitchen.

"We should get moving," Mac said, pushing his chair back as I entered the room.

"Yes, we should."

I knew Holly: She would not give up her questions as easily as that.

"We'll drop in on our way back," Mac said, as we headed for the door.

Like hell; she'd corner me if we did and I'd be toast.

"Good," Kevin replied. He shook Mac's hand. Kevin leaned over and kissed my cheek then caught sight of my neck. "What the hell?" he drawled. "Holly, have you seen this?" He tipped my head back with two fingers placed under my chin. Tipping up my chin was tiresome, real quick. It's no big deal, a scratch if anything.

"It's nothing," I protested, "Really, it's nothing!"

Holly moved closer and peered at the mark on my neck. "When did this happen?"

"Two days a go," Mac interjected. "The Unsub is getting bolder."

"Be mindful," Kevin warned him, "If he's brave enough to do that, then there's no telling what he may do next."

Ya think! I looked at Mac. There was no need to upset anyone with the Unsub's latest exploits.

Mac drove. As we neared home, I pulled my gun from my holster, checked the magazine and chambered a round. Mac glanced at me.

"Just checking," I mumbled, pushing the weapon back into my holster.

"Figured," he replied. He had already turned his attention back to the road.

Confession time. "I have a bad feeling."

"Snap," Mac said.

As we turned into my driveway, I felt an unusual sense of alienation. It didn't feel like home.

"Don't go right around," I said. "Park near the front door so we can leave quickly."

When I unlocked the front door, my hand shook. Together, we approached the kitchen door. I pushed it wide open and stood in stunned amazement at the sight in front of me.

The entire room was spotless. It was my kitchen, except for the smell of hospital grade disinfectant and a knife missing from the block on the counter.

"Wow," Mac commented.

"Crime scene clean-up do good work," I said, turning away from the now sterile room. It may be clean, but it still felt wrong. A maniac had vanquished my sanctuary.

"Does that mean ..."

"Yep. Your place will be returned to normal as soon as forensics is finished." I tried hard not to use the words 'crime scene' in regard to Mac's home.

"Whew."

I didn't ever want to go back into his guest room, clean or not.

"Come on. Let's go upstairs to my office. The sooner we get started, the sooner we can leave." I shut the kitchen doors behind us. The urge to leave grew strong.

We ran up the stairs. I switched the computer on. My office felt warm and inviting. It still felt like home in there. I pulled open the top drawer of my desk and collected a handful of CDs. Above my computer monitor hung a napkin poem Mac had written at our first face-to-face meeting. He noticed it right away.

Mac said, "I recognize that napkin."

"I love that poem."

He shrugged. "It's just a scribble. What do you want me to do?"

"Check the bookcase, Mac." I read the labels on the CDs piled on the desk. "Anything dated this year, or that mentions Cobwebs."

Mac piled CDs next to me. "We should have made coffee," he said. I had the feeling he wasn't going to offer to spend any time in my kitchen.

"I'll go." I stood up. "You do this." I shoved a CD into the ROM drive.

He sat in the chair I had vacated and looked up at me. "You'll be okay?"

"Hell, yeah," I replied from the doorway, hoping I sounded convincing.

I didn't much feel like being in the kitchen either. This is my house and I'm okay; how could I not be okay?

I started the coffee. While I waited, I inspected the kitchen. Visions of the last time I saw it superimposed themselves over what I could now see. My mind conjured up the crime scene. As I stared at the floor and remembered the spectacle, it became very apparent that Caine was right. The kitchen had been too clean. I'd seen only one set of footprints and they were Carter's, there should have been two sets. No way could the assailant have got out clean. He could not have avoided the blood. His feet would have left bloody prints. Unless it was him wearing Carter's shoes and he carried Carter in and then out. A drugged Carter and a smart Unsub.

I pulled my cell phone from my pocket and called Caine. "Me again, as if you didn't know. I've had a thought about the first crime scene."

"Your home?"

"Yes." I paused to gather my thoughts. "One set of foot prints, forensics matched to Carters shoes. Right?"

"Right."

"What size shoe?"

"I'll get back to you, Ellie. I can't access that information at this time. I know where you are going with this. You think they wore the same size shoe, and the Unsub carried him?"

"It's a thought."

"It's a good one. What'd Carter weigh? One-ninety? That's a hell of a dead weight to lift."

"Yeah, but he only needed to do it once and he could've dragged him in, he probably wasn't bleeding then. On the way out he was in pieces that would've been easier to handle."

"I'll get back to you."

Twenty minutes later, I stomped back up the stairs carrying two mugs of super- strong black coffee and was met by an, "Ah, finally!" Mac took the mugs from me and set them on the desk. "It's been forever since we've had decent coffee." He picked up a mug and sipped the hot liquid. "Oh yeah, that's what I'm talking about."

I rolled my eyes; he sounded like a dork. "Found anything yet?"

"Nope, don't think we have gone back far enough yet. I'm setting aside disks that mention Dhs, you never know."

"Good plan."

Mac stifled a yawn. I brushed past him and opened the window. I lingered for a moment breathing the fresh mountain air.

"I should've bought the laptops."

"What if we check your drive and then take all the CDs we've found back to the motel? Then we can both search."

"Let's do that." I leaned back against the windowsill and watched Mac scroll through files on my hard drive. "Would you pass my coffee?" I asked.

He handed it to me and smiled. His smile melted into me and quickened my heart. I would walk over hot coals three times a day for the rest of my life just to see him smile like that at me.

"Thank you."

"You're welcome."

I had a seriously bad feeling about being back at home. It was fueled by an undercurrent of concern about being back in Rockbridge County at all. I'm okay, but something else isn't.

Common sense told me we should be safest here. Nobody would expect we'd return to the scene of the first crime. There was no reason for the Unsub to return here either. Unless he was stalking us. I pushed the thought out of my mind.

"Ellie!"

"Uh huh." I think Mac must've called my name a few times before I heard him.

"Blank disks?"

"Bottom drawer."

Mac went back to the download task.

I leaned out the window and watched a squirrel in the back yard.

Something tapped me on the back. I jumped and bashed my head on the window sash.

"Ouch!"

Mac almost fell off the chair laughing. "You all right?" he asked, struggling to control himself.

"Yeah." I felt silly, but I was undamaged.

"Good." His warm, throaty chuckle ceased. Mac took my hand and pulled me onto his lap. "I think we have everything. If you want to get going, we can."

"Cool. I'll get some clothes and stuff while we're here."

"Not necessary, babe."

"Shush," I whispered, burying my head in his neck as his arms tightened around me. The subtle scent of his cologne combined with the warmth of his body stirred feelings that were hard to ignore.

"I think I'll take a shower," I whispered, breathing in

his scent.

Chapter Nine

Ghost Riders In The Sky

An hour later, I went back to my office. From the gun cabinet I took two fresh magazines and another box of ammunition which I hid among the clothing in the overstuffed bag. I slung the bag over my shoulder and had the CDs clutched in my hand. Mac and I stood by the open front door ready to leave.

Mac spoke, "When you turn your computer on, does it connect to the Internet?"

"Yes," I replied, inwardly cursing my cable connection. Usually I cursed the connection due to poor service so this was a new experience.

"You didn't send any emails or go to the chat room?"

He knew I hadn't.

"No."

"Well then, let's go."

We stepped out into the cool breeze. I locked the door then had a thought and asked, "Did I turn it off?"

"I dunno," Mac replied.

I unlocked the door again. "Come with?"

"Yep." He followed me back into the house and up to my office.

The computer was still running. When the mouse moved to clear the screen saver, it revealed the little mail icon in the task bar.

"Oh no!" I clicked on the icon and opened my inbox.

"Check the time it was sent."

"An hour ago," I replied, opening the email: *And the Cat came back she couldn't stay away.* "Oh Man." I groaned. "How?"

Mac shrugged. "Turn it off," he said. "He's playing stupid head games. It's like the tequila thing, he's guessing."

I looked up at him, and hoped it was a game designed to frighten and not a prelude to more horror. I forwarded the email to Caine and switched off the computer.

We left the house again and re-locked the door.

My turn to drive. I pushed the key in the ignition and turned it.

Nothing happened.

I flipped my hair out of my eyes and turned it again.

Nothing.

"Now what?" I wondered aloud.

"Loose lead? Pop the hood, love. I'll take a look." He leapt from the car.

Mac raised the hood. I heard him gasp. I scrambled from the car to Mac. The horror on his face spoke volumes.

A disembodied head sat on top of the battery with its dead eyes wide open and frozen in terror. A bloodied scrap of paper protruded from the cold blue lips. Who'd have thought a head would fit?

"Who?" Mac said.

I blinked several times as I tried to make sense of the horrid sight.

"I don't know." I shook my head. I handed Mac the keys. "But I guess someone else is missing from the chat room."

"What does it say?" Mac asked.

I held my hair back to prevent it falling onto the head and peered at the note.

"'Can you fix what's broken, when you're unable to see? Look into my eyes, hear my plea.'"

Yuck. I shivered and stepped back. Mac slammed the hood down. My stomach flipped as a thought lurched around my brain, what if it had been squashed? I dismissed the thought; there was plenty of room under the hood.

"It didn't smell too putrid, must be a recent kill." My words echoed against the house. "Did it look male to you?" I asked, grabbing my bag from the car.

I heard Mac gulp and swallow as he unlocked the front door. Once back inside, Mac locked the door behind us.

"I don't know. It just looked ghoulish," he said.

"I thought it looked ghoulishly male."

"Who is it?"

"I don't know. I guess it's someone from the chat room. I haven't seen photographs of everyone, just those that had them in their profiles. He doesn't look familiar."

I traded feeling grossed out to morbidly curious and amused. "It's freaky looking." And smaller than I thought a head would be. Not that I gave much thought to the size of disembodied heads, but that's twice now I've come across a head.

I called Caine. "He's killed again. We're at my place."

"Can you leave?" His voice bore the same flat tone I'd heard earlier.

"Not sure. My Explorer is in the garage," I replied and crossed my fingers that my truck was free of any body parts.

"I'll notify Kevin and the State police. I'll send someone out from Lexington. If you two can leave, then go."

"You want us to leave a crime scene?" I struggled to understand what he had said.

"Yes," he said. "Get out of there, and do it now. He may be watching, so for God's sake take care."

My skin crawled as I slipped the cell phone back into my pocket.

"Did you hear him?" I asked Mac. Time to get serious. I pulled my hair back into a ponytail.

"Yeah."

"Okay, we'll go through the back door and head for the garage. There's a side door, we'll use that." I explained my intentions as we walked through the kitchen. I stopped at the back door with my hand resting on the door handle. My eyes flicked to the window in the door as I turned the handle. "Oh, Christ!"

Blood covered the outside of the frosted glass in the top of the door. A face pressed against the window.

My gun was in my hand, index finger on the side of the barrel.

"I think I saw eyes," Mac said. "This is insane."

I glanced at him. He had a firm grip on his .357. I

heard running footsteps outside. The crunch of gravel determined direction.

"Front door."

Mac was already on his way.

I slid the heavy bolt across the backdoor just in case and hurried after Mac.

"He's still running," he whispered.

The footsteps faded.

Mac stood to one side of the front door and could just see out of the side window.

I fished into my pocket for the phone and made a 911 call. I asked for a patch straight through to Kevin in his car. "The Unsub is here. Sounds like he's running around the fucking house."

"State police are on the way. I have four deputies with me. Twenty-five minutes, Ellie."

"I think he pressed his face against the glass in my backdoor. There could be prints."

"I'll make sure any evidence is protected."

"Hurry the hell up." I disconnected and shoved the phone back into my pocket.

"Can he get in through any other doors?" Mac asked.

I shook my head. "Unless he breaks a window." My mind ran over the layout of my home, checking all scenarios.

But there was another way.

"There's another door at the back of the house through a storage room. It's a solid door with an internal bolt." An unfaltering air of calm swept over me. "I'll go check."

Seconds later, I stood in the storage room. Something scratched and banged on the door leading to my back yard. I released the interior bolt. The noise outside turned my blood to ice. A loud squawk pierced the air. The scratching ceased and screeching started. Wings beat against the door. Anger rose in waves. I slid back the last bolt and pulled the door towards me. The noise from the door was deafening. The screeching reached scream pitch. Feathers flew in all directions from the extended wings. I winced as I pulled the trigger. A single round ended the struggling bird's torture.

"I'm sorry, Abigail."

The bloodied carcass nailed to my door jerked.

"You sadistic fuck!" I screamed into the yard before slamming the door and shoving the bolt across. Abigail's body thudded against the wood.

"Ellie!" Mac called. "You okay?"

I hurried back to him.

"He nailed Abigail to the door!" I said. "She was still alive!"

Absolute disgust registered on his face. He leaned back on the wall and ran a hand through his hair.

He glanced sideways at me and asked, "Who is Abigail?"

"My chicken," I said. It was unbelievable anyone would be so cruel to an animal. Wasn't it bad enough that Carter and his insanity had caused me to trample all over Abigail's eggs? Now my chicken hung like some horrid voodoo warning, her lifeless body flapping in the wind.

Mac exhaled. "Oh man! I thought it was a person." He checked himself. "Sorry, Ellie."

It had become eerily quiet. At that instant, it felt as though we were in the eye of the storm. The silence created some sort of bizarre void. Minutes dragged by.

Mac jolted to full alert. "Did you hear that?"

"Sounds metallic," I replied. I searched the recesses of my mind to give shape and form to the noise.

"It's coming from over there." Mac pointed towards the far side of the kitchen.

"Oh fuck!" I yelped. "Gas. The tanks for the underfloor heating are in that part of the basement." Why was he messing with the gas?

"Where's the bag?" Mac looked around the room.

I reached over the back of the sofa grabbed the bag, and then slung it over my shoulder.

"If he's in the basement, he may not be able to get out before we get to the garage."

Mac grabbed my shoulders. His dead-serious eyes stared into mine. "You want to take that chance?"

The chance to live versus a fiery death? Now that's a tricky one. I am so glad he can't hear my thoughts.

"We don't have a choice."

Mac unlocked the door. We ran around the front of the house and kept to the far side of the driveway, close to the old barn. The grass verge deadened our footsteps somewhat.

The double garage doors loomed in front of us. I could still hear a metallic ringing sound coming from the basement.

I pulled Mac around the side of the building and through the small door. I peered into the back of the Explorer, ever conscious that there was a body somewhere.

I grabbed the spare keys from the shelf and threw them to Mac. "The remote for the garage door is on the dash," I said.

He climbed into the driver's side. I jumped in next to him and threw the bag onto the backseat.

He pressed the remote for the garage door. "How fast does this door open?" Mac asked. He turned the key. The engine sprang to life with a throaty roar then purred.

"Not fast enough," I replied. "He will have already heard us."

The door seemed to move in slow motion.

Mac planted his foot on the accelerator. We tore forward and wiped out the door. It must've made a hell of a noise but all I could hear was the scream of revs and the tires tearing up the gravel. Stones pelted the underside of the car. Somehow, Mac controlled the turn onto the road. In the distance, we could make out rolling lights and hear faint sirens.

Mac grinned at me. "Cavalry is coming."

"They can't go in there. The whole damn house might explode any second!"

Mac angled the car across the road, turning it into a makeshift roadblock. We waited. My cell phone rang.

I frowned as I checked the display. "Jesus, Mac ... 703?"

"Mom," he said.

Mac answered the call, "Help desk."

I heard a woman's voice say, "It's not funny this time, either!"

A fireball shot into the sky. A second later, the sound of the blast hit us.

Mac said, "Not now, Mom." He flung the phone into the glove compartment.

Kevin pulled up beside us and rolled down his window. "You all right?"

"Yeah," I replied. "You see any vehicles parked along the road or pass anyone on this road?"

He shook his head. "You think he got out before the explosion?"

"He's not ready to die, Kevin. He's having too much fun."

Kevin nodded. "Then he must've had a vehicle somewhere."

"We'll check driveways on our way out. There's a head, possibly cooking, under the hood of the car by the house."

"Jesus Christ!" Kevin looked ill. "Anything else?"

"He nailed Abigail to the storage room door. The casing you'll find by her is mine. I had to shoot her. He nailed her up alive."

Another explosion ripped through the air.

"Both tanks have gone. Guess it's safe to drive on up now." Kevin grimaced. He reached forward and lifted the radio handset. "ETA on the fire truck?" He paused.

Something crackled back at him. His ears were more

in tune with the crackle than mine were and he replied, "Copy that."

Kevin waved his arm out the window. Two police cars rolled past us and turned into my driveway.

"We'll be in Lexington looking through files," I told him. "Coordinate this with the FBI. They should be here soon."

"Will do."

"Catch you later, if he doesn't get us first." I waved as Mac straightened up the car.

We paid close attention to driveways and wooded areas that we passed. I looked for concealed vehicles and found none.

Mac said nothing. He was concentrating on the road ahead.

"It's going to be okay, right?" I asked. It felt very strange to know my home no longer existed. I was homeless.

He turned his head and smiled. "We're together, and we're alive."

I knew then everything would be okay.

Chapter Ten

Deuces Are Wild

"We have to do this file search tonight, don't we?" Mac asked. He surreptitiously attempted to hide a yawn behind his hand.

"We should." I attempted to disguise my own fatigue. "But honestly, after today and the state we're in, we'd probably miss the very thing we need to find."

Mac stood up and stretched. My mind replayed the day's events and I knew the minute I lay down it would increase the speed with which the images of horror manifested.

"Damn, my body is tired," Mac said.

"Why does horrible shit make us laugh?"

Mac's astonished expression suggested my question came from left field.

"I guess it's just our way of dealing with it. We've seen some weird shit. How often do you find a human head on top of a battery?"

"Well, it was a first for me. Wonder if it cooked?"

"Euwwwwww."

"Do you suppose the brains would boil or something inside the skull?" I asked. My finger traced intersecting lines on the Formica tabletop. I looked up to see if Mac had heard me.

"That's one of the sickest questions I have ever been

asked."

"But would it?"

Mac couldn't answer. He laughed so hard tears trickled from his eyes. They tumbled over his long dark lashes and over his cheekbones. I found I wasn't far behind him. Images of legs on wire and heads cooking sent me over the edge.

Mac regained composure enough to answer. "If it was exposed to high heat for a sustained period, the liquid in the tissues would evaporate very quickly; thus dramatically shrinking the brain."

I had visions of a shrunken head and some bizarre tribal ceremony as he spoke.

"All that would be left would be the tissue minus the liquid, which comprises about seventy percent of the brain mass."

"Ah, now I see."

"If the heat was sustained much longer, after the liquids had evaporated, then the tissue would contract even further and burn to a crisp. It would look something like a crumpled piece of leather, but crispy," Mac explained with frightening authority.

"No boiling then?"

"No, no boiling." He shook his head. "I don't know what bothers me more: That you asked the question in the first place, or that I could answer it."

With shrunken-head thoughts lurching through my brain, sleepiness hit like a sledgehammer. My eyes would not stay open any longer. We curled up together on the comfortable bed and succumbed to the exhaustion our bodies and minds felt.

Friday morning arrived with a loud banging on the door.

“Mac, do you suppose psychotic killers knock first?” I checked through the peephole in the door.

“Why? Is there one at the door?” he asked, and sounded almost awake. He trained his gun on the door.

“Nah, just Caine,” I replied, undoing the security chain then unlocking the door to let him in. I glanced down at myself before he stepped in. I wore a long tee shirt, my moment of panic subsided. I was decent.

“Morning,” he announced, “I come bearing caffeine.”

I took two of the styrene cups from the tray he carried and passed one to Mac.

“Thanks,” we replied in unison, and set the cups on the small bedside table.

“You’re welcome.” Caine sat himself at the table.

Mac and I dressed at speed.

“Did you get anything in those files?” Caine asked. He lit a cigarette then sipped his coffee.

“We don’t know yet,” I told him.

I crossed the room and opened the curtains, letting in what little sun the morning offered. When Caine didn’t admonish me for my tardiness concerning the files, I knew there was something up.

“What?” I gave him a questioning look and sat at the table.

“The Marriott body had traces of ketamine.” He rolled

his cigarette end around the ashtray then raised his eyes. "We think it may be some Cobwebs' regular who went by the name of Pebblerock."

Ack! I remembered him making a comment about that poem I had posted while we were at the Marriott. I couldn't raise any joy at being right about the identity of the body.

Caine carried on without waiting for a response. "Have you checked your credit card account recently?"

"Work account?"

"Yes."

"No. Haven't checked it at all since Delta finished the Blue River case. That was what, three weeks ago?"

Caine nodded. "You are absolutely positive?"

"Yes. I wrote you a report on my expenditure after the last assignment and have had no reason to check it since."

Caine continued, "Because we couldn't work out how he found you at the Marriott. I checked your account. It was a long shot but now I know we have something."

"What?"

"Someone logged into the card member service as you, twice, in the last forty-eight hours."

"Well, it wasn't me," I replied.

"We ran a trace on the log-in." Caine paused and stubbed his smoke butt out. "The first time this person logged in as you, it was done at the Richmond public library." He looked over at us. "We checked the computer logs and matched the user to a library card. Ellie Connelly was the name."

"You're kidding!" I was stunned. No way!

"The second trace led us to the Fairfax library and to another library card holder by the name of Ellie Conway-Connelly."

"Now that's a mouthful." I grimaced. No way would I hyphenate.

"Any addresses? Did he have an attack of stupid and give us a break?" Mac asked.

"Richmond, the address on file for the card was 1970 East Parham Road."

I knew that address. My mind stumbled over Richmond and came up with an answer. "FBI field office."

"Yeah," Caine replied. "The Fairfax library card gave us Vienna Woods. He was less inventive that time."

"How the hell did this sicko bastard get my account info and password?"

"We need to have your home computer analyzed to be sure, but more than likely the result of a key logger."

The thought of some hacker sneaking a key logger into my computer turned my gut. I felt violated as much as I would if that same person rifled through my underwear drawer. Who's to say he hadn't?

"My computer was in the house. The house exploded," I told him. Someone watched every key stroke I made. I gulped down some coffee and hoped it would subdue my churning tummy. It didn't. I shoved my chair back, jumped up and hurried for the bathroom.

A few minutes later I heard a quiet knock on the door

and Mac's voice, "You okay in there?"

No, I'm not okay. I just wasted perfectly good coffee. And found out some freak watched everything I did on my computer. I wiped my mouth, brushed my teeth, and then flushed the toilet. Another knock this time louder, followed by a determined voice, "Ellie?"

I twisted the handle and swung the door open.

"I'm okay."

He looked worried and pleased all at the same time.

I felt jittery, like my insides were cold and shivering.

Mac's arm slid around my waist. "You're pale."

"Go figure."

"Smartass," he said and planted a kiss on the top of my head. "Caine has more to share."

Great! I had a feeling none of it was good. I didn't trust myself to speak again. Damn, that hacker/killer/Unsub bastard and his violating ways. I could feel my hands shaking as I tried to light a cigarette. My mind spun as if it was no longer part of me. Words flung into the darkness. They slowed until one word stood out as it floated through, food. I need to eat and I need to eat now. A voice mumbled next to me, and then it mumbled again.

I reached for the ashtray only to discover I didn't have a cigarette in my hand. I blinked several times to clear my vision and determine what was happening. It wasn't a cigarette in my hand. It was a fork. When did my cigarette become a fork?

"Eat."

I heard the same voice that mumbled minutes before.

It was Mac. I stopped trying to understand, ate the eggs, toast, and drank the orange juice that appeared before me.

I swallowed the last mouthful of egg. I could think again, but I wasn't sure I wanted to. Caine and Mac had the laptops fired up and were searching files.

"Where did the breakfast come from?" I'd work my way into thinking.

"I ordered it on my way, had one of the boys pick it up and bring it on over," Caine replied.

I considered his reply. Obviously, my brain had stepped out and missed the breakfast delivery. Okay, on with the real questions.

"Whose is the head?" I asked draining the last of the juice.

"May take some time to figure that out, no one's been reported missing thus far, so our search area remains very broad."

"The Marriott body had a head." I'd never forget opening that bag.

"Yes."

"What about regulars missing from the chat room?"

"We have to wait and see. So far the only comment from our agents in the room is that Dhs hasn't recited anything, or made any comments since you posted that poem."

"Unusual," Mac replied. "He's prolific with his weird poems and also likes to freak out people with strange comments."

I raised my eyebrows at him. "Maybe he wasn't there at all."

Caine asked for another CD. I passed him a pile.

Five CDs later Mac found something. "I got it," he said, and scrolled through a file containing four hours of room conversation. He stopped just after the Welcome home poem to read who had made comments. "Stormy, Bitter, me." He shifted his eyes to find mine. "Someone called Addict_man."

Caine leaned back in his chair. "What do you two remember about this person?"

I could see Mac's thoughts ticking over. "I remember him, he was kinda pushy, a regular for about a month and kept asking if he could have a hammer."

I recalled him, too, for different reasons. "He used to message me all the time, wanting to send me poems, and he struck me as desperate to fit in. His poetry was more a collection of randomness than actual poetry, and very dark."

Caine looked from me to Mac. "Did either of you befriend him at all?"

We shook our heads.

Mac replied, "No. He wasn't the friendliest of people and would get all upset if Ellie wasn't in the room for whatever reason. Or if she was spending time talking to the rest of us."

"Interesting," Caine said. "When did he stop coming?"

"Ah," Mac replied. "That would've been when Ellie was away for about three weeks. He came in for the first week, constantly asking where she was, and then he began accusing others of being her. He actually said that he believed she was avoiding him and hiding." Mac leaned back in the chair. "I don't remember seeing his nickname again."

I shuffled my chair over to see the screen. "Do you mind?" I angled the laptop towards me and checked the log I always kept of who was in the room. "Dhs was there too."

I read further, looking for something Dhs might have typed in the room. "Look." I nudged Mac. "Dhs replied to a comment by Addict_man, their fonts are different."

"Yup," he said. He sounded thoughtful. "Can you find something that Addict_man recited?"

I found a short poem that almost sounded like a nursery rhyme when read aloud. Caine came around to see the screen. "Copy that poem to an email and send it to the Questioned Documents Lab. We'll see if they can figure out if it's the same guy who's leaving you little poems now."

I reviewed the poem once more before sending it off. I decided to check his online profile and it didn't take longer than two minutes to find it. There was no picture and no real information. He stated his interests as poetry, especially Cobwebs' chat room and OtherwiseCat.

"Now that's just creepy," I said, and showed Mac. "No invites to join him in chat or to install messenger."

"Maybe there were until recently," Mac replied. "Look at the date at the bottom of the page."

I scrolled down. "Updated yesterday, always one fuc'n step ahead!"

A pop-up informed me I had new mail. I clicked the icon and opened the mailbox to reveal yet another email from the Unsub. The subject line caused instant alarm: *Three blind mice.*

I opened the email and read the contents aloud, "'Three blind mice, three blind mice, see how they run, see how they run. They all run around scared at night. I cut off someone's head with a carving knife. Did you ever see such a sight in your life as three blind mice?'"

"Would you say he's watching us or trying to freak us out?" Mac asked, he stood up, crossed the room, and drew the curtains.

"We didn't prepay the room." I reminded Mac. "We haven't used the credit card since we left Arlington."

"Yeah, I know. But he was in Mauryville yesterday."

Caine looked up. "We have no way of knowing if he's watching for sure. But just in case, I have agents in the motel across the street and several more arriving soon."

I reread the email for the second time.

Caine continued talking, "You know the drill, Ellie. Only polite conversation if you run into them outside. It's unlikely you'll recognize them anyway. You spend little time in the Hoover building and I requested agents based in DC."

I replied, "Yeah, I know ... nod and smile."

I watched for several moments as Mac paced back and forth across the room. I could tell he was lost in contemplation and let him be. I turned my inquisitive mind to Caine. “So tell me about the agents across the street?”

“They started at seven this morning. We gained permission from the motel owner late yesterday, and have two agents in the house attached that overlooks the street, posing as painters.”

I changed the subject. “About the crime scene.”

He knew which one. “Your home?”

I nodded. “What did you get on the shoes and foot prints?”

Caine flipped open his notebook and rifled through a few pages. “Carter wore a size twelve. They were on his feet in the trunk of the car. His shoe prints were on the floor in your kitchen. The Unsub wears a size ten, maybe, if that was him at the café.”

“So it was or wasn’t Carter who made the shoe prints?”

“If he wears a size ten shoe, then it may have been the Unsub, wearing Carter’s shoes, who made the prints.”

“How do you know? Mac asked.

“The pressure points on the shoe and therefore the print were different from the wear marks on the sole.”

“How is it possible that he knew to do that?”

Caine’s mouth twitched. “The same way he avoided leaving trace evidence at the scene. With some kind of protective clothing and probably foot coverings.” He played with the ashtray. “This guy is a fucking ghost.”

Ghosts don’t come prepared to kill. I let the whole protective clothing thing settle in my mind as I tried to recall the person who attacked me. What was he wearing? My mind drew a blank. I had no memory of seeing him.

Mac stopped pacing. He sat down at the table.

"Tell!" I knew him. His pacing halted because he'd settled upon an idea.

"What if we tried to lure him out into the open?" he asked, and rocked his chair back to a precarious degree.

Caine leaned forward resting his elbows on the tabletop. "Sounds like you have something in mind."

"I do," Mac replied. "We think he's close, right?" He looked up at us. We nodded in agreement. "He's using *our* chat room, killing people we know. Ellie already used the room to initiate a response from him, but all that gleaned is a possible nickname." He paused.

Caine paced up and down. "Go ahead, Mac."

"Why not use the room to trap him?" Mac said.

Caine slid back into the chair and leaned towards Mac. "How?"

"I could spend a few hours in the room, doing regular host-type stuff, as though everything's fine. Ellie and I know when he's in there. My idea involves Ellie parking close to the Interscape Café, but out of plain view. If I announce to the room that I'm staying in Lexington for a few days and need to go out for a bit, but will drop by the Interscape Café and check on the room. It's what a good chat room moderator would do." He made eye contact with me then carried on. "Which is what I'll do. He seems unable to resist taunting us, so let's give him an opportunity. Maybe we can catch him."

Caine rocked back on his chair. "A couple of points.

One, the building is too big for one person to watch. It will require Ellie plus at least one other agent. Two, we must consider the possibility of him being already at the café when you get there, and that puts you and any patrons in a very dangerous position."

I interrupted. "How long do you need to secure the café?"

"Two hours," Caine replied.

"Well, let's do that while Mac is in the chat room setting the scene. Before his announcement."

"The biggest problem is that he may be watching and may follow Ellie, in which case the whole thing falls flat."

"I have a solution," I said. "Let's have Mac mention that I have gone grocery shopping. Have someone tail me. I will *go* shopping, and if he does follow, we'll pick him up then."

Mac came up with a twist on my idea. "What if I mention I'm meeting you at the café after you're done shopping? Up the ante for him, he gets to have us both in the same place, he likes that."

"Yep, he does, sick shit that he is."

I watched Caine's face as he thought. I knew he was coming up with a revised game plan. "Ellie you shop ... with a protection detail that will hopefully remain invisible and not tip off our Unsub. Join me, when you're done. You'll be late meeting Mac, which gives him an excuse to log into the chat room while he waits."

"Excellent." Mac seemed quite perky at the thought of swaying the balance of power.

"What time is it?" Caine asked.

"Ten," I replied.

"Let me organize everything. Mac, get yourself into that chat room and do what you do. I want surveillance in place before you mention your little outing to meet Ellie for coffee. I will call at midday. I'm going to shoot for a two-thirty set-up and want everyone in place, barring you and Ellie, by twelve-thirty at the latest."

Mac nodded.

"Ellie, you go shopping at one-fifteen. I'll confirm time when I call."

I nodded. It felt good to be proactive instead of reactive.

Caine rose from his chair. "I'll be in touch. You did well, Mac."

"Thanks," Mac replied.

Caine's mouth twitched at both corners as he left the table. I recognized the twitch as his equivalent to an all-out grin. He reached into his pocket and handed me two credit cards and a roll of cash.

"I set up a new account for this situation, credit only."

I looked at the Visa and American express he pressed into my hand. "Thank you."

"You're welcome. Here's five hundred dollars in cash. Keep all your receipts."

"I always do."

"If you need anymore, let me know. I am the only one with access to the new account." Caine twitched. "I'll call you soon."

I walked him to the door and locked it after him.

I heard my phone ring from the counter top. Mac frowned as he picked it up and read the display. "Why doesn't she ever listen?"

I shrugged and dropped the roll of bills and the credit cards onto the table.

Images of the woman wildly clicking the print icon on her computer, while cursing the printer for not obeying her instantly, popped into my head.

I wrestled the phone from Mac's grasp, "Its Ellie here, Mrs. Connelly. Mac and I are a little busy right now. But if you would like, I can come up in a few days and I will fix your printer for you." I have a five-pound sledgehammer that should fix it. If it doesn't, I can get some power gel: The explosion might take out half the house but it would damn well fix the printer problems.

I hung up, and blocked her number on my phone.

Mac sat on the bed watching me.

"And?"

"And she didn't really listen at all, so I blocked her number."

He toppled back onto the unmade bed. "Good thinking."

I grabbed Mac's hand and tugged. "Come on, get in the chat room and be charming."

He pulled back. I fell onto him. He grinned and said, "We have a few hours."

"And they'll evaporate fast if we don't move!"

I rolled off him. Mac sat up. "Tease!"

“Am not!” I retorted. I hauled myself off the bed and searched through our bags for clothes. Mac chuckled and went back to the table. I heard him typing as I searched. He was doing the host thing and catching up with the remaining regulars. I showered and wrapped a towel around my hair. I went back to the main room and dressed. The towel fell on the floor as I dragged a tee shirt over my head. Wet hair stuck to my back, which made me wonder why I didn’t think to drop a blow dryer into my bag of tricks. I’d searched the bathroom and found a notice in a drawer saying a hair drier was available at the front desk for a reasonable fee. Guess they had a lot of theft.

“I’ll be you for a bit if you want to take a shower,” I said.

I leaned over Mac’s shoulder to see who was in the room. There were noticeable gaps among those we had considered friends. I ignored the building sadness at the loss of lives. “Did you hear me?”

“No,” his voice was a little husky as he replied, “What did you say?”

“I said I’ll be you for a bit if you want to take a shower.”

“Oh.” He reached up and removed strands of wet hair from my face. “That’s not at all what I heard.”

“Do tell?” I prodded him to move from the chair.

“I heard ‘take a shower with me?’” He gave me a long look that ran from head to toe. “I see you managed to do that all by yourself.”

"Go! Shower!" I pointed to the bathroom.

"Damn, I thought you were propositioning me."

I grinned. "If this all works out I sure will be."

"Tease."

"Hit the shower, dude." I nudged him out of his chair.

"All right, all right." Mac stooped down and kissed the top of my head. "Be back soon. Try not to get into any trouble."

I feigned horror at his comment. "As if!"

"Just be me, not you," he said as he walked away.

I became Mac in the chat room and made charming Mac-like comments. I enjoyed reading the recited poetry and watching the conversation thread between poems. After a few minutes, I had the hang of being Mac and enjoyed myself. My phone rang. The noise alone almost toppled me from my chair. I checked the display and was surprised. Aidan.

"Hey, Aidan."

"Ellie, where are you?"

"Why?" I asked.

I squinted at the screen. Someone had used a pink font and it was difficult to read. Had I been Otherwisecat and not Galileo, I would have insisted that they change it to something more suitable. It took great self-control to resist reprimanding Sweetpea for her ridiculous choice of color.

I could hear Aidan's voice in my ear but had to ask him to repeat, he sounded huffy as he did so.

"I thought I saw you on the road to Mauryville, yesterday."

"It's possible." I exhaled, and decided to pay more attention to my brother's call and less to the room.

"What are you doing back down that way?" Then I heard the concern in his voice.

"We had to pick up some stuff from home." I felt zero need to elaborate on that or anything else that had happened.

"We? Is Mac still with you?"

"Yep."

"Good," he replied in a calmer voice. His intonation suggested he had yet to address his real reason for calling.

"What's up, Aidan?"

"Mom."

Ack, that's all I needed. I felt my back stiffen. "How bad?"

"She's upset. You haven't called, and she hasn't seen you in weeks ... Blah, blah, blah."

I chewed my bottom lip. Upset was code for nuttier than a Snickers bar.

Aidan continued. "She's not real bad yet but I can feel it building."

I typed a quick comment into the room: Well read, just as Mac would after someone had recited. They didn't need to know I had no clue what the poem was about.

"You still staying at their place?"

"On and off, yes."

"Go home. Be out of range."

"But what about Dad?" His reply alerted me to the real problem he was struggling with, his guilt at leaving Dad to deal with Mom.

"Aidan," I said. "Go home. Dad can take care of her. He's been doing it a long time, and it is not your problem." I paused and could hear his breathing.

"I feel bad leaving him when she's worked up."

More code; worked up means borderline manic.

"I know. Just go, Aidan. You don't have to put up with her shit anymore. You're an adult. Walk away."

"Okay." For the first time in a long time, I realized I missed Aidan's company. I hated not being there for him.

"Go home, catch up with friends, have some fun. I'll go see Dad and her as soon as I can."

"Be safe, Ellie." The phone call ended and left me staring at the screen.

I placed the phone on the table and continued being Mac in the room, even though I knew he was standing behind me. He'd been there for half the conversation. I didn't have to explain anything to Mac. We shared a common family background – insane mothers. It was a lot to rise above.

We bore scars from less-than-perfect and nowhere-near-normal childhoods. Over time, we managed to develop a healthier perspective of the insanity that had ruled our lives for so long. My answer was distance. I kept a physical and emotional distance between the woman known as Mom and myself. Despite the distance, I remained very close to my Dad; it was a juggling act which Aidan couldn't pull off. He was blackmailed into contact and still clamored for the mother he wanted and needed. I knew by the time I was eight that 'Mommy Dearest' was all we were ever going to get.

Mac, too, had a close relationship with his father and saw his parents regularly. He tolerated his mother. Finding her antics mostly amusing, she'd swapped violent insanity for a more quirky and entertaining form of dementia, with fewer outbursts of uncontrolled anger.

Mac had replied to a poem in the chat room. I hadn't even noticed his hand on the keyboard.

"You okay?" he asked. I ducked under his arm and moved from the chair.

"Yeah, just ramblings and mom bullshit," I said. "I think we need more coffee. I'll make some."

"Good idea."

I knew he watched me as I moved to the tiny sink and cleaned out the coffee pot. An unusual, subdued tension had begun to creep into the room.

Mac had gone quiet. Apprehension pervaded every space of the motel room, interrupted only by the sound of cups placed on the tabletop, the mechanical tapping of computer keys and the occasional flick of a cigarette lighter.

Caine called at midday, saying everything was set. All surveillance was in place and Mac had the go-ahead to construct the farce. Caine reminded him to converse with people in the chat room about how bored he was. At the appointed time, he would mention that OtherwiseCat was leaving to do some grocery shopping and afterwards he would meet her at the café. We stared at each other as the call ended.

I spoke, "Has this been the longest day so far or what?"

"Hell, yeah," Mac replied. "Only an hour before you leave."

"I hope this works." I sat next to Mac and glanced at his screen. I also hoped the agents following me stayed close and remained undetected.

His hand touched mine. "You're not sure, are you?"

"Nope." My reply was honest. "I am hoping this catches him off guard and he shows because he can't resist the opportunity." My tone lacked assurance, and I knew it.

"I know; me too. Guess we'll find out."

"I want you to wear a wire." I had been thinking about it, and I was worried. "I'm going to call Caine and have you rigged for sound."

Mac frowned. "There are agents everywhere."

"Humor me, okay? I want to know myself that you're all right," I told him, while I pressed in the quick-dial code for Caine's phone. I watched Mac's expression sour further as he listened to me ask Caine for a voice-activated radio microphone. Caine agreed and said someone would drop a parcel at the motel reception desk within ten minutes.

I ended the call and glared at Mac. "And," I paused. "I'll have the car. You'll be walking over to the café. I just need know you get there safe."

He gave me a strange look then grinned. "You think I

am in danger of being molested on the streets of Lexington?"

"You never know your luck."

Ten minutes later, I collected the parcel Caine had promised. Back in our room I opened the small box and removed what looked like a lapel pin.

"There is a tiny, tiny switch at the back of this pin." I turned it over to show him. "I'll turn it on before I leave."

I attached the pin to his collar.

"How loudly do I have to speak?"

"Normally. It'll pick up everything from a slight whisper to more usual speaking levels."

"How clear?"

"Very; no one will miss anything you say."

"That almost sounded like a warning." He pulled me to him.

"It wasn't." Or maybe it was. Just a little one.

My phone rang. Caine was ready to run a sound check and wanted the mic on. I flipped up Mac's collar and turned the tiny switch to the 'on' position.

"You're live."

His eyes widened. He looked as though he'd never speak again. "Don't tell me you've suddenly become mute?"

"Not quite," he replied. "Just a little nervy. It's more real now."

"Go sit over by the computers and say something quietly," I instructed.

A few moments later, the phone rang again.

"Checked okay," Caine said

"Cool, he may as well leave it on. It's almost time for me to go."

"Yes, I'll see you soon."

"Okay."

I ended the call.

"Okay, I'll get ready," I said to Mac.

I gathered all the necessary items, my gun, holster, a jacket and wallet. From the box Caine sent over I removed a very small earpiece. I turned it on and pushed it into my ear letting my hair fall to cover it.

"Mac?"

"Yeah?" he replied, looking across the room at me.

"Just checking," I said with a smile.

I stamped my feet a little to ensure my boots were snug.

"Want a hand with anything?" he asked. "There's not much happening in the room right now, and typing 'I'm bored' doesn't require much preparation."

"I'm done," I replied. I wore a shoulder holster concealed under my black leather jacket. My hair was loose to prevent anyone close to me seeing the small earpiece. I stood in the middle of the room and did a quick run-through, making sure I accounted for everything I needed. "You take my cell phone so Caine can get hold of you. I'll exercise the company credit cards and buy a new one."

"All right. Sounds like a plan. You set?"

"Yep."

Mac walked me to the door. "Be careful." He wrapped

me in his arms and kissed me. “I’ll see you soon, babe.”

“You sure will. Remember I’ll be fashionably late. I think I’ll ditch the Explorer, too. Get us a rental. It’ll make it a bit harder for this nut-job to spot me.”

“Good idea, but I don’t want another festering, old redneck disaster!”

I winked at him. “Okay, no Fords.”

Mac waited by the door. He waved as I drove off.

CHAPTER ELEVEN

HOLD ON I'M COMING

Grocery shopping would be a good idea, seeing as room service was a luxury we no longer had. My plan was simple: Grocery store, electronics store then drop off the Explorer at the mechanic's place and pick up a rental.

I parked in the last available parking space outside the grocery store and was pleased not to have to walk far. I caught sight of a reflection in the large window. Two parking spaces away an agent I knew climbed out of a beat-up old car. It was comforting to know they were around.

I had no idea what I was shopping for as I entered the store. I strolled down aisle after aisle hoping inspiration would grab me as I surveyed the multitude of enticing, packaged foodstuffs. Ahead of me, I saw a familiar figure.

"Hey, Mr. Parker. Thought you did your shopping in Mauryville."

He lifted his head and smiled. "I usually do, Ellie; had some things to take care of in town today."

I nodded and scanned the shelves. Maybe a list would have been a good idea or I could have at least asked Mac what he wanted.

"The whole town's talking about that sorry business out at your place," Jed Parker said, as he scrutinized the label of a competitor's honey jar. The satisfied look on his face suggested his labels were better.

"Really?" Uh huh, of course they are; small town gossip and speculation makes the world go around.

"Yes, indeedy. Even ole Doc Tompson is talking. He told me he saw that fella."

Okay, so now I was interested. "How'd he know it was him?"

"He spoke to him."

"Really?" I tried not to appear too interested, but this was something new.

"Yeah. He said he spoke to him. He said his name was Carter McDonald."

Whoa, back up ... Carter's name was not McDonald. His name was McClaren.

"McDonald?" I repeated.

"That's what Doc said. Also said he was a vet from Illinois."

A vet? What the hell? Now he's Carter McDonald the vet. It's has to be someone else, surely? Coincidence maybe? Ketamine lurched into my conscious thought. Vets have access to ketamine. Carter had ketamine in his system. Note to self: Have someone to talk to Doc Tompson.

I tried to sound nonchalant as I asked, "Did Doc say what Carter wanted with him?"

"He never said," Mr. Parker replied. "Probably vet business."

Vet business; the man was supposed to be a chef. A chef, not a vet. There is something screwy with this whole scenario. Surely, an alias would have been uncovered during the preliminary investigation.

"Don't suppose you know when Doc saw him?"

"I do. Doc told me it was the night before the ruckus out at your place."

I thought for a second about the last known sighting of Carter. "Did you see Carter the next day?" I knew they'd followed him to Parker's and then lost him.

"No, Kevin and the boys were all over my place looking for someone, told me they found his car. No strangers came into the store or came to the house."

My mind threw up visions of Kevin and the boys, *Dukes of Hazzard*-style. I'd be damned if I'd be Daisy. Best if Holly took that role. I shook the intrusion from my already over-taxed mind and nodded. "I'd best get a move on, Mr. Parker."

I checked my watch and reminded myself if I didn't get out of there I really would be late. Every now and then, I could hear Mac muttering in my ear, which was unnerving. I kept expecting to hear, "10-4 little fat buddy," come out of his mouth. I had to shake the *Dukes of Hazzard* visions.

Mr. Parker placed a gnarled hand on my elbow. "Not before I tell ya about the dance, Taylor's barn, two weeks on Saturday."

I grinned. "Tell me there's venison pie for supper and I'm there."

"Hell, yes, and honey mead."

"We'll be there," I assured him.

Jed's worn face broke under a wide smile. "You and that Mac fella?"

Oh man! "Yeah."

"I heard tell he's a good one." Mr. Parker nodded. "Kevin said he thinks mighty highly of that man of yours."

I smiled. "See you at the dance, Mr. P."

I grabbed a few cans of some kind of casseroled muck. The label looked inviting, but I suspected the contents would resemble cat food. I hurried down the next aisle in search of fruit. I needed fruit. I escaped the supermarket and dropped the bag of groceries onto the back seat of the car. I walked a few doors down to the electronics store and struggled to maintain my composure, while I listened to a conversation Mac had with someone about the planting of bulbs. I also heard street noises; it sounded like he was on his way to the café and had stopped for a chat. I attempted to wipe the smile off my face as I entered the store.

Mac had made it to the café and ordered his coffee. I had an urge to ask him to order for me, too, but knew he couldn't hear me.

I chose a new phone, handed over a credit card, and filled in the paperwork for a new connection. Mac could keep my other phone. This one we'd keep free from Manic Mother calls.

Next stop, the mechanic. I'm sure dollar signs pinged up in Floyd's eyes when he saw the state of the Explorer. I'd bet money on him working for Boss Hogg. I'd bet money on him being related to Boss Hogg, possibly a first-cousin marriage. I had to get the Dukes of Hazzard thing out of my head.

"What do you need Ms. Conway?" he asked. The man seemed to be in a permanent state of filth.

"I need you to *not* rip me off, Floyd, you got that?" My tone conveyed instant death: The only way to deal with Floyd.

"Yes ma'am."

"I want George to do the panel work, not one single scratch or ding is to be left in this truck."

He inspected the damaged panels, running his grimy, oil-stained hands all over what was once my immaculate vehicle.

"You been ramming shit in this thing? You've smashed up your lights. You should have bull bars."

"Whatever," I replied, and quickly dismissed the idea and Floyd's notion of making extra cash out of me. "I want you to change the oil, change the filters, check the brakes, the belts, and ..." I gave him a long hard stare, "... *NO* joy riding in my car!"

He shuffled from foot to foot looking a little embarrassed. "Yes, ma'am."

I kept my smile to myself. Something told me I was close with the first cousin hypothesis.

"I need a rental."

His eyes lit up; before he could say anything I continued. "I'll be back in a bit, and give you the keys then."

I left Floyd to his embarrassed pondering, and strode

up the street to the rental company. Like hell I would rent a car from Floyd.

I picked out a car and drove back to Floyd's garage. I took everything from my car and flipped the keys to Floyd.

Once settled in the rental, I cranked the window. "Not one cent will be paid until I have test driven that car, and thoroughly inspected the panel work."

"Yes, ma'am."

I grinned as I pulled out of his lot. Yes ma'am, no ma'am, three bags full ma'am. I suspected that had I looked in my rear view mirror, a bird would have flown my way.

I slipped into a parking space under a large maple within clear sight of the Interscape Café: My predetermined surveillance spot was a good one. The agent I'd seen earlier drove by and disappeared around a corner. I checked my watch; still not late.

The front entrance of the red-bricked café looked inviting and the mingled smells of roasted coffee beans were divine. My mind screamed espresso as I settled in.

I called Mac and told him I was there. "Hey you, I'm here. Make it look like I'm telling you I'll be late. Make sure you add this number to your phone, okay?"

"Will do and I'll be waiting," he replied. The smile that curled my toes came through in his voice.

"Miss you."

"You too, see you when you get here."

I hung up and watched a few cars go by, then called

Caine. "I'm in position; you got anything?"

"Not a dickey bird. You got a new phone. Good thinking."

"I have something for you. Did anyone speak to Doc Tompson out in Mauryville?"

"Shit, Ellie, I'd have to check the case notes."

"I think you should and find out why Carter used the name McDonald or, if he didn't, find out who the hell Carter McDonald is."

Caine interrupted me, "That's the third time that car has been by in the last fifteen minutes. Did you get the tags?"

"Yes. I'll call them in."

I disconnected the call to Caine and dialed our central communications call center.

"Special Agent Conway badge number seven-nine-seven-two requesting QV." Okay, so we don't *always* use plain English but 'query vehicle' takes too long to say.

"Go ahead SA."

"Personalized Virginia plate reads L-M-A-O. Lima Mike Alpha Oscar."

Seconds later, I got my answer. "White Mazda sedan, registered owner Darius Harcourt Senton, Virginia Beach address."

"Thanks, Conway out." I hung up. Watching the road as the car came back around again, I made a connection.

"Dhs, oh man!" I called Caine back while observing the car park up the street. He seemed to change his mind and drove off again.

"L-M-A-O is chat-speak for 'laugh my ass off'… The car is registered to a Darius Harcourt Senton of Virginia Beach … his initials are Dhs. Coincidence?"

"I'm on it," he hissed and hung up.

Mac sighed in my ear and whispered, "The Unsub is in the chat room." Then I heard the email alert sound on the computer and him click twice then whisper again, "'He waits – but will she come?'" Mac groaned. "Fuck me. He's got to be watching."

I put the phone back to my ear and called Caine again, my stomach twisted. "Did you hear Mac?"

"Of course."

"Could he be in there?"

"No one but Mac has entered the café since midday."

My thoughts ran wild. "What if he's been using the café the whole time, he could have already been in there."

I listened as Caine spoke to the agents in the café. "He may be among the patrons." Brief and to the point, as usual.

Then he spoke to me again, "Heads up, Ellie. That white car is back."

I watched and memorized a partial description of the driver. Backwards red baseball cap, sandy hair, freckled face, young looking, wearing a faded, beige-checked shirt.

Two men walked towards the Interscape Café on foot. I watched with interest but they passed on by.

The white car parked up the street and someone exited the vehicle. I called Mac as the person approached the café parking lot, then turned and headed down the side of the building.

"Look out the window by you," I said. "Is someone there? A male wearing a red baseball cap backwards?"

I saw Caine run past me. He hurried up the street to the white vehicle and waited out of sight.

"Jesus!" Mac exclaimed. "There was, and he's running!" Mac started chuckling. "He runs like a girl."

"Order me a coffee, Mac. I'll be in shortly." I disconnected the call and drove up the street to join Caine. I arrived just as he stepped from the shadows of a building and confronted the man.

"Going somewhere?" he asked, as the scruffy individual tried to unlock the driver's door.

"Home," he replied, with downcast eyes.

"Where's home?" Caine asked. He opened his jacket just enough to reveal his gun and badge.

"Natural Bridge," the young man replied. He stared a hole into the ground.

Caine rolled his eyes at me. We both knew this kid was no killer. He didn't have the confidence to lie nor was he brazen enough to face us.

"Come on over here and give me those car keys," Caine said, and held his hand out. "What's your name, son?"

"Jimmy," he replied. "Jimmy Turner." He handed Caine the keys and stood on the sidewalk with his arms hanging by his sides.

I now had a better chance to look at him. His hands were rough and unkempt.

His clothes seemed several sizes too big and well-worn. The pattern on his flannel shirt had long since faded into a nondescript beige blur. There were oil and grease marks on his torn and ragged-bottomed jeans.

"Well, Jimmy Turner. I think your mama is going to be disappointed in you."

"I didn't do nuthin'." Jimmy's voice cracked a little.

"Let's start with driving a car that doesn't belong to you and move on from there, shall we?"

"I'm under arrest?"

I smiled at Caine and whispered in his ear, "Jimmy's none too bright."

"No, Jimmy, you are helping us with our enquiry," Caine said. "How old are you, son?"

"I'm twenty," he replied. He kicked at stones with shoes that had seen better days. For the first time Jimmy raised his eyes. He drawled, partly under his breath, "I'm not your son."

Caine's mouth twitched. "Well, son, you and I are going to have a chat."

I motioned to Caine to step back with me for a moment. "I'm going to go have a coffee with Mac. The real killer may show." I'd heard some very strange things over the earpiece and I knew Caine had, too.

"Yeah, do that. You think Mac's okay?"

"He seems odd, and it's not like him." Odd? He was whistling 'Three Blind Mice' in between bouts of random noises. He'd moved on from odd and had begun to freak me out.

"Go find out. I'll have a talk to this young man, and

then get someone to remove and impound the car."

I said goodbye to Jimmy. He seemed a little special. I drove back to the café and parked in the lot. I found Mac where I thought he would be. There was something peculiar going on with Mac. He was sitting facing a computer and didn't see me approach. His hands were tapping out a beat on the desk as he chuckled to himself.

I took my earpiece from my ear and turned it off then dropped it into my shirt pocket.

"Hey, Mac."

He looked over at me and appeared to have difficulty focusing for a second or two. "Ellie!" He leapt to his feet and grabbed me in a bear hug and swung me around before putting me down.

"You okay?" I asked while I made sure I was on my feet.

"I'm great!" He sat back down and reached for the coffee in front of him. I intercepted the cup and moved it away. He slurred, "Hey. Get your own."

"I will in a minute, have to call Caine." I walked away a few feet and watched him as I held my phone ready to make a call. He was not behaving anywhere near normal. Mac lit a cigarette and sat staring at the burning embers. My phone rang. Caine pre-empted my call.

"And?"

"He's high. I don't know how but he is."

"I'm sending two agents over to you. They have been in the café for a few hours now."

"Thanks."

"He okay?"

"Seems to be. He's quite entertaining ... I'll deal with this, you sort out Jimmy."

I hung up and dropped the phone into my pocket.

Mac called out to me, "Ellie! Dance with me?"

I smiled indulgently at him. I had no doubt he could hear music but it wasn't playing in my head, and he hated to dance.

"Check it out, Ellie, this is way cool." He held out the burning cigarette and touched the ember with a finger.

"Mac, stop it!" I snatched the smoke from his hand and looked at his finger. "You've burned yourself."

"It doesn't hurt," he replied, inspecting his finger.

"It will later."

Footsteps came up behind me. I glanced over my shoulder as two agents came into view. I turned to face them and smiled. "Lee?" It was at least four years since I'd seen Lee. He was bigger than I remembered, but hadn't aged at all. There was still a familiar smidge of Rambo mixed with rock star in Lee.

"Hey, Ellie," he replied.

"Will you get a glass of iced water, please?" I asked, and held up Mac's finger for him to see.

"Be right back."

Mac found Lee's presence amusing. "Oh, cool, General Lee."

I looked up at the second agent. It had been too long. He grinned at me then spoke to Mac, "I'm Sam, General Lee's partner."

Mac smiled vacantly.

I attracted Sam's attention with a question, "Did you see who brought Mac his coffee?"

"A pretty, little dark-haired chick. I'm on it," Sam said, then strode away in the direction of the kitchen, leaving me stunned. The older he got the more he looked like Mr. T, minus the bling, of course. I shook *The A-Team* theme song from my head as I wondered if Sam was scared to fly in an airplane.

Lee came back with the water. I set it on the desk and plunged Mac's finger into it. Mac leaned back in his chair, his head tilted up, smiling at whatever he could see on the ceiling.

"What's up there?" I asked. I hoped to find a clue as to what was happening in his head.

"Rainbows and butterflies. See? The small rainbow is trying to be a big rainbow." He pointed. We looked. After in-depth inspection of the ceiling all I saw were the old ceiling lights and the need for fresh paint.

Lee and I looked at each other. "He's tripping," Lee mumbled. "Look at him ... He's relaxed, feeling no pain, hallucinating."

Sam came back holding a young girl by the elbow. He was short of breath and flushed. I gave him an enquiring glance.

"She ran when I asked her about the coffee." Sam pressed the girl into an empty seat and spun it to face us. "This is Julie. She has something to tell you, Conway."

"Go ahead, Julie." She looked all of eighteen and

scared. I gave her my undivided attention, which wasn't easy with Mac asking me to dance every two seconds. He didn't just want to dance: He wanted to dance on a rainbow.

"He said it wouldn't hurt him, it was a joke." She paused and looked at Mac, then up at me. "I was supposed to give him his coffee at the end of my shift then go home, but they asked me to do extra hours to cover for someone."

I rolled my eyes. "I don't really care why you are still here. What was in the coffee?"

"It was a clear liquid."

I was losing my cool with the half-wit. "What kind of liquid?" I snapped.

"I don't know; it was in a little bottle."

"Where's the bottle now?"

The girl shrugged.

Mac sang again. This time it was 'Somewhere Over The Rainbow.'

"What did this man say to you, exactly?" I asked, and leaned forward towards the girl. I wanted to pull my gun, hold it to her stupid temple and squeeze the trigger. Why would anyone put something in someone's drink? People are dumb.

"He told me to put the stuff in his coffee and then take it to him. He said it wouldn't hurt him."

"How much were you paid?"

"Twenty dollars."

Sam's large hands hauled her to her feet and he

searched her pockets. I noticed he'd already pulled on latex gloves. He found a twenty-dollar bill in her jeans' pocket.

"This it?" he asked.

"Yes." Her voice trembled. Tears built up in her eyes.

Sam dropped the note into a small baggie and sealed it, then shoved her back down.

"When and where did this happen?"

"Out the back, around lunch time. I was outside having a break. He must've been over by the trees behind the building."

"Describe him."

Lee was ready, pen poised over his notebook. Mac had quit singing and was talking to the rainbow people.

"Tall. As tall as him." Julie pointed to Lee. "But not big like him, more medium-sized."

"So you're saying he's around six feet four inches and medium built?" Lee clarified her answer.

She nodded and said, "He was white, thirty maybe, old."

I guess to an eighteen-year-old, thirty does seem old. Some days thirty feels old.

Mac chuckled. "It's General Lee." Then managed to spill the water all over himself.

Sam swooped in, with surprising agility and a bunch of napkins and mopped it up.

Mac chuckled louder. "You're Mr. T?"

Sam grinned. "I'm whoever you need me to be, you just be happy, yeah?"

Mac's hand reached up and touched Sam's bald head. "How do you get your head so smooth and shiny?"

Sam's grin grew even wider, exposing his brilliant white teeth. "A bit of elbow grease goes a long way. You ask those rainbow people of yours."

Oh man! My head was starting to pound. I needed coffee. I was in a café and I didn't have a coffee! I listened to the girl and to Mac's ramblings.

"He was nice looking, had blue eyes and very dark hair. He had on jeans and a mid-blue hooded sweater."

Since when was 'nice looking' a description we could use?

A slow dawning occurred: Decoy. The bastard had screwed us again. Two decoys for what? Jimmy wasn't a killer. Why drug Mac?

The answer was obvious: To keep us busy and off balance.

Julie said one more thing; I heard it echo through my head. "Cornflakes."

"What?" I asked. "What about cornflakes?"

"He told me the stuff in the coffee was like liquid cornflakes."

I closed my eyes and took a slow breath. "Ketamine," I said and stared at the girl."

Lee tapped my shoulder. "If he's been given ketamine then by the look of him he's had just enough to put him into K-land; it should only last an hour or so."

"K-land?"

"He's tripping, With K you either go to K-land, which

has been described as a magical wonderland ... or you do the K-hole thing, which is like a near-death experience or so they say." Lee kept his voice low and even. "The thing now is, let's make sure he stays happy ... even tones, no raised voices. We don't want him agitated and we don't want to turn this trip into a scary thing."

"Okay. Will he remember this?"

"Maybe, some do, some don't."

Mac interrupted us, "Heeeeey, General Lee?"

"Yeah?"

"Wouldn't you be really, really old now?" Mac spun around in his chair with his head back watching the ceiling the whole time. "The rainbow people said you were really old."

"Yep, I'm an old bastard, Mac," Lee replied. "Mind if I sit with you a bit?"

"Nope." He tipped his head further back and asked the Rainbow people if they minded; apparently they didn't mind either. "See the little tiny rainbow person?" Mac pointed to the ceiling. "That's a new one, you can tell 'cos the colors aren't as bright as the others."

Lee perched on the desk and conversed with the rainbow people and Mac. For one surreal instance, the whole thing seemed very normal.

Sam hauled Julie to her feet a second time and said to me, "I'll take this girly outside. We'll get a full description of this man to Caine and he'll decide whether we press charges or not."

I glared at him. "She will be charged. I'm thinking we

start with reckless endangerment and move on up from there."

Sam smiled, turning a little, so the girl couldn't see his face. "Mac's one of us, huh?"

"Yep."

"Drugging a federal agent carries a high penalty. I wouldn't want to be you, kid. Administering a Schedule-3 controlled substance to a Fed ..." he said. He spun her to face him and shook his head from side to side. I could've sworn I heard him whisper, "Pity the fool!"

The girl looked ill. "I'd better get her out before she pukes."

"Okay. I'm staying here with Mac."

Lee moved to get a chair, which he pulled past Mac to sit on the window side of him. I sat on the other side. It was killing me knowing the bastard drugged Mac, but he was pretty damn amusing. There was a growing need for coffee. The low levels of caffeine in my system were threatening to tip my mood into a downward spiral.

"I'm going for coffee," I told Lee and Mac. I stood up then stooped and kissed Mac's forehead.

He smiled up at me. "You're my girlfriend."

I smiled back. "Yes, I am."

I ordered us coffee and watched as it was made. Something forced its way into my consciousness causing me to tug my phone from my pocket and call Caine.

There were no niceties as I vocalized my thoughts, "Jimmy Turner ... decoy one. Mac being drugged ... decoy two. Why?"

"To throw us off balance," he replied with customary calmness. "To pull manpower away from his target or prove how clever he is."

"What the hell does he want?"

"We're getting closer to finding that out. Every time he does something the odds of discovery go up. I'm almost done with Jimmy then I'll meet with Sam and the girl."

"We're stuck here till Mac feels better." I looked at the counter: Our coffee was ready. "I'll talk to you soon."

"Leave his mic on, so I can monitor the situation."

"Will do."

I shoved the phone in my pocket and paid for the coffee. I picked up the tray and headed back to Lee and Mac.

Mac was talking when I arrived back. I almost dropped the tray when I heard him say, "Just stop clicking the damn thing!" I heard his mother's voice getting louder and angrier. Mac said, "Why is it so hard for you to follow simple instructions?"

I glared at Lee and snapped, "We were keeping him happy ... what's with the phone?"

"It's his Mom," he replied. "How bad can it be?"

Okay, it was unfair of me to be snappish with Lee; he didn't know about Mac's mother.

"Trust me, Lee!" I grimaced and turned my attention to Mac. "... is that your Mom?"

Mac didn't attempt to shield the phone as he spoke to me, "She's fuc'n nuts, Ellie; silly bitch keeps clicking and clicking and screaming and clicking."

Uh oh. I smiled at Mac and slipped the phone from his

hand into mine.

"Mrs. Connelly, it's Ellie." I could hear her angry raspy breathing down the phone. "Mac's not very well. I'll get back to you soon and explain."

She screamed at me, "He called me a bitch!"

"I'm sorry. I'll explain later." How the hell I would manage that I didn't know. She was not going to let this one go in a hurry.

She yelled some more, "He can't speak to me like that!"

"I have to go now."

I hung up and once again blocked her number. This time I kept Mac's phone in my pocket. He was leaning back in the chair making random comments to the rainbow people about how he was the HP help desk.

Lee looked over at me. "He seems calm enough." He wasn't so much calm as mellow. Mac was in a happy place.

"For now," I replied. "Wait till this wears off and he finds out what he's done."

I sipped my coffee and smoked a cigarette, letting Mac have a drag every now and then. I didn't want him holding anything that could hurt him.

I turned my chair so I could see Mac and into the café. My mind sifted through the most recent events. My car. Oh man, he got me out of my car. So much for swapping the Explorer, the clever little shit knows what I'm driving again.

I looked at Lee. "Could either of you see my car before

you came over to help me out?"

"Yeah, we both could. We saw you park and come in." His congenial expression fell, "Shit!"

"Who else is in here?"

"No one, now. There were four of us. Caine called two to help him. Sam's outside with the chick. I'm with you." Lee's brown eyes widened, "We've been played. We under estimated the motherfucker."

"Well fuck!" So far, we're not doing too well. The FBI foiled again by a lone nutter and his ability to distract.

Lee's phone rang. I knew it was Caine.

"I'm on it, boss," Lee said then hung up. He lifted his eyes to mine. "He wants you and Mac to stay in here. We've got four more agents arriving in less than ten minutes; when they arrive I'll go out and check the car."

I had trouble believing that all this was just so he could hide another body in a car in a public place. I don't know why it was difficult for me to believe. Maybe I just didn't want to.

My phone rang. I was very tired of hearing cell phones ring. It was Caine again. "I got a call back from Virginia Beach. Darius Senton left his home early yesterday morning. There have been no sightings since. No signs of struggle in his house. He lives alone. Neighbors reported seeing him leave in the company of another man. Nothing seemed out of the ordinary at the time."

"So is he the Unsub or is he dead?" It would be too easy for him to be the Unsub.

"Good question, which hopefully we can answer soon."

Caine sounded tired. He even sounded annoyed.

"Anything else?"

"Just another complication. DEA are screaming at me. They've lost an agent. He disappeared thirty-six hours ago."

Nope. I didn't see how that was our problem. They should've been more careful. It's not our fault if they were careless and misplaced someone.

"And?"

"You're going to love this ... don't yell at me!" He paused for a breath, "They had an agent in Cobwebs. Ever seen the nickname 4urxtc?"

"Yes, a regular for maybe nine months or more."

"Well, he's missing. They're hollering that we jeopardized an ongoing investigation into Carter's activities within the chat room."

"Like hell we did. They understand the man is dead, right? Rather makes the investigation into his activities difficult, doesn't it? If they had info, they should've come forward. What happened to sharing pertinent information? I didn't even know there was an agent in the room."

Lee tapped my arm and pointed to the computer screen in front of Mac. "You got mail."

"Open it while I'm talking to you," Caine said.

I opened it and read the subject line then the body of the text. "'Chicago' is the subject. Then he says 'How's K-land, Mac? They've all told me it was a fun place to be. Have another gift for you, Otherwisecat. Remember Chicago? He broke your arm. 4urxtc won't bother you anymore.'" My heart was doing more than pound now. It was threatening to stop all together. How would this fuckhead know about Chicago? I could hear Caine breathing.

He took a deep breath, let it out and said, "How's Mac?"

I tested my voice, "Okay." I don't think it shook too much.

"We'll talk about this later. Meanwhile let's expect another body to turn up soon. If and when that happens I'll deal with DEA." His voice was even. He didn't sound annoyed by the new development. I couldn't think if that was a good thing or not. I couldn't think.

Lee took the phone from my hand, and said something to Caine. I don't know what he said. My brain had stalled again.

Chapter Twelve

Objects In The Rear View Mirror May Appear Closer Than They Are

Mac began to return to normal. I noticed it when he looked at me fully focused and said, "Gonna tell me what's going on?"

"How do you feel?"

"A bit floaty." He frowned. "I feel like I have missed something."

"That's to be expected." I looked up. Lee nodded so I figured it was okay to tell Mac what had happened. "Our stalker-slash-killer managed to get ketamine into your coffee."

"He what?" Mac was back. His voice echoed the disbelief written all over his face.

"You were drugged. Luckily Lee was here and knows a bit about ketamine and its effects."

"Lee? General Lee." Mac said, shifting his gaze to the bulky agent sitting next to him.

"Yup, that's me." Lee clamped a meaty paw on Mac's shoulder.

"Jesus! What did I do?" Mac bit his lip and looked at me. I wasn't sure he really wanted to know. "How embarrassing was I?"

I grinned. "You were fine. You and the rainbow people were happy as could be."

He groaned and sat up straighter. “I didn’t dance did I?”

“No. You didn’t. You kept asking me but we didn’t dance.”

He heaved a sigh. “What a relief; you know I can’t dance.”

“Can’t sing either,” I replied. His horrified expression made me smile.

“I didn’t!”

I nodded. “You did; you were most entertaining.”

“Shush.” Mac groaned. A blush rose in his cheeks.

Lee’s deep throaty laugh flowed. “Mac, you were just fine. No harm, no foul.”

I tried hard not to laugh.

“I have a weird question.” Mac looked at us both. “Did either of you see Mr. T?”

I choked under the effort needed to remain composed. Lee roared with laughter.

“What did I do?” Mac asked with a resigned sigh.

Lee answered, “I have never seen anyone rub Sam’s head like that before and get away with it.”

Color flamed in Mac’s cheeks. “He’s a real person?”

“Oh yeah, he’s real all right.”

Our laughter subsided. Mac was embarrassed and we weren’t helping any.

“What now?” Mac asked reaching for the pack of Winston’s in front of him. Lee and I watched as he lit a cigarette.

“What?” he asked. Guess our curious expressions gave

something away.

"Nothing," I replied. He was okay and didn't seem drawn to the burning ember or spellbound by the lighter flame. I reached over and turned off the computer. I didn't want Mac seeing the latest email, not yet anyway. I had already forwarded a copy to the lab.

Some sort of commotion reached our ears from the front of the café. Lee's back straightened as he listened.

"They must be here," he commented.

I nodded.

"They who?" Mac asked, stubbing out his cigarette and preparing to move. He seemed back to normal.

"Extra agents," I replied. "We've been waiting for more agents."

We moved as quickly as we could through the tables and past interested patrons. Lee caught my arm as we negotiated through the throng near the door. "Watch him, Ellie. He may not be all the way through the trip yet."

"Does this shit flash back like LSD did in the sixties?"

"Not that I can recall but I'm not a hundred percent sure. I figure he's had an hour and a half or so." Lee glanced at Mac. "It's always possible that the hallucinations haven't completely gone but he seems to be through it. Err on the side of caution."

"Okay."

We had emerged through the front door to the café. In front of us, we found a woman lying on the ground with several people kneeling beside her. I saw an FBI identity card clipped to the shirt pocket of one of the men kneeling. I motioned to Mac and Lee to follow me as I made my way around the edge of the small gathering to the agent.

"Need any help?" I asked as I knelt down by him.

He glanced over at me. We exchanged brief confirming looks. We recognized each other. Kurt shook his head. "Paramedics are on the way. This lady here fell in her rush to get back inside the café."

I almost didn't want to ask. "Why was she in so much of a hurry?"

He looked at me, and then his eyes hit Lee and Mac, "Take a look in the trunk of the red Pontiac over there."

My stomach threatened to revolt. "Last time I looked, it contained my groceries."

He replied under his breath, "I wouldn't want dinner at your house, Conway."

I leaned over to whisper in his ear, "You're not invited. Was there a poem?"

A hint of what he'd viewed reflected in the depth of his tired eyes. "Yes."

"I'm sorry." I meant it. It wasn't fair that we had some insane freak leaving bodies in cars for his personal gratification and traumatizing innocent people.

We headed over to the car and found three agents gathered around the trunk.

"Hey," I called as we approached. Two agents jumped as they spun around. The third lifted his head and acknowledged me with a nod.

"Sorry, didn't mean to frighten y'all."

"You sure you wanna see this, ma'am?"

"No, but I'm going to," I replied.

Lee spoke, "Move aside gentlemen. Agent Conway here is taking a peek." They parted and stepped back. Mac and I moved in closer. Lee positioned himself close to Mac, just in case.

We peered at the headless body. Damn it was weird looking.

"Looks like we found the owner of the head," Mac stated.

I turned to the agent nearest me. "Have you got any gloves?"

He fished a pair of latex gloves from his pocket. "They're large, will probably swim on you," he said handing them over.

"Thanks, they'll do." I slipped them on. The gloves resembled saggy, white elephant skin as they fell in folds and wrinkles from my hands. It was an effort to hold the gloves in place as I reached for the bloodied piece of paper stuck to the neck of the corpse, where once a head had resided. I held it up and read the scrawled handwriting.

"This is entitled 'Stumped'. 'Did you connect the letter in the left-hand side? Have you identified the head I fried? Sticking your neck out would be unwise'."

I could see Mac's appalled look as he stared at the paper in my hand.

"I can't believe you touched that," he said avoiding all

reference to the content and title of the poem. I saw something else too. I detected a tremor in his shoulders. A slight crinkle by his eyes told me he was trying not to laugh.

I looked away. The danger of an uncontrolled outburst of laughter from me was soaring. I put the note back where I found it and watched as the gloves fell from my hands landing on the rim of the trunk. From my perspective they appeared to be climbing into the trunk. I used all my will-power to maintain some semblance of professionalism. My defenses crumbled as the macabre humor of the situation escalated.

I heard Caine's voice somewhere behind me. I checked Mac with a sideways glance to avoid his eyes. I could still see his shoulders trembling.

I did my best to look at the ground and not back at the cause of the problem. I didn't even trust myself to look at Lee. Caine announced his presence with a small cough over my shoulder.

"What do we have?"

No one spoke. I had hoped Lee or Mac would speak up.

"Ellie?"

He sounded as though he expected an answer. I tried to make my voice as normal as possible by taking a deep breath. "This could be Dhs. There's a poem that suggests as much." I could feel the laughter bubbling up in my throat. I clamped my hands over my mouth trying to control myself. I could barely remain upright, and my ribs ached as I struggled to catch my breath.

Caine bellowed, “Conway, get a grip!”

I caught his icy stare as he spun around and stalked to his car. We all heard the car door slam and the engine start. I tried to breathe deeply to calm down; it didn’t work.

I walked away to the edge of the lot to compose myself.

A few minutes later or maybe longer, it’s hard to know when hysteria takes hold, Mac and Lee appeared. Mac sat down on the cold asphalt beside me. He lit a cigarette and passed it to me. Slowly but surely calmness returned.

“We still may be down a body,” I said. “There was only one here, right?” I refused to let my mind go anywhere near the headless corpse thing again.

“Yep, only one,” Lee replied. “He’s probably saving the other for tomorrow.”

I grinned. “Yeah, thanks for that.”

“No problem.”

I reached over to Mac’s collar and turned the microphone off. He smiled at me but said nothing. I was tired of everything we said being broadcast to Caine and who knows who else. A cold gust of wind caused me to shiver. Mac draped his arm around my shoulders and hugged me to him.

Lee crouched down beside us. “You two may as well head off.”

“Don’t even start!”

He grinned. “It was unintentional, I swear! But seriously, you may as well go back to the motel and hang out there until Caine comes up with the next phase. We're all going to be sitting around waiting for the medical examiner and forensics."

"Okay," I replied. Mac stood first and pulled me to my feet.

"You feel okay, Mac?" Lee asked as he scrutinized his face.

"Yeah, I'm fine."

I kicked at a small stone with the toe of my boot trying to hit it into a nearby puddle. "Did anyone see anything?" I felt hopeful.

Lee shook his head. "You're not going to believe this, but so far we haven't found anyone from the café who saw a damn thing; apparently the trunk of your car swung open all by itself as that poor woman passed it."

Maybe this Unsub is a ghost after all. "Surely he has to screw up soon and leave us something."

"Let's hope so. You guys want an escort?"

I shook my head. It wasn't necessary. We were both armed and the Unsub had probably had his fun for the evening. "Thanks Lee."

"You're welcome, take care. Watch out for each other." He shook Mac's hand then mine. I had forgotten how big Lee was, his hand swallowed mine. He walked back towards the throng of agents around our rental car. General Lee and Mr. T waved us off. We headed up the street. The wind picked up and there was a definite chill in the air. Winter was close. The shadows on the ground became darker as the weak sun gave up and hid behind large gray clouds. It didn't take us long to reach the creamy-brick motel. I looked up at the motel sign at the front proudly welcoming us to The Mountain Oasis. Why anyone would give motels names like Oasis or Mecca was beyond me. Every city I have ever visited had at least one Oasis and often several versions of Mecca. I ended the thought train before it derailed my already taxed mind.

Mac unlocked the door and swung it wide open. A wall of warmth hit me as I stepped over a folded newspaper in the doorway. Mac picked up the paper and kicked the door shut behind him. I flopped down on the bed, propped myself on one elbow and watched him. He dropped the paper on the table and then turned his attention to making coffee. He looked great and didn't seem to be suffering any ill-effects from his trip. He turned back to the table and spread out the newspaper.

"I can't believe its still Friday. Was this the longest day ever or what?" he said. I watched his eyes scan the newspaper headlines. Frown lines creased his forehead, deepening as he lowered himself into a chair. Until then I was happy observing but now I had to know.

"What?" I asked, sitting up.

"The Unsub has written to the newspaper," he stated and seemed unable to believe what he read.

"Read it to me."

"'Hello to you all. What a game. What a prize. Ain't it fun? Isn't it time you opened your eyes? Let me introduce myself I am the Son of Shakespeare. Maybe I'll write again, share a poem or two. My Post-it note poems were well received by the FBI. A word to the wise: the ones I protect must be left alone.'"

Mac paused; he exhaled loudly then said, "That's all except the signature, Son of Shakespeare."

I lay flat on the bed with my fingers laced behind my head and stared at the ceiling. Son of Shakespeare? The ones I protect? What a crock of shit!

"Took him a while to involve the media," I said. "And now he's made it more difficult for us all."

"How?"

I heard Mac fold up the paper. He'd had enough news for one day.

"Panic for one, it's no longer a controlled scenario. Network news teams will be all over this like rats." I lifted my head to see Mac's face. "And now we *may* get copycat killers."

"I can't believe this dork thinks he's a poet. Son of Shakespeare!" Mac was disgusted. "Son of a Bitch, more like."

I rolled over and crawled up the bed chuckling to myself. I stretched out on my tummy with my head on the pillow turned towards Mac. My hair kept falling over my face.

"You look comfy." His voice was soft.

"You look too far away." I smiled and reached my hand out to him. He stood up and moved closer taking my hand. I pulled him close to the bed then sat up.

"Take your shirt off," I instructed.

He dropped it on the floor.

"Lay down."

He blinked at me. I patted the expanse of bed next to me. "Just lay down on your tummy, right here."

Mac raised an eyebrow but did as I asked. I climbed over him. Our bags were at the end of the bed. I unzipped my bag, removed a bottle of massage oil.

"What're you doing?" I knew he couldn't see me unless he sat up.

"You'll see," I replied. I took the top off the bottle and tipped some of the contents into my palm. I climbed back onto the bed, and straddled Mac at the hip. I rubbed my hands together for a few moments warming the liquid and releasing the aroma of exotic flowers into the room. I slipped my hands onto his shoulders and rubbed in the oil. Kneading the tight muscles under my fingertips, I worked all the tension from his shoulders and upper back. Mac groaned as I worked my way down his spine, radiating the warmth from the oil and my hands outward.

"Okay?" I asked as I unlocked the pent-up tightness and knots.

"Ohhh, yeah."

He reached his left arm back and took hold of my right hand. "Come here." His voice rasped. I let him guide me as I fell, landing next to him. Mac put one arm over my head and hoisted himself above me.

"You're just full of surprises." He smiled. His eyes sparkled.

"I have my moments," I whispered.

He lowered his lips to mine and kissed me. The heat

from his body burned through the thin fabric of my tee shirt.

CHAPTER THIRTEEN

SOUND OF SILENCE

I rolled over as Mac pulled his arm out from under me.

"Mac?" I mumbled.

"Shush, I'm just getting a drink. I'll be right back," he replied. I closed my eyes and heard him turn on the faucet, then place a glass on the counter. He rattled the windows and the doors. Mac opened the bathroom door. I heard the light switch flip a few times and then he cursed, "Useless fuc'n light bulbs."

I crawled out of bed and poured myself a glass of water while Mac was in the bathroom. I didn't bother with lights, the streetlights outside shed enough light. I stood by the tiny kitchen counter and drank a full glass of water. The bathroom door squeaked open.

"Hey."

"Hey, yourself. What're you doing up?" Mac asked, he closed the distance between us and wrapped his arms around my waist. His chin prickled my shoulder a pleasant way.

"Thirsty." I leaned back on him enjoying the warmth and closeness of skin against skin.

"Bathroom light is out. Do you suppose they'd have spare bulbs anywhere?" he whispered and his breath tickled my ear. He kissed my neck in a most distracting manner.

"Cabinets under the sink?"

Mac flipped the kitchen light on and searched through the cabinets eventually finding a light bulb.

"I'll be right back."

"Hurry, I need the bathroom."

He reappeared seconds later. Light shone from under the bathroom door. "There you go. Light works: The bulb was missing." He shrugged. "Maybe they meant to change it this morning but forgot."

"Yeah." I hurried past him into the bathroom pushing the door almost shut behind me. I watched several flies from my seated position. They buzzed about the light bulb. It occurred to me there weren't several flies at all, there were a lot of flies, and I begun to notice an unusual rank odor. I called out to Mac.

"What's up?" he asked from just outside the door.

"One sec." I flushed and opened the door. "Get in here and tell me why there are flies buzzing all over. Tell me you didn't cause the smell in this room!"

Mac grinned at me from the doorway. "I swear it wasn't me."

"Well, it was someone, and it wasn't me, either." I washed my hands and splashed a little water on my face. My mouth felt like the bottom of a parrot's cage. I squirted a dollop of toothpaste onto my toothbrush and gave my teeth a quick scrub. From the mirror above the sink, I caught sight of the shower curtain. I spun around and stared at it. I dropped the toothbrush into the sink. Cold dread curled in my stomach.

“You want to look in the shower?” I asked.

Mac moved closer into the room.

“Hell, no,” he said, with an unsure glance at me.

“How could he get a body in here?” I was thinking out loud. “Unless it was here before we came back from the café?”

“But agents were watching,” Mac reminded. “Across the road, remember?”

“In theory the motel was under surveillance.” Surveillance is boring; attention wanders. “He could’ve posed as housekeeping and come in here with a trolley. I wouldn’t put it past him. The guy is smoke!”

We stood together watching more flies emerge from the top of the curtain and buzz about the light bulb. I had hoped we’d enjoy at least a day’s reprieve before anything else happened. I watched another few flies emerge. Dammit!

“Oh, fuck-a-doodle-do. I’ll do it.” I edged forward with my hand outstretched and flicked the far side of the shower curtain. It barely moved. “Welcome to Friday night in Lexington.”

I stepped forward with more purpose. What’s the worst it can be? I ripped back the curtain in one fast movement. I had to swallow hard and clamp my hand over my mouth and nose. I heard Mac gag next to me. I gulped back bile and stared at the slumped body in the shower cubicle. Flies crawled all over it. I moved as close as I could. I tried not to breathe. Disgusting didn’t even come close to describing the mess. I couldn’t see anything distinguishable. I leaned in and lifted back a piece of torn fabric from what I thought was a sleeve. Maybe there'd be a watch or something that we might recognize. Vomit rose in my throat as I held the fabric out of the way enough to see what appeared to be a tattoo, a mermaid.

Roy Matheson, DEA.

Oh, Jesus dammit. Roy is dead. 4urxtc was Roy!

"Roy."

I stumbled back in an effort to get away. My feet slid on a small towel. I felt Mac's hand brush past my arm as I fell.

I heard my name and Mac said, "Oh shit, this isn't good."

I tried to say 'I'm okay' but the darkness swallowed me.

When the night comes, it comes with vengeance. No gentle billowing of soft clouds, just thunderous black storms, pounding and unrelenting, shaking my soul.

"What else did he do?"

My arm hurts. It's not real. It's a dream. My arm hurts.

"What else did he do?" The dream voice was insistent.

"Shut up! He didn't do anything."

A door closed somewhere; it got darker. How can night get darker? A night light would be good, an anti-demon night light would be even better. It's not always as it seems.

Thunder rolled around me. I took a breath. I'm okay. It was just a storm. Momentary panic grasped at me. I couldn't feel Mac. The panic subsided; something told me he'd be close.

The thunder stopped. I was flying. Gliding through the air and then sinking into warmth. I heard his voice. Not what he said, but how he said it. I was right: He was close. I loved his voice.

The darkness lifted a little then fell again like a guillotine. It was a trick. There was no reprieve, and there was no light. The darkness wasn't going to set me free or let me go back to the safety of Mac's arms. It had a purpose, its purpose was to disorientate and torture.

"What else did he do?" Why was the dream person doing this to me?

"Shush! He did nothing. Nothing happened!" Did I even speak? My voice sounded hollow inside my head. Maybe it wasn't my voice. I didn't recognize the voice speaking to me.

"You protest too much, holder of secrets."

"There are no secrets," I squirmed, "Nothing happened."

"Things are not always as they seem, Conway. What are you hiding?" The unrelenting torment by this dream person was almost more than I could cope with.

"I have nothing to hide, leave me be!"

"How did he break your arm?"

"What are you talking about?" The non-stop inquisition was beginning to annoy me. This is my dream!

"Carter broke your arm."

Whoa, what? I want to wake up now. I don't want to dream this dream. It's not real. It's not real. How dare someone step into my dream and say such things?

"No. There was a fight." Okay, it's my dream so I'll change it. I shall dismiss the dream person. "You can go now, goodbye!"

"I'm not going anywhere. Someone killed me."

I blinked in the dim light trying to make out features. It wasn't enough for someone to say they'd been killed. I've had a week of people being killed; this could be anyone. For some reason that thought gave me zero comfort and the dream continued. I needed Ghostbusters: The obvious answer.

"Who are you?"

"I was there. Who found you?"

My throat constricted as pure panic took hold. "No!"

"Who found you?"

"There was a fight." It was a fight. Why won't the dead guy listen? Why is he in my dream? My stomach churned. Breathing became difficult as my throat tightened even more.

"Who found you?"

"I don't know." I felt cold. I was cold and my arm hurt. I was freezing as if the air had turned to ice around me.

"Can you feel it? The biting cold?"

"Yes." I was so cold I couldn't shiver and I couldn't move. It was dark again. Pitch dark.

"Let me open the door, so you can see."

"I don't want to see." I closed my eyes.

"You have to see." He was adamant.

"No." Hot tears stung my frozen face as they sprang

from my tightly closed eyes.

"Please?" The voice changed; he pleaded. Light flooded across me. I blinked to clear my vision. A man appeared in front of me. Blood ran from a cut above his right eye. He wiped it away. I saw the tattoo.

"Roy?"

"I found you," he said, as he nodded.

I took a breath and looked around. My eyes hurt. I couldn't move my head properly. Where was I? A bathroom. I looked down at myself. Where were the rest of my clothes? I was half-dressed. My arm hurt. I looked at my right arm. Handcuffed to the shower rail, there was something very wrong with my arm, the angle was all wrong. I looked back at Roy.

"You don't remember do you?"

"No."

"I was there looking to buy from Carter."

"Drugs?" I asked. The shock of seeing myself began to fade. It's a nightmare, nothing more. Maybe some kind of ectoplasm trap would deal with the ghost of bathrooms past; because he sure wasn't leaving of his own accord or even on mine.

"He was giving me the run around. I suspected he'd been supplying Xeo."

Nightmare, nightmare, not real. My body shook uncontrollably.

"I was leaving. I had spoken to Carter several times during the evening. I was about to leave when I heard a scream."

I didn't want to hear this. I clamped my free hand over one ear, no more!

He took my hand and held it. "The fight happened when I opened the bathroom door and found you."

"No!" I shook my head.

"I went looking for the source of the scream. I found him with you."

"No. That's not how it happened. I was using his computer. You and he came in yelling at each other. There was a fight." See? I did remember what happened. Just a fight and my arm was broken.

"I'm sorry. Things aren't always as they seem. I'd been after him for a few months before you became involved."

"It was just a fight." Why won't he listen to me? Stupid dream! Why can't I change it? My arm hurts, my head is going to explode, what sort of warped damn dream is this?

"I couldn't arrest him for what he did to you. I was undercover and for all I knew you could have been, too."

"Nothing happened." My voice seemed to echo back off the cold walls; it bounced through Roy leaving a trail of pale light.

"I didn't walk away. Don't think I did. I took you to the hospital. I called Grafton, you had his card in your wallet, and then I called your brother. I found his card, too."

Roy began to fade, his edges blurred. "I'm sorry, Ellie, I'm sorry."

I shook my head. "Don't be, it was a fight." It would always be a fight, always and forever.

"Things aren't always as they seem. I wish you could remember but I also hope you never do. Stay safe, Ellie." His feet disappeared into the mist.

"I'm sorry you were killed." My words seemed to take shape and surround him as the gray dissolved his form. For a fleeting second, he was a merman.

Sadness crept from the edges of a bleak memory. People were dying and I didn't know why. I closed my eyes a second time and locked away the nightmare. My closed eyes offered scant relief from the searing arm pain or the invisible daggers breaching my skull.

Mac. I wanted Mac. Wanted him to erase the night and stop the guillotine from decapitating me, and most of all to say, "It's only a dream."

Weariness washed over an uninviting dreamscape until there was nothing. The pain in my arm drained away. Replaced by a soothing yellow glow.

Somewhere from the deep night a smooth voice filtered through the shadows and drifted into my semi-conscious mind.

What I wanted, what I needed was right there if my eyes would just open.

A warm comfortable feeling spread from the pit of my stomach radiating outward as I recognized the words. "Ellie, please wake up." Words accompanied by the gentle touch of lips on my lips and the soft scent of familiar warm skin.

My eyes were tired; Opening them at first was difficult and more effort was required. Focusing through a haze I recognized his smile.

"Welcome back."

I took a breath.

"Hi." Not exactly profound.

"How do you feel?" He studied my face. I looked into his hazel eyes and wondered where he'd been all my life. I wasn't sure how I felt. Safer now I could see Mac but a little confused as well. I tried to lift my right arm. It seemed heavier than normal. My eyes searched Mac's for answers, knowing he'd supply them without me voicing the question.

He smiled. "You broke your arm and cracked your skull, have a concussion and you've got a wicked damn bruise on your right thigh."

I blinked trying to clear the swimming blobs of light in front of my eyes as I tried to assimilate this new information. "Where are we?"

"Stonewall Jackson Hospital."

"Why?" I forced my eyes to remain open as I tried to understand what the hell was going on.

"Babe, you're hurt. You've been unconscious for several hours."

"I don't remember," I said. I tried very hard to keep a feeling of panic from my voice. Mac brushed a stray hair from my face. He sat on a chair right next to me. His arm reached over my head and a light flashed at the edge of my vision. "What did you do?"

"Pressed the call button, need to tell them you are awake."

I searched his eyes for something familiar and found heaven. His eyes smiled drawing me into their depths. He didn't move until a nurse appeared next to the bed. Then he sat back a little to allow the nurse easier access.

"Hello, Gabrielle, glad you have joined us," she said smiling as she took my wrist in her cool hand. "How do you feel?"

Why does everyone want to know how I feel? I don't even know how I feel. She should be able to tell me. Isn't it her job to know such things? I watched her. She looked around forty. My father once described women in their forties as being of a sensible age, and she looked sensible, with short, wavy, dark hair and a wide, pleasant smile.

"Let's see how you're doing." The nurse produced a small flashlight from her pocket. She shone it across my eyes. I recoiled as pain erupted with great force in my head. Great: Just what was needed; more bright lights exploding in front of my eyes. "Sorry," she murmured.

I waited for the next instrument of torture to appear. She produced an electronic thermometer. "This will take two seconds," she said poking the small cone-shaped end of the machine into my ear. "Excellent!" she smiled at me. "So far, so good."

I sighed. I didn't mean to but the light made my head hurt. She watched me with clinical interest.

"How's your head?"

"It hurts," I replied. "What's your name?"

She smiled again. "Sorry, Gabrielle, I should have introduced myself. My name is Annie."

It suited her.

Annie held up her hand in front of me. "What do you see?"

"Two blurry fingers or maybe hairy sausages."

Mac whispered in my ear, "Smartass."

"Good, now I have a few questions for you. What is your name?"

"Gabrielle Conway."

"What year were you born?"

"Seventy-six." The questions were surprisingly easy for a pop quiz.

"What year is it now?"

"2000 and something."

I hoped that was the end of the questions requiring numerological answers. I had zero clue what the actual date was and anything more difficult than the year I was born and my age was beyond my comprehension. I knew Mac was chuckling to himself. He was well aware of how challenged I was by simple things like the actual date or day, with or without a head injury.

"Who's the president?"

"George W Bush," I replied. I also knew he was the forty-third president and his father was the forty-first and I didn't vote for either of them. I chose not to elaborate quite that much. I could see Mac waving frantically and holding up fingers but was having a hard job making my eyes stay still.

"Okay, we're done for now. I'm going to write up your chart. You're doing great." Annie patted my left arm and then looked over at my right arm. "How does that feel?"

I moved it and wiggled my fingers. "It's okay." I saw the cast for the first time. It was bright yellow like the sun.

Annie smiled. "Don't often see yellow casts, makes a nice change." She closed the door as she left.

Mac nudged me. "We're on to the forty-fourth President now."

"Whoops." You'd think I'd remember something like another inauguration.

"You even voted for this one. Do like the yellow?"

"Yeah, did you choose it?" I lifted my arm gingerly for closer inspection; it sure was yellow.

"Nearly went with Barbie pink." He grinned. "I had a feeling you'd smack me with it if I did though."

"How long have I been here?"

"Since the wee small hours."

"What day is it?"

"Still Saturday, not long after dawn."

I smiled. My head felt floaty, my arm felt odd, but having Mac with me made everything okay.

"Were you scared?" I asked. I smiled, yet silent sneaky tears ran from the corner of my eye onto the pillow. Eyes can't be trusted.

Mac wrapped his arms around me lifting me off the bed. "Yeah, you scared me," he whispered. "I'm happy you are awake."

"Good, now put me down, I'm not a doll! And tell me what happened?" I felt nervous; snippets of a disturbing dream slipped in and out of my mind before I could grasp their meaning. "The last thing I remember was you changing the light bulb in the bathroom and now we're in hospital."

"You've missed the fun bit, babe." He moved so he was sitting on the edge of the bed. I was struggling to focus. He grinned like an idiot. "You used the bathroom and accused me of creating an odious smell in there." He attempted a wounded look but failed. "Then, you pulled back the shower curtain and we discovered the body, at which point you stepped backwards and tripped or slipped on a hand towel and fell, hence the hospital."

"Ohhh," I said. "Whose body?" Something pushed its way from the edges of a murky shroud. Roy.

"You said it was Roy. Guess we'll find out if we ever get any FBI in here."

I slid down the bed. How did I remember it was Roy? I looked up at Mac. "Where's Caine?"

"Our motel."

My eyes started to close.

"Rest," he murmured. "I'll be here in this very comfortable-looking chair." He pointed to a chair by the bed. "I think it's conformed to the shape of my backside, by now."

Footsteps sounded, coming ever closer. I opened my eyes to see a man in a lab coat standing by the bed. I glanced at Mac. He nodded at the man.

"Hello," he said to Mac. "I heard she was awake and scoring well."

Scoring? Did I take a test? They could wait until I'm fully functional.

"You seem surprised," Mac said.

"I'm very pleased. Not everyone comes back from a four." His eyes narrowed somewhat. "Certainly not so quickly, it's a big jump from four to fifteen."

What the hell was he talking about? Four to fifteen what? It made no sense.

"Who are you and what the hell are you talking about?" I said trying to sit up. It was way too hard. I managed to get my shoulders off the bed then lay back down.

"I'm Leon Kapowski," he said. "Your physician."

"Uh huh, and?"

I saw him and Mac exchange glances before he spoke to me again, "Do you know what the Glasgow coma scale is?"

It didn't sound good.

"Are you about to tell me my head is made of sawdust?"

He smiled a little. "No, I was about to explain how the scale works."

Oh man, medical mumbo jumbo! Can we just skip it? Move right on. I'm sorry I asked the stupid question to start with, I really don't care what four, or fifteen are. I sighed and wondered if it was audible. By the look on Mac's face I guess it was.

Leon hadn't taken his eyes off me since he started speaking but now he waited for me to give him permission to carry on.

"Okay, tell me," I said, and hoped my mind would stay with me for a bit. I was having as much trouble controlling my field of vision as I was my mind.

"It's how we classify head injuries, four is very bad, and fifteen is great."

Cool. I went from *very* bad to great that must be a good thing. Let's move on. I have no clue how long I will be able to maintain this minimal level of concentration.

"Gabrielle?"

"What's with the name? It's so formal."

"Look at me?"

I was trying to look at him.

He spoke to Mac. "Have you noticed her eyes? How they seem to wander all over the place. I take it she doesn't usually have one eye looking at you and one eye looking for you?"

"Not usually, no."

I wiped my hand across my mouth. I'd been swallowing a lot. For some reason I had more saliva than I'd ever had. I was becoming a drooling wreck. My worst fear was coming to fruition.

"I think you were drugged."

"Does that mean I'm not going to be permanently drooling with crazy eyes?"

The doctor smiled. "I've seen this before but usually in post-operative patients. A high dose of ketamine can cause this particular grouping of symptoms, once you start to come out of it."

"I thought I hit my head and as unbelievable as it seems actually fractured my thick skull?" My head hurt. If I didn't hit it then why did it hurt so much?

"You did, but even with a skull fracture and diffuse brain injury you should've been more responsive from the beginning and you weren't. I think we'll find you ingested ketamine prior to falling." Leon said.

"A diffuse what?"

"Concussion, it's a concussion," Leon replied.

"That sounds better than the other thing."

Mac's eyes remained focused on mine, must've been quite hard for him to maintain eye contact with my eyes wandering all over the place, god knows I was having trouble. "The only thing you did that I didn't do, was brush your teeth."

I almost smiled but held it back. I had no explanation for why cleaning my teeth was suddenly amusing.

"We need to find out if the toothpaste was tampered with," I said.

"Can you do that?" Leon asked.

"FBI will take care of it." I said. Mac slipped his arm around me and gave me a big squeeze.

"I'll be back soon, you rest," Leon said. By the time I looked up he was gone, just like the Lone Ranger. I fought the zany thoughts that tried to break out. I forced away the thoughts of the masked man, 'Hi ho Silver and away'.

I whispered to Mac, "Guess it was my turn. But it could've been either of us, if it was the toothpaste."

He whispered back, "Maybe we should get a new tube every day!"

"Okay." My eyes closed.

"Don't move back, you'll fall off the edge of the bed," he cautioned. I heard a noise and the bed moved slightly. "You can move now. The rail is up."

A fresh mountain breeze blew orange and yellow leaves over the steep path; some tumbled back behind me. Leaves trapped by small stones crunched underfoot as I trudged upward. My goal was an outcrop of rocks at the very top of the path. A place I knew well. It was somewhere I could sit and watch the river below as it twisted and babbled through a field of purple wild flowers. The smell of pine was strong in wooded pockets along the trail. I was trampling oak and maple and yet could smell pine. Life was mysterious. Scarlet rhododendron flowers peeked at me as I passed. I'd never liked them and the thought of them soon falling and turning to slippery brown mush amused me. The warm sun and nasty red flowers soon would be forgotten. Snow would soon blanket much of western central Virginia, brought by the fast-approaching winter. I paused and looked at the scarlet blooms. The rhododendrons were out of whack. Cool autumn air tugged at my jacket.

They shouldn't be flowering yet. Something very peculiar was happening in Virginia. Bunches of scarlet flowers nodded as if they agreed with my thoughts. I pressed the mysterious seasonally-confused flowers from my mind. All too soon my path to serenity would become a treacherous icy slope and the wild flowers I adored would be dormant until the spring thaw. Higher and higher I climbed towards the sun and blue sky.

Voices floated upward. No one ever came this way. I didn't want anyone up here now, either. This was my sanctuary. I felt that this maybe the last time I would sit and watch the Maury River meander below me. I was saying goodbye to Rockbridge County.

I climbed the last few feet and paused, breathing clean air. The voices continued yet I could see nobody. I stepped off the trail and ducked under overhanging branches. I grabbed a gnarled old tree for support and descended through a small tunnel created by foliage. I emerged onto a platform of solid rock suspended, as if by magic, over the river valley. I checked for snakes before sitting on the edge of the outcrop, my legs dangled way above the river. Wild flowers ran to the very edge rippling in the gentle breeze.

The murmur of the wind: Was that the voices I heard? My mind traversed a twisted path littered with destruction. Faces appeared in the meadow springing from wind-sown seed and accompanied by voices of undetermined origin. One voice rose. It wasn't anger I heard, it was annoyance mingled with escalating fear. A female voice.

I didn't understand why voices were intruding into my world. My world! Dammit why can't I have some peace? I observed the faces of the dead as they faded in and out among the flowers. My eyes drifted to the water. Sunlight caused ripples to sparkle amidst the sparkle; more faces appeared, all male.

Her voice didn't match the distorted faces in the flowers or the indistinct river faces. Maybe she was Roy's mermaid. That seemed like the only logical explanation.

Sun warmed my back as I pondered the new development. Everything seemed to twist in my mind. I wasn't sure what was real anymore or even if I should be concerned about that. Was it my voice I heard trapped forever in the wind? Where was I? I knew what I could see and yet I could hear neither birds chirping nor any other sign of wildlife in the woods above me and behind me. I could see the river but not hear it. Was I dreaming? Was I dead? Is this heaven? My mind filled with images of Mac. I didn't want to be dead. My life had just started.

I stretched my hand out and laid it flat, expecting to contact solid rock or maybe chiffon-like cloud. My fingers grasped something soft, not rock at all. Not warmed, sun-drenched rock but cool soft fabric. I blinked. The river below became a murky haze. Faces swam as I blinked again hoping to restore the vista I so enjoyed, but it was gone.

A vast expanse of a smooth neutral something replaced it. What was I seeing? No flowers, no river, no trees or rocks, what was it? Floor? I was standing on floor in a doorway. I looked behind me and saw a sink and toilet, and could hear the cistern filling. In front of me on the floor, I saw booted feet.

I recognized the heel of the boots. My eyes traveled

upward from heel to legs to waist. I knew the person Mac grappled with. He had him face down on the bed, with one arm bent up behind his back. The river danced before my eyes then disappeared.

"Aidan?" Did I say that? Did I speak?

Mac looked from me to the man now gasping and trying to turn his face towards me.

"Jesus!" Mac released his arm and hauled him to his feet. "Aidan!"

I stared at the sight in front of me as I became more aware of my surroundings. How I got from a rocky outcrop to a hospital room was a mystery. How my brother got there was puzzling. Simple math would have perplexed me right out of my skull at that instant so I felt more than justified in finding the situation a little strange.

My hand was resting on the end of a bed. It wasn't rock or cloud. Something didn't feel right. My legs didn't feel right. Why oh why, was my body so disobedient? I knew my legs were rebelling to the point I was about to fall. No wonder. I guessed it was the long walk up that steep hill that made them so reluctant to stand.

"Jesus, Aidan, what the hell are you doing sneaking around the Intensive Care Unit?" Mac asked regaining his composure.

Aidan smoothed his rumpled clothing then sank onto the bed. "I was looking for my sister!" he replied with a sidelong glance at Mac.

Mac exhaled then looked over to me. "Damn!" He

reached out to take my hand and help me move closer to the bed. I took a few uneasy steps.

"I've been all over the awful hospital. Her name wasn't on the door," Aidan said as Mac helped me sit next to him. I felt myself sway a little.

"Put your arm around her so she doesn't fall," Mac told him, "I need to use the bathroom."

Aidan grabbed me as I started to slip sideways from the bed. "Hey, stay with me here."

It took great effort to look up at him.

"Aidan, why for you here?"

He laughed. "Why for? Jeez, Ellie, how hard did you bang your head?"

I tried smiling.

"Let's get you back into bed," Aidan said. He encouraged me onto the bed and pulled the covers over my legs.

Sometime later Mac appeared in front of me. His shadow blocked the light so I could see his face and he was frowning. "What's the matter?" he asked then added, "Damn, you're pale." He turned to Aidan. "Pass the white container on the bedside cabinet."

He handed it to Mac and Mac settled the container on my knees; within seconds I vomited into it.

"Hit the buzzer, Aidan; twice," Mac instructed then added. "Move your ass."

He took the container from me. I was cold and shaky. He sat on the end of the bed.

I recognized the nurse as she bustled in, Annie. She seemed surprised to see Aidan.

"No visitors except family in the ICU," she announced.

"I'm her brother." Aidan was snappish.

Annie glared at him then turned to Mac. "Do you need something?" Her whole manner changed. Her voice was soft and concerned.

"Ellie vomited, a lot. She doesn't look too well."

The woman picked up the container from where Mac had left it and placed it in the sink by the door. She approached me.

"Gabrielle?"

I flinched. Her voice surprised me.

"How do you feel?"

I squinted it was hard to focus on her face. "Sick." A fresh white container appeared in my hands.

"I'll get you something for the nausea." She spoke to the men and asked them to dim the lights and keep an eye on me. That was lucky because I couldn't keep an eye on myself without removing my eyeballs and setting them on a shelf somewhere. I stayed semi-sitting. Lying down would've involved movement and movement was bad. Hadn't I done enough for one night?

Aidan and Mac talked in hushed whispers from chairs close to the bed.

"Did Caine call you?" Mac asked Aidan.

"Yeah, he told me not to come; as if!" Aidan leaned forward resting his elbows on his knees. They shushed as footsteps approached down the corridor.

"Nurse maybe?" Mac whispered.

"Heavy footsteps for a woman," Aidan replied. "Could

be a male nurse but nurses tend to wear soft-soled shoes, too."

The footsteps moved away.

"We're supposed to have a couple of agents on the door," Mac said. "No one's shown up yet."

"He wouldn't try anything here, would he?"

I replied to Aidan, "Why not? This moron is unfazed by anything so far. Imagine that, a body turning up in a hospital. Would they notice an extra one?"

"Nice thought, Ellie. Thanks for sharing," Aidan said.

"Okay?" Mac asked me.

"Yep," I said. I'm okay. "I'm tired of you two annoying me. I could do with being left alone."

Mac ignored my comment and returned to Aidan's question. "Ellie's right, there's no reason why he wouldn't, he's a psycho."

Again, we heard footsteps travel the corridor with slow precision. They came to a halt at regular intervals.

"Its sounds like someone who's lost," I mumbled, "Staff wouldn't walk like that."

"True," Mac replied. "They tend to know where they are going."

I heard Aidan move and the chair squeak. He leaned back to get comfortable. We all heard a female voice in the corridor asking someone for identification. Aidan walked past me. He stood by the door. There was an escalating argument happening outside. Mac joined Aidan. I watched Mac disappear and closed my eyes to block out distractions and listened to what was happening outside the room.

"Problem?" It was Mac.

An undetermined male spoke and sounded annoyed, "Nothing to do with you."

"I was talking to the nurse," Mac said, with clear cold precision.

"I'll be with you in a second." It was Annie. "Just wait here."

It was definitely Annie. I hoped she had meds for me. I could do with something to stop these waves of nausea. I grabbed the plastic container and vomited again with renewed force. My head swam. Maybe I fell in the river.

I heard Mac's voice, he sounded pissy, "And her name is?"

Annie spoke, "He said his sister is Gabrielle Conway."

How many brothers do I have? Let me see, tricky question. One. I have one. Aidan and I looked at each other for a split second then he left the room.

I closed my eyes. I was alone. There was scuffling going on outside my room. Vomit rose in my throat. Someone touched my arm. I opened my eyes half-expecting to see a knife plunge into my chest. Close, but no cigar. A needle slid into my arm.

"You'll feel better in a few minutes," Annie said. "Your boyfriend is dealing with someone in the corridor. He's waiting for security."

"Where's my brother?" I asked.

"He's with him."

I felt light-headed. Had the covers not held me down I

would've been up on the ceiling. Was this the smack to the head? Or the aftereffects of ketamine?

"Would you like me to stay with you?" Annie asked. She straightened the bed covers then whisked away the soiled container and brought me another fresh one.

"I'll be okay," I assured her. "What was in the needle?"

"Something to stop the vomiting and some pain relief. We'll be monitoring you. Fifteen-minute observations. I know that's going to be annoying but I will do my best to disturb you as little as possible."

"Thank you."

I liked her. She was pleasant and efficient with a great smile. I closed my eyes. I don't know how long I slept before I heard Aidan's voice.

"Well?" Aidan asked.

"Well?" Mac repeated back at him.

I chuckled.

"Thought you were sleeping," Aidan said to me.

"Nah, just resting." My eyes opened. It was an effort not to squint. "Any clue who that moron was?"

Mac shook his head. "Yet another sucker, I suspect." He smiled. "I was worried it was another diversion. I'm glad you're okay."

"Annie came in and gave me something for the nausea and pain."

"Feeling better?"

"Uh huh." Floaty, spacey, it's almost fun. Thanks to the Unsub I now had an idea how Mac felt when he was drugged at the café.

"Good."

We all froze and stared at the door. More raised voices in the corridor outside.

The door opened. Caine emerged bathed in pale light. He had a halo for a second or so before he moved from the doorway.

He leveled a cold stare and pointed at Aidan. "I told you not to come here." He held his hand up to stop Aidan's reply and turned to Mac. "You did well. That man you stopped is Eugene Summers. He received fifty dollars to locate Ellie's room and cause a disturbance. Mr. Summers has an attitude problem and has breached his parole. He's been taken into custody."

"Did he have a description we can use?" I asked. Hoping that was what I actually said and that the words came out in the correct order.

"Yeah, and again it doesn't match any we have so far. Except this time there was mention of three deep scratch marks running down the man's neck." Caine rolled his eyes. "It was dark he couldn't see clearly."

"What the hell happened to our FBI doormen?" There was a sharp edge to Mac's voice.

"I have no clue. I sent two agents over here twenty minutes after you left in the ambulance. No one's seen or heard from them since. We didn't know they were missing until the police called about old Eugene."

"Oh, man," my voice groaned, at least I thought it came from my mouth. I had to tell them something. "Parking lot, grounds ... Eugene may have done more than find me." That was hard work. I liked floating better than trying to concentrate.

Caine directed himself to Mac. "Is she stable enough to be moved?"

Mac shook his head. "Not yet. Maybe by tonight."

Tonight, did that mean it was daytime already? It's awful dark for daytime. Maybe there were no windows in my room. I stopped trying to work it out.

"We must move her as soon as possible. I suspect the Unsub followed the ambulance here. I don't want you two followed again."

"So now what?" Mac's voice was low and filled with semi-concealed annoyance.

"A decoy."

There was silence, the sort of silence that indicated thought. My thoughts were scattered to the wind. Nothing made sense anymore. It occurred to me that I may have drowned in the river. Roy's face came into view. A question needed answering.

"Caine?"

He looked at me, stony faced as always, no apparent twitch. "Yes."

Words flowed without real conscious thought on my part, "Roy told me he called you and Aidan when I was in Chicago. He said he had been investigating Carter for a few months before I showed up."

Caine wasn't stony anymore: He frowned. "When did Roy tell you this?"

"I don't know, he came and saw me."

"Ellie, think very carefully. When did Roy tell you this?"

"I think it was tonight. He said someone killed him."

Caine's eyes widened. Damn! I shouldn't have said anything. It must've been a dream. Panic rose as I watched Caine rub his face with his hands.

"He was killed within the last twenty-four hours, his body was in your shower, and you are telling me he spoke to you?" Gone was the usual tone I expected from Caine. He replaced it with utter disbelief. I see dead people.

"Just answer my question! Did he call you?"

"Someone called me. An anonymous Good Samaritan told me you were injured and suggested that a toxicology screen be done."

"You don't know who it was?"

"No."

"Aidan did you get a call?" My gaze shifted to him. He looked uncomfortable.

He started to shake his head but changed his mind at the last second. "Yes."

The rest of the conversation with Roy bounced through my disjointed mind. He told me the truth. Toxicology – is that why I don't remember. Did Carter drug me?

I didn't want to ask but something told me I needed to know. "What showed in the tox screen?"

Caine shook his head. "We don't need to go here, it's going to do more harm than good."

Funny how things become clear all of a sudden. I believed there was a fight. I didn't have exact details, just enough to make me think that's how it was. They told me there was a fight. Roy, Caine, maybe even Aidan, concocted the story.

"Tell me, Caine."

His eyes landed on mine with force. "Rohypnol."

I'm okay. I don't remember anything happening. So if I don't remember, it didn't happen. I'm okay dammit! But Roy was right. Rohypnol has a specific use so it's highly possible that something else did happen. I'm still okay.

I could sense Mac's question before the words escaped his lips I answered it, "It's a date-rape drug sometimes called coma capsules, or Roofies."

He didn't say a word. I peered at Aidan. He was a little sad-looking.

Words fell from my mouth in an effort to stop the tears, "We have to stop this son of Shakespeare prick before he kills again. Roy was a good guy."

Caine didn't ask again how I managed to talk to a dead DEA agent. Instead, he turned his attention to Aidan.

"I want you to go home. Ellie's fine; she's in good hands."

"I can stay and help." Aidan offered.

"No. I don't want you becoming a target. Please Aidan, your sister and Mac have been through enough."

Aidan nodded and stood up. He reached his hand out and shook Mac's, "Keep her safe."

"I intend to," Mac replied.

Aidan kissed my cheek. "Be okay."

I smiled. "I'm always okay, you know that." For the

first time since he arrived I could see him clearly. "The new sweater suits you. You should wear turtlenecks more often. Black makes your eyes stand out more. They seem a brighter blue."

Aidan smiled.

"Next time you visit Holly, wear the black."

He grinned. "'Night Ellie. You seem to be feeling better."

I listened as Aidan's footfalls faded away.

"You rest up, kid. I'm going to organize your decoy and everything else." Caine turned towards the door then spun back; his eyes glistened in an odd way. "Don't hate me for what I did."

"Were you protecting me?" I knew the answer already.

"Yes."

"I would never hate you, Caine. Sometimes I dislike you; your intentions were honorable, that's what counts."

I surprised myself with that answer. Maybe the drug was some kind of truth serum. Caine's mouth twitched so I smiled back.

He wasn't so bad: More teddy-bear-like than he would have anyone believe. He felt a lot more than everyone around him suspected; the cold hard SAC was a façade. You had to know where to look to find the cracks. I know where to look. I'm okay.

"We'll move you tonight." Caine left the room.

Mac stretched out in a chair. I closed my eyes and wondered if I'd see Roy again. It's not so bad seeing dead people.

My eyes opened a while later. I lay still listening to noises. Hospitals aren't quiet places. How anyone could sleep without sedation I didn't know. The fact that I couldn't sleep for long told me the ketamine was probably all but gone from my system.

A small lamp, no brighter than a night light, partially lit the room. The corridor lights shone in through the glass in the top of the door. I turned my head. The inside of the pillow rustled. Yet another reason people needed sedating to sleep. Plastic protected pillows.

Mac was in the chair partially obscured by the curtain, his legs stretched towards me.

"Hey!"

I waited for a response but he didn't reply.

Maybe he was asleep. I decided to leave him to sleep for a bit; he must have been exhausted.

My attention turned to my cast arm. I inspected it. It was very yellow. Would it glow in the dark? A chuckle erupted from me at the thought of a cast bobbing about a pitch-dark room all by itself. My left arm itched. It wasn't my whole arm that itched but inside my elbow and the back of my hand. I discovered white sticking plaster in both locations. No wonder it itched. It was time to try out moving my right arm. It moved okay. I was even able to grasp the edges of the tape and pull it off. It left behind welts that itched like crazy.

"Mac!"

My throat was dry. I watched his legs. They didn't move.

"Mac!" My voice was loud that time.

He still didn't wake.

With extreme care I sat up. I needed a drink and there was a desperate urge to pee. I had no idea how much fluid they had pumped into me.

Enough to make me need to pee with urgency and yet I was still thirsty, go figure! I swung my legs over the side of the bed. This gave me a chance to examine my thigh. No wonder my legs were stiff. There was a huge bruise spreading from just above my knee almost to my butt.

I looked at Mac again he seemed in no hurry to wake so I wobbled my way to the bathroom unaided. I reckoned he'd bellyache a fair bit about that when he woke but I needed to go, now.

He was still sleeping when I returned. I chuckled as I crept over to him and whipped back the rest of the curtain intent on giving him a fright. He was still in the shadows. I leaned forward. He had his stupid cap pulled over his face.

"Mac," I whispered, expecting him to jump as I touched his hand.

He felt cold.

A horrible feeling spread through me like wildfire. No! Not Mac. Not Mac. Oh God!

A Post-it protruded from blue-tinged lips. Someone screamed. Everything stopped. '

A cloud of nothingness descended from above.

Chapter Fourteen

Calling All Angels

I lay staring at the ceiling with no clue where I was; for the first time ever I didn't care. It didn't matter where I was. Nothing mattered.

My eyes followed the swirling pattern in the plastered ceiling. It wasn't a hospital: They didn't have plastered ceilings. Maybe it was some kind of private sanitarium. Yeah, a nice secluded nuthouse. That seemed reasonable given recent events. The spirals began to revolve and made me dizzy.

My head moved on the pillow. It wasn't plastic-lined. From where I lay, I could see a bureau and a gilt-edged mirror above it. Fancy furnishings indeed. Floor-length curtains obscured almost an entire wall. They appeared to be pale-green embossed satin. There was something familiar about those drapes but I gave up trying to place them. My gaze shifted and roamed the walls: paintings, several paintings. They weren't prints; they had too much life to be prints. Wherever I was, it was nice. If it was a nuthouse it was costing the government plenty.

It took sometime before I had enough courage to move my head the other way. There was a door. A regular, solid, door. It matched the door I saw on the other side of the room by the mirror. Something moved in the corner of my eye. My gaze moved further around the room, more paintings and another door, this time different, a closet maybe. A chair, Mac, a bedside cabinet with a tiffany lamp set upon it. I dragged my eyes back to the chair. Mac. Legs stretched towards me, eyes closed.

What was the last thing I remembered? I blinked back tears as hard as I could. A little voice deep inside whispered, “Psychotic break.” Another voice screamed for Mac to wake up. I shut my eyes. I knew when I opened them again the chair would be empty.

I felt my body shudder. My face was wet from tears and a voice I so wanted to hear said, “I’m here.”

I rolled over. I didn’t want to see the empty chair.

Again I heard his voice, “I’m here.”

A hand took mine. I knew that touch. I searched my broken mind for answers. The only one that made any sense was psychotic break, some kind of mental lapse due to shock. I expected a nurse to appear and sedate me. They did that to my mother when she took little breaks.

The hand that held mine moved. Two hands were on my shoulders, then one underneath me. My body moved. He rolled me onto his arm and lifted. How could it be him? His face was inches from mine. “Ellie, I’m here!”

My hand reached up, struggling free of the covers and past his sweater. Fear gripped me as my fingers touched his face. It was warm and stubbly. His eyes filled with tears. One escaped and dripped onto my cheek.

No words came. I couldn’t speak. I was either insane or Mac was alive, which was it?

There was a knock at the door. It opened and Mac’s

father peeked in. "Just wanted to see if you needed anything." His shadow fell over Mac and me as he stopped at the foot of the bed.

I looked up at him.

"Mr. Connelly?"

He spoke Mac's name as if he were here. If he can see him he must be real. Was Roy real? Oh man! My hand stayed on Mac's face. He kissed my palm. "I am real."

He held me so tightly, how could I doubt him?

"It wasn't me, love, I was talking with Leon."

Leon the doctor: I remembered him.

"When I left there was a nurse with you. She was supposed to stay till I returned. She must've been called away. I swear I was gone ten minutes."

"It was your baseball cap." There was no way to stop the tears as I remembered what had transpired.

Mac's voice was calm and smooth as he spoke, "I know. I was coming back when I heard you scream. I stepped into the room and found you unconscious on the floor holding my hat."

The bed sank as Mr. Connelly sat down. His arms went around us both.

"You had a terrible shock, Ellie. You're both safe now."

"I thought it was Mac."

He nodded. "You're safe here."

Here? Where's here? Are we in Rockbridge still? Did Mac's Dad come down?

I watched them. They looked at each other but didn't speak. Or did they and I couldn't hear? I wanted to know where we were.

Something odd happened. Maybe I missed him leave or perhaps he never came in but Mr. Connelly was gone.

"Mac, Where are we?"

"The last place on earth Ellie. The last place on earth."

A slow dawning occurred. "We are at your parents? Did hell freeze over?"

"I think it must have." The pensive look from a few minutes before faded. His eyes smiled. Could a dead person smile like that? Could we both be dead and not realize it yet? Am I the only one who knows that was logical and being in Fairfax wasn't.

"What?" The look returned. "What's happening in your head?"

Before I could silence them my words were hitting the open air. "What if this is a dream? How do I know we're not both dead and only think we're alive?

Mac's hands cupped my face. "Can you feel me?"

"Yes."

"Can you hear me?"

"Yes."

His hands stayed on my face holding me as he looked into my eyes.

"I'm alive. You're alive and this is real." He never flinched or moved his gaze. "I understand how confused you are right now, I do." His eyes filled with pain.

"Don't let me turn into my mother." It was my fear and it always lurked in my mind. And now it felt like reality was unhinged and flapping in the autumn breeze.

"No chance." He smiled again.

"Promise?"

"If that's what you are worried about, I can assure you it will never happen."

Damn, the truth serum was still in effect. "I feel discombobulated and everything's jumbled up. I'm scared it'll always be like this. If I close my eyes you'll disappear."

"Where would I go? I ain't leaving you."

I tried to smile. His thumbs wiped away my tears. "It's going to be okay."

A loud complaint erupted from my stomach which made him smile then chuckle. "Let's feed whatever the hell is trying to get out of there. I think it will help." My stomach reverberated again. It appeared to agree with Mac.

A sigh came from somewhere; it could've been me. There was a distinct fog hanging over my aching head. In the middle of the fog a voice said something about eating and doing it now. I don't know if it was an audible voice.

"Here." A glass of orange juice was in my hand. "You must be thirsty too."

The glass magically rose to my lips and the room-temperature liquid slipped down my parched throat. The empty glass disappeared. The juice tasted better than I ever remember it tasting before.

"Okay?"

"Yep."

In a day or so we'd be laughing about this as we lay in

our coffins.

"You're smiling." Mac whispered, placing a piece of toast in my hand. I ate, his eyes never left mine. Relief flowed through me as the juice and toast kicked in. If I'm dead, it's okay. If I'm dreaming, please don't let me ever wake up.

I munched through another piece of toast before speaking again.

"I don't know what day it is."

"Hardly surprising, you've slept through most of the last two days. It's Sunday, late afternoon."

"Have they caught the Unsub yet?"

"No."

"Where is your Dad?" I wondered if he was ever here at all.

"Guess he's gone back to see Mom."

The Connelly men and their insane women: Damn, they had bad luck. The fog lifted, slight panic built on a momentary fear. I was about to wake and find myself alone.

I pushed the fear away; my head ached and I didn't need fear as well. "Tell me why we are here?"

Mac smiled. He brushed crumbs from my tee shirt. "Caine's idea. He spoke with my Dad; Dad insisted we come home."

I groaned as snippets of the last few days surfaced. I needed a sledgehammer; I had to fix that printer once and for all. The conversation with Mrs. Connelly. Whoops, the bitch thing!

"They know you were drugged, huh? When you called your Mom a bitch?"

"Nothing like a little truth to drop someone in the shit! Caine explained the whole thing to them."

From outside the door I heard her say, "Is she okay?" I barely recognized the woman when she wasn't yelling abuse about her printer down the phone.

A few scattered intrusive thoughts forged forward. The scariest was, is he real? At least the thoughts were calmer now and easier to set aside.

"Mac?"

"Yep."

"You're alive?"

He smiled; I'm sure he wanted to scream 'Yes, dammit, I'm alive: Now get over it!' To his credit he didn't. "You heard the mad woman's voice?"

I nodded. Never nod with a headache!

"You think anyone could pry that woman from her home and drag her all the way to Rockbridge?"

"Hell, no."

"The dead guy is in Stonewall Jackson Morgue. I'm here in Fairfax with you."

"What happens now?" I had no idea how long I had been lying around in this unhelpful semi-conscious state or how much I had missed.

"Caine's on his way over. They still don't have the Unsub. He'll fill us in when he gets here."

My eyes roamed the room. It would be a shame to see this house sullied by the death that followed us.

"Who was it in the chair?"

"There was this guy who used the nickname, Died-Monday. They think it was him."

"What did the poem say?"

I had a flash of a note stuck to dead lips and refused to think of the lips as belonging to Mac, no matter what my mind tried to tell me.

"We'll talk about it later. Let's not get into it now."

Chapter Fifteen

Lay Back In The Arms Of Someone

"I should get up." I attempted forward motion. Mac pushed my shoulders back onto the bed.

"Oh, no you don't. You are in no condition to cope with this house right now." He smiled wickedly. I knew there was a story I could tell by the twinkle in his eye.

I raised an eyebrow. "Tell!"

He struggled to keep a straight face. "We arrived very early this morning. I got you settled right away and went back to face the music in the dining room. I thought Mom would have a few things to say to me. But she was still asleep." He paused. "Anyway ... I was standing by the dining room table while Dad made coffee and it occurred to me that there was something not quite right about their very, very, neat and tidy house. You know how Dad likes things; he's a neat freak." Mac grinned. "The entire table top was covered with at least fifty set mouse traps. I questioned Dad about this strangeness. He told me it was a crafty plan to stop the cats jumping on the table."

"Perfectly normal!"

"Yep, said he set them up a week ago and that every night he could hear them going off, pop, pop, pop, but not as much the last several nights because the cats are learning."

"So are these traps there all the time?"

"I think so." He looked thoughtful for a minute. "I'm sure they were still set when I went through the room a few hours ago."

I forced my thoughts to more serious matters. "Your parents know how dangerous it is, having us in the house?"

Mac nodded. "They know. Dad said he would prefer us here rather than alone at some strange hotel."

"Of course he does: The killing hasn't started yet. We shouldn't be here, Mac. We shouldn't. This is not smart."

"It'll be okay, Ellie, if we can cope with the madness that tends to wash over this house." He brushed my hair back from my face. "You look brighter. Feeling better?"

"I am, thank you." I chewed my lip. "Thank you for looking after me."

His eyes lit up making the green in them more apparent. "You know despite the gruesome sights and pure terror we have been subjected to ... I enjoy your company." He leaned in and kissed me. "No matter what the situation, I'm glad we're in this together."

Someone knocked on the bedroom door.

"Come in," Mac called.

The door opened and his father entered the room. He smiled at us. His smile was similar to Mac's. In fact, they looked a lot alike. Mr. Connelly was an older, heavier, shorter, more weathered version of Mac.

"You feel better Ellie?"

"Yes, thank you, Mr. Connelly."

He beamed. "I came to see if either of you have any

preferences regarding dinner."

Mac and I grinned at each other causing the older man to chuckle and roll his eyes. "What was I thinking? You two would eat road kill if you were hungry enough."

I grinned back at him. "Ain't nothing wrong with bunny pie. I'm not hungry yet. I had that toast earlier."

"Ignore her. By the time dinner is ready she'll be hungry again. Anything, we're not particular." He gave me a sidelong glance. "I've never seen anyone put away as much food as Ellie can in a day."

"Nothing wrong with a healthy appetite, son," his father replied, nodding wisely, as fathers do.

"How about I help?" Mac volunteered.

I grabbed his arm. "Only if I come, too. I need to be vertical!"

I watched him think. His brow creased. "Okay, but ..." There's always a 'but' why is there always a 'but'? I waited for the 'but' to reveal itself. "You sit and watch us, if you feel weird at all, say something."

"Deal." I considered I'd been let off lightly. I could feel a wicked grin settle on my face, "There's something about a man cooking ..." I whispered so only Mac could hear.

Mac helped me up and replied, "Really? You seem to be getting better in leaps and bounds."

Mr. Connelly was waiting for us by the door. I noticed him watching me as I walked towards him, not so much watching as scrutinizing. It didn't bother me. I reasoned he had a right to do so; after all, I was in his home with his son.

"There's not much to you, is there?" Mr. Connelly commented as we neared him.

"Guess not," I replied with a wry smile. "I probably harbor a large tapeworm. No doubt that would account for the large quantity of food I consume." My head was annoying me. Being vertical wasn't all it was cracked up to be. I screwed my nose up at Mac; it's rude to comment on how much a lady eats.

"Damn, girl, we best feed you and that worm before you disappear all together." Mr. Connelly said with a wink. He stepped aside to let us pass. I witnessed a subtle exchange of glances between the Connelly men and knew what it meant. They were going to have one of those deep and meaningful father-son chats. One of those talks that began with a simple question about bleeding brakes and changing oil, flowed onto a discussion about the best cordless drill on the market, twisted through the complexities of installing a new house alarm and finally arrived at the all important, 'How serious are you two?'

Mac sat me at the dining room table.

I surveyed the set mousetraps and said nothing. What the hell could I say? Interesting table decorations you have, Mr. Connelly. Perhaps you could paint them different colors and turn it into some kind of mosaic tabletop design?

I was sure *House Beautiful* wasn't about to drop by and do a full-color photo spread on this particular table, unless of course, he did do some kind of mosaic thing.

Mac's mother appeared covered in fine sawdust. Mac

hurried into the kitchen; I knew by the expression on his face he didn't want to hear the explanation.

"How're you feeling, Ellie?" She asked lighting a cigarette.

"Much better thank you," I replied. Mac may not have wanted to know but curiosity was killing me. "You look like you have been busy."

She sat at the end of the table. Dust fell over what little polished surface there was between the mousetraps.

"I'm making wooden bows," she said. "You can come down to the basement later and see. They're ornaments for the house, thought they'd be pretty."

"How many have you made?"

"I've got about fifteen finished." She held her hands out in front of her, a good twelve inches apart. "They're about yay big."

I smiled. I thought I was doing well to control myself enough to simply smile. "Y'know you could name them, so everyone has their own bow."

Something soft flew at my head from the vicinity of the kitchen I looked over and found Mac trying to attract my attention.

"Did you want me?" I asked with much innocence.

"Yes." I had never heard the word 'yes' delivered with that much inflection before.

I stood up and excused myself. Walking to the doorway was a challenge but I got there. "Problem?"

Mac whispered in my ear as he wrapped his arms around me, "Don't encourage her! Name them? Jesus,

Ellie, I don't want my name on one of those oddities she's created."

"Really?"

"You're evil," he rasped in my ear as he hugged me, "Cough, if you need me to save you."

I returned to my seat and watched Mrs. Connelly light another cigarette. She was unaware of the one still burning in the ashtray. She didn't notice my leaving or returning and had continued the conversation alone.

I let my mind wander and pretended to listen to Mrs. Connelly's ramblings. I remained focused enough to "uh huh" and "mmhmmm" every now and then.

Mac and his Dad were engrossed in conversation. I roused myself from my stupor in time to hear Mac explain how to wire room sensors. I drifted back to the semi-darkness that still lurked inside me. It offered zero insight. The murmuring from Mrs. Connelly stopped. She paused for breath and lit another cigarette. I counted three cigarettes, all burning down in the ashtray, not including the one in her mouth.

A hand fell onto my shoulder. Mac's Dad was standing next to me.

"Come with me a minute, Ellie," he said. "She'll be right back," he told his wife who hadn't realized he was there. In the kitchen Mac applied the final additions to a salad.

"Mac, come out to the garage," his father whispered.

All three of us left the house. None of us spoke until we reached the comparative safety and seclusion of the garage. I looked around and surmised that Mr. Connelly's cars lived better than many people do. It was warm in the garage. I suspect he heated the room. He'd lined the walls too, making the whole place feel cozy. We walked to the far end past the cars. There stood a table and chairs, behind them a bookcase and next to that a magazine rack. I saw newspapers folded in the rack. This was Mr. Connelly's retreat. Mac pulled out a chair for me. His Dad told us what was on his mind.

"The way I see it," he began, "you two are in a pickle. I know the FBI are doing everything they can ... and I'm not being arrogant or an ass ... but I think the three of us can maybe go a long way to solving this case."

I nodded and resolved never to do so again.

"The thing is Mr. Connelly. I ..." I looked at Mac. "No, We don't want to endanger you or your wife. And if it were my choice we'd be in a hotel right now." I maintained a calm tone.

Mr. Connelly nodded. "First up, I'm Bob." He smiled. "Never have taken too kindly to the mister prefix."

"Fair enough," I replied.

"Second of all ... you two need help. I do understand your reluctance to be here, and appreciate that you are concerned about us. At the same time ... it's about time you both used your brains and came home."

Mac grinned. "Dad," he said interrupting him, "this sicko taunts us and deposits parts of people we know in places for us to find."

"I know, boyo," his father said. "Humor me. I'll be less

worried if you are here."

Mac sighed. I knew the expression on his face, a resigned expression. He didn't want to be here anymore than I did. I held his gaze and he smiled. It was going to be okay.

"Well, we're here and, unless Caine has another idea, we'll be staying for a bit." His eyes never left mine as he spoke.

"Grafton is on his way over?"

"Yes," Mac replied still locked in my eyes. "Will you join us when he arrives? I value your input."

"Sure. We best get back to the house. Beatrice can talk the legs off a table and probably hasn't noticed we vanished. But all the same we should go in."

Our stomachs keened stereophonically. Mr. Connelly chuckled. "We best get some food into you both," he said. "The only time that woman is quiet is when she's eating."

We headed back into the house and set about clearing mousetraps from the table in preparation for dinner. Beatrice hadn't noticed us leave and was still talking nineteen to the dozen and smoking like a train.

She looked up at Bob and forcefully said, "Why don't you keep your hands off my stuff, dammit!"

"What now?"

"You know what I mean!" She huffed. "You took my can of red paint and my quarter-inch brush!"

"I didn't take it," he replied. "It's on the shelf in the basement, with your other paint cans. The brush is in the drawer with your other brushes!"

"See?" She complained, looking at Mac. "He did take them, otherwise how would he know where they were?" I watched Mac hurry back into the kitchen. He did not intend being dragged into his mother's accusing spree.

Mac's father rolled his eyes. "I picked up the paint from the coffee table in the living room and put it away!"

"See you did take it!" She seemed delighted to have a confession but was still angry. "Keep your hands off my stuff!"

Bob ignored her and went back to the kitchen. I heard him mutter under his breath, "It was two days ago. Jesus, woman! When will you ever learn to put things away?"

I watched Mac set the salad on the table. I could tell he was struggling to keep his comments to himself. My own highly-developed self-preservation instinct kicked in. I zoned while Beatrice ranted.

Bob swooped in and removed the ashtray laden with cigarettes that had burned down. That caused another outcry from Beatrice, "I haven't finished with that!"

His arm reached out and swiped the burning cigarette from her hand as it waved in his direction. "Now you have," he replied, stubbing it out and tossing the contents of the ashtray into the trash. He placed a fork in her still-flapping hand. "We're eating now," he told her. Mac slid a plate in front of her.

"About time," she complained.

Mac smiled at me as he took his seat.

"This looks great," I said. Mac piled salad onto my plate next to a juicy steak. I watched in child-like wonder as he pulled my plate towards him and cut up the meat for me. "Thank you."

"You're welcome," he said. "Eat up."

We ate in silence. My mind threw up random excerpts of general eccentricity. The other shoe was about to drop; I could feel it. I looked across at Mac. I felt Caine's presence. Words fell in some sort of disjointed order from my mouth.

"Mac-door-Caine."

He glanced up from his plate as a loud knock sounded at the front door. He gave me a 'damn you're spooky' look.

"I'll get it," he said making his escape. I glanced at his plate as he left. Once again he had devoured his food at an inhuman rate. I looked at my own plate: I wasn't far behind.

I could feel surreality taking hold of me and seemed powerless to stop it. Caine and Mac appeared. Both looked grim.

"'Little Bo peep, you lost your sheep, and don't know where to find them; leave them alone and they'll come home dragging body parts behind them.'"

Caine arched an eyebrow in my direction. "Nice, Ellie."

"They're dead, Caine, he killed them; that's two FBI agents added to the mix."

He didn't say a word.

"Ol' King Cole was a merry old soul and a merry old soul was he; he called for his pipe, he called for a knife and he called for his fiddlers three.'"

Caine and Mac froze. They stared at me. So I stared back.

"Ellie?" Caine sounded odd. He'd added a new tone to his repertoire. I couldn't place it at all; from anyone else's mouth I would have considered it to have a fearful quality. Caine was never afraid.

"What?"

"You should be resting."

"Plenty of time for resting when I'm dead," I retorted. How rude. I've had enough damn rest. Meanwhile there's a killer loose. "Am I the only one who thinks we are playing fiddle to accompany a killer? Every move we make, he's there. He's ahead of us, behind us, with us; how? How can he find us so readily? How does he place bodies under our fuc'n noses? Does any of this bother you?"

Mac's eyes widened and filled with uncertainty. I didn't think I was being irrational. They were perfectly reasonable questions.

"I'm fine," I assured him.

"For the record, you almost sound fine," he replied taking my hand and encouraging me to stand.

I looked around. Mac's Mom was talking between each mouthful and appeared unaware that I had spoken at all.

His Dad, however, had laid down his utensils and was watching with interest. He spoke with calm clarity, "If you three fiddlers would like to go on back to your room. I'll be along." He flashed me a wink.

I knew then I wasn't alone in my observations.

Mac stooped to bring his mouth close to my ear. "You

sure you're fine?"

I nodded and sighed at my stupidity. You'd think I would learn.

As soon as we were inside the room Caine spoke, his voice flat and tired, "Our decoy agents in Richmond ... we've lost them. I'm hoping they turn up alive."

"Jesus," Mac hissed, he leaned on the door. "How the hell did that happen?"

"He must've known it wasn't you two from the outset," Caine replied. "I've got the DEA fuming and breathing down my neck wanting to know why this prick killed Matheson."

"What else?" Mac asked.

We both sensed there was more to come. We were looking into the face of a very worried man. For a change he wasn't so hard to read.

Caine frowned. The lines on his face deepened. "I want you both to log in and check your mail. I'm betting he has a message for you after his last little spree. Maybe we can find out where the bodies are."

"And?" I asked. "Was I right? Were the agents at the hospital dead?"

"Yes. We found the two agents who were supposed to watch you at the hospital. Agents McLean and Morley were drugged, stabbed, and left in the trunk of their car. The car was within the hospital grounds."

"You keeping a tally?" I glared at Caine. "'Cos I'm starting to lose count here."

He was sitting on the bed his hands resting on his

thighs. I watched his fingers tense.

Caine spoke, "A question. Most of his poems are short and quite childlike in their composition. He's used and distorted several nursery rhymes. What does that suggest to you?"

I tried to piece together all the little pieces of information we had gleaned so far. It wasn't easy: My mind attempted to rebel and wreak havoc on its own accord.

I replied, "A troubled childhood." I'm sure my own little restructured poems weren't far from his mind.

"Why does he leave the bodies for you?"

I shrugged. "Maybe he likes me. How the fuck would I know?" I was in no mood to play twenty questions on the topic of multiple murders.

"Pretty close. We have a psych profile if you're interested."

"Just spit it out!"

Caine almost smiled. "The brainiacs have decided this sonofabitch was an abused kid, perhaps still gravitating back to the abuser or another abuser. His poetry began as a cry for help but nobody picked it up. He may have read things into your poetry, Ellie, and yours as well, Mac, which suggested a similar background."

"Uh huh," I replied.

"Neither of you dwelled too much on such things in the poetry room, as far as we can tell from the transcripts and poetry we have read. You both come across as strong characters who have moved on. He hasn't. He looks at you both as heroes, his heroes."

"Why kill our friends and acquaintances?"

I was beginning to think that maybe, just maybe, this was usable information for once.

"They suggest he has appointed himself the guardian of the chat room. He has discovered his power lies in the deaths of those who may or may not have offended you."

Well, that just sounded like a load of horse manure, and I wasn't about to plant roses.

"In the deaths? Or the killing?" Mac asked.

"Killing: He now has power he never had before. He decides who lives and dies." Caine pursed his lips as if he'd just sucked a lemon. "And he seems to be embracing his new power with open arms, proving his worth to you by killing anyone who is, was, or could be a threat."

I grimaced. "A threat to what?"

I had an urge to scream. How the fuck did he know about Chicago? How did he know about Carter? How did he know Carter was dealing in ketamine?

I didn't scream. I formulated a pressing question and stated it with unfelt calm. "Is it possible that this sick bastard is FBI or even a cop?"

"It's possible. Who ever he is, he's smart. He appears to know too much and can find you too easily. Being in law enforcement would help explain his ease in locating you."

Mac asked, "Is this personal? Could he just as easily have picked another room and another set of victims?"

Caine shrugged. "That's the thing Mac, we have no solid suspects, and we have no way of knowing for sure if this is personal; for now the safest option is to assume it is."

"He's mobile, right?" Mac asked rhetorically.

I watched thoughts form in Mac's eyes.

He said, "We're pretty sure he's using satellite ... so he could be any-fucking-where."

"That's what worries me most right now, and why it took me so long to get here. I don't want to be the one who leads him to you."

"Who knows where we are right now?" I asked.

"Only me. In a few minutes I am going to ask you both to log into the chat room."

I am sure my blood began to freeze in my veins. The last thing I wanted to do was spend time in that godforsaken room looking for nicknames that would never again appear.

"He's using others. Could he be using others to locate us as well? If he's as smart as you think, he'd have tailed both you and Aidan from the hospital. One of you is bound to have face-to-face contact at some point." My eyes flicked up to Caine's. "Do you think he followed the ambulance to the hospital?"

Caine's eyes fell. He picked at his fingernails. "I think so. I think that's how he got the agents I sent after you. He's creating crime scenes all over."

Mac moved. He took the laptops from the backpack. His Dad popped his head around the door. "Need anything?"

"Extension cords," Mac replied with a glance towards

the door. "Where's Mom?"

"Basement creating havoc," he replied. "Be right back with those cords."

"Thanks."

I lay back on the bed. I had a sneaking suspicion that we would never get ahead of this jerk-off. Were we doomed to play the fiddle for a nut-job, accompanying his insane killing spree, never free to live again? Half my mind seemed to agree that I had a right to feel sorry for myself while the other half admonished my self-pitying weakness and told me to get a fuc'n grip.

"Ellie? Earth to Ellie?"

I rolled over towards Mac's voice and half opened an eye. "Uh huh."

"We're set. Waiting on you."

But I don't want to! I don't want to go in there again. I don't want to. I don't want to check my mail. I just want it to stop, now! I'm not okay dammit!

My internal voice chided me for acting like a four-year-old and insisted that I pull my act together and get my ass up; it didn't work as well as it used to. My conscious self showed a sudden disobedience that took me by surprise.

"I can't."

Did I say that? I must have: The room felt cold. I waited for the wrath of Caine to descend bringing forth thunder and lightening.

Nothing like that happened.

Caine asked for my password.

The email alert sounded and I wished I was deaf.

I heard Caine read the email aloud. I'm sure that was his intent and I wished he'd be quiet. A growing feeling of ill-ease built inside me. It was familiar and yet took me a while to place it. Two things were missing and much missed: Nicotine and caffeine. They would improve my borderline temper.

The email alert sounded again. The piercing chime irritated every inch of my body.

Then a voice close by said, "Coffee, Ellie?"

I sat up and felt surprisingly good, not great, but definitely better.

"Better?" Bob asked.

"Yes, thank you," I replied. I smelled coffee.

"Head aches a bit, I take it," Bob said, sitting on the bed by me and passing me a mug of coffee.

"Not really, it's pretty good," I said and took a cigarette from the pack he offered me.

For the briefest instant I considered quitting. Then dismissed the thought as craziness and lit up.

"Go easy, you haven't had one in a while."

He was right. I sucked in the soothing nicotine-laced smoke. Much better. I finished my coffee and the cigarette, enjoying every flavor-filled second. Mac and Caine sat at a small table in the middle of the room. I joined them.

I tapped Caine's shoulder. "Scoot."

He stood up and let me sit in front of the laptop.

"Sign into the chat room, Ellie," he instructed, and then turned to Mac. "Can you sign in as someone other than Galileo?"

I noticed Caine checked his watch as he spoke.

"Yes, I can. Do you want me to?" Mac replied.

"Please, I would like to see how this prick reacts when he thinks Ellie is alone."

"I'm in," I told them. "He's here. You want me to say anything in particular?"

Caine twitched. "Pretend you're talking to Rachel, tell her you don't know where Galileo is, you haven't seen him all day."

I watched the glare Mac directed at Caine. "You're playing with fire," he warned then said. "I am in the room as Socrates."

I made idle chit-chat in the room. In casual conversation I mentioned I hadn't seen Galileo all day and hinted at concern for his absence.

"Mac answer her ... tell her he's moved on. Perhaps he grew tired of her."

"Jesus!" Mac replied. "You're really pushing it."

Seconds later both of us received emails from the Unsub; this time they were different. I read mine aloud, "'I thought you understood you should be together.'"

Mac read out his, "'No, no, no, this won't do at all. I worked hard, you can't ruin this now.'"

"Oh shit!" Caine exclaimed. "Guess we know one thing that he wants now and with more certainty. You guys together."

I stared at Caine. "Mac needs to be here as Galileo. You've proved your point."

“Doing it,” Mac said.

Mac signed out then signed back in with his usual nickname. Very quickly after that, my email alert chimed again.

I opened my mail and read aloud, “‘You lied. You do know where he is.’” I paused and looked over at Bob. “His parting comment … ‘Tell Mom and Dad I’ll drop by later.’”

Bob shrugged at me.

His voice took on a no-nonsense edge and he replied, “Let him come.”

Caine checked his watch again. This time I called him on it. “What’s with the watch thing?”

“I’ve made it harder for this prick to trace your satellite blips. I figure he’s using tracking software and cruising till he gets a signal.”

Mac raised an eyebrow in Caine’s direction. “Explain!”

Caine twitched; it was almost a real smile. “There are twenty agents working in pairs scattered around Fairfax County, who all signed into different chat rooms within the same platform at approximately the same time as you two. The signals don’t need to be coming from the same room just within the same platform. Four of them are in Cobwebs now. They’ll all pop in and out of Cobwebs at different times.”

Mac smiled. “They’re using satellite right?”

Caine nodded. “They’re all using exactly the same set-up and satellite provider as you two use. Which is a service used by the FBI. We checked that first; I wanted to limit the number of innocent people caught up in this satellite net. He would've been watching for your signals to pop up and now he has his little screen covered in blips. With no clue about which two are yours. His little screen will be covered in blips about now. He can cruise and track blips across the county. It should take him a while to find the needle in the satellite haystack."

I surveyed the list of twenty-three people in the chat room; twenty-three people and one invisible killer.

"What happens when he homes in on the correct signal?"

Several people left the chat room and a few more came in.

"I am hoping to have a little chat to him about killing my agents," Caine replied.

"This could take all fucking night," I muttered. "Why not kill all the signals and just have our two out there? Get it over with."

"I hear you, Ellie. I don't want him thinking I'm leading him. I want him to think we're protecting you, not leading him to the slaughter."

"Like I care," I snapped. I know I sounded bitchy and cranky, but tough, this had been dragging on and we were getting nowhere. "Giving a shit would be a large leap for me to make."

I watched the room conversation for a little while. Half-hearted at best; it wasn't riveting stuff. There was nothing at all attention-grabbing until I noticed the conversation stalled and one party asked why he or she had gone so quiet.

Mac jumped in and typed: *Maybe they've been disconnected, it happens all the time.*

It was true, it happened so often we coined a phrase to describe it, 'moofing'. We watched as a reply came from the other party in the conversation a guy called LostAdam, a regular.

You're right I did get disconnected, but it was my head.

I looked at Mac. He sucked in air. His eyes widened. I looked back to the screen and saw the reason. LostAdam recited a poem but it wasn't his style. In fact, it was very familiar. I had that same horrible, cold, sinking feeling that had been with me on and off since Carter's death.

Something bad just happened.

"Mac?"

Mac called Caine over, "Can whoever you have in the room find out where LostAdam is?"

"Problem?"

"See for your self."

Caine hunched down and watched as Mac scrolled back to show him the conversation. "That doesn't sound good. What's with the poem? It's way too good to come from the sonofabitch killer. I'll get them on it."

Words wouldn't form as I read and reread the poem. It was Mac's poem, he wrote it for me. No one had ever seen it, unless that person had been in my office before the explosion.

Where is the shroud, I always knew? I looked but there was only sun, something not seen for so long. Again I ask, what be-

came of the dark? When I awoke in the middle of my night.

"I wrote that poem," Mac's voice hovered just above a whisper. "I wrote it for Ellie. No one else has seen it."

He looked to me as if to confirm what he'd said.

I nodded.

Caine said nothing. His mouth tightened into a hard line. He pulled a two-way radio from his jacket. Caine walked across the room talking to whoever was on the other end.

Some kid started posting a most dreadful poem in the chat room about cutting, ack! Why do they do this in our room? I typed before thinking and told her to suck it in and blow it out. The world doesn't revolve around her – not today, or tomorrow, either.

Does the world revolve around a moron who likes to kill? Quite possibly. Still, I don't get the whole cutting thing, what's the point? Just seems like a way to make a big mess and I am sick of these kids coming into our chat room and spewing this crap. It's a poetry room, people! Not a room for those with mental issues.

When I looked up Mac frowned at me across the computers. "That was mean," he said.

"It was the truth."

"What sort of encouragement is that?" he asked.

"How many times has this kid posted similar poor-little-me shit?" I let my tone convey that he knew very well how often this happened.

"I know, she needs to toughen up and get over herself somewhat, but Ellie ... there's a killer watching everything you type."

"Life's a bitch."

Why do I spit forth my thoughts without censoring them? Why can't I just use that social filter thing everyone else seems to be able to implement?

"Jesus!" I huffed, and typed into the chat box: *Sorry kiddo, I shouldn't take my bad temper out on you. Thanks for sharing your poem.*

It was a mere second later that I received an email from the Unsub.

I read it aloud, "'Maybe she needs to be put out of her misery, she upset you. I fear Adam is truly lost.'"

"Caine, find that kid," I yelled at him across the room. "And he mentioned LostAdam!"

Mac looked up and announced he was chatting with her. "She's in Vienna. I have her address."

Caine had his cell phone poised in one hand and radio in the other. "Give me her address. I have a couple of agents in Vienna."

Mac read it out to him then told the kid to disconnect from the Internet.

I felt awful for endangering her life. I felt awful for many reasons. Who had access to my office? Who had read that poem? I went over and over the last time we had been in Mauryville. The Unsub was there, but outside; there was nothing to suggest he'd been inside at all and I remembered seeing the poem hanging on the wall. Jesus! I stopped the churning in my stomach by swallowing hard. The kid sprang into my mind again.

"What's her name?"

"Crystal," Mac replied. "She's seventeen."

Caine interrupted us as he and Bob headed for the door, "Stay on line. Bob and I are going to make coffee while we wait for the callback on the kid."

"Okay," I replied.

I could barely bring myself to look at the screen and was struggling to understand why I had acted so rashly in the chat room. Even taking into consideration my well-known lack of tact, I had surpassed my own meanness. I stood up and walked over to the bed.

Distorted nursery rhymes ran through my cloudy mind. "'Little Jack Horner sat in the corner, eating his Christmas pie, he stuck in his thumb and pulled out a plum, saying what a good boy am I. His mother smacked his head and made him cry. You're not a good boy, you should die!'"

"'Jack and Jill went up the hill to fetch a pail of water, Jack fell down and broke his crown, and Jill went tumbling after. Mother laughed, she was to blame, Jill jumped up and spun around, don't you ever touch him again!'"

I fell back onto the bed. Mac's hand rested on my head. I looked up at him a little surprised that he was there. I thought he was still watching the chat room.

"Where did they come from?"

"Where'd what come from?" I asked, matching his soft tone.

"The rhymes."

"They're in my head. How'd you know?"

My eyes closed. I thought he could read my mind.

"You were singing."

"Sorry." Mystery solved.

"Don't be, where'd they come from?"

"I used to make them up when I was a kid." I tried to keep my voice even, it wasn't easy, those weren't memories I wanted to revisit. "Whenever Mommy Dearest did something to Aidan I would write a rhyme. By the time I was twelve I had a whole notebook of them."

"Are you all right?"

"Yeah. I'm just dandy." I'm okay. Another one bought the dust. How many dead now? Why are people dying? I shoved all horror aside and focused instead on Mac.

"Uh huh," he didn't sound convinced. "Like to try that again?"

"Nope." I grinned. "I'm thuper. Thankths for athking."

"You casting aspersions on my sexual orientation?"

"Hell, no," I replied. "I am well aware of your orientation."

Mac's hands encircled my neck as he pretended to choke me. "I should hope so too."

"Perhaps I need a reminder, a refresher even." I lifted my head to meet his and kissed him.

Chapter Sixteen

Run To You

I sat on the bed. It was nice to feel clean, dressed and more human. I appreciated Mac's help: It's not easy showering and keeping a cast dry on one's own. Time seemed to be dragging. Sunday night was becoming the longest night on record. Mac ran his hands through his hair in an attempt to further tidy himself before opening the door for his father and Caine.

"Everything all right?" Bob asked. He looked from Mac to me and gave us both a wry grin.

"Fine," Mac replied. "How's the kid?"

"Safe," Caine said. "How's the chat room?"

"Don't know. We just finished showering," he replied.

"I've had a report back from two agents on Oakton – said they had an unsolicited pizza delivery about half an hour ago. Sounds like he maybe narrowing the field."

"Anyone else see anything?" I asked, noting Mac was still recovering.

"Not yet. Aidan called my cell wanting to speak to you."

"Is he okay?"

"I think so. Said he's at home, hasn't been back to your parents' place."

"Good." I felt a sigh forming and pressed it aside. "Does he know where we are?"

"I didn't tell him, nor did he ask. He only wanted to know that you were okay."

"LostAdam?" I almost regretted asking because I knew it wouldn't be good news.

"We found his residence, he was in McLean. We think someone died at a computer in the house. He lived alone and possibly was wheelchair-bound. His living room resembled a slaughterhouse. No body yet, either."

Caine's phone rang. He answered it and walked to the other side of the room as he spoke in a low tone. I couldn't make out what he was saying. He disconnected the call and turned to face us.

"Another pizza delivery from a different pizza company. Tyson's Corner was the location."

Caine pulled a map from his inside jacket pocket and knelt on the carpet with the map spread in front of him.

"Counting your two, there are eighteen more signals for him to trace scattered across the region." Caine pointed to the map. "The farthest out being Reston. Eighteen signals, nine locations."

"Do you suppose he's driving about with the bodies in the trunk?" Mac asked.

I shuddered.

"Chances are," Caine replied. "If he sticks to his signature he has to have them somewhere close to be able to leave them for you to find."

Silence fell like a shroud over the room as a car alarm sounded. It was loud and felt close.

Mac looked at his Dad. "Is that one of yours?"

Bob shook his head. "Similar but not mine, the garage alarm would have sounded first."

We heard Mrs. Connelly call out. Caine leapt to his feet. "Bob, we should see if Beatrice is all right."

Caine seemed a little edgy to me. The way he leapt at the sound of Beatrice's voice was unusual. I surmised that this was a very unusual situation and we were all a little edgy. Why should he be any different?

"She's misplaced something," he said, with a here-we-go-again tone to his voice.

"She sounds angry," Caine replied, as he opened the bedroom door.

"Yep," Bob said, and followed him out. "That's how she always sounds."

I knew Mac wasn't about to go check on her with them. He leaned back in his chair to make himself more comfortable.

"It could take hours before the sonofabitch gets to us." Complaining wasn't going to help but I was feeling grouchy and borderline bad-tempered. There was still a lurking strangeness, suggesting none of it was real, that this was all an illusion or delusion.

"Yes, yes, it could."

I yawned making Mac follow suit.

"Lay back, close your eyes and rest a bit. I'll wake you when the Unsub sends us pizza."

"I'm okay. Don't fuss."

He threw his hands up in surrender. "If you say so."

"Mmmm, I could eat two whole pizzas about now." I

wasn't hungry but that didn't mean I wouldn't eat pizza if it turned up. "They'd better be Meat Lovers from Pizza Hut, pan crust with barbecue sauce."

"Hell, yeah," Mac replied.

It had become oddly quiet outside our room. I couldn't hear his Mom's customary hollering or his father's patient yet firm responses.

"Are you thirsty?" Mac asked.

"I am."

"Let's go see what we can find to drink."

"Sounds good to me."

We walked along the hallway into the living room. There was nobody around. We checked the dining room and found that, too, devoid of human occupation.

"Wonder where they are?"

"Basement," was my guess. I dragged Mac into the kitchen. "Thirsty here!"

Mac took a bottle of juice from the refrigerator. He poured us a tall glass each and managed to spill juice all over the spotless scrubbed counter- top.

I took my glass and went to sit at the dining room table. On my way from the room, something outside the window caught my eye. I stopped and looked again. Whatever it was, disappeared. Mac was wiping down the countertop and didn't seem to have seen anything.

"I thought I saw something outside the window."

Mac looked out. "All I see is dark."

Yeah, well, me too, now!

"Hallucinations," he offered as an explanation.

"Yeah. Could be."

Mac chuckled.

I sat at the table and drank some juice. I watched Mac pick up his glass and turn off the kitchen light.

He froze in the dark room, staring at the window.

"What?" I asked.

"I thought I saw something."

I flicked the dining room lights out. From the kitchen doorway I peered through the window, looking past Mac's reflection into the night.

"Can you see anything now?"

Mac was studying the vista beyond the reflective glass. He turned, and grinned. "Nah. I think I am a bit spooked is all. Just the wind moving the branches."

We stood facing each other in the darkened room.

"That's understandable," I said. Unease built rather quickly and with it came a familiar phrase, 'things aren't always as they seem.' "Are the doors locked?"

"Should be, Dad's forever locking them ..." He paused. "And my crazy mother is forever unlocking them. Best we check." I watched his hand slip to his hip and then a blur of confusion settle on his face. I knew what he was looking for and where our guns were.

"In our room."

"Well, fuck!" Mac cursed; he crossed the kitchen floor and checked the back door lock. Satisfied he hurried back and grabbed my hand. He led the way through the dark dining room and out into the dimly-lit hallway. We walked towards the front door.

It too was locked but not bolted. Mac reached up and slid the bolt home. We stopped at the top of the stairs on our way down the hall. There was nothing to hear.

"What the hell?" Mac's confusion grew. "I should at least be able to hear my mother yapping."

You'd think, considering the woman never stopped talking, not even to pause for breath. Something was niggling at me, gnawing away inside my head. What if he was tracking us another way? What if that email referring to Mom and Dad wasn't a stab in the dark?

What if he knew all along where we were? A growing feeling of dread spread through my stomach.

"Weapons," I said, and hoped I didn't sound as worried as I felt. We turned off lights as we passed switches. That plunged ninety percent of the house into darkness. Mac picked up our guns from the dresser. I took mine from him holding it awkwardly in my left hand. Mac was in danger of a friendly-fire hit if I had to shoot left-handed.

"Damn. I hope I don't have to shoot. This could go badly."

"How badly?"

"It'll hurt you more than it'll hurt me!"

He almost smiled then moved past me to the closet and pulled a heavy box out into the room. He removed a flashlight and checked it worked.

My mind spun through the thoughts that wouldn't leave me alone. How else could he have found us? We could be carrying a GPS bug. I stared at my gun. The temptation to throw it across the room was strong. What did I have with me the whole time? I felt as though my life was draining away.

"Mac?"

"Shit, you okay?" He was right in front of me holding my arms just above the elbow. "Ellie? You feeling all right?"

Hell no, I don't feel all right!

I struggled to form words and keep my voice composed. I asked, "What have I had with me all the time?"

"Sit." He pressed me to sit on the bed, so I did and waited for his answer, which would match mine. "Your wallet, badge and gun."

"Would you get my wallet and badge?" It was difficult keeping alarm from my voice. There was something odd going on in the house and we could've been carrying a bug this whole time. He could already be here.

Mac placed the items on my lap.

"Have I changed the magazine in this gun since this began?"

He shook his head. The stone-cold feeling grew in my tummy, forcing itself upward. I searched my wallet: There was nothing to indicate any tampering at all. My badge was the same, no evidence of anything hidden in the seams of the leather case or anywhere else. That left my gun or more accurately the ammunition in the magazine.

"What are you looking for?"

"GPS bug about the size of a vitamin pill." I released

the clip and dropped the magazine onto the bed. “If he’s bugged me, the only place left that I can think of is a doctored round.”

“You really think he could have? How many people have access to your weapon?”

“Not many. If I am carrying a GPS bug inside a bullet then it points to someone close to me.” I removed all the rounds from the magazine and ran my fingers over them. All brass. All intact. It was unlikely that a GPS transmitter was inside a brass casing. The metal may interfere with its ability to work. I reloaded, satisfied that I wasn’t carrying a dummy round or a bug in my magazine. “Where else could it be?”

“What else hasn’t changed?”

I shrugged. “I need to think and we need to find your parents and Caine.”

Wishing hard seemed like my only option at that point. So I wished that the Unsub wasn’t here and that they were okay.

“Let’s do it. We’ll worry about this bug later.”

“Agreed.” I forced the thoughts of GPS aside for the meantime. We had no proof a bug existed. Where could it be? If it was a bug it was too late to destroy it anyway.

Mac pocketed his cell phone and picked up the flashlight. He flipped the light switch as we reached the door. A blanket of darkness descended over us along with an unnerving silence.

I touched his arm and whispered, “We’ll secure the house room-by-room starting up here, bedrooms, living areas, then basement."

"Okay."

"Safety off, finger out of the trigger guard. At each room we come to, keep to the hinge side of the door." Even though I was whispering my voice seemed to carry in the dark. I half expected to hear an echo.

"Okay," Mac replied.

We walked on and kept close to the wall as we closed on the first bedroom down the thick carpet in the hallway. My nerves jangled so much I am sure they sounded like bells ringing from a church tower. Someone was tugging on the rope and swinging those bells for all they were worth.

I extracted the flashlight from Mac's hand. It was hard to hold it with a cast, but awkward though it was, I managed to keep it steady. My left hand held the gun. I let the gun rest on top of the cast. It wasn't brilliant but the light and gun were roughly in the same direction.

I turned to Mac, shining the light in his face. "Sorry," I whispered. "On 'two' reach forward and fling the door open for me, hard. Make it smack the wall behind. Keep to the hinge side of the door."

"Okay," he replied. On 'two' Mac swung the door wide. I stepped through keeping my back to the wall moving around the perimeter of the room scanning up and down and side to side. My heart calmed as it became obvious there was nobody there. I motioned to Mac to enter. Together we checked under the beds, in the closet and behind the curtains.

"Nothing," Mac said. I guessed his heart was pounding big time. We left the room and shut the door behind us. We moved to the next bedroom. I passed Mac the flashlight.

"Your turn."

He whispered to himself, "Gun and light, same direction, back to wall."

"Yup," I replied as I counted and then flung the door wide open. It smacked against the wall behind it.

Minutes later we were done. Upstairs was secure. We stood at the top of the basement stairs.

"Dad has alarm sensors down there, the beam kind."

"Uh huh. Guess we'll find out if the alarm's on."

We started down the stairs. I could smell something. My stomach gurgled as I placed the aroma. "Can you smell pizza?"

"Yeah," Mac replied. I could just make out his face in the dim light. He was worried and chewing his lip. We stopped outside the first door we came to.

"Storage room," he said. I could tell he just wanted to find his parents. Stopping to search rooms slowed the process unbearably.

"Let's get it over with."

I half expected the basement alarm to sound any second. Mac secured the room. We both searched the two large closets. All we found were boxes upon boxes of Christmas decorations but no sign of life.

We followed the pizza smell down the hallway. Mac secured the next room we came to. The odor of pizza grew stronger as we neared the workroom. Mac flung the door open. It crashed back into something sending an avalanche of stuff tumbling to the floor.

"Shite!" he exclaimed. "She'll have a major fit about this."

The reek of fresh paint inside the room masked the pizza we smelt out in the hallway. Mac shone the flashlight in a sweeping motion around the room. There were cans of paint open on the workbench. I felt compelled to point them out.

"She's always leaving stuff lying around, maybe nothing."

"Where the hell is everyone?" I turned around. Where could they have gone? "Mac, how can three people just vanish?"

"Not easily," Mac replied, he lowered the beam and scanned the floor again. "Jesus!" he hissed, "What the fuck is that?"

The light settled on a flat, square box on the floor past the workbench.

"Pizza box," I replied without thought.

"Christ!" Mac exclaimed, and opened the box. It contained a half-eaten Hawaiian pizza. Still warm.

"Phone!"

I held out my hand; he gave me the phone.

I punched in Caine's number and waited. The call diverted to his message service.

"Well, that's odd," I muttered as the call flicked over to his answer service. I left a short message, "Where the hell are you?" and disconnected the call.

Why would he have his service pick up messages in the middle of this mess? It didn't make sense at all. He had regular update calls flowing in and he needed to be available. Bad thoughts were raging despite my trying to settle them. It didn't make sense.

I handed back the phone and asked, "Where could they be?"

"I dunno," Mac replied, unable to take his eyes off the pizza box.

The pizza was making me hungry, and I don't even like Hawaiian pizza. Fruit and meat just shouldn't be together.

I shoved my gun into my waistband.

Mac spoke, "The only place left is the garage."

"Then let's go!"

We stopped at the top of the stairs and listened to the house. It gave nothing away. The entire house remained silent. Graveyard still.

"Jesus, this is eerie."

"Yeah," Mac said, and took my hand.

He helped me negotiate the darkened rooms all the way back to the kitchen and the backdoor. "What if?" Mac began to say as he turned the handle.

"Let's cross that bridge when we come to it," I replied. "'What ifs' are not helpful."

He opened the door. We walked along the path. Trees rustled as the cold wind stirred the foliage. Mac turned the flashlight beam at several trees as we passed. Just in case. For a split second I thought I smelled spicy cologne in the breeze. As we approached the garage we saw a golden glow emanating from under the side door.

"Hinge side," I reminded him, tugging my gun free of my jeans.

I took a breath and looked at Mac for a second. I nodded. He swung the door back hard. It slammed into the wall behind. The crash reverberated around the garage, followed by an exclamation from a male voice, "Jesus!"

"Dad?" Mac called back.

I followed the sound of the voice to discover Caine and his parents sitting around the table. They all looked well and unharmed. I saw Mac's posture change. He replaced concern with anger. I closed the door.

"You've been here the whole time?" Mac asked. I heard a slight tremor in his voice as he tried to remain composed.

"We've been talking to Mr. Grafton," Beatrice replied, she sounded perky, almost jovial.

Mac pushed his shoulders back, standing straighter. His hand was around mine. He squeezed my fingers at the edge of the cast. He looked at Caine.

"We found a pizza box. You didn't answer your phone," he informed them with much control.

"Would've been nice if you'd told me you were leaving the house!" I said.

"Shall we take this party back inside? And once we're there, I want a good explanation for everything." Mac reached around and opened the door.

There was no argument. One by one the garage occupants filed past us into the darkness.

"There were no lights on when we left the house," Mac said stopping just before the back door. There *were* no lights on yet light flooded out onto the path where we stood, emanating from the kitchen window.

"Stay here," Bob and Caine said in unison. I saw Caine's lip twitch as he spoke again, "Sweep and secure. On my mark, take left."

A *Rockford Files* remake happened before my eyes. Rockford and his sidekick stepped through the kitchen door.

Mac's Mom was talking nonstop close on my right about the nice young man who had bought the pizza and how kind he was. "How did he know I felt like Hawaiian pizza? He was very thoughtful don't you think, Mac?"

"Yes, very," Mac replied.

She barely paused for breath and was off again on a new ramble. This time she muttered on about how clever the cats were and how she had seen them turning on lights and opening doors.

Bob reappeared smiling. He honestly looked as though he was enjoying himself with old Rockford. He spoke to us, "Come on, it's all clear." We passed Bob in the doorway.

"As long as you're sure," I replied. There was no keeping the amusement from my voice.

I heard the door lock behind us. Mac and I headed back to the bedroom and laptops. Bob was behind us ushering Beatrice along in another direction.

We waited in silence for Bob to join us. When he did I turned to Caine, who waited in a chair.

"Why didn't you answer your phone?"

"It never rang."

"I was redirected to your message service."

"Ellie, it never rang," he repeated, "What number did you call?"

Mac took the cell phone from his pocket and checked the last number called then read it out to Caine.

"That's my number." He checked his phone. "It doesn't say I missed any calls." He listened to his messages. Then called his message service. We all saw him check his watch and then he said, "I did not forward my calls to the service!"

"Make sure I get my calls, dammit!" His voice raised a notch, "Don't, 'But Sir' me! Change my authorization code."

He punched a series of numbers into the keypad then did it again. "Thank you," he snapped and hung up.

"How the hell did that happen?" I became aware of Mac's eyes on me. I glanced at him: He was frowning.

"Fuck knows! It could have been him but how would the bastard get my access code?" Caine stood and paced up and down the room. "Six more pizza deliveries."

"Why were the lights on?" Mac asked.

"Well, we don't know that either. One of the cats?" Caine replied. "There was no sign of an intruder and nothing to indicate that anyone had entered the house, bar the kitchen light magically turning on." He stopped in front of us. "Quite frankly we don't know shit!"

"Was it him who sent the pizza here?" I had to know.

"No." We all looked at Bob as he spoke, "I checked our phone log. Beatrice ordered it herself then became confused."

"Whew." He hadn't found us yet. "But that could mean he's still looking for us."

"Yep and those bodies aren't getting any fresher," Mac replied.

"Oh man! No more putrid corpses. Couldn't he keep them on ice, so they're nice and fresh when we get them?" I stopped and stared at Mac. "How many bodies are we talking about?"

"Three, now. Two FBI and one chat room patron."

"That's a lot of stench to have in a car. Even in the trunk."

I gave it some consideration, in truth only two of them would be borderline stinky. LostAdam might still be fresh. I turned to Caine. "Hey, Caine."

Caine looked up. I could tell he too was thinking.

"What would you do with three bodies while you searched for the people you wanted to deliver them to?" I asked.

"Ice 'em," he replied. "I'm on it." He sat at the table and tapped on one of the laptops. "Four refrigerated trucks have been stolen in Virginia over the last twenty-four hours. One in Manassas, two in Richmond, one in Fredericksburg."

He picked up his cell again and made a call to the Fairfax police department asking them to keep an eye out for the trucks.

I lay back on Mac. Caine was busy on the phone and computer. There was nothing much we could do except wait. Caine's phone rang constantly as information on the stolen trucks and surprise pizza deliveries came in.

Bob knelt on the floor in front of the map, marking off pizza deliveries and sightings of the trucks. If half the FBI in Northern Virginia were mobilized to stop the trucks, then sooner or later we'd get a hit. The pizza deliveries were getting closer so maybe we wouldn't have so long to wait after all.

I wanted pizza, even pizza sent by the Unsub would do.

A loud knock from the front door echoed up the hallway. Mac leapt to his feet, followed by Caine and Bob. The three of them hurried down the hall. I crept after them. I managed to keep out of sight and slipped into the living room doorway. From there I could see the front door and hear all that went on.

"Do psychotic killers knock?" Mac asked, as they approached the door.

"A psychotic killer with manners would," Bob replied. "Mac, out of sight. You and Caine hop into the coat closet."

I moved a little so I could see. Bob readied himself to open the door. He hid his gun behind his back. There was a man on the doorstep.

"I need your help, Dad," he said, and pushed past Bob

to gain entry. “Why was the door locked?”

“Not now,” Bob said. “We’ll talk tomorrow. I’ll drop by in the morning.”

The light outside the front door illuminated the horror on the man’s face. I recognized him as Eddie, Mac’s older brother.

“This is important!”

“I’m sure it is,” Bob said. “I’m busy this evening.”

Eddie grabbed his father’s arm. “You can’t tell anyone, but I think the Son of Shakespeare is after me,” he declared his eyes wide and somewhat crazy-looking.

Oh dear, Eddie, that’s the *wrong* story to be telling your Dad tonight. I watched Bob shake his head from side to side. I saw resignation on his face.

Eddie had an overactive imagination. Mac told me often of the wild claims Eddie made on an almost weekly basis. Last week Eddie was in hiding due to being on a gang hit list. His story was so incredible and changed so often it was entertaining for me to hear. The week before, Eddie was a hero for saving a small girl from the middle of the road just as a car was bearing down on her. An obvious hit-and-run attempt, according to Eddie. It took Bob only two days to get the real story from Eddie’s boss. Eddie was driving the car and had swerved to miss the child who was using a marked pedestrian crossing at the time. Yet somehow in the retelling, Eddie became a hero. Mac told me he suspected Eddie was fast becoming as unbalanced as their mother.

“Look at me!” Bob’s harsh tone made me jump. “I

don't have time for your imaginings right now!"

"I'm not imagining it," Eddie protested with much annoyance. He stepped closer to his father. "He's after me. I was in a chat room and I think he was there, and someone knew I'm a deputy sheriff."

"Eddie. Go home to your wife and kids." Bob was very firm. "This is not a good time."

I heard a noise coming from the coat closet. By the look on Eddie's face, he heard it too. He stepped closer and opened the door. Caine and Mac almost fell on him.

"Hi," Mac said, as he struggled to regain his balance.

"What the hell have you been doing?" Eddie's whiny voice was laced with suspicion.

"Coming out of the closet," Mac quipped.

I held my hand over my mouth so as not to roar with laughter.

"Oh ... oh," Eddie replied. He took a stagger.

"I was joking, you moron," Mac said, he reached out and slapped Eddie on the back of the head.

Eddie gave him a shove.

"Yeah, he was joking," Caine confirmed. "Weren't you, sweetie?" He blew him a kiss.

Mac pointed his finger at Caine. "Don't you start with me!"

"Well, we have things to take care of, Bob," Caine said, winking at Mac

"Okay," Bob replied. "Eddie's just leaving. I'll be down in a second."

Mac and Caine leveled with the living room door. Mac

glanced sideways. Guess he didn't expect to see me there. He gasped. Caine spun to face me. I held my finger to my lips and stepped aside so they could slip into the room. We all watched the show together.

Eddie continued unaware that we were watching. "I'm not leaving. What if he knows where I live? Did you think about your grandchildren at all?"

"That does it. I have heard all I care to listen to. Go home and sleep it off."

Eddie's manner changed. "What's going on? You're hiding something. Oh, I know what it is." He appeared almost gleeful for a moment.

"It's nothing that concerns you," his father replied.

"Why's Cormac here?" Eddie was trying to see down the hallway but his father blocked his view. Eddie was agitated, shifting his copious weight from foot to foot. "You have always liked him more than me."

Mac whispered, "Here we go! This is the point where Dad says a silent prayer for strength."

We listened to Bob. "He's staying with us, that's all there is to it."

"Who's the suit?" Eddie cocked his head to one side and squinted at his father. That action made him appear more insane, as if he had some terrible facial tick.

"A friend of your brother's," Bob replied. "Enough, Eddie. Go home."

Eddie opened the door. "I need your help," he stated, stepping onto the porch.

"You need to go home and sleep," Bob reiterated. "I'll

see you tomorrow and then you can tell me all about it."

We watched Eddie walk away then all hurried back to our room before Bob caught us eavesdropping. Mac waited for his father by the bedroom door.

"Okay, Dad?"

"He's getting worse," Bob said. "He and reality seem to be directly opposed right now."

I interrupted them to excuse myself. I was thirsty and had a dire need for a glass of cool water. "I'll be right back."

It was less creepy with the hallway lights on and easier to find my way to the kitchen. I didn't bother turning the light on in there. I had a glass of water while standing at the sink. Poured another and watched the trees outside blowing in the wind. I saw Mac's reflection appear beside me.

"Watch with me," I said not turning around.

"Watch what?"

"Just wait," I said.

We looked past the reflections and focused on the night beyond. The wind blew, rustling the leaves on the trees.

"There!" I pointed. The leaves parted to reveal a shape in the tree. It vanished as quickly as it came.

"Oh my God!" Mac exclaimed. The wind blew again. "Is that a face?"

"I think so." I was unable to take my eyes off the tree. "Damn. Eddie must've acted like a purpose-sent decoy."

"Stay here." I saw Mac hurry away in the reflection in

the glass. Before long, he was back with Caine and Bob.

"Look outside, watch that big tree," I said. I still stared past the reflections and into the night.

"Why?" Caine peered into the darkness from beside me.

"There maybe a body in it," Mac replied.

"Yeah." There was no surprise in Caine's tone. "I checked your email. There's a new one asking how you liked your latest gift, and saying he now sees he was right about Mom and Dad." Caine was squinting at the branches trying to see what we saw.

"Great!" I hissed, "How the hell would that dickwad know we'd be at Bob's, and how would he know where to look for them?"

Caine looked at me strangely.

"Don't look at me like that; there are literally hundreds of Connelly's in VA and more to the point, Bob and Beatrice are not listed in any phone book."

Caine frowned. "He already commented earlier about Mom and Dad."

"Yes, he did. I suspect that wasn't a stab in the dark, so to speak." I dragged my eyes from the window to look at him. "So did he trace us, or did he know already and just play a little cat-and-mouse-pizza game?" I went back to looking out the window. I knew what I suspected. "By the way, I want pizza, I feel cheated!"

A macabre face appeared, its frozen, dead eyes staring through the shifting branches.

"Shouldn't we do something about that?" Mac suggested. I could see his face in the windowpane. He was watching with morbid curiosity. The body swayed almost to the point of animation.

"Yeah," Caine replied then added. "Wonder where the other two are?"

Bob passed Caine the telephone receiver from the counter top.

"Thanks," he replied. Caine stepped away from the window and made several calls.

Mac and I stood shoulder-to-shoulder, peering into the darkness, waiting to catch another glimpse of the ghoulish figure. I refused to think of this new horror as an agent and perhaps someone I knew.

I sensed something in Mac, when our shoulders touched I felt a subtle tremor in his body.

"What?" I whispered in his ear.

"Come with me," he whispered back taking my hand.

No one noticed as we slipped from the room and scurried back to our room. We sat facing each other on the bed.

Mac appeared to be having great difficulty controlling a grin that was forming on his face. It looked like quite a struggle from where I sat.

"Let me tell a story from my childhood," he said as evenly as he could. "Mom, as you know, is a little nuts. Anyway, when I was about nine, I guess she became very angry with the squirrels that were destroying her flower beds." He paused. "This particular day she decided to deal with the problem, she sat out in the front yard with a twenty-two, a bucket, and a six-pack of beer." He looked at me. "She was already drunk."

My mind filled with images of Beatrice on that fateful day.

Mac carried on, "Mom is a really good shot and before long, her bucket was filled with squirrel carcasses. So she stomped off to the backyard hollering and carrying on about how she hates squirrels and tosses the contents of this bucket into the bushes." Mac shook his head. "You've never seen anything like it. Their little fuzzy bodies stuck on branches, hanging like some bizarre goddamn Christmas decorations. Tiny beady eyes, blankly staring back."

I saw why Mac was having difficulty in the kitchen when faced with the ghoulish sight out of the window.

"That's dreadful," I mumbled

"Yep."

"I don't think I can go back to the kitchen," I told him. "If I start giggling Caine's going to have a red, white and blue fit."

"Yep," Mac said. "We're already in trouble over stumpy."

I looked at him and was helpless to stop the rising mirth. It grew into uncontrollable laughter. We collapsed exhausted on the bed.

"Think anyone heard us?" I whispered. At least I thought I was whispering.

"It's late at night, the house is silent." Mac was trying not to make eye contact. "Sound travels."

"So we're in trouble again?"

"Most probably," he replied.

"Don't you wonder where the other one is?"

"Well, yeah," he said. "I'm sure we'll locate it."

We froze as heavy footsteps approached our room, and watched in silence as the door opened.

Caine stepped in. "Everything all right?"

"Yes," I replied.

"Good." He nodded. "Medical examiner, forensics, and the local police are here. It'll be morning before they're done."

"Do you know where the other bodies are yet?" Mac asked, exhibiting much restraint.

"No clue," he replied. "Check your mail and let me know if you get anything from our friend."

"Sure."

Caine left. I guess he went back to direct the investigation and annoy people who were trying to do their jobs. Mac said he wanted to talk to his Dad, to check he was okay. He kissed me. "I'll be back."

"I'll be here," I replied, grinning.

I sat back down in front of the laptop and checked my mail. It was an uneventful exercise. Yet again, someone wanted me to grow a penis. Why couldn't this Son of Shakespeare target spammers instead of poets? Now that would be a worthwhile public service.

Chapter Seventeen

Damned

"Do I sound paranoid, Dad?"

I strained to hear Bob's answer but couldn't make it out. A smoke ring rose from the ashtray next to me and dissolved. The wind had died down to intermittent puffs of cool air. Monday evening was dreary and dull. Police had spent much of the day standing around while forensic technicians did their thing. I'd spent most of the day trying to get answers.

Mac spoke again, "You must've seen the way he looks at her. I'm leery but is it unfounded? There are too many things we don't know and it just seems to me that he's overly attentive."

Bob's voice was a little huskier than Mac's I had to listen carefully. "Boyo, I've been down this path, I know where you are headed."

I concentrated on Bob's voice. "I've also considered that this could be the work of a cop or a fed."

He paused. I heard a lighter flick.

"Y'know, boyo, you were investigated seven ways from Sunday the minute you became involved with Ellie. He knows everything there is to know about you and you better believe that if he had found something he didn't like, you and Ellie wouldn't be together now."

I watched another plume of smoke rise from the cigarette in my hand. Did I believe that? They were discussing Caine and yeah, he was a little overprotective at times. But would he engineer the destruction of a relationship? Mac's voice alerted me to pay attention. "Ellie thinks someone planted a GPS device in something of hers."

"And that would have to be someone close to her," Bob said.

Mac actually thinks Caine is the killer! I stubbed my cigarette out but remained where I was.

Mac spoke again, "Tell me for sure it isn't him, and couldn't be him."

"What I can tell you may raise your suspicions, not allay them," Bob replied, his voice dropped. I had to strain even more to hear him. "Grafton had a daughter. Fourteen years ago she was murdered."

I could almost hear Mac thinking before he spoke, "How do you know?"

"I remembered the name and wondered if it was the same Grafton, so I dropped into the police department after he called me on Wednesday evening and borrowed the computer."

I'd forgotten how good retired cops are at getting information.

Caine had a daughter. In eight years he'd never mentioned a daughter or a wife; he'd never mentioned any family. How well did I really know Caine?

"And Ellie?" Mac asked.

"Watch him when he's near her. You'll see what I see.

He adores her, he's fatherly towards her."

Oh please, he cares about all of us! We're a tight team and he holds us together.

"You think he'd kill to protect her?"

"What father wouldn't do everything they could to protect someone they considered their child?"

My head spun. How could they think Caine would kill like this? Bile burned in my throat as Mac continued.

"He knew six months ago that Carter drugged her. When his name came up again it could have sent him over the edge."

Bob stopped Mac. "This is pure assumption, Mac. We have no evidence to make a suspect of Caine. Unless there is a GPS device in some personal object of hers and if that's the case, anyone she is close to becomes a valid suspect."

"The credit cards, Dad, someone accessed her account and made it look as if that's how the Unsub found us. Caine had access."

"Made it look, or did find you that way?" Bob needed clarification.

"We believed that's how he found us in Crystal City. We think he was using a key logger, we can't prove it. The computer that would have had the key logger on it was destroyed in the explosion at Ellie's home."

"We need to know for sure if there is a bug."

I sat shivering in the shadows as I considered the conversation. Eavesdropping is never a good idea.

Mac was right about three things and there was a

fourth he didn't yet know. He received a call from Roy, he had access to my credit card account, he had access to everything of mine, and he had access to explosives. 'It's not always as it seems' echoed in the empty recesses and dark shadowy patches of my mind.

Don't let the seeds of doubt grow into a tree without facts.

Mac and Bob's footsteps neared my secluded position. I knew they were about to discover me. There was nothing else for it. I waited to be discovered. I was damn sure the look on my face was going to give away my eavesdropping; so be it. What scared me most was that I was giving any credence at all to Mac's suspicions. I looked up and waited as they came into view.

"Hi." I figured that was enough. They both stopped in their tracks. Mac's expression needed no explanation.

The only place I could think a bug could be was in my toiletries. That was all that was left. The one item that I thought could be tampered with, which I hadn't lost over the course of the horror, was my mascara. It's one of those things, you get one you like and you keep it close. It was also something I carried in my gym bag and, while I was working out, that bag was in the locker room. It wouldn't be difficult for someone to access my locker.

Even as the idea forged into existence I didn't believe it was possible. "Mac, in the bathroom is my black mascara. If there's a bug, that's the only place I can think it could be."

He disappeared. Next thing I knew Mac was passing

the mascara to me.

I handed the tube to Bob. “Don’t suppose you have a way of verifying this?”

He appeared thoughtful, “I may do.”

“Moving that mascara is going to lead the Unsub to wherever it goes,” I warned.

Mac interjected, “If it’s bugged.”

“Yep, but the more I think about it the more sure I am. He could not find us so readily without some kind of tracking and positioning system.”

Mac sat on the step beside me.

I continued, “The devices we use are coded and numbered. Each signal is unique so there is zero confusion when tracking. All our cars have GPS tracking capability, as do most of our cell phones, laptops and palm pilots.”

Bob lay his hand on my head. “I have a friend who’s a dentist. His office is close by, he lives behind it.”

“How fast can you get that x-rayed?”

“I’ll be back in twenty minutes. He’s just around the corner.”

“Be careful, we’ll stick with Caine. If it’s him he has no reason to monitor the signal, if it isn’t, you’re in danger.”

Mac kissed me on the cheek and stood up. “I’m going with you.”

Bob smiled and firmly said, “No, you’re not.” They hugged before Bob vanished into the night, his footsteps muffled by the grass verge of the driveway.

“Come on.” Mac took my hand and helped me to my feet. “Let’s go back inside.”

We used the front door rather than trying to get by the agents, crime scene investigators, and medical examiner by the back door.

Mac checked on his Mom, she was sleeping. We tiptoed from the room.

"How can she sleep through this?" I wondered aloud.

"She's medicated. Otherwise she doesn't sleep at all."

"Oh." That made sense and after seeing her in action I guessed the only real peace Bob found was when she slept. If I were him I'd be tempted to medicate her during the day as well.

Mac and I located Caine and made sure he knew we were going back to our room; while we were with him I asked about the identity of the victim.

"One of ours." Caine's lips pressed together. He was a very unhappy camper. "One half of the decoy team that aided your covert escape from Rockbridge."

"Who?"

I hadn't recognized the cloudy dead eyes I'd seen earlier. He was dangling from a tree, partially obscured by branches and I didn't get a good look. I knew the next time I saw him he'd look fabulous. It amazed me how morticians could make the dead appear as if they're simply sleeping.

"Lane McNab."

"He was supposed to be me?" I knew him; he wasn't a big guy and was a few inches shorter than me.

"Yes, he was. We had him wear a cap like yours with a long blonde wig under it."

"How'd he get him in a tree?" He would've been five feet six tops and his frame was slight – almost weedy – but dead weight is hard to maneuver.

"He looped a rope around McNab's neck then threw the rope over a thick branch and pulled. It was tied off to a lower branch. It wouldn't have taken him long to hoist him up. With no dogs and lots of trees and shrubbery in this neighborhood, he could've easily come in through neighboring properties, unseen."

"But carrying a dead weight, a man?" As soon as the words left my mouth, I realized he might not have been whole.

"Half a man. His lower body was missing from the waist down."

I had nothing to say to that. "We'll be in our room."

Mac and I walked away.

I shushed Mac as soon as he started to speak, "Let's wait till we know."

His face betrayed his need to apologize for the conversation I'd overheard and there really was no need for him to do so.

I sat on the bed and watched him pacing up and down. I was surprised there was no track worn in the carpet. We suffered the longest twenty minutes in history. We even checked our email twice but there was no word this time from the Unsub. Just as the waiting began to take its toll we heard Bob's voice outside the door, "I'll be right with you, Caine, let me just talk to Mac for a second."

The door opened, Bob hurried in and handed me the

mascara. “This is it, and the number on it is ZYC-4225.”

I held the innocuous object in my hand, I didn’t know if I was shaking externally but all my internal organs jumped at once and took their time settling. I decided it was time I changed mascara brands. Bob excused himself to speak with Caine.

“Now what?” Mac’s arm slipped around my waist as he sat behind me on the bed.

“I’ve got to get to Washington. I need to run that number.” My stomach churned with the possibility of the device being one of ours.

“Can’t you do it from here?”

“Nope, I don’t have access to the entire system from my laptop.”

Mac was thinking. I could feel his chin on my shoulder and his jaw clench. “I’m presuming you don’t want Caine or anyone else knowing where we are going?”

I had given this as much thought as I was able and had a semi-formulated plan, which I shared, “There is a way. We can use the tunnel.”

Mac moved to face me. “The old tunnel under Fairfax hospital?”

“Uh huh.”

“How far does it go?” Mac asked. “Can we get into DC under the river?”

I nodded. “After you told me a few years ago about the tunnel, I did some checking; remember I said there was a tunnel under the White house?”

“Jesus! It goes to the White House?” The surprise was

evident in his voice.

"It links to the White House-Capitol Hill tunnel."

"Jesus!"

"It's a bit of a walk and maybe wet in parts but it is a quick way to get into the city undetected."

Mac frowned. "Ellie." He shook his head. "There is no way we can walk that far and get back in a reasonable time frame."

"I know but here's the cool thing ... Fairfax hospital is right across Gallows Road from Mobil Oil Corp, yes?"

He nodded.

"They have an underground parking garage. Our tunnel goes under Mobil, there's a gate inside the parking garage."

And I used to think my mind contained useless information, gleaned solely to amuse myself.

"Okay."

"You used to ride motocross, yes?"

He nodded again.

"Know anyone who'll lend us a bike?"

Mac grinned. "Hell, yeah, I do."

"There you have it!"

"Apart from a bike we need anything else?"

"Bolt cutters."

"I'll get Dad to get the bolt cutters from his garage."

"Groovy."

"What are we going to do with that?" Mac referred to the mascara in my hand.

"Leave it at the hospital; that's where everyone will

think we will be." I smiled and tapped my head. "Looks like this concussion of mine is going to need monitoring."

Chapter Eighteen

Needles And Pins

Mac shut the bedroom door. His Dad was down the hallway ready to intercept anyone heading in our direction. We had a plan to put into action. It involved calling his friend Davy and borrowing his Suzuki motocross bike.

I love it when a plan comes together. The theme from *The A-Team* rushed through my mind, I was feeling about as nuts as Howling Mad Murdoch. I ended the *A-Team* vision with a well-placed 'pity the fool' and let my mind drift into *MacGyver* and settle. This was way more of a MacGyver situation than an A-Team one.

Mac moved the telephone to the bed and dialed. He pressed the speaker button as he did so.

"Speaker?" I queried.

"We're running out of time, this way I can carry on getting our stuff together."

"Okay." I settled myself back against the pile of pillows and waited for the ringing to stop. My stuff was together, I had my gun, badge, wallet and mascara. I stuffed the mascara and my wallet into my jacket pocket.

A sleepy voice came from the telephone, "Hello?"

"It's me," Mac replied.

A waspish reply replaced the sleepiness, "Go figure!" Davy sucked in air and continued in a manner that conveyed real concern. "Where the hell have you been? I've been calling, I even went by ..."

I watched Mac's face as he listened. He was frowning but said nothing and shoved his arms into his brown leather jacket. He adjusted the collar with a deft flick of his wrists.

"There was police tape all over, I went to your Dad's and he tells me 'Davy, don't worry'– what the fuck?"

"It's a long story."

"I bet. It's nearly eleven p.m. You woke me up. I got time."

"Can I borrow the RM?"

"Now?"

"Uh huh."

"You want it now? The middle of the fuc'n night?"

"Yep."

"You in some kind of trouble?"

Mac looked at me, with a 'How do I answer that?' kind of expression. I shrugged. His expression changed to 'You're a fat lot of help'.

Davy's voice was clear as he asked again, "Mac? You in deep shit?"

"Nah, ankle depth is all. I need the bike, Davy."

"You got it, where and when?"

"Mobil on Gallows Road in half an hour. We'll meet you just inside the main entrance."

"We?"

"Me and Ellie."

"Ellie the blonde chick you had coffee with at Borders about a month ago?"

I spoke, “Hey Davy, and yeah, that Ellie.”

“Ah. Hi, Ellie.”

“The bike?” Mac fastened the dome snaps on his sleeve cuffs.

“I’ll be there. This is a story I really wanna hear.”

“Thanks Davy, take care.”

He turned the speaker off and returned the phone to the top of the bureau.

“You set?” Mac patted his pockets.

“Yes, sir,” I replied, and grinned. “Your wallet is on the bed.”

“Thank you.” He paused and looked at the bed. His eyes narrowed. “Lie down, and look sick, dammit!”

“Okay.”

I lay down and attempted to look sick. I’d been feeling better and better so it wasn’t as easy as I first thought.

“I’m going to get Caine and Dad. Sick, remember?”

“I can vomit if you want.”

“I don’t think that will be necessary but thanks so much for the offer.”

I let my eyes close as I wondered what Mac had in his pockets: A pack of gum? And some string maybe? A Swiss army knife? I wouldn’t have been surprised to find he did have sticks of gum, string and a Swiss army knife: He was very MacGyver-like. MacGyver dreams carried me into real sleep.

I was successfully returned from dreamland by Mac whispering in my ear, “Keep your eyes closed. I’m going to carry you out to the car. Caine’s watching.”

I listened to Caine give instructions about staying with me, then the car door closed and the engine started.

When I opened my eyes, we'd passed the end of the street and were headed towards the hospital.

Mac and I were in the back seat. I was lying down with my head on his lap. I sat up.

"Everything go okay?" I asked.

"Yes. He didn't argue at all."

Of course he didn't. It's Caine. I'm part of his team. He's all about the team.

Mac spoke to Bob who was driving, "How far away are we now?"

"Almost there, boyo."

"You're enjoying this aren't you, Bob?" I couldn't help it, he was like a pig in muck and it was obvious.

"Yes, ma'am."

"I see Davy's truck," Bob said as he turned into Mobil.

"Me, too," Mac said. "Two bikes? No way!"

We exited the vehicle and joined Davy by the tailgate of his truck. Davy was a big guy, tall and solid in appearance. His head sported a dark-colored ball cap. I wouldn't have been surprised had it been a coonskin cap. A red flannel shirt was peeking out from under the turned-up collar of his sheepskin-lined brown corduroy jacket. Mac and Davy shook hands and did the man-hug thing. It involved a lot of backslapping. I just bet he had a rifle in his truck. Drizzly rain settled on us, not enough to be wetting but just enough to be annoying. I expended great effort to rid myself of the *Ballad of Davy Crockett.*

"You might need help with whatever it is that got me out here at zero-two-thirty." Davy said then turned to Bob and me. "Good to see ya, Ellie. Bob."

I smiled at Davy not quite trusting myself to speak yet, for fear of what craziness might pop out of my mouth, along the Davy Crockett path.

"I appreciate it, Davy, I really do, but not this time," Mac replied and turned his attention to the bikes. "No way! That can't be my old bike."

Davy grinned. "Hell, yeah, it is. Still got y'number on it an' all."

Mac was speechless, His mouth moved but sound eluded him.

I felt the need to intervene. Mac's jaw flapped in the breeze. I hoped I could speak without breaking out with the *Ballad of Davy Crockett*. Just don't say his name.

"We appreciate your help; we have to move – we don't have much time."

"I hear ya, Ellie," he replied, and undid the tailgate then removed the tie-down straps from Mac's bike. Everything was slippery from the light rain.

"Bob, before you head back, fill Davy in as much as you can."

"Will do."

Mac was running his hands over his bike leaving a finger trail in the wet. He knelt down and traced the number still visible on the side, number thirty-seven. I wished I had a camera to capture the look of disbelief on his face. He straightened up when Davy tapped his shoulder.

"Lids," he said handing us a helmet each, "Safety first." For some reason, hearing those words come out of Davy's mouth amused me.

Bob helped me put on the backpack. It was light and contained essentials, bolt cutters, flashlights and a first aid kit. We were both wearing holsters and guns. I had the magic mascara in my jacket pocket, which I pulled out and handed to Bob. "Find somewhere safe for this, in the hospital."

"I know just the place, don't worry about it."

I had confidence in Bob and believed nobody would find the bug and our signal would suggest we were in Fairfax hospital.

"Three hours, we'll be back within three hours."

A plume of blue smoke poured from the exhaust of the bike. The smell of two-stroke filled the damp air. I fastened my helmet and climbed up behind Mac. Like most motocross bikes, this one was built for speed not for the comfort of pillion passengers. I kicked the pegs down and felt lucky to have them at all, then tapped Mac's shoulder.

"All set?"

"Yep," I replied.

I slid my arms around his waist, shoving my hands in his jacket pockets for warmth.

We cut the first lot of chains with the bolt cutters a matter of minutes after entering the underground parking garage. I had estimated we would find eight gates. We found and opened seven. Some were very old. The iron was rusty but not the chains securing them. It was a quick trip into Washington. I began to count markings on the wall knowing we would soon approach the White House underground. There were rusted-iron ladders rising up the sides of the cold, damp tunnel at irregular intervals.

I tapped Mac and said loudly, "A hundred yards."

"Okay."

We planned to leave the bike and climb one of the ladders. With any luck, it would emerge right next to the old executive building or, more precisely, between the executive building and the White House. Would be good if the old rusty ladders held our weight, too.

Mac killed the engine. We removed our helmets and left them with the bike. I was sure we had reached the correct ladder. Even so, my fingers were crossed.

We were in a dark damp tunnel that seemed to run on forever. The only discernable markings being faint numbers that dated back to the civil war, so I wasn't entirely certain where we were.

Mac's hand slipped the flashlight from mine. He shone the beam all the way up our chosen ladder. It was intact, which was a good sign. He gave the ladder a forceful shake. It didn't fall. He applied a little weight to the bottom rung, then a little more. To our relief it held. Mac grabbed the edges of the ladder and jumped on the bottom rung. It shook and groaned but held firm. He shone the flashlight back up to the top again.

"What's up there?"

"Manhole cover."

"Okay." He shone the beam around a little more. "Will we be visible when we exit?"

Not if I use my superhero power of invisibility.

"It's sheltered; we should be okay." I crossed my fingers tighter.

"All right, up you go," Mac said as he shoved the flashlight into the backpack then slung the backpack over his shoulder. "I'm right behind you. Count off eighteen rungs then wait."

I started climbing. It was pitch dark and the rungs were slippery causing me take extreme care with my footing.

I reached the eighteenth rung and called down to Mac, "Eighteen."

A question I should have considered earlier popped into my mind as I clung to the cold ladder, how were we going to open the manhole? A second later, I felt Mac's feet on either side of mine, and his body pressed against me. He reached over my head. The ladder groaned under us as he applied force to the manhole cover. I swear that man has superhuman upper-body strength. The cover above our heads creaked ominously and gave way to the force applied by Mac. With much MacGyver skill, he climbed over me as he shoved the cover aside.

All I could see was a dark form crouched above me. His hand reached down. "Come on." I climbed the last few rungs and water dripped onto my face. Miserable rain fell. As soon as I cleared the tunnel Mac slid the cover back. We stood in the dismal Washington night and surveyed our position. I was right. We were where I hoped we'd be: On the White House side of the old executive building.

"Let's get going." Mac took my hand. "Who knows what's lurking in the shadows of the city at this time of night."

We walked, hand in hand, towards the Hoover building. The streets appeared mainly deserted, apart from a few small groups of unsavory-looking characters. They served to remind us why no one in their right mind would walk through Washington DC after dark. Unless they were armed and on a mission. Yeah, right! Like that would protect us. Damn, I did it again! My mind picked up on the *Mission* and the *Blues Brothers*' theme song rampaged through my head.

We're okay.

The rain became steady by the time we reached the Hoover building. We hurried up the steps and into the foyer. I grabbed Mac's hand as we walked to the elevator leaving a trail of water behind us.

"Why is there no one around?" Mac asked as we stepped into the elevator. I pressed the second floor button.

"Dunno. I don't often wander about here at this time of night."

The door opened onto another deserted floor.

"It's creepy."

"Yep," I replied, leading the way down the corridor to a large office at the very end. "This is it." I tried the door.

Locked. I fished a key card from my pocket and swiped it then swung the door open.

Mac's eyes widened, "Where'd that come from?"

"Fell out of Caine's wallet earlier this evening." I shut the door behind us. The only drawback to using Caine's card was that the computer now registered him as being in the building. Which had a plus side: It meant it didn't register me.

I hurried through the expansive office to a desk at the far end and a computer. I sat down and began to check the number written on my hand from the bug. Mac inspected the display boards and read all the current case information. It took twenty minutes to follow the trail left by the GPS transmitter number. It was part of a consignment of devices sent for destruction. Four weeks earlier ten devices, including that one, arrived at the Richmond field office. Agent Tim Gardner signed them in. Six hours later he signed them over to a company called Dataraze. All ten devices appeared accounted for at that point. Two days later Tim Gardner received a written report stating that all ten devices had undergone destruction at the Dataraze site.

I needed to find out more about this company. They had government contracts and had done for ten years. There were no reports of anything going missing but, then again, if we hadn't found this bug there still wouldn't be anything missing.

"Mac, ever heard of Dataraze?" I looked up when he didn't respond, he was reading a bunch of papers. "Mac?"

He turned towards me. "Yeah."

"Have you heard of a company called Dataraze?"

Mac chewed his lip as he thought, "I think they are a subsidiary of Global Underwriters. I'd have to check to be sure."

"Okay." Global Underwriters was a company I knew. Aidan was an assessor for Global Causality, another of their subsidiary companies. "The date on the destruction receipt is the same day Carter turned up in DC, I need to check Caine's day planner."

"When you are done, you need to read this stuff," Mac said. He thumbed through more papers.

"I'll be with you in a few minutes."

I needed to be able to say it wasn't possible for Caine to have had anything to do with the GPS bug defying destruction. I opened his day-planner and went back four weeks, then opened mine. With both screens open at once it was easier to see how the day had gone. We were close to wrapping up the Blue River case; that morning we had a staff meeting. Everyone involved was there. I looked down the list of names, all bearing checks stating they had shown up.

Caine and I had a short meeting afterwards. He then met with our legal department. I went to meet Mac for coffee at four p.m. Caine logged a call from me at six p.m. I returned to the office at eight-thirty p.m. Caine was here, there is no way he could have made it to Richmond and back that day. And the previous two days we were in Baltimore.

The Unsub had been using others; if it was Caine, why would he have to be anywhere near Richmond? So where and when did the GPS bug disappear, and why wasn't it noted on the destruction report? I checked back on the destruction order, and then looked up Dataraze's contract. This was the fifth year in a row that they had won the contract to handle destruction of electronics and not just secure-paper destruction. I wanted to visit the company in person. Find out first-hand what their security procedures were and who it was who last handled that shipment.

I erased my activity on the computer and logged out. Annoyance burgeoned. I still couldn't rule out Caine, even though I was his alibi.

I joined Mac. "Find anything?"

"Four descriptions: None of them matching; only one with scratches on his neck. Cat hair."

"Cat hair?"

"Yep, cat hairs were found on the clothing of all the bodies and from the bedcovers in my guest room." He passed me a forensics report.

I skimmed over it; he was right, and they said it was from the same cat, apart from some hairs taken from Mac's cat for comparison. "Our killer may have a cat."

Caine didn't have a cat, or at least he never spoke of one and sure as hell never had cat hair on his immaculate dark-gray suits.

"Ketamine and cat hair."

"There's something else, Ellie, on the list of possible

suspects: Kevin, Holly, Aidan."

"Are you there?" Great. My brother and my friend; they don't seem to think this is a stranger thing then. I wondered why my parents weren't on the list? I rolled my eyes; if Mom were a smarter insanity-ridden person, I would've picked her first off. That one was a no-brainer.

"Yep. I was cleared within the first twenty-four hours."

Kevin had a cat. Holly had a cat. Aidan had a cat. We knew Carter was a dealer, but why did all the bodies contain ketamine and why drug Mac? It made less sense now I knew more, if that was possible. Why kill a DEA agent? I sat on the edge of the boardroom table in the middle of the room, wondering if I could be any more perplexed. Why kill FBI agents? I felt an urge to slap myself in the head but resisted because my head was having enough trouble.

"You know what?"

Mac gave me his full and undivided attention. "What?"

"I'm lost."

"Check this out." Mac handed me another pile of paperwork. "Surveillance records."

I skimmed over the opening paragraphs then stopped. "They have to be fuc'n joking."

"I think they're serious."

My mind came to an abrupt halt; short of a swift kick nothing was going to be operational again tonight. I clutched the white paper in my hand, the black typeface leapt at me: Aidan Conway, electronic surveillance transcript, sheet one of twenty-five.

Don't kill the messenger. I calmed my inner turmoil before speaking again, "How did they get authorization for the wire-taps?"

Mac frowned at me. "I haven't seen anything else relating to Aidan."

"Find any surveillance ordered on Holly or Kevin?"

"Nope."

I took the pile of papers over to the photocopier. I needed to take a copy with me to read when we had more time.

"Mac, can you check the file these were in? There has to be an official request for this surveillance."

I stapled the pile of copied paper, folded it into thirds and shoved it in the waistband of my jeans.

"There is nothing else that mentions that surveillance."

I handed him the transcript to return to where he had found it.

"I can't discount Caine to my own satisfaction." I couldn't believe I thought the thought, let alone said it aloud, "Could he be setting up Aidan? And why the hell would he?"

"Fuck knows."

"If it isn't Caine, then he has no clue about the GPS device we found - if I give it to him ..."

Mac stopped me "Working for a company that is under the same umbrella as the Dataraze Company is not sufficient evidence to incriminate Aidan."

I almost smiled. "Ah, the voice of reason." I thought back to Mr. Parker telling me about Doc. "You find anything suggesting anyone spoke to Doc Tompson?"

"No."

I searched the whiteboard on the wall in front of me for some reference to Doc and found nothing. Didn't anyone bother checking into the McDonald-McClaren connection? DEA were a possibility, perhaps part of the investigation landed in their jurisdiction. I wracked my brain trying to think of a friendly face in DEA I could approach. It dawned on me that none of them were going to be too friendly seeing it was my fault Roy was killed. Flag that for later.

Copies of the post-it poems were stuck in order of discovery on the wall. I read them one by one until I came to the one no one mentioned to me, the one from the hospital in Lexington. Bile rose as I read it to Mac,

'I've seen you in my dreams, Voodoo doll manifests, That I tear at the seams, Threadbare from my handy work, I make another stitch, Just enough to keep you breathing, As I torture this digital bitch.'"

"It's one of his better efforts," Mac commented.

I could feel his eyes on me even though I was still facing the wall.

"Yes, it is." I read it again. *As I torture this digital bitch.* "Computers? Surely they must've bought back the victims' hard drives for analysis!"

"Let's get looking."

Mac and I pored over piles of notes and reports until he found something, "Okay, here," he passed a summary to me. It didn't take long to read.

"Apart from Carter, all the victims' computers contained a key logger, the same key logger."

"That makes sense. How else would he find them? The FBI had trouble tracing these people, but this bastard tricked people into downloading key loggers and waited for the information to fall into his lap," Mac said.

"He hacked into our chat room and went about getting key loggers onto everyone's computers?"

"Looks that way." Mac shook his head. "He knew everything that was going on; these machines were infected months ago but not all at once."

"Jesus, Mac, they checked your drive too and the same key logger showed up. Did you read the rest of this report?"

"No."

"Says this is a custom-designed key logger: They think he created it himself so it was undetected by all the spy software we run. It was traced to our poetry community, to pictures in the album of someone called Poetman." I placed the paper down on the table. "No way could this be Aidan, he can't even operate a video player!"

"We don't know a Poetman."

"No, we don't. We know of an Addict_man. And the last name Carter used was Addictedtolove. Well that was the last one I banned anyway, right before he came knocking on my door."

Mac looked at his watch. "Anything else you need to see?"

"Not right now. Right now I need to be in Richmond to

check out this Dataraze place, I want to know how and when and who liberated the GPS device from its designated destruction path."

"Don't suppose there are tunnels all the way to Richmond?" He looked quite hopeful for a second.

"Nope." I replied, putting everything back where we found it. I watched raindrops run down the window. We'd missed something. Evidence, we'd missed some evidence. "Mac, did you see a report on the DNA?"

"Nope."

"Now that's odd. What the hell happened to the DNA sample?"

He shook his head. "I saw zero mention of it. But I found something about Summers, that guy at the hospital who caused all the commotion."

"What?"

"Aidan and I were out there with him – he saw us both, but he did not identify Aidan as the person who paid him to find you." He looked at the papers in his hand. "Caine asked him if he could identify the person; Summers said no. We were both right there. He didn't even glance towards Aidan."

"We better head back."

Rain pelted against the windowpanes. It would be a wet walk back to the tunnel. We left the room, taking the stairs this time to avoid encountering anyone in the hallways. I was having difficulty with the whole concept of Aidan being a serious suspect, especially as Caine reported Summers did not know Aidan. Almost as much difficulty as I had with Caine being a suspect in Mac's eyes. I'm okay. I just need to find whoever was responsible for stealing that damn bug. Rain dripped steadily as we left the building.

Washington was still dark and scary as we hurried back up Pennsylvania Avenue to our secret tunnel and safety. Wouldn't it be cool to live in the tunnel and never have to deal with people? Tunnel life appealed to me. Hell, I'd be happy in a mountain cave. Anywhere that didn't have killers and conundrums that taxed my achy, tired mind would be good.

'Things aren't always as they seem' became a haunting phrase that tormented my thought processes and yet provided no answers. The disappearance of the only actual physical evidence, DNA, ate away at me.

Chapter Nineteen

Keep The Faith

The journey back to Virginia through the tunnel was as uneventful as the journey to Washington, just wetter.

The Aidan thing was festering in my head. The murders were messy. Especially Carter's; the killer had left slash-type incisions, the blood pattern all over the kitchen and the type of wounds indicated that the killer would have blood on him somewhere, possibly a lot of blood. Aidan came to visit Holly that day. He didn't have bloodstained clothing. He said he had a job out in Lexington. He was wearing a mid-gray suit and a lemon shirt. There was no blood on him. My mind toyed with a possibility that made me feel icky. He was wearing a suit that day, when we saw him. Aidan carried spare clothes in his car, a pair of jeans, tee shirt, sweatshirt and a pair of steel-capped boots; some times being an insurance assessor was a messy job.

I pulled the plug on that line of thought. What struck me as very odd though was the lack of human trace evidence. They found cat hair but never any human hair. Did the killer not have hair? Or was his head covered at all times? I would've expected to find a few human hairs especially if there was a struggle. I scratched him. Therefore, there was a struggle. If indeed it was the killer and not some other person. Unless we find him we won't know.

I found my internal 'kill' switch and turned off all thoughts regarding the murders. We were almost back at Mobil and would have cell phone reception shortly. The tunnel blocked our cellular signal; as soon as we emerged from the underground parking garage we would call Bob to come get us.

Rain poured from the night sky as we left the parking garage. Large puddles lay on the asphalt gleaming under the soft glow of security lights. We intended to hide the bike in the wooded area close to the entrance of Mobil. Visibility wasn't great through sheets of torrential rain but as we neared the pre-arranged point to leave the bike. I was stunned to find Davy waiting for us, right where we'd left him. He'd turned the truck around and was facing Gallows Road.

"Anything exciting happen?" Mac's conversational tone suggested he expected Davy to be there.

"It did. About half an hour ago four police cruisers pulled into the hospital after a refrigerator truck." Davy rocked back on his heels and jammed his hands into his jeans' pockets. "You wouldn't know anything about that, would ya?"

I wondered if either of us betrayed our thoughts with our facial expressions. Something in Davy's tone hinted that we might indeed know something.

I dragged a cell phone from my pocket and called Bob.

"We're back, what's up?"

"I'm at the hospital, in the Gray parking lot. Been here

the whole time. There's another body."

I groaned. "Anyone figured out we weren't there?"

"Not yet. Use the Gray entrance. Keep away from the emergency department entrance, there are cops all over."

"Will do." I hung up and pocketed the phone.

Mac chatted to Davy, and tried to say nothing about our predicament.

"Mac, we should go. Bob's waiting."

He shook Davy's hand. They did the man-hug thing again. Davy turned to me. "Look after him."

"Always."

Mac grabbed my hand and we disappeared into the trees that lined the road. We walked along Gallows Road until we were level with the Gray hospital entrance. Police flashers lit up the front of the emergency department.

With darkness and rain providing cover, we slipped across the road and into the parking lot. Bob was waiting at the far side in deep shadow.

Mac flung the back door open and we clambered into the warm car.

"When did they find it?" he asked his Dad.

"Twenty minutes ago."

"Should we go in and pretend we were always there?" I more wondered aloud than asked.

"Nope," Bob replied. "I've already told Caine that I have taken you out of the hospital and that the Unsub must've been confused this time 'cos he dumped the body in the wrong room."

"Poem?"

"Oh yeah, another gem from the freak, I wrote it down for you."

"Was it one of the missing bodies?"

"I got a good look at it. I don't think this was an FBI agent."

Chapter Twenty

A Stranger With You

"What the fuck are we doing?" I yelled at Caine across the bedroom.

"Settle!" he snapped.

"I want to know." I let the annoyance resound in my voice. I knew I bordered on outright anger but dammit, I had a right to be angry. "It's fucking Tuesday morning, that watery shit coming in through the curtains is sun ... bodies have been turning up for over a week!"

"We're doing everything we can." Caine turned to Mac. "Can you calm her down before she ends up back in hospital?"

"Ellie's fine and we want answers." He was respectfully forceful.

Caine leaned forward, and rested his head in his hands. "I have forty goddamn agents and as many police officers and state cops that I can get my hands on, not to mention DEA, and this prick keeps slipping through the net."

Yeah, let's not mention DEA. I wish he hadn't said net. I wish the theme to *Dragnet* wasn't now playing in my head, 'just the facts ma'am.' I shushed it.

"Where are the other bodies?" I was prepared to believe we still had one and a half unaccounted for, one and a half FBI agents.

"We haven't found them yet. That truck at the hospital was empty, yet another decoy; the body that was dumped there was not transported in the truck. It was LostAdam from your chat room."

Let's not dwell on hospitals either, lest someone realizes we weren't there at all.

"Jesus!" I threw myself back on the bed and stared up at the swirled-plaster ceiling. "Do we at least know what kind of vehicle he's driving?" Someone must've seen a car in this area before we found the tree body. It's easier if I don't think of him by name. I'm okay.

"Out of the four vehicles that were sighted in this street last night, the only one that didn't belong was Mac's brother's car." Caine paused. "About that, Mac ..."

I half expected Caine to say that Eddie was now a suspect; made as much sense as Aidan being a suspect.

"Eddie was stopped leaving the street and it was apparent he was drunk. He's being held at the local police station; they've impounded his Beamer."

I turned my head to see a grin spread across Mac's face. "Hearing that almost makes up for having this Unsub still roaming Fairfax."

"He's quite pissed about the whole thing."

"Go figure," Mac replied, chuckling, "Does Dad know?"

"Yep, he said he can stay in the police cells for as long as they'll have him."

Mac chuckled even more at the news – his older brother, the deputy sheriff, in jail overnight.

"Oh, how the mighty are fallen." Mac leaned back on

the wall with a grin on his face.

I contemplated how Eddie would spin this story on his release. It'd be one hell of a tale, of that I was sure, no doubt he'd tell anyone who would listen he was stalked by Son of Shakespeare and how he ended up in protective custody.

Meanwhile back in the real world we were the playthings of a psycho.

I turned my attention and Caine's back to the situation at hand. "Have you found anything usable from this scene?"

"No."

"He can't be this good. Sooner or later this sonofabitch will screw up and leave us something traceable." I bit my tongue to stop myself adding 'like cat hair'.

"Forensics has been all over the yard, and found nothing," Caine said.

"It was night, something could have been missed," I snapped a little more than I intended.

"I suppose that's always a possibility."

Mac walked around the room then stopped and faced me. He was chewing his bottom lip as he tended to do while thinking. The spark in his eyes caused me to become very attentive.

"What?"

He walked towards me. "You said once that this guy could be an agent or a police officer."

I wondered where the hell he was going with this, considering I knew he suspected Caine and he still wasn't off the hook as far as either of us was concerned.

"Yes, I did."

"Hmmm. It's not necessary for him to be a cop to know a lot about how they work, or to scan frequencies and listen to what's going on. Lots of people have police scanners." He paused as if to organize his thoughts. "He's targeting specific people, or he began targeting specific people. I have a feeling he killed Carter because he knew about his drug business, and yes, enjoyed his new power ... but the other deaths were to cover up the first one. Carter's death is the key to this puzzle."

"You think he knew Carter?"

Mac nodded. "That's what I think," he said and looked into my eyes. "Either he knew him or he knew of him and had met him at some stage."

I tried hard not to roll my eyes in case Caine saw me.

"Why does he seem so determined that you and I be together?" I joined Mac in his game.

Caine interrupted, "If we knew that, we'd know more about how this sick fuck operates. The best we can come up with so far is that you've both displayed resilience and strength."

"How does he know that? How does he know who we are? You can't get a clear picture of someone from a month in a chat room." Mac sat on the bed next to me. "I think he knows us, and I think he knew Carter. This is someone we have met in person."

Caine continued this thought process aloud, "He's proven he can get close enough to you both to drug you individually." He nodded at me and then said. "Yes, before you ask, there was a substantial amount of ketamine in the toothpaste you had at that Lexington motel. You'll love this bit of information: He replaced your tube of toothpaste with a doctored one. The paste was mixed thoroughly with a high dose of ketamine then injected back into the tube." Caine seemed almost pleased the Unsub showed such a high degree of planning. "With the advent of plastic tubes, it's not difficult to refill them, especially with a large syringe. No doubt he enjoyed that. But you're still alive, and he's bitching about wanting you together ..."

"So we're going to be his *pièce de résistance?* He has some amazing double murder planned that will knock the FBI's socks clean off?" Seemed to be the way he was heading. "That fills me with joy, not!"

Caine stared at me. "I wouldn't have put it quite like that."

Caine wasn't coming forward with any of the information I knew he had. He could have jumped in at anytime and told us we'd all had key loggers on our computers and it was possible the Unsub came to know us quite well, but he said nothing of the sort. He didn't knock my theory on why the Unsub wants us together.

I mustered my best thinking face then threw him another bone. "This investigation must have covered common ground!"

"We thought so," Caine replied. "There really wasn't any common ground apart from the chat room."

I turned to face Caine. "Really wasn't? What does that mean?"

"Either there is or there isn't," Mac said. "What do we all have in common apart from the chat room, or who do we have in common."

To his credit, Caine looked uncomfortable as he formatted his reply. "Aidan is a suspect."

Mac and I looked at each other hoping we both appeared sufficiently surprised by Caine's announcement.

"That's it? Of all the people it could be, do you think Aidan is a possibility?" I waited to see if anything else was going to come to light.

Caine glanced at his watch, "I'll be back in an hour; we'll talk more then." He seemed uncomfortable. "I'm late for a briefing."

He left the room.

"You get the impression he doesn't want to talk about this?"

"Yep," Mac replied. "If I was him I wouldn't either."

I lay back down.

"I'm going to go see Dad for a few minutes. Rest for a bit, Ellie."

Rest? With my mind in turmoil, he suggests resting. Yeah, sure, no problem. I'll just close my eyes and pretend nothing's going on, everything's fine.

Chapter Twenty-One

Lie To Me

What was that annoying damn noise? My hand felt around the immediate area hoping to locate the source of the aggravating high-pitched tune. As I extracted the offending noisemaker from under Mac's pillow, the tune became frantic.

The display flashed with Holly's name, I answered it.

"Hey, Holly. You checking in?"

"Yep. You're all over the news, no names though. The sonofabitch has written to the paper again."

"Poems?"

"If you can call them that, nasty rhymes. Nothing like the poems you and Mac write."

Hang on a cotton-picking minute! We don't show people our poetry, not any body, not even best friends. We share our poetry in the Cobwebs chat room and with each other. End of story.

Ack! I had to ask or it would drive me crazy, "When did you see our poetry?" I hoped my voice sounded casual, chit-chatty. There was a poignant silence at Holly's end.

"Holly?"

"I can't tell you, it's a secret."

"Tell!"

"I can't, you'll find out when the time is right." She

changed the subject leaving me confused. "Hey, you will never believe this: Aidan invited me to the dance."

It sounded like she didn't believe it herself. Something cold clawed its way up from my stomach and then there was this secret causing problems, too.

I forced a smile onto my face as I replied, "Dance?"

"Uh huh, the one at Taylor's barn."

The penny dropped. "Ohhh, that dance."

"So what do you think?"

"About Aidan asking you?"

"Dah, yeah!"

"I think it's about time he asked you out."

The cold kept clawing up until it reached my brain. I closed my eyes for a second to let the thought emerge and wished I hadn't. Thinking isn't always what it's cracked up to be.

"How'd he know?" I assumed there'd be flyers and posters all over town.

"Mr. Parker invited him."

"Good ole Mr. P."

"So how are things with Mac?"

The interrogation was about to begin, I felt the familiar prickle as my hackles rose and I slipped into defense mode. Normally only my mother caused such a response and I wasn't sure why I felt defensive at Holly's simple question.

"Good."

"You guys still, you know?"

I smiled. "Yeah, we're still you know!"

"Cool."

"When did Mr. P invite Aidan?" I attempted to sound curious, with nothing more than a sisterly interest in her reply.

"I think it was that day you and Mac were here."

I probed further, "The day Carter gave Kevin's boys the slip?"

"Yes, that day. Aidan said he'd visited Mr. P to get some honey for your Mom."

The cold became ice; before or after Carter's death? Nobody mentioned Aidan being at Parker's that day. Why was that? It must've been on his way out of town. The icy feeling wouldn't leave.

"Ellie?"

I blinked several times. "Yeah."

"Something wrong?"

"Not at all," I replied. "I think its great you're going to the dance with Aidan. Mac and I will try and be there."

"We all miss you down here, any idea when you can come home?"

"I don't know." Now that was an honest answer and much better than me spitting 'I don't have a fuc'n home anymore, remember?'

What the hell was wrong with me? Why was I so defensive and irritated? I needed a good slap. Get over it! I hate secrets especially when I don't have the energy to pursue an answer.

"I'd better get moving. Take care."

"You, too."

I hung up and dropped the phone back onto the bed. Within seconds, I began to pace up and down the room. I hoped the pacing would bestow brilliant ideas on me, as it always seemed to for Mac. I didn't like the thoughts I was thinking at all. The last place anyone saw Carter alive was Parker's farm. Aidan bought honey that day. Who knew?

Carter visited Doc Tompson the night before. Any chance he could've got his hands on a supply of ketamine during the visit? If he had the ketamine with him, the Unsub could have taken it.

Questions buzzed at a frenetic pace through my mind. How did Carter get from Parker's farm to my place? What if Aidan gave him a ride? How else could he get there and become a murder victim? A vehicle of some description had to be involved. Someone nobody would think twice about seeing or even find his presence at all noteworthy.

Wait!

Wouldn't Aidan being there have been noteworthy that day? By nine that morning, the whole town would have heard about the ruckus at my place. The whole town would have known but not Aidan. Unless Mr. P told him. He would have assumed Aidan had come to make sure I was all right. Parker could not have known I didn't want my family informed. Is that how Aidan knew who Mac was also?

The bedroom door opened. I ceased my pacing.

"What's up?" Mac's voice suggested someone else was nearby. As he walked towards me, I spotted Caine in the hallway talking to Bob and Beatrice.

"Nothing."

Mac wrapped his arms around me drawing me into a warm hug. His voice rasped as he whispered into my ear, "Everything okay?"

I whispered back, "Aidan bought honey from Mr. Parker the day Carter was killed."

"Ohhh, I take it we're not sharing this info with Caine," Mac replied.

"Not until I know what's going on and if this is relevant."

"Fair enough."

I was beginning to wonder if either of us would get time to read the copy of the electronic surveillance report I had hidden under the mattress.

Chapter Twenty-Two

Hey God

We were almost out of the door when a cell phone rang. I recognized the ring tone. It was Mac's phone again; hardly anybody had my new number yet. Mac retrieved the device from where I had left it on the bed.

He answered the call then handed me the phone and said, "Richmond hospital."

I gave him a 'this can't be good' look and answered the call, "Special Agent Ellie Conway."

"This is Richmond hospital coronary care unit, Are you Simon Conway's next of kin?"

My heart sank all the way to my boots as I swallowed terror and answered, "Yes."

"Your father has had a heart attack. He is in a serious but stable condition in Cardiac Care Unit, and is asking for you." This cannot be happening!

"Tell my father I'm on my way. I'll be there as soon as I can." I hung up and passed the phone back to Mac. I could feel the tears prickling behind my eyes. It was a losing battle. I bit into my lip. A surreal calmness surrounded me. "We have to go."

"And we shall," Mac said. "I'll go see my Dad about borrowing a car."

He vanished from the room. I stared at the open door for a few minutes and assessed my befuddled mental state. I concluded I was as well as I could be under the circumstances and began packing at speed. Thoughts of the killer evaporated. I concentrated on getting home to my family.

Mac returned as I was struggling with the zipper on my bag. It was stuck fast and no amount of cussing helped. Raised by a military father, I knew how to curse insubordinate inanimate objects and was astonished that it didn't immediately work. I finally got the fabric together with my good hand and pulled the zipper with the fingers of my broken arm. Apparently cursing like a sailor does work, given time.

"I'll do it."

"I've done it!" I replied.

Mac smiled. "It's okay to let me help you."

"I know, but I didn't need help."

"We're taking Dad's car. He won't say anything to Caine."

I blinked trying to clear the tears so I could see. Mac pulled me into his arms, words I didn't want to say came from nowhere, "I'm scared."

"Understandable, let's get going."

"I'm not ready to lose him."

"He's tough, Ellie. Remember that, he's tough."

Yeah, old seamen don't die they just end up sitting in a corner smelling gross and reminiscing about great battles.

Footsteps sounded in the hallway nearing our door. The door swung open and Bob stepped in. "Come on."

The transcript popped into my mind. I slipped my good hand under the mattress and shoved the papers I had retrieved into the inside pocket of my jacket.

Bob and Mac stowed the bags in the trunk of the car in the garage.

"You give your Dad my best, Ellie girl."

"I will," I replied as Bob passed the seat belt over me.

Bob clicked the seat belt into place then asked, "What do you want to do with this bug?"

"Give it to me. We'll take it. May as well take the Unsub with us." The more the merrier.

Bob pressed the mascara into my palm. "Be careful."

"We will."

He shut the door and stood looking over the car at Mac. "Drive safe, boyo. Let me know when you arrive."

"Yep. We'll be okay."

"I know you will."

Bob walked around the car to Mac. They hugged and I heard Bob say, "I'm proud of you."

"Talk to you soon." Mac climbed into the driver's seat and turned the ignition key.

Bob waved. That was the moment when I wondered if any of us would survive this mess.

I determined it was going to be the longest drive home ever undertaken. The first time I checked my watch we'd been on the road a full half-hour. As Captain Compass was driving, there were no guarantees we'd make it at all despite my insisting he put our destination into the car navigation system. At least his father had the foresight to have GPS navigation installed in his car. TomTom would be working overtime to get us to Richmond Hospital.

An uneventful hour passed.

"You hungry?" Mac flicked the wiper blades as rain splattered the windscreen. It wasn't enough to warrant them being on all the time but just enough to be annoying.

We left before lunch and hadn't eaten since having a very early breakfast.

"McDonald's?" There had to be a drive-thru somewhere.

"Okay."

We'd hardly spoken since we left Merrifield. I guessed Mac was wondering what we'd find in Richmond, as I was. So many things were rampaging in my head it was difficult to get a single clear thought, Dad, the bug, Mom, Aidan, Caine, where was the second agent's body? What happened to the evidence? How did anyone get authorization for a wiretap on Aidan? Everything clamored for my attention. I didn't notice that we'd pulled off the road until Mac spoke. We were in the parking lot next to a McDonald's; about ten cars were lined up in the drive-thru.

"Looks like we've got time to decide what we want," Mac said.

We debated the merits of McDonald's cheese dogs and how good their coffee was for almost twenty minutes. By the time we were ready to order the line had thinned to just us.

Mac wound down his window at the drive-thru speaker and turned to me. "What'll you have, babe?"

"Cheese dog and coffee."

Mac placed our order. He settled on a cheese burger, fries and coffee. The female voice from the drive-thru speaker began to repeat our order back to us.

A clear, male voice broke in, "Let's see what we have in the trunk today, what will you have? A slice of Agent McNab on a sesame seed bun?"

Mac and I stared at each other for a split second. I was sure I couldn't have heard what I thought I had heard.

The voice continued, "Cheese dog and coffee, made with fresh index finger and onion rings. I do hope you can identify the food. Perhaps Agent Kilby is more palatable."

"We'll pass thanks," Mac replied.

"Oh, come on, live a little, Galileo."

My insides froze, who ever it was knew who we were.

Mac wound up his window and put his foot down. "I'm not hungry," he said and tore out of the drive-thru. "We helped him set us up by hanging around too long before ordering. He's using that damn bug to follow us."

"I'm not into eating anyone I may have known," I replied and checked the side mirror as we left. "Do you think that really was him?"

"Not willing to wait around and find out."

I grabbed my phone and placed an anonymous call to the state police. I didn't want to talk to Caine. He didn't need to know where we were. I gave them the address of the drive-thru and told them it was possible there was a Son of Shakespeare body involved. After all, we still had two unaccounted for.

"Was he physically in there or did he hack into the drive-thru speakers, like those kids did a while back?"

Mac shook his head. "Search me. He must've been close or he wouldn't have known it was us."

"How'd those kids do it? Could our Unsub hijack the speakers that easily?" I wanted to believe he wasn't there and body parts weren't going into the onion rings.

"They modified an old CB radio to broadcast on the fast food frequencies. It's not difficult; he's already proven he's smart."

I was freaked out by the whole experience and had a feeling it would be a long while before I went to another drive-thru. My stomach rumbled. It had been looking forward to a cheese dog. Mac heard it too.

"Think we should risk another drive-thru?"

"Nah. I'd sooner starve."

"Understood."

Forty-five minutes down the road, we found a store. Mac parked in the open, I stayed with the car. He ran in and grabbed a couple of coffees and some sandwiches.

On the front window of the store was a concert poster, advertising a Grange concert. There was a pang of dissonance within me as I considered that rock concerts were for normal people who lived normal lives. Our brief stop was uneventful.

Further down the road I called Aidan from my cell

phone. I didn't know if he knew about Dad.

"Hey."

"Ellie?" He sounded concerned, as he always did. I listened, there appeared to be background traffic noise.

"Yeah. I want you to meet me at Richmond hospital. Dad's sick, he had a heart attack." I could hear him breathing for what felt like forever. "Did you hear me?"

"Yes."

There was traffic noise.

"Do you want us to pick you up?"

"That's not necessary. I'll meet you there." He paused. "Where's Mom?"

"Don't know; with him?"

"Okay. I'll see you there." Aidan hung up.

A frown line formed as I gazed at the phone in my hand.

"That was odd."

I switched the phone to vibrate, not ring; that way I could easily ignore a call from Caine.

"What?"

"I called his home number but I thought I heard traffic noise, like he was in a car."

"Maybe he was in the front yard."

"Maybe. I just never thought of his street as being that busy." I shrugged. "Fuck, it doesn't matter. I probably imagined it."

"He's a suspect: Caine said he all but discounted any involvement." Mac sounded so calm. He was my rock, my salvation, and my sanity all rolled into one.

"Uh huh."

I lit a cigarette and watched the scenery flash past the window. I wished we could disappear into the mountains and never have to worry about people again. My idea of heaven was a little cabin in the mountains, all alone with Mac. No electronics, no gadgets and no computers. Screw the mountain idea; I want to go back to New Zealand. Pictures floated into view in my mind, I remembered the house and the walk down the long steep driveway to the sea. All the rhododendrons in the garden reminded me of home, even though I dislike them. The memory of two cell phone- and computer-free weeks spent in Mahau Sound in Marlborough, made me long for a vacation. I wondered if Mac would enjoy a New Zealand trip. I glanced at Mac. I saw him, supportive, wonderful, funny, caring and gorgeous. He should be running as far from me as possible. If there ever were two gene pools that should never mix, they were ours. Why on earth did I ever think we could turn our friendship into something bigger? A more controlled voice edged through the negative murk in my head: Shut up Ellie, he knows what he's doing. Have a little faith.

The conversation in my head slowed to a background grumble as I tried making conversation with Mac.

"You only took a week off work, right?" I asked.

"Yeah."

"Won't your clients be pissed about now?"

Mac was a stock trader. I didn't think the market would wait for him to return to work. No doubt his clients' stocks wouldn't wait either.

"Yep." He was still calm as he smiled at me. "Guess I'll find out when we get back just how good the FBI technical analyst is."

"Caine arranged an analyst to look after your clients' portfolios? Do they know?" I asked.

"No. I didn't have much time to organize my leave."

I smiled a little. "Shit happens, huh?"

"It sure does. This is the longest break I've had from trading, and I can honestly say I am not missing it yet."

"Really?"

"Uh huh."

"I wanted in on the cemetery rape case."

"I know. I could tell when Caine told you about it."

"Was I that obvious?"

"Yeah, you were."

I shrugged. "I am sure they'll cope without me, and I'm sure Caine's keeping an eye on the investigation." I couldn't help but wonder how it was going. Two team members were down. I was stuck playing fiddle for a serial killer and a colleague was on maternity leave. Caine's attention was on trying to keep me alive and not on Delta's case. I reminded myself the team would function perfectly well regardless.

Mac asked, "Would Delta have been assigned to this case if you weren't involved?"

"Yes. It definitely falls within our brief, almost any serial crime, murder, rape and armed robberies. Rape gets more press coverage so most people know of Delta from the rape cases we've been involved in." I exhaled watching the smoke billow towards the gap in the window. "Anyway, it seems I'm front and center in this investigation."

Front and center I may be, but useless I truly felt. Zero objectivity and a dumbass head injury do not make for a helpful agent.

"Don't it though." Mac stopped at an intersection. "We take a right, yes?"

"Just trust the TomTom. It knows the way," I replied tapping the small screen on the dashboard.

"I know, it's just we're in a city now and you might know a quicker way?"

"I can't believe we made it. TomTom or not!"

"I still don't get how cops always know where they are," Mac said, following the TomTom directions.

I squinted through the rain.

"It's a life and death thing. If your life depended on you knowing where you were at all times ..." I laughed. "You'd be dead wouldn't you?"

Mac grinned. "I'm afraid I would be."

It'd been a peaceful trip phonecall-wise. I loved that blocking numbers made annoyances vanish.

I never did fix that printer.

Oh yeah, the transcript. I wrestled the papers from my pocket to study. By the time I turned the first page I was sure they weren't actual taped conversations. It was bogus! Why? It didn't even say anything incriminating; it was bullshit, but not Aidan's particular brand of bullshit.

"Someone is playing a very dangerous game! These conversations never happened."

"What?"

Mac glanced over at me then back to the wet road ahead.

"My brother doesn't talk like this," I said. "There are conversations here that Aidan and I supposedly had over the last few days."

Mac expelled air through clenched teeth and said "That's impossible."

"Yep."

"Why the fuck would someone invent a transcript?"

"Because the surveillance is crap. I don't believe he ever was a suspect, someone ... let's say Caine, wants it to appear as though he is."

"To what end?"

"No idea." My head reeled at the possible implications: Missing evidence and fabricated evidence. It was possible that Caine was trying to keep the real evidence out of sight to limit knowledge or, was he setting up Aidan? Stop!

The actual tapes have to be produced for the District Attorney if they are going to arrest Aidan, and that would be impossible because there is no way those tapes exist. Foreboding clawed its way from my stomach enveloping the whole situation: Was Caine trying to throw someone off the real investigation?

Does he really think it's someone in the Bureau?

We parked in the hospital parking lot. I glanced at my

cell phone. The display said I had missed four calls, all from Caine. I had a solution for my moment of guilt. I snatched up both cell phones and threw them into the glove compartment for safekeeping. I knew I needed to talk to him but this was something I wanted to do face-to-face where his eyes couldn't lie. There would be time to discuss this with Mac. He'd have already boarded my thought train anyway.

"Let's go," Mac said jumping out of the vehicle. He opened my door for me.

"Thank you."

"You are very welcome." Mac locked the car. Pocketed the keys and took my hand. Together we walked through the main entrance of the large old building to the patient enquiry desk.

At the nurse's station in the Coronary Care Unit, I asked for my Dad, "Simon Conway?"

A nurse opened a chart and then looked up at me. "Gabrielle?"

"Yes." I flashed my credentials.

The young nurse nodded. "Your father is in room two-ten."

"How is he?"

"As well as can be expected, don't over tax him," she replied.

I held Mac's hand tightly and remembered to breathe as we walked down the corridor looking at room numbers. I peered through the window of room two-ten. Dad was semi-reclined in a bed with wires and tubing all over him, including oxygen prongs in his nose. My mind quickly threw up some protective walls to shield me from the possibility that he may not survive. Mac's arm slid around my shoulders.

"Do you want to go in alone?"

"No!" I couldn't hide how horrified I was at the suggestion. I hate hospitals: They are where people come to die.

Mac swung the door open for me. Why are hospitals so overheated? The minute I stepped into the room I felt hot and clammy.

"Dad?" I touched his tube-free hand. His eyes flickered open.

"Hello, sweetheart." His voice sounded softer than normal, somewhat weaker in tone; his eyes settled on the hard-to-miss, bright-yellow cast on my arm. "Is that what happened in Lexington?"

"Yeah, it's nothing, an incomplete fracture. I'll only have to wear this for about two weeks."

His skin was grayish and he looked very ill. I was used to Dad being tanned and bright, full of life.

"That doesn't sound bad."

"It's not, it's just annoying. You don't look so good, Dad."

He chuckled, "Don't feel so good, either." He turned his head a little to see Mac. "How are ya, Mac?"

"I'm good."

"How's your Dad, Mac?" It seemed difficult for my father to talk: He sounded quite breathless as he spoke.

"Sends his regards, we just spent a few days with him."

"I know," Dad replied.

Mac raised an eyebrow. "You know?"

Dad coughed a little. "We've known each other a lot of years."

Mac and I were very surprised at his revelation. Mac pulled two chairs closer to the bed.

"You've never mentioned Bob Connelly before." My eyebrows rose, too.

Dad smiled. "Sure I have, kid; Tank and I go way back."

I looked at Mac and thought back to all the times Dad had been hunting or fishing with his old buddy, Tank. Mac's eyes narrowed, leading me to believe he had similar memories. I watched as his face lit up with recognition.

Mac grinned and said, "You're the Colonel?"

"Yes, that's me."

"Damn, it's a small world," Mac muttered. "Who'd have thought ...?"

"Tank called me when you left, said you were on your way." He sounded very short of breath and his color worsened, more bluish than he had been.

"What's wrong?"

He struggled for enough air to speak, "I'm sure they turn the damned oxygen off ... every now and then ... to see how many of us survive."

"Shush, rest."

"Not yet, Ellie. Time enough for rest when I'm taking a

dirt nap."

I glared at him. He'd be doing that a lot sooner than he expected if he didn't behave.

"Have you seen your Mom?"

"No, I thought she would be here."

"I haven't ... seen her in two day ... she doesn't know, Ellie."

"Two days," Mac repeated.

"It's not unusual," I told him, "In fact, two days for her is nothing. She disappears periodically." I leaned into Mac and whispered, "But it's never long enough; the bitch always comes back."

"I'll find her, Dad." I watched his eyes close. "I called Aid. Thought he'd beat us here."

Simon opened one eye. "No, Ellie. We argued last time I saw him. He's angry with me."

That wasn't good. "Over Mom?"

"Yes."

"I'll talk to him," I replied. I am my brother's keeper. "We should have picked him up on the way."

"Let him be," Dad said.

"All right, but we'll go get him and I'll find Mom."

"Try Aunt Caroline's," he said. "She still goes there when she's manic." Dad looked beaten down and flat-out exhausted.

"She's off her meds again?" I tried to keep the disappointment from my voice. I wished my mother would act like a normal person, just once.

"I thought she was ditching them a few weeks ago ...

and now I am sure."

"You got sedatives at home for her?" I asked. I knew what to expect if Mom was off her meds again and in the midst of a manic episode.

"My bathroom ... bottom vanity drawer ... small black case." Dad became distressed; his eyes filled with tears.

"It's okay, Dad, I know what to do."

"I know ..."

He closed his eyes again. His breathing sounded labored.

I leaned over and kissed his unshaven cheek. "I'll be back soon, Daddy; everything will be just fine." I waited by the door for Mac.

Dad reached a hand up and laid it over Mac's. "You sure are Tank's boy. He's mighty proud of you."

"It's good to meet you, Colonel."

I blocked the host of voices in my head as they attempted to scream in unison, "This really sucks." They weren't helpful. My less-than-perfect family demanded my attention and I didn't want to give it. I wanted to stay here with Dad. I did not want go out looking for my wayward, promiscuous mother and my brother who was too stubborn to visit Dad. I mentally slapped myself good and hard. Get over it! It's my duty.

We drove in silence across town to Aidan's house. Two drive-by's later, we determined his car was indeed in the driveway and made the surveillance van down the street.

"I bet that van is empty."

"You think we should risk it by knocking on the door?"

Mac asked.

"Ummm no, there's an alleyway that leads to the back of these houses from the next street."

Mac parked around the corner.

"We'll climb his back fence," I said.

Mac nodded.

As soon as I saw the fence, I realized that scaling a six-feet-high fence, one-armed, was a little ambitious. I had Mac. Together we managed to clamber over the wooden fence and drop unseen into the yard.

There was no answer to my knock on the backdoor. I couldn't hear any movement inside. Keys, I needed the keys. There were four large flowerpots on the steps by the back door. I tried to remember which pot held the spare key. Eeny meeny miny mo. The third pot from the top was my choice. I scrabbled through the dirt hoping the key was still there.

It was, but buried deeper than I recalled. I wiped dirt from my hand down my jeans then unlocked the door. We wandered through the house, keeping away from the front windows. There was no sign of life.

"Odd," I mumbled to myself, flicking through a pile of bills lying on the dining room table. I stopped at a bill from Orbit Satellite Internet. "Funny, must be for work." I refused to consider anything more sinister. He must've succumbed to the pressure of work to carry a laptop.

I went into the kitchen leaving Mac scanning the bills. There was something wrong with the house, most notably with the kitchen.

"He hasn't been here in a few days," I said.

Mac appeared in the doorway. "Say that again, I missed it."

"He hasn't been here for a few days."

"How do you know?"

"It's too damn clean. The cleaning lady comes twice a week and leaves the house looking like this, within hours he has messed up and used the kitchen. What day is it?"

"Tuesday. It's Tuesday afternoon."

"She comes Saturday mornings and Wednesdays."

"Maybe he's been over at your parents' place or out looking for her?"

"He didn't know Dad was in hospital or that she was missing."

"Good point. Maybe he cleaned up and went for a walk?"

Like hell! He didn't clean anything or walk anywhere. "Highly unlikely. Come on let's go home and get the stuff."

I buried the key and pressed the dirt back down in the pot. We left the same way we arrived.

I let myself into my parents' home. I called out but there was no answer. I found the black case in Dad's bathroom and handed it to Mac.

"What's in it?"

"Open it and have a look," I replied as I checked to see if anyone had been in the house recently. I cleared the answer machine too, nothing of interest there, either.

"How does this work?" Mac held a small glass vial between his fingers.

"See the long narrow top?"

He nodded.

"You snap it off then fill the syringe. It's designed to break cleanly." I showed him my right thumb covered in a myriad of small scars. "It's a fallacy." I grinned at him. "I've learned to always snap the top off, by holding it in fabric of some sort, usually the bottom of my shirt."

"How many per syringe?"

"One. One is enough to settle Mom."

"Okay, we ready?"

"Ready as we'll ever be." I so wasn't looking forward to it. Looking for my crazy mother was never fun.

We began our search at Aunt Caroline's, which Mac discovered was a place not a person.

The old diner stood at the far edge of town, smack in the middle of an industrial zone. I took a deep breath and planted a synthetic grin on my face. We walked into the narrow building. Its tattered red and black décor spoke volumes about its age and clientele, as did the menu, written in now-chipped paint above the long narrow counter.

No need to update the menu, they were still serving the same high-cholesterol food. Only now, it had moved to the realms of comfort food.

I scanned the room. My eyes searched for a familiar beehive hairdo which matched the distinctive nasal voice I could hear. I checked my plastic smile as I spotted the woman four tables away. Her bleached-to-a-crisp blonde hair was piled on top of her head, as it had been since the sixties. Bright-red lipstick bled into deep crevices around her lips. Her faded, blue eyes, accentuated by more eyeliner than Michael Jackson wore.

The woman had stuffed her large well-padded body into a pale-pink uniform that she may have fitted thirty years ago. It was complete with frilly apron that was, amazingly, still white. The whale of a woman spun around almost as if she sensed new blood. Her pudgy hand clasping a coffee pot for all it was worth as the contents sloshed and threatened to spill.

"Saints be praised!" She shrieked and moved at surprising speed towards us, "Ellie!"

"Hey, Cindy." My smile became real. Okay, I liked her in small doses and it had been a while.

Cindy pulled herself up. She set the coffee pot on the counter, adjusted her hair-do and smoothed her rumpled clothing. It didn't help.

Her plump, manicured hand extended to Mac.

"Your mama said there was a new man."

I watched her eye Mac with expertise that came from years of dealing with men of all types. "Well, no wonder you ain't been home, doll." Cindy winked at me. Her long, fake, eyelashes seemed to make the wink last longer.

Yep, that's the reason. I got a man, no need to go home ever again. I did an internal eye roll. Of course, it has nothing to do with some psycho-bastard-Unsub, or not wanting to see my psychotic mother. Dah me! Boy, I am stupid. As if she would know whether I had a man or not.

Her daydreaming had created a life for me, again.

At least she didn't invent a lesbian life this time.

I felt the need to keep a tighter rein on my thoughts for fear they'd pop out. I knew from experience that my mother didn't cope well with the truth. Such a shame because I was a champion at dishing it out in vast quantities, especially around her.

Mac grinned and was as charming as ever. "Pleased to meet you, Cindy"

"Oh, the pleasure is all mine I assure you." She fluttered her long black eyelashes for all she was worth. For a brief moment, they appeared to be spiders trying desperately to run away. What I needed was a giant-size can of Raid.

"Have you seen Mom?" I watched with amusement as Mac tried to extract his hand from Cindy's dumpy grasp.

"Ohhh, you wanna introduce your man." She gave yet another wink of her frightening lashes.

"Sure do," I replied. I controlled my desire to set those spiders free, and run like hell.

"Mama is out back, Ellie; she been staying with me a few days."

"Do you mind?" I indicated that Mac and I would like to go through the kitchen to find her. I would've been fine just walking out and going back to see Dad.

"Of course not, doll. You go show off that fine specimen of manhood. She'll be delighted." Cindy winked again.

I shuddered.

"She's the life and soul, that woman."

Cindy's eyes fixed on Mac's shoulders. I couldn't fault her awed gaze, his shoulders were fine indeed.

"I just bet she is." I bit my lip to stop myself adding anything else. She always was the life and soul of any party just total shit at the family stuff.

I grabbed Mac's hand and led him back behind the counter and through the kitchen to a red door. The paint was peeling in patches showing a pink undercoat; it seemed fitting.

Everything had seen better days, clientele, staff, the building, the menu, all worn and tired. I knocked then opened the door; much to my surprise it didn't squeak.

"Mom?"

The dingy interior smelled of stale tobacco and gin. The diner décor spilled over into here. It was pleasant enough, almost comforting, in some weird way.

"Mama, you here?" From across the room I heard a muffled sound. "Mama?" I edged closer to the origin of the noise. "I have someone I want you to meet."

A head popped over the top of the sofa almost giving me a heart attack.

"Ellie!" Mom squealed, and leapt to her feet rearranging her clothing. She paused and threw a blanket onto the sofa.

I started to move closer but she headed me off. She rushed at me with her arms wide open. Mama caught me in a hug then turned her attention to Mac. With her occupied I peeked over the top of the sofa: A male face peered back at me. He'd seen way better days. I glared at him. Yuck.

"Mama, we have to go. Daddy's sick."

Mom clamped onto Mac's arm fluttering her old eyelashes and patting his hand. I wanted to slap her and scream 'Remember Dad, you know, your husband?'

"We can sit for a bit and catch up, Ellie," she crooned.

I think not. Not here, with her latest conquest hiding on the sofa. "We will, Mama. We can catch up in the car. We'll go get coffee and catch up all you want." I trotted out my patient, smooth, unruffled voice.

"Would be nice to chat with you, Mrs. Connelly," Mac added.

"We can have coffee out in the diner with Cindy." Her eyes were roaming. The more flustered she became the wilder her gaze appeared. "I don't want to leave, Ellie."

I don't want a crazed woman as a mother. We don't always get what we want. I adjusted my tone to pacify the insanity I felt building.

"We'll bring you back, I promise." Too late to cross my finger: The lie was already out there. "I promise."

Mom smiled at me almost serenely. "You've never broken a promise to me, Ellie, not ever."

I did a double take, who was this woman? She sure had an odd grasp on reality. We managed to steer her towards the door and out into the diner. We even made it to the parking lot with little drama.

When we reached the car, she started to back away. "Its red, Ellie, you know you shouldn't have a red car!"

she squealed, "Red cars are bad." This was more like it. I remember this woman. "Oh, this is very bad, Ellie. I see blood, blood all over the road." Her arm waved frantically in no particular direction. "Red is bad, there'll be tears before bed tonight."

I glanced at Mac. He produced the black case and passed it to me from behind his back all the while talking to my deranged and distressed mother, "It's not red. It's that funny orange color." His voice stayed soft and gentle.

I smiled as I loaded the syringe. He was almost color-blind and the car was cherry red. Mom argued. Mac became more patient. Without fuss, I pulled up her sleeve and pressed the needle against the skin inside her elbow. Mom had great veins, they were always easy to find; today was no exception. She was still upset about the red car and took a few seconds to register the needle.

I kept her focus on her perceived problem so she didn't pull away. "It's just a color, Mama,"

"What was that, Ellie?" she asked.

"Just something to help you relax." I gave her a reassuring smile. "It's okay."

"It's red."

"It's just a car."

Mac helped her into the back seat.

"Put the child lock on, babe, just in case," I whispered. Something pinged like old elastic in my mind and I knew, without a doubt, that children were not an option in my life. There she was, my mother, proving to me once again that her gene pool needed serious cleaning.

"Okay." He locked her in.

I twisted around in my seat to talk to Mom, "How're you feeling?"

"A bit sleepy." Her head bobbed as the car moved.

"You can sleep soon."

I took Mac's cell phone from the glove compartment and looked up her doctor's phone number. The exercise reminded me to transfer my address book to my new phone. I mentally added that to my list. It didn't take the doctor long to answer.

"Doctor Dunn, this is Gabrielle Conway. Mom's off her meds again."

"How far away are you, Gabrielle?"

I looked out the window and then at my watch. "Ten minutes, give or take."

"I'll have an orderly meet you at the emergency department."

"Thank you." I dropped the phone back into the glove compartment and chewed my lip. I hated what was going to happen next.

A whisper from Mac broke into my thoughts, "What happens now?"

"She'll stay in the medium-security psychiatric wing for a few weeks until her meds have her stable again." Then, in a month or so, she'll go off her meds because she thinks it's a conspiracy to keep her quiet and stop her having fun. It'll start all over again.

"Are you okay?" His hand reached out and touched my leg. "How're your arm and your head?"

"I'm okay. I just want to get back to Dad."

"All right."

"What?" I watched him check the rear view mirror then adjust it and look at Mom. I turned to see, she was asleep. He readjusted the mirror.

"She never mentioned your arm? It's a bright-yellow cast and she never said anything."

"Ohhh that ..." I chuckled. "Mom doesn't see me, never really has."

"Never?" This surprised Mac.

"Okay, so that was a slight exaggeration; she notices enough to criticize, blah blah ... you're too thin. You've lost weight. Why do you hide behind your hair?"

Mac chuckled. My hand flipped out and smacked his leg. "I have weighed the same since I was fifteen-years-old; that was also the year I decided on a fringe."

"You are just fine the way you are."

Mac pulled up in front of the emergency department. Two orderlies were waiting with a wheelchair. They assisted Mom from the car with relative ease.

Mac and I followed behind as they wheeled her off to the elevator. We exited on the fourth floor and found Doctor Dunn waiting at the admissions desk. He passed me a clipboard and a pen. "You know the drill, Gabrielle."

I filled in the relevant areas of the form and signed it, leaving blank the section that related to length of stay. Would be nice if, this time, it could be forever. I knew it wouldn't be, but a girl can dream.

I passed him back the clipboard. "Thank you, Doctor

Dunn."

He spoke to Mom, "Nice to have you back, Jenny, let's get you settled."

She didn't respond.

"What did you give her?" he asked me.

"IV valium, one full vial."

"Good girl," he replied.

I bent down and kissed her cheek. Mac and I walked away and as always I never looked back.

Mac broke the silence as we made our way back to the car, "How many times have you done that?"

I shrugged. "Too many to count. It's a lot easier when she's doped up."

We found a more suitable parking space close to the main hospital building and covered the short walk back inside and up to Dad's room in Coronary Care Unit.

I paused at the window. "Does he look worse to you?"

"About the same, about the same," Mac replied with one of his comforting smiles.

"Hey, Daddy," I whispered taking his hand.

The whiteness of the hospital pillows and sheets added to the frailty I now saw in my father, a stark reminder that he wasn't superhuman after all.

His eyes opened. "Hiya, Ellie, everything okay?"

"Yes, Mom's back in hospital, she'll be fine. You seen Aidan yet?"

I still had concerns about Aidan and didn't want to have to worry Dad any further.

"Not yet, he'll show." Dad's eyes partly closed. "Sorry

you had to see Jenny like that, Mac."

Mac smiled and replied in typical Mac fashion, "Not a problem."

There were two chairs in the room this time. We dragged them close together and closer to the bed.

"You two look tired," Dad commented; even sick, his eyes missed nothing.

"It's been a rough few days," Mac replied.

"This old ticker of mine sure picked a fine time to fall apart."

"At least we got away from Caine for a bit." I glanced around the room. We've seen way too many hospital rooms. "We should be safe here."

Mac squeezed my hand; it was a don't-speak-too-soon squeeze, and he was right, I had forgotten about the mascara in my jacket pocket. I had to find out who liberated the bug from the designated destruction path it was on. A big part of me wanted everything to go away so I could concentrate on Dad. I'm okay. He'll be okay. We'll all be okay. My internal pep talk was starting to look lie wishful thinking.

The warmth of Mac's touch made me smile as I willed the tears of frustration, and fear for my father, to remain hidden.

Chapter Twenty-Three

We Are Family

I scanned the window by the door for the hundredth time since we'd returned, this time Aidan stared back at me. I smiled, and beckoned to him to come in; I was relieved to see him. He may not have been home for a few days, but he wasn't dead.

He opened the door and entered with trepidation, his eyes pained and demeanor sullen.

"Hey, Aidan," Mac said; his voice cut the air.

"Hey." His response was somber as he approached the bed.

"Aidan?" Dad's voice was stronger than it had been all day. He was trying to show him that he was okay.

"I'm here, Dad," he replied.

"Where have you been?" The strain of keeping his voice even and strong showed but he did it.

"Had a bit of a tidy up and dropped some old clothes into the Salvation Army." he replied with a touch more confidence, "Busy at work."

Aidan had edged closer to me. I stood up then sat on Mac's knee, letting Aidan sit down. I noticed three almost-healed scratches on his neck.

"You been tormenting that old cat again?" I resisted the temptation to ask if he'd killed anyone lately. I still didn't believe he was capable and asking, even in fun, would be in rather poor taste considering the circumstances.

Aidan appeared confused; his hand sought the marks on his neck. “Oh, yeah. He hates the flea powder, even though fleas make him cranky.”

“He always was a mean creature,” Dad commented, “I don’t know why you keep him around.”

Aidan shrugged. “He likes me as much as he likes anyone, I guess.” He looked from Dad to me, “Where’s Mom?”

“Up on the psych floor.”

“Did you do it?”

“Yes.”

Dad reached a tube-pierced hand out to Aidan. I knew it was a struggle for my brother to touch his hand, it was a pride thing. He was a stubborn idiot at times. I felt unexpectedly pleased when Aidan held the hand that reached out to him. I caught his eye and winked, he smiled back.

Aidan’s scratches were unsettling, I knew they shouldn’t be because his cat was evil and it wasn’t unusual for Aidan to have deep scratches. We never saw the cat, or any sign of the cat whilst at Aidan’s house.

“Where’s the cat?”

“What?”

“I dropped by your place, but I just realized I never saw that evil monster.”

“He’s in a cattery.”

I watched Dad breathe. His eyes closed, he still looked

gray, and his lips were tinged with blue. Cat's in the cattery: If he was my cat he'd live in one permanently.

I touched Dad's shoulder and asked, "Daddy, do you need anything?"

He opened his eyes and looked into mine. "What else could I possibly need?"

I smiled. "Not bad for someone as ill as you seem to be."

He held my gaze. "Appearances can be deceiving, Ellie, my girl. Don't take for granted what's smack in front of your face."

I digested Dad's words with difficulty. My internal screen saver scrolled familiar words through my mind, 'it's not always as it seems.' I could hear Mac talking to Dad but wasn't listening. The need for coffee crashed my thoughts. I rejoined the conversation when I heard Dad speak to Aidan.

"I wish I'd known you were going to the Sally Army, Aidan. I have several boxes to drop off myself." Dad mumbled.

"So you were out when I called," I said to Aidan. "the traffic noises – you weren't even at home."

He looked at me as though I'd lost my mind before replying. "I forward calls to my cell whenever I'm out. You were the one who suggested I do that."

"When?"

"Must've been a good whack to your head; all your brains fell out."

"Tell me when," I asked again, ignoring his retort.

"I didn't know I had to retain information from six months ago, Ellie. If you'd told me I was going to be interrogated I would've made sure to remember the details."

"You are such a dick sometimes. Six months ago?"

Aidan grinned. "Approximately six months ago."

"Simon, we can drop off the boxes for you," Mac offered, successfully interrupting my conversation with Aidan. I knew by the fidgeting he was doing that he, too, needed coffee.

"That would be great," Dad replied, his voice rasped a little more than it had earlier.

"Maybe you should sleep a while, Dad. We'll be back this evening." I told him, "We need to sort out where we are staying."

"There's nobody in the house, Ellie; you know you are always welcome."

"We'll drop our stuff back home then."

I nudged Aidan. "You staying?" I used a tone that left little doubt that it was an order, not a question. I bent down and whispered in his ear, "I need you to stay with Dad." That was the clincher. He would never turn me down once I said I needed him to do something.

"I'll stay here with Dad till you get back," he agreed.

"We'll be back soon. We'll bring sandwiches and coffee. Do you need anything, Aidan?"

"Yeah, there's a book on the coffee table at my place, would you grab it please."

"No problem."

"Don't be long," Aidan said; his voice betrayed his anxiety.

"You'll be fine, time you and Dad talked."

I kissed Dad's cheek. "You need a shave. I'll arrange it on my way out."

"Thank you, sweetheart." His eyes closed again.

Chapter Twenty-Four

Jack And Jill

I collapsed on the bed in my childhood room. Nothing much had changed. I lay and stared at the ceiling. The glow in the dark stars I'd stuck up a lifetime ago were still there. Hundreds of stars adorned the ceiling.

Mac flopped down beside me.

"What was Ellie like as a teenager?" He also gazed up at the greenish-yellow stars.

"Smart-mouthed, contrary, full of the angst of a teenage girl, sometimes withdrawn, but not too bad a kid, I don't think."

My mind did a brief mambo through the trials of teenage life, peppered with patches of outright insanity courtesy of my manic mother.

Mac rolled over and propped himself up on an elbow. He gazed down on me with soft, caring eyes.

"We're survivors, Ellie."

"Yes, we are," I affirmed.

I looked into his eyes and thought how easy it would be to become lost in the flecks of gold. They reminded me so much of tiny stars. Real life broke in; things needed doing. "We should unpack, then find those boxes Dad wanted dropped off."

"I've got a better idea," he said. "How about you close those very captivating blue eyes of yours and rest up for a bit?"

I wasn't tired but maybe just being still would clear things enough to provide some insight into what was happening.

"Okay."

He started to move.

"Don't go far."

"Thought I'd just get comfy and stay right here, okay?" Mac did just that he shuffled down on the bed and pulled me close to him.

I let sleep come. My mind took a whirlwind tour of both recent and past events as it sifted through garbage searching for what should be preserved. Images burned as they converted into little video clips and arranged themselves in a more palatable context. Glossy apparitions spoke volumes as they reeled through my dream movie theatre.

I watched in awe as files opened to catch single thoughts and moving pictures, logging everything for further exploration. Everything had a categorized place for future need based on most pressing and relevant information. Once sorted and sifted, the movie reels began again, playing footage. Editing, rearranging, turning the complex into simple concepts, easily understood by the waking mind.

I felt Mac stir beside me; his arms wrapped tighter around me. I blinked a few times as partial dream excerpts clung to the edges of my waking mind.

"Orbit Satellite Internet," I said.

"What about them?"

"Scratches on his neck," I added with more clarity, "Everything can be explained."

I felt Mac's body freeze beside mine. He knew what I was talking about. I pulled a dreamscape from out of its shadowed box file.

"When we were high school – Aidan was a couple of years behind me – these asshole kids from my class had been giving me a hard time about Mom. I ignored them, they were jerks, and it didn't matter. But one afternoon, Aidan decided to take matters into his own hands. I wasn't there but I heard what happened from a friend of mine the next day."

"Go on," Mac prompted.

"She told me she came around the corner of the gym and stopped because she couldn't believe what she saw. Two of the guys who'd harassed me were on the ground. She swore they weren't moving. Aidan was kicking them in the head, taking turns with each one. He was saying, 'No one is going to destroy her happiness, you motherfuckers!' Karen said he repeated it over and over. She was terrified." I closed my eyes. "She would never be in the same room as him after that. One of those kids almost died from the brutal beating he received from my brother."

"What happened after that? Was he charged?"

"No. He went to counseling and to another school. I graduated soon after that." I opened my eyes to find Mac studying my face. "I don't know of any other incidents like that."

"Where are you going with this?" His voice was gentle yet confused.

"As I see it right now there are two possibilities: Caine, or an unknown who could be an agent. But there are situations, such as the beating, that could be used against Aidan," I explained. "Aidan said he dropped off clothing today, maybe we should check that out. Someone fabricated surveillance. What if that person followed him and dropped off something else?"

"Something like a missing body?"

"Yeah, that's what I was thinking," I said. "If Aidan is pulled in for questioning his whereabouts will be scrutinized. Everything he's done will be out in the open. That includes seemingly innocuous things like dropping off clothing to the Sally Army. Someone will search for those clothes."

I wondered how far this person would go to implicate Aidan.

"What now?" Mac asked.

"Would you call the hospital, check Dad's okay and that Aidan is still there, please?"

"Of course, I'll do it now, then?"

"We're going to find those clothes before someone else does."

He hurried from the room to make the call and returned a few minutes later.

"He's still there, Dad's the same."

"Thank you."

Mac picked up a high school yearbook from the bookshelf and flipped through it while I changed into warmer clothes. "What are you looking for?" I pulled a clean fleecy top over my head.

"You, as a teenager."

Oh man, we don't need to go there. I attempted to grab the book from him but he ducked out of the way.

He had it open at the back page and was reading comments and well wishes, "One day you'll notice me. Tommy." He looked at me from over the book. "Who is Tommy?"

"Not a clue." I shrugged. It was a long time ago and of about as much interest now, as it was then.

Mac searched through the book. He held up a page and pointed to a kid. "Damn, Ellie! You overlooked him?"

I eyed the picture, disheveled dark hair, heavy black-rimmed glasses. "Mmmm."

"He even has a pocket protector."

"I don't remember him." I took another look, "Ohhh yeah. He was in the science club." I shuddered as a memory surfaced. "He followed me a few times, and he was really intense and creepy."

Mac chuckled and said, "Any clue what happened to him?"

"Nope."

Mac closed the book. "Come on, let's go."

"Let's start with the Sally Army stores between Aidan's and the hospital," I suggested, "But first ... we drop by a drugstore, for latex gloves, both small and large paper bags and a waterproof marker pen; oh, and we'll swap cars. Let's take my Dad's car."

Caine would know by now we had Bob's car and he'd be looking for us.

"All right." Mac nodded. We cruised up to the first drugstore on the way to our targeted area. I purchased everything we needed with cash. I saw no need to alert Caine as to our whereabouts, with credit card transactions.

"Paper bags?" Mac asked as we loaded the supplies into the trunk. His question didn't surprise me. I knew he'd been thinking about it while we were in the store.

"For evidence, should we find any. If it's bloodied it must be in paper because plastic bags keep the blood from drying and allow bugs to grow."

"This is one giant learning curve."

We headed on our way to the next stop.

Mac pulled up in front of the first Salvation Army store. It was large, with plate glass windows across the front bearing the Salvation Army logo.

We entered the store. I approached the counter and spoke to the assistant, "My brother may have dropped off some clothes this afternoon."

The woman interrupted me, "Ah, don't tell me, and he bought in the wrong box?" She said with a wide smile, "It happens a lot."

I grinned. "Yes, he did."

"Everything we've had today is stacked down the back, on the far right." The woman pointed across the store.

“Thank you,” I replied.

“We’re closing soon,” she called after us, as we hurried over in the direction the woman had pointed. There were several boxes piled up in the corner. Mac lifted down the first box and set it on the floor. We snapped our gloves on, not easy over a cast. Five boxes later, nothing had jumped out or even seemed familiar.

“Shall we move on?” Mac sounded a little disheartened.

“Yeah.”

We pulled our gloves off and dropped them in our pockets.

“Thank you,” I said, to the woman at the counter on my way past, “He can’t have dropped them here.”

“Try the store closest to the hospital. We also have clothing dumpsters by the hospital.”

“Thanks.” I followed Mac from the store.

“Store or dumpsters?” Mac opened the car door for me.

“Store, let’s do the easy thing first.”

“Sounds good to me.”

Steady rain fell as we pulled in out front of the next store.

I made a decision, “Let’s flag the store till later, we’re losing light, and I’ve a feeling about the dumpsters.”

“You sure?”

“Yep.”

Rain was now pouring from the gray sky and showed little sign of letting up as Mac parked close to the big red dumpster. It bore the Salvation Army shield in brilliant white which glowed brighter under our headlights.

We sat in the car and stared at the bins while I willed the rain to ease off. It was almost dusk and the rain wasn't helping visibility any.

I took out a flashlight from the storage drawer under my seat. Dad always kept a fully-charged flashlight in the car.

"We'll need this, its dark inside those things."

I surveyed Mac's shoulders then scrutinized the large flip-top dumpsters in front of the car. I realized he wasn't going to fit, the lids were smaller than I remembered. I'd be the one flipping upside down into the dumpster and I'd been in enough dumpsters to know even those supposedly containing clothing also held unmentionable filth. The rain eased a little so I slapped on a brave face.

"Let's get this over with." I squinted out the window. "You'll have to give me a leg up; don't think I can jump with this damn cast."

He looked at me in horror. "No way! I'm going in."

"Hun, you won't get through that little door," I replied with a grin and waved a hand at his broad shoulders.

He looked over at the bins then back at me. "This is highly unacceptable," he said. "I am not happy about you dropping into a freaking dumpster."

"It's not the first time, and I doubt it'll be the last. My small frame has always been in high demand for awkward-to-reach places."

Mac shook his head. "I'm not impressed with this

idea,"

Me neither. "Let's get this exercise in stupidity over."

We stood on the sidewalk by the dumpster. Puddles lay all around us and rain dripped from the sky. I pushed on the lid and swung it out of my way. Mac placed his hand on it to stop it banging on my head. I peered inside.

"Doesn't look very full. Why do people drop trash into these things?"

I could see what looked like file folders and newspaper. Something in the dumpster smelt rancid. It occurred to me that it could've been a dead animal.

"Laziness; people are lazy. You going in?"

"Yeah. That lid's gonna smack me on the head any second, huh?" I was having difficulty trying to figure out how Mac intended to help me into the dumpster and hold the lid.

"I hope not," he said. "Push the lid out of the way with your cast as you slip a leg over the edge. Once you are up there I'll hold the lid."

"Clever." I winked at him. "I thought I'd go in head first and flip over."

"The hell you did!"

I dropped into the bin feet first with the flashlight in my good hand. The inside of the bin was dark. A dank, drippy darkness overcame me. I shone the beam around. My flashlight did nothing to alleviate the creepiness.

I could've sworn I heard a scuffling noise from beneath the paper and trash. Trash equals rats. I didn't ponder on how they would get in the dumpster; I just accepted they were there.

A foul smell sucked all the oxygen from the air. Maybe a dead rat or cat.

Damn, there was a noise. “Mac, I don’t think I’m alone!”

The lid moved letting in more of the dull wet light. “You okay?”

“Yeah.” I moved papers and trash out of the way and searched for clothing. I convinced myself I heard rats. I could shoot rats, so no problem. I didn’t think I would find anything to link Aidan to any clothing. My brother was no killer. I doubted I would find any clothing bearing blood stains matching any of our victims, either. I stepped carefully. My right foot sank into something soft. More trash. I lifted my foot which released a plume of the stench.

“Oh, man,” I groaned, covering my mouth and nose with my sleeve.

“What?” Mac’s voice echoed into the dumpster.

“There’s something rotten in here.” I kept my sleeve over my mouth and nose, and kicked at the garbage using my feet to push rubbish out of the way.

I didn’t go any closer to the stench than I had to. Heavy plastic crinkled as I moved. I shone the flashlight by my feet and saw the edges of black polythene. I kicked more trash away. My foot connected with something solid. I redirected the flashlight beam and it still took me a second to realize what I was looking at.

Someone’s head was in contact with the toe of my boot

and the eyes popped out like boiled eggs. “Oh, yuck!” It was more a high-pitched yelp than actual words.

“What?”

“Mac, get me outta here!” Panic surged in my voice as I staggered back to the opening and tried not to fall. I dropped the flashlight. Too bad. There was no way I was going to pick it up. It became dumpster trash. I reached up to Mac. He grabbed me just above the elbows and hauled me over the top past the lid.

Mac steadied me then let go. I stumbled away from the dumpster wondering if I looked as green as I felt. I leaned against the car, facing into the street. I gulped for air and swallowed hard.

“What the hell happened?” There was a panicky edge to Mac’s voice.

I raised my hand to my face. I could still smell it. The putrid stench was in my clothes. I tore the zipper open on my jacket, ripped the garment off, and threw it on the ground as far away as possible. Mac spun me around.

“What?” He tilted my face up to see my eyes.

“It’s revolting,” I said still swallowing hard, “Can’t you smell it?”

He shook his head.

“It’s everywhere.” How could he not smell it? “It’s the most disgusting thing I have ever smelt in my life.” The odor clung to me. I’d become enveloped in the noxious vapor.

“Take a deep breath. You’re not making much sense.” He was calm and I could feel nothing except building panic. "Breathe."

I took a breath, spun on my heels and vomited into the gutter.

Mac waited until I straightened up before saying anything else, "What's on your boot?"

I looked at the back of my foot. "Nothing," I replied with much relief.

"No, the other one." He pointed at my left foot.

I lifted my foot and took a closer look and was sorry I did. A foul stink rose from my boot. Even Mac could smell it now. He reeled backwards, clamping his hand over his mouth and nose.

I heard my voice before I could censor it, "I believe it's a section of human intestine."

I pulled on a pair of latex gloves and opened the car door. I sat with my legs over the pavement and removed my left boot trying not to dislodge the human remains clinging to it. Stuck to the sole I discovered a small piece of yellow paper. I removed it and could see black handwriting, partially obscured, beneath a thin coating of blood and other body fluids.

I read it to Mac, "'One man's trash is for the finder to measure, as I stare at you, it's you I treasure.'"

"Guess that removes any doubt of this being unrelated." Mac kept his eyes on mine. I knew he was trying not to look at the bloodied post-it note that I held at arm's length.

"Pass one of those small paper baggies, please."

Mac opened one and held it out to me. I dropped the

vile scrap of paper into it and Mac folded down the top.

"Grab the pen. Write the time, date, where the evidence was found, and your initials."

I watched him write; he didn't look well. I sat for a moment trying to compose myself. The trunk slammed shut rattling the car. Mac reappeared. I threw the left boot on top of my discarded jacket, and followed it with my right boot and the gloves.

The decomposition of the body caused confusion. From the putrification I'd witnessed it appeared that death might have been as long as three weeks before; I had stepped in it boots and all. Bile rose in my throat.

"I can still smell it," I said to myself, as I struggled to undo my jeans with one hand.

Mac reached in through the driver's door and fumbled in the glove compartment for a cell phone. Light rain continued to fall. I could hear the beeps as he pressed buttons.

Then a moment later, I heard him say, "It's Mac. We have a problem." I indicated to him to press the speaker button so I could hear.

Caine replied, "I thought you would."

We heard traffic noise, what sounded like large trucks and occasional cars.

"Where are you?" Suspicion resounded in Mac's voice.

"I'm about four cars back from Bob, looks like we're heading into Richmond."

Mac asked, "How far out are you?"

"Just past Kings Dominion, hang tight, Mac. I'm almost there." Caine paused. "Shall I guess where to meet you, or will you tell me?"

I frowned. It was unusual to hear such a sarcastic tone from Caine.

"Head towards the hospital; you may as well continue following Dad." Mac looked up the road towards the large hospital complex. "About two-hundred yards from the main entrance, on the right is a row of dumpsters, mostly big red Salvation Army ones. We're parked in front of them."

"Is the problem there also?"

"Oh hell, yeah, it ain't going anywhere, either."

"Is this related?"

No, we called you for fun!

"Yes and Ellie stood in it."

"Oh, gross," Caine retorted. "Poem?"

"Uh huh."

I swallowed hard to stop myself gagging. I couldn't believe I'd stood in someone's guts. Oh yuck!

"I'll send the police to secure the scene. You can go when they get there, I'm sure Ellie needs to clean up."

That was it. Even though there was little in my stomach I retched violently out of the car door.

"Thanks." Mac said to Caine then handed me the phone. "He wants to talk to you."

I held the phone to my ear and listened to Caine. "I've been trying to get hold of you. We found the other half of McNab; he was left on the doorstep of a house in Fairfax with a pizza perched on top of his legs."

"No word on his partner then?"

"Agent Kilby is still missing."

"Thanks."

I turned the phone off and handed it to Mac, he put it away. I lit a cigarette and watched him come around the side of the car towards me. Raindrops had settled on his black hair and shimmered like tiny crystal stars. He shook his head, dislodging the sparkling rain. Drops flew in all directions. They were cold and stung slightly as they hit my bare legs.

"You want me to gather your clothes and put them in the large paper bags?" Mac asked.

"Not really. Caine can deal with it. Unless you want to." I could tell he didn't; who in their right mind would want to touch that putrid-smelling pile?

"Okay?" Mac asked, and crouched beside me.

"Okay," I repeated and nodded. "That body is old. This maybe the first victim, which means Carter wasn't. And that discovery makes this a whole new ball game."

I watched the smoke from my cigarette twist and dodge the misty rain, as I waited for Mac's observations.

"Can you think of anyone from the chat room who disappeared before Carter's death?"

"Not offhand."

"Me neither. Aidan may be carrying a tracker too."

Mac nodded. "Yep. I was about to say that."

I changed the subject.

"It's a small world, huh?" I saw the smile on his face and guessed he had followed my thoughts back to our fathers. "Funny to think how close we must've come to meeting years ago." I gazed into his hazel eyes.

"Yup," he replied.

"Guess there's a reason we met when we did and not as kids."

Mac smiled. "Maybe."

I heard a siren. A few seconds later, two police cars rolled up beside us. Mac stood up to greet the officers. A tall and very overweight police officer swaggered towards us. I watched wondering how many donuts he'd consumed to reach that size and how he could pass the annual fitness test. The exceptionally large officer stood beside Mac.

"Are you Mister Cormac Connelly, or no?"

At that point, I was grateful he wasn't talking to me. The feminine voice didn't match the large man who spoke.

Mac took a second to respond, "Yes, I am Cormac Connelly and this is Special Agent Conway." He indicated towards me. I was doing a statue impersonation, gripping the seat and trying desperately to not think about anything. But the thoughts kept coming. How can such a big, swaggering police officer speak like a girly? Mac passed his credentials to the officer. The cop glanced at them then handed it back with a nod and a wink. It could have been a facial tick.

Oh, please don't let him speak again.

"Everything seems in order."

"The body is in the second dumpster over there." Mac

pointed. “We’re going to clean up. The FBI will be here soon. This is part of an ongoing investigation.”

“Are you from up north or no?” His voice squeaked as excitement took over. “Are you on the chat room killer case or no? Is this all part of that or no?” His eyes positively sparkled with interest or did he just fancy Mac?

“Yes, we are,” Mac replied.

The officer pointed to my clothes on the ground. Oh god, he was going to speak again. I bit my lip hard.

“Are they evidence or no?” He winked again. If I’d closed my eyes I would’ve sworn that it was a woman speaking.

How was it possible for that effeminate voice to come from something so large and seemingly masculine? Too much estrogen maybe? It was all too much. I couldn’t even look at Mac. I tasted blood in my mouth; in my effort not to laugh I had bitten into my lip. Maybe he suffered a truly vicious wedgie at school and parts of his anatomy never recovered. I suspected his underpants were pulled right over his head and tied in a bow.

“They belong to Special Agent Conway. Let the FBI deal with them.” Mac opened the trunk and handed the cop the bag with the evidence. “Give this to SAC Grafton, and only him.”

I watched the officer: He was readying himself to speak again. Mac caught my eye and I glared at him.

He must’ve understood my panic. “SAC Grafton is on route ETA...” Mac glanced at his wristwatch, “Approximately twenty minutes.”

He then nudged my legs to encourage me into the car then shut the door with a bang. I had the impression he wanted to leave as much as I did. He slid into the driver's seat. Another officer was standing by Mac's door. He smiled at us as Mac turned the ignition key and dropped the car into reverse. I could tell by the look on Mac's face that it took immense control to drive without exceeding the speed limit. I knew he wished to be as far from the police officer with the dainty voice, and the dumpster, as fast as humanly possible.

We maintained a closed silence until we were almost at my parents' home. I couldn't take anymore. "I was afraid I was going to be pulled into his gravitational field – I'm only little – I may never have broken free!"

Mac roared with laughter, "Yup, he could've sucked us both in, babe."

I spluttered and choked, finally catching my breathe enough to speak. "Imagine that, being trapped orbiting planet girly-man-cop for eternity."

Tears rolled down my face as pure hysterical laughter overrode the horror of the dumpster episode.

Chapter Twenty-Five

Blue Eyes Crying In The Rain

We ran across the parking lot. Water splashed up with each step soaking the legs of my jeans. It was a relief to be in the main foyer of the hospital and out of the torrential rain. I leant in towards Mac and planted a kiss on his lips. "I'm going to check on Mom, I'll meet you back in Dad's room."

"You want me to come with you?" His hand still held mine, our fingers entwined. I smiled at him. I knew his father would be with mine by now.

"Nah, go see your Dad, I'll be along in a few minutes."

"As long as you're sure."

"I am. I just need to see that she's settled." I wanted to make sure she remained doped up and semi-conscious so there was no chance of her demanding to visit Dad. He wasn't in any condition to deal with her.

Mac walked away. Holly's observations were correct: He possessed a very fine backside. While watching Mac I dragged my wet hair back into a ponytail to stop it dripping down my face. I could've stayed there until he disappeared into the elevator but the sooner I checked on Mom the sooner I could join him in Dad's room.

It didn't take me long to get up to the secure psychiatric wing. I checked in with the nurse's station then asked them to buzz me through to the actual ward.

Her room was about half way along the tunnel of doom. All the doors on this ward remained locked to keep the loonies contained. All rooms had windows from the corridor for observational purposes. I stopped at the window into Mom's room. She was sleeping. I hit the red button on the wall that unlocked the door, then the green button to keep it from locking behind me. No way was I going to be trapped in there with her. I glanced towards the door; knowing I could escape at the first sign of movement gave me comfort. My reflection in the window caused me slight distress. I decided the light was unflattering and there was no way I could look as terrible as my reflection suggested. I fought to keep the dumpster body out of my conscious thoughts. Best not to linger on the reflection, next thing you know I would've lost weight and be hiding behind my bangs as my mother so often accused. I turned my attention to Mom.

"Mama? You asleep?" She didn't answer. I took that to be a yes and breathed a sigh of relief as I watched for a second or two. She was facing away from me. There was something child-like, even innocent, in the way her long blonde hair lay over her shoulder and across the white pillow.

I hiked the covers up as much as I could and tucked them closer to her, lifting her hair out of the way and letting it fall across the pink blanket. I moved around to the other side of the bed to leave her a note on the pad on top of the bedside cabinet.

I was alarmed when I noticed her open eyes. "Mom?" I

shook her shoulder. An arm flopped over the side of the bed. “Mom!”

I hit the emergency call button three times. A crash team barreled into the room. Some doctor spoke, “How long has she been like this?”

I reacted sharply. “I don’t know. I just came in myself.”

What do I look like: A fuc’n doctor? No! I am like the anti-doctor I take people apart instead of putting them back together. Where do these thoughts come from? I only shoot people who really deserve it. Mostly.

My gun wasn’t in my hand so I didn’t shoot anyone this time.

There was a flurry of activity during which I left the room. I stood watching through the window unable to comprehend what had happened.

Time stopped.

Noise faded.

A cone of silence lowered itself over me. So thorough was the cone’s blocking ability that I could not hear the words spoken to me by the doctor. His lips moved but no sound reached my ears. With a loud crashing of internal glass all noise returned.

“Gabrielle, we were unable to resuscitate. Your mother is dead.”

I blinked. “What?”

“She’s gone.”

I looked through the window. What the hell was he talking about? She was right there. How could she be gone? I can see her.

"Gabrielle?"

She's right there! I can see her. I can see her. The window distorted, bending and blurring. My head spun. She's right there! Wake her up for God's sake! How hard can it be? She only had one vial of valium. Wake her up! Darkness fell with a thud.

Chapter Twenty-Six

Mac The Knife

"Mac, where's Ellie?" my father asked, as I settled into a chair next to him. The Colonel, aka Simon, was sleeping. Aidan stared out of the window. Some days went on forever, and this was the longest Tuesday I'd ever lived through. There was a hospital dinner tray by Simon's bed.

"Checking on Jenny," I replied. "How was the drive down?"

"Was okay. The Colonel was pleased to see me. We're planning a fishing trip once he's up and around again."

I seized the opportunity. "Why didn't you tell me you knew Simon?"

"It never came up."

"Never came up?"

My father smiled. I knew I would get no more out of him.

I looked over at Aidan.

"Aidan, you okay?" He hadn't spoken or moved his gaze from the darkening view outside.

"Yes. How long will Ellie be?"

"Not long I shouldn't think. Did you talk to Simon?"

"No. I just stared out this window watching the rain, the entire time you and Ellie were gone."

His reflection smirked.

"I see smartass is a family condition."

Aidan laughed. "Friend me on MySpace we'll go for a beer."

"You have a MySpace? Ellie reckoned you were technologically challenged and didn't much like computers."

He shrugged. "She doesn't know everything: She just thinks she does."

A young nurse appeared in the open doorway and hesitated before approaching us. I glanced at Aidan. He wasn't in any hurry to talk to the nurse. I rose to my feet and stepped into her path.

"Can I help you?"

"I hope so. I was asked to locate Mac Connelly, are you him?"

My heart stalled then jump-started. "Yes."

"Would you come with me, please?"

"Sure." I shrugged at Aidan and my Dad, and then followed the young woman from the room. She seemed nervous which made me nervous.

"Is there a problem?"

"Miss Conway is upstairs in the psychiatric wing. Doctor Dunn asked me to fetch you."

He wouldn't send for me concerning Ellie and why would he send for me regarding Mrs. Conway? It should be Aidan out here. "Did you mean to come and get Mr. Conway?"

"No, I was told Mac Connelly."

Something's up and it doesn't sound good. "Why?"

"I don't know."

"Give me a minute to tell them where I'm going." I indicated at the room with my head.

"I'll wait here?"

"Yeah, thanks."

She didn't look as though she should be out alone and certainly didn't look as though she was old enough to be wearing a nurse's uniform.

I ducked back into the room. "Hey Dad, I'm going to go find Ellie. Hold the fort." I averted my eyes. He'd know in an instant there was something up. The man knew everything.

"Sure, Mac. I'll let the Colonel know where you are when he wakes from his nap."

"Won't be long." I shot a quick look at Aidan; he was back to staring out of the window as if it held all the answers. I nodded towards him, knowing he could see me in the window. "Back soon with your sister."

"Sure, I'll be right here, with the old man."

I heard Simon reply, "Watch who you're calling old, boyo."

I followed the young nurse. She said nothing. Just as well: I wasn't in any mood to strike up idle chit-chat. My mind ran an inventory as we walked, locating things that were very important of late. The cell phone was in my pocket, my credentials in my wallet. I patted my back pocket reassuring myself of the presence of my wallet, and my gun was on my hip. I had all eventualities covered. Maybe.

The nurse stopped just outside the elevator doors and

pointed to a room down the hall.

"They're in there waiting for you."

"Thanks."

I returned the kid's smile then turned to the door. The sign said 'treatment room' which had an ominous ring to it. I knocked then opened the door. I recognized Doctor Dunn who was sitting on a stool by a gurney where Ellie lay unmoving. My heart dropped so fast I expected to fall with it.

"She'll be fine, Mac," he said standing up.

She didn't look fine. "What the hell happened?"

"She passed out."

My mind shuffled pertinent information into order. "Did she hit her head?"

"Yes, I don't believe the impact was significant to do damage."

Oh yes it could. "She has a skull fracture."

Dunn looked from me to Ellie. "That changes everything. I'll order a head CT immediately."

He slid over, grabbed the phone from the wall, and made a call. I brushed Ellie's hair off her face. "When will you learn," I whispered. "You're not ten feet tall and bullet proof."

The doctor hung up the phone.

"What happened?" I asked.

"Her mother died."

Died? People don't just die. She had a mental illness not a medical condition that could've killed her.

"Where is her body?"

"Still in her room."

"I want you to seal the room until the FBI can get here and conduct an investigation."

The doctor paled. "Do you really think that's necessary? We conduct our own investigations into patient death."

"Not this time, this time the FBI will conduct the investigation." I dragged my wallet from my pocket and showed him my credentials, "It's not only necessary, but essential." I was beginning to feel like an actual special agent. I was surprised how comfortable that felt.

He made another call.

I waited until he was done. "Can I use that phone?"

"Yes. Dial nine to get an outside line."

I scrolled through the address book on my cell phone and found Caine's number then punched it in to the phone on the wall.

It took him several rings to answer.

"It's Mac. We need you at the hospital."

"Serious?"

"Ellie's mother is dead. Ellie is unconscious: She hit her head again."

He didn't hesitate. "Where do I go?"

"Psychiatric wing."

I could hear traffic and an ambulance siren while I waited for him to speak.

"I have arranged guards for her Dad – military police – I don't know who else to trust," Caine said.

"Jesus! You can do that?"

"I know people. Simon is military, it's no big thing; nor is it too much to ask considering all he's done for this country."

"How quickly can you be here?"

"I'm almost there now."

I hung up and sat with Ellie while we waited for a call back about the CT and for Caine. A nurse came in and told me there was a call for Ellie. She transferred it to the phone in the room.

"It's Mac, how can I help?"

"Mac? Is Ellie okay?" It was Aidan.

"She banged her head." I didn't want to give him time to ask questions, "Hey, Aidan, has anyone shown up in the room?"

"Not in it, no, but we have two military cops on the door; they arrived a few minutes ago."

"Okay."

"What's going on?"

"Has to do with the sonofabitch killer, Aidan. Ellie and I will be back as soon as we can."

I wanted out of this conversation before he asked anything else. I said 'bye' and hung up. I looked at Ellie. There were things I needed to do; I removed her holster and her badge then went through her pockets and took the mascara, her wallet and her cell phone. All the small things fitted into my pockets, which left me with the gun and holster. There was nothing else for it, I would have to wear it.

There was a knock on the door. The doctor opened it.

He spoke then turned to me.

"They'll take her down to radiology now. Do you want to go to?"

"Yes," I replied. Stupid question. As I left the room behind them I spotted Caine striding towards us.

He made eye contact with me. "Stay with her."

"I intend to."

"Where is the body?"

I pointed to Doctor Dunn, "He can show you."

Caine nodded. "Keep me informed."

His eyes rested on Ellie as the gurney passed him heading for the elevator. Again I saw the expression my father described as fatherly interest. Was that enough to make him kill? I knew he hadn't killed Ellie's mother, and why would he ask for guards for her Dad if he were the killer? Is it possible I was wrong about Caine or is that what he wants me to think? But was everyone wrong about Aidan?

Once again, I had to hurry to keep up with a gurney carrying Ellie in a hospital. I hated that she was hurt. The elevator halted at the first floor. Ellie mumbled something. I gave her hand a reassuring squeeze.

"Its okay, babe." My reply was automatic, just so she knew I was there.

We hurried through the doors to the radiology suite. Ellie was taken straight in for the head CT. I paced the floor outside pausing only to answer more stupid and some not-so-stupid questions from helpful staff. No, I don't want coffee. Yes, I know guns aren't permitted inside the hospital. No, I still don't want coffee. Her last hospitalization was at Stonewall Jackson hospital for a skull fracture, concussion, and broken arm. Why was Ellie discharged against medical advice from Stonewall Jackson hospital? Because some freak left a body in her room and compromised her security. No coffee thanks! My mind lingered over thoughts of Ellie. Each thought caused a razor-sharp pain to pierce my heart. I don't want coffee. I want her to be well.

I saw the double doors to the CT suite open and breathed a sigh of relief as the gurney bearing Ellie trundled over to me. She turned her head towards me and smiled. Thank you, God.

"Hey, how's the head?"

"It's okay."

The radiologist spoke, "Nothing out of the ordinary is going on in that skull of hers."

"Good!"

"Nothing more than a moderate concussion, anyway. The fracture is healing."

"Thank you."

"You're welcome. She needs monitoring for twenty-four to thirty-six hours. I made a call and CCU is prepared to take her. She'll be in the same room as her Dad."

"Thank you again."

"No problem."

Ellie struggled to sit up.

"Stay put." I pressed her shoulders back down.

"I don't want to lay here, I feel stupid." She grimaced

at me.

"I don't care what you want, do as you're told."

Ellie narrowed her eyes and glared. "I'm getting up!"

"The hell you are!"

Someone cleared their throat causing us both to look left. "I have a solution," said the radiologist, "A wheelchair."

I looked at Ellie; she was determined to be contrary over this, which I took as a good sign. She really was okay. "That may work if Miss Contrary can control herself for five minutes."

"I'm not contrary!"

"The hell you aren't!"

"Wheelchair?" The radiologist offered again.

Ellie screwed up her nose.

"Your choice Ellie: A wheelchair, or the gurney?" I was trying to keep my voice even and reasonable. She sure appeared okay but I had previous experience with a concussed Ellie. What I wanted to prevent, more than anything, was a repeat of the last time, which scared the hell out of me.

"Wheelchair," she said with annoyance. I helped her sit up.

"Just sit there for a minute to get your balance before you try standing." A wheelchair miraculously appeared beside me.

The nurse put a foot at right angles to Ellie's feet to stop her slipping, turned her to sit in the chair then lowered the foot rests.

She draped a blanket over Ellie's legs. "CCU has been notified; a bed has been prepared in your father's room." She stepped behind the wheelchair and kicked off the brakes. "I'll take you up there."

"That's lucky," Ellie said. "Because Captain Compass would probably get us lost."

And with that, I knew without a doubt that Ellie was just fine. The nurse giggled quietly.

Outside the elevator doors in the foyer to the Coronary Care Unit, I tapped the nurse's shoulder and indicated for her to stop. Ellie gave me a questioning look as I crouched in front of her, steadying myself by resting my hands on her blanketed knees.

"Before we go in, do you remember what happened?"

Her eyes searched mine. She chewed her lip but said nothing.

"Ellie, do you remember?"

Her voice shook as she told me. "I went to check on Mom."

"What happened then?" I had doubts as to whether I should tell her or not but I knew Aidan was going to ask.

"I went into her room and the next thing I remember is seeing a radiologist and you."

I steeled myself and spoke the words as kindly as I could. "Your mother died. Caine is there now trying to figure out what happened."

Ellie's eyes widened, making her appear very alabaster-doll-like. "Died?"

I nodded.

"People don't die from bipolar disorder."

"I know; that's why Caine is there."

Her eyes roamed, confusion settled upon her face. "Can we go to the museum yet?"

Something rose up and tried to choke me. I struggled to keep my voice calm, "Not yet, but soon." First, I need to find whoever put you through this and dissect his abdomen with a chainsaw; then we can go to the museum.

"She's really dead?"

"Yes."

I observed an eerie smile creep across her face. "Ding dong, the bitch is dead."

Oh Jesus! "Ellie you need to implement your social filter before you see your Dad and Aidan."

Her smile changed from creepy to real, "Its okay, Mac, I won't say that in front of them, no matter how true it is."

"Just checking."

"I know. I'm okay Mac. I am okay." Her smile sure seemed convincing but if I had a penny for every time I had heard her say that over the last week or so I'd be a wealthy man.

I looked up at the nurse. "Can I use my cell phone out here?"

She nodded. I made a quick call to Caine and suggested we say nothing of Jenny's death until after Simon's operation in the morning.

Chapter Twenty-Seven

In My Father's Eyes

The room hummed with questions when we arrived. As promised there was a bed for me next to Dad's.

"Let's get Ellie settled, and then I shall explain," Mac said.

The nurse tried to help me stand. I snapped, "I can do it."

"I need to help you," she replied.

"I can do it!" I stood up by myself.

"Just let the nurse do her job," Mac said.

"Back off," I said, hoping to catch both Mac and the nurse with one comment. "I don't need help."

The nurse left as soon as I climbed up onto the bed. I refused Mac's fussing. I'm okay.

"What happened?" Dad asked.

"Ellie passed out and hit her head."

Ah, a half-truth from Mac.

"Ellie? You all right?" Dad turned to face me. He had limited head movement due to the oxygen tubing.

"Yeah, Dad, I'm fine, this is a precaution because of the skull fracture." I indicated the bed. "I'm really okay."

He smiled. "You need to slow down a bit, take it easy. Let Caine carry some weight."

"Advice heeded."

I watched Aidan. He'd said nothing. I could tell he was

listening even though he stared into the dark beyond the rain-lashed windowpane.

Mac sat on the end of my bed.

"Daddy, I have to ask; this is bugging the hell out of me ..."

I knew what I wanted to ask but for a split second I held my breath. I wondered what was really going to pop out of my mouth and hoped it wouldn't involve any 'ding dong the bitch is dead' type phrases.

"What?"

Concentrate, Ellie!

"Why does Bob call you Colonel? There's no such rank in the Navy." I made it: A simple reasonable question with no ding-dongs.

Dad smiled a little. His breathing seemed better than last I saw him, "It's a long story."

"We have time," I replied. I thought if Dad told me a story I'd be able to stop thinking about Mom and the Unsub and the mess we were in.

Mac's Dad coughed, "You want me to tell it, Colonel?"

"Don't make me sound too bad here, Tank."

"That's a big ask," Tank replied.

"Your turn will come."

I watched Bob stretch his legs out in front of him. He assumed a story-telling pose, I had a feeling we were going to learn some entertaining family history of ill-spent youth.

"Back when we were younger and more rambunctious, we both received a call from Blake, a buddy of ours, he wanted us to go on down to his place for a little get-together."

"How young?" I asked.

Bob looked at Dad. "What were we Colonel: Twenty-five or twenty-six?"

"Yeah, about that."

"We both agreed it was a great idea so off we went; turned out to be quite an adventure. We had a couple of bottles of Jim with us and we had one hell of a night. Your daddy was so toasted he was blind."

Dad coughed, "I don't believe you were far behind."

Bob laughed and nodded. "We were messy. At any rate, the next morning I woke to the sound of Simon hammering on the door, seems that the doorknob had come off and the rod had fallen out ... we were trapped and he didn't look good. All our hammering was to no avail. Blake was dead to the world somewhere. Simon was down to the wire. His choices were limited, so he opened the window; we were two stories above ground so I knew there was no way he was climbing out of the window in his condition. He knew that too and leant out and puked pure bourbon onto the ground below."

We were all laughing.

"Some hours later, Blake realized we were trapped and fixed the door. We'd both gone back to sleep before that happened. We cooked breakfast and started to clean up the hellish-awful mess we'd all made the night before. Blake went on out to the yard, he came running back in hollering that someone had killed all his chickens. We scooted out to investigate. About as quick as two severe hangovers would let us. We found seven dead chickens. Turned out that the chickens had eaten Simon's vomit!"

He paused, winked, and then said, "No body kills chickens like the Colonel."

I moaned, "Oh that's gross. I'll never eat chicken again."

Bob was laughing. "First time I'd ever seen chickens marinated from the inside out."

"So that's how you got your name?" Aidan was grinning as well.

"Yes," Dad replied smiling, "We were young once you know."

I looked at Bob. "So what's your story?"

"You trust me to tell this, Colonel?"

"Go ahead. I'm right here to put the kids straight if you paint yourself too pretty."

"We have this buddy GW, his family has money, but he's a good guy. This happened maybe a year after the chicken killing. We knew GW was going to be in Washington on business, there'd been a rumor suggesting as much. The Colonel here called him up and said we were thinking of going fishing, did he want to tag along. GW was all for it and said to come and meet him, we'd have a few drinks then head out early the next morning. Easy we figured. Simon was doing a stint at the Pentagon and I was in Fairfax County. In we went to meet GW in the hotel bar. He was running late so we had a few drinks."

Dad coughed and gave Bob a prod.

"We had a few shooters and a few more shooters and I had a few more than the Colonel."

"That's better," he commented.

"About an hour and a half later we called GW's room, he said he was sorry and we should go on up. He didn't just have a room he had a whole suite, was very nice. He told us to make ourselves at home, have a drink and so forth while he took a shower, and then we'd go to some bar he liked. I found this golf club. GW must've been getting in some putting practice."

Dad interrupted, "I think I need to explain this bit." He struggled somewhat for breath but carried on, "Bob here picked up the putter, wielding it like a baseball bat and took a swing at the golf ball, only he missed the ball and let the club go. It sailed through the air and smacked straight into this big fish tank on the other side of the room. There was water everywhere, with poor tropical fish flapping on the carpet amidst the broken glass. GW came running wrapping a towel about himself. He stopped in his tracks when he saw Bob's face and the mess and burst out laughing."

"He was a good sport," Bob said and took over the story telling, "Anyway he got dressed super-fast, hid the golf club and ball, then told the hotel staff that the fish tank must've had a crack in it. The three of us hightailed it out of the hotel and ended up in GW's favorite bar, still laughing."

"I think I'd better tell the rest seeing you have little memory of the following events." Dad said, with a smile.

"By this stage of the evening Bob was smashed, in fact he was more smashed than that fish tank. He wandered out onto the street and was proceeding to water the sidewalk when a cop car happened along. We realized he was missing only to find him just as the cops detained him for being drunk in public. We did the decent thing and followed along, thinking we could bail him out but the cops decided to leave his sorry ass in the drunk tank overnight."

I was beginning to see a lot of tanks in this story.

Dad carried on, "We waited, as good friends would. We had an okay time; the cops let us use their dartboard and even gave us coffee and donuts. Anyway we'd been hanging around waiting for about two hours when this cop come up to us and says we should get our buddy and take him home he's causing too much trouble and they didn't want to have to charge him with assault. He'd started three fights in the tank. On our way home, I came up with an acronym TANK, The-Asshole-Never-Knew. Bob had no idea he'd started fights or had been in the tank. He was so drunk he couldn't remember a damn thing after arriving at the bar."

"Tank is an acronym?" I asked. "Anyone hearing the names 'Tank' and 'Colonel' would assume a military connection, as we did."

Dad roared with laughter which culminated in a near-death coughing fit.

Simon said, "We were young once."

Once Dad settled and stopped coughing I directed another question to him, "Who is GW?"

"He's a buddy of ours."

"He's not that GW is he?" My eyes shifted from Dad to Bob and back.

They both laughed.

The door opened and Caine stepped in, I saw him and held up my hand, "One sec, family business." I turned back to our fathers, "Is he that GW?"

Bob bellowed with laughter, "We can neither confirm nor deny."

Dad said, "We're not at liberty to say."

I grinned at them both then spoke to Caine, "Sorry, we've been hearing some old stories."

"Are you well enough to help me out for a few minutes?"

"Yes."

"Good. Mac, can you give us a hand too, please?"

"Sure." Mac smiled at Aidan. "See what else you can get out of these two, Aidan, I suspect there are many, many stories we'd be interested in."

Aidan replied, "I'll do my best."

"We shall return."

"As for you two," I directed myself to the fathers. "You do know I expect a full explanation on this GW thing."

Chapter Twenty-Eight
Don't Take Your Guns To Town

"Ellie should have a wheelchair," Mac said as we stepped into the corridor behind Caine.

"No!" I said. "I'm perfectly capably of walking. You can knock off that invalid shit."

Caine stopped, turned and looked at me with discerning eyes. "Do you need a wheelchair?"

"No!"

He looked a Mac. "You heard her."

We followed Caine through the hospital corridors which appeared to be a never-ending maze that twisted and turned. I wished the Lone Ranger would appear and save the day. Short of that, I hoped there would be some answers waiting for us when we arrived at where ever we were going.

Caine stopped outside a solid wooden door. We were on the management floor of the hospital. He flung open the door and beckoned us in. At a large table in the center of the room sat three agents I knew well. They all looked up and nodded. At the far end of the table sat another person known to me, but not expected at this gathering.

"Ellie, how are you feeling?" she asked, indicating we should all sit.

"All right, thank you, Executive Assistant Director Owen."

I was impressed with my ability to say her title and not muck it up. With luck, I covered my surprise at seeing her with my smooth move into introduction phase.

"This is Cormac Connelly. Mac, Executive Assistant Director Owen, of the Criminal Investigation Division." Mac stepped forward and shook her beautiful, manicured hand. As always Executive Assistant Director Owen was picture perfect, making me feel like I had crawled backwards through a thorn bush before landing on my ass in dog poop. She smiled charmingly at us both.

"No doubt you are wondering why I am here. When Special Agent in Charge Grafton told me an agent of ours was involved in the Son of Shakespeare case, we made a decision to safeguard the relationships inside this division and prevent any conflict of interest clouding the case."

"You're running this?" I blinked, trying not to appear stunned. To my knowledge, the Executive Assistant Director never became involved in specific cases. What if she chipped a nail? What if a strand of hair broke free and got in her eye? I bit my tongue so hard at that point: An image of Owen dragging her beautiful sleek red hair back into an unruly ponytail while running down an alleyway leapt to the forefront of my warped mind. As if she could run in those heels! She was still talking. I dragged my focus away from the amusing mind scene and back to her.

"I conducted all internal inquiries, oversaw the polygraphs and DNA testing of the entire criminal investigation division."

Damn that was one hell of a task. That meant Caine was clear. Whew!

"Why are you here?" By the glare Caine gave me, I realized I sounded snappish, which was unintentional; however, she didn't seem to notice.

"The next phase of this case must run without a hitch and without any prejudice on the part of the Division or we'll destroy any chance of convicting this felon."

It sounded like she knew whom it was. "You have information on an identity?"

"I have information that brings us closer to discovery."

A photograph passed down the table to me. The dumpster body. It was a woman but still I didn't see how this brought us closer to anything, except, to my knowledge he hadn't killed any other women. The photograph sent no rushed messages to my mind except total revulsion from standing in this woman's guts.

"Do you recognize this person?"

I wanted to shake my head but didn't, for fear of leaving a trail of brains across the wall behind me, convincing everyone else I was okay was a lot easier than actually being okay. "No."

She slid another photograph over, "How about this person?"

I sank back into the chair holding the photograph in my hand. I found myself staring at a familiar face. Even though I hadn't seen her in over five years, I recognized my best friend from High School. My eyes went back to the first picture.

"Karen Brown," I replied, and compared the pictures. It was the same person. The realization that I had stood in Karen's guts didn't sit well in mine. My stomach threatened to mutiny at any second. Caine pressed a glass of water into my left hand.

"Sip it," he cautioned.

Owen spoke, "She married several years ago, and became Karen Midlow. She was an advertising executive."

"And?" I placed the photograph on the table and leaned back in the chair, sipping at the cool water.

"Her body was covered in cat hair fibers. They're an exact match for your brother's cat. Some of the hairs contained skin tags, we have DNA and, as with all the bodies, the cat DNA is a match for Aidan's cat."

I felt my whole body stiffen. Cat DNA, Jesus! No way was this going to land on Aidan. I guessed they couldn't arrest a cat on suspicion of murder. I studied her face for a few minutes. This cannot be happening!

"Get Aidan in here. There is no way in hell he is the Son of Shakespeare."

Mac's hand was on my arm, a gentle pressure that cautioned me to be still.

Caine slid into the chair on my right and spoke, "Who else knew about the connection between you and Karen?"

"I don't know, but Aidan didn't kill anyone."

"Where's the video footage from the psych floor?" Mac asked, "Was there anything useful on that?"

I watched Caine.

"Aidan was there. He visited his mother ..."

I clenched my teeth and hissed, "He did not kill her!"

"I know," he replied, his gruff voice calm. "He never went in the room. He watched her from the window accompanied by a member of the nursing staff. Ten minutes after he left someone else entered the room, dressed as staff and unchallenged. We showed the picture to all staff and doctors on that floor; he was not recognized."

"Show me," I demanded.

Owen passed me a picture. Mac and I scrutinized it. I had no idea who it was.

"I need a private word with Ellie," Mac announced taking my hand.

Caine and Owen both nodded in agreement.

Lee, who had said nothing since we'd arrived spoke, "There's a small room through that door on your right, it's private."

"Thanks, Lee." Mac stood and pulled my chair out for me.

We left the quiet table for the sanctuary of the other room. "Do you believe this?" My head was spinning at the mere thought of them considering my brother as a serious suspect.

Mac paced several feet then came back. "What will happen if we hand Caine the GPS?"

"I've withheld information; I could lose my job and be charged."

"Can we explain to Owen that as far as we were concerned Caine could have been a suspect, which is why we said nothing?"

This is so not a good situation. "Might have to try. I need someone to go to Aidan and search him and everything he has with him, he must have a GPS tracker on him somewhere, too."

I was sure he didn't dump Karen's body but he said he'd dropped off clothing. Could someone have followed him? Did the same person track us to our mother's room and wait until Aidan visited before killing her?

"Well, if we come clean now, we can have him brought here."

"They won't let us be in on the interview."

"They tape everything though, huh? We can watch from in here if they set up a closed circuit TV."

"Might be a big ask considering I've been sitting on evidence for a few days."

Mac treated me to an evil grin. "We can play the concussion card if we have to. You have a skull fracture, and are recovering from an earlier concussion; even better you were drugged with ketamine – you have enough medical testimony alone to more than compensate for the 'forgetting' to tell Caine about the GPS ... and I'm sure he'd go for the video thing."

"It's not going to be his decision, its Owen's. Caine has a conflict of interest in this case. There is a good chance she won't allow him in on the interview."

I watched Mac assimilate the information. His brow creased, he pushed his hair back off his face, running his hands through it. Somewhere inside me a light went on, a warm glow spread upward carrying with it the strength Mac possessed and Waylon Jennings singing 'Luckenbach Texas'. Oh great, now I hear country songs!

For a second I thought Mac heard it too.

He wrapped his arms around me and whispered into my hair, "I vote we come clean about the GPS now and tell them we think Aidan was bugged as well. Then without even pausing, run the taped interview up the flag pole."

"Deal." I hugged him hard noticing he was wearing two holsters. So that's where my gun went. "Hey ... where is the bug?"

"In my pocket."

"Thank you."

"You're welcome," he said, his breath ruffled my hair. "When this is over, I want to take you away."

"I'd love that."

"Ready?"

"Yeah." Most of me wanted to go away now, right now. The two of us just walk out and never come back. Crazy talk, as if I could leave Aidan to the vultures. Fuc'n cat DNA.

"One sec ... do they have enough to arrest, or hold, Aidan right now?"

"Not as far as I know; they have circumstantial evidence at best, they can ask that he help them with the inquiry but he doesn't have to agree to an interview; in this instance it would be best if he did."

"You're sure?"

“No, I’m not. I guess they could arrest his mean-assed cat.” The thought of that damn cat in handcuffs floated my boat. I don’t recall ever disliking an animal as much as that one.

“Let’s do it.”

I steeled myself against the coming storm. We had a fight on our hands.

A grayish haze settled inside my head, blurring details and thoughts into blobby masses. Mac remained beside me when we went back to the torture chamber, presided over by the head witch hunter, Dana Owen. I had a feeling that Owen wanted everything neat and tidy and packed away in a little box. This isn’t a fold-it-away-neatly type of case!

In that regard, it mimicked the mess inside my own head.

Chapter Twenty-Nine

Mystery Train

Owen's eyes settled on mine from across the table; she appeared contemplative, which I hoped was a good thing for us. Her elbows rested on the table as she tapped her long French-manicured nails together, click, click. I bet she clicks pens too. It grated on my raw nerves. With much resolve I told myself that snapping at her to 'stop' would not help our cause.

"All right. But I don't want Caine, you or Mac present during the interview."

My eyes closed as I offered a silent prayer of thanks before speaking, "Thank you ma'am. Can Lee set up a video link so we can hear and see what's happening?"

"Yes."

Why is she being so nice? Who cares why as long as she is, that's what matters. And at least the infernal clicking has stopped. I watched Lee leave the table and take a small case into the other room.

I weighed up the risk of telling her how to do her job and my need for this to be thorough. Screw it; this is my brother's life we're all playing with. I reminded her of the discussion we had before she agreed to the interview. "Everything Aidan is carrying needs to be closely inspected; this guy is good. If he can devise a way of hiding a GPS in my mascara there's no telling what else he could come up with."

"Understood, Ellie."

I let my head rest in my hands, hoping to ease the throbbing.

Mac whispered in my ear, "You okay?"

Owen spoke again, "If you need to lie down, Ellie, I think we will all understand."

Why is she being so nice? It's not right.

"Mac ..." I think that was audible.

"What do you need?"

I need this to go away. I need everything to stop. I need Aidan not to be a suspect. I need coffee. I need quiet. Uh oh! My hand reached out and shoved Mac away. I turned sideways in the chair trying to quell rising nausea. No amount of swallowing was going to help. A white container appeared, not a moment too soon, held in Mac's hands.

Way to be professional, Ellie.

"You done?" he asked and handed me a tissue.

"Much better thanks."

"You should be in bed. This is a bad idea."

I lifted my head to see him: He was pale and looked unwell. I guessed I didn't look too flash myself. My head was swimming.

"I'm okay, carry on."

Owen was talking on the phone; a few minutes later she hung up. "I doubt you'll agree to go to your room. I have asked for a doctor to join us for the duration of the interview."

"That's not necessary." And some kind of violation of FBI interview practice, to bring a civilian in during an interview. We don't do that kind of thing!

"Yes it is, and he is not a civilian."

I never said that aloud; damn woman is in my head!

"You know Special Agent Kurt Henderson?"

I knew Kurt, last time I saw him was outside the Interscape Café with a woman who had fallen.

Mac gave me a questioning look and asked, "Kurt?"

"He was at the Interscape. But I didn't know he was a doc."

"Well, he is," Owen replied. "And he's downstairs now, reading your file."

Okay, fine, whatever.

"He'll join us in a few minutes. Sam is bringing Aidan up in ten minutes. That should give us plenty of time to get you all settled in the other room."

Mac held out his hand, helping me stand. "We're going in now, there's a sofa Ellie can rest on."

Lee was still working in the room. I lay on the sofa. It was cooler and quieter in there.

Mac and Lee chatted a bit, and then Mac helped him get the equipment organized.

My mind dredged through silt, mud and a dreadful panicky feeling. "Who said, for every human problem, there is a neat, simple solution and it is always wrong?"

"H L Mencken," Lee said. "I thought she wanted this folded away a little too quickly, myself. I'll be in there, Ellie. There'll be zero room for her to railroad your brother into a bunch of murder charges."

My fear was real. Who ever was responsible will be facing the death penalty. Killing federal agents in the State of Virginia was not a smart move. There would be no room for plea-bargaining, not with so many deaths attributed to the person and four federal agents. I didn't want that to be my brother's fate because someone had an axe to grind. "He doesn't know Mom's dead."

"I'll tell Owen. We'll keep away from that as much as we can. I doubt it will be necessary to bring up your Mom's death." He shut his case. "We can re-interview should we need to."

"Done?" Mac asked straightening up.

"Yep," Lee replied. They shook hands.

I let my eyes close as the room fell quiet.

When I next managed to break free from the fog Kurt was sitting on the floor by me.

"Hi."

Simple greeting but the response eluded me as I concentrated on roping in my wandering mind. It just needs to learn not to go off alone. Not until it proves it can take care of itself.

"Ellie? Did you hear me?" He shone a light into my eyes.

Fantastic! Just what I need, torture! I thought the torture chamber was in the other room. Dah!

"Kurt, quit with the light."

He smiled. "Thanks for joining us." He looked different wearing a white lab coat with a stethoscope around his neck. Guess he borrowed it from someone.

"Is it Halloween already?" I tweaked his stethoscope. "Nice touch, Doc." I quelled the urge to call him Hawkeye and stopped the theme from MASH before the never-ending repeat cycle started in my mind.

I took a few moments to focus. Caine was sitting on a chair not far from the sofa. I had the feeling that if I wasn't so dumb-assed and stubborn, I'd be doing better. It wouldn't have killed me to admit to being injured and take the wheelchair offer. I seem to take stubborn to new and dizzying heights every day.

"What have I missed?"

"Aidan is in there. They're searching him now," he replied not shifting his gaze from the TV screen.

"Is he doing okay?"

"He seems fine, cooperative, he said a few minutes ago that he just wanted to help anyway he could."

"Have they asked him anything yet?"

"No." Caine held his hand up indicating I should shush for a bit. Then leaned forward and turned the sound up. "They found a device." He squinted at the screen then at me. "Inside his cell phone. You were right."

I couldn't help the smile that spread across my face, and said a quiet prayer of thanks to whomsoever it was that looked after us. We all watched as Lee took the device and settled in front of a laptop. A few minutes later, he announced to the room that this new device had also been destined for destruction.

"So now what?" Mac asked.

“Question time. Did you see the look on Owen’s face?”

Mac nodded.

“She’s not a happy camper,” Caine replied, he sounded worried.

“Has anyone bothered to try and find the man who entered Mom’s room?” I couldn’t keep the bitchy tone from my voice.

“We’ve had no luck.”

My mind danced over what I thought was a possibility and words fell from my mouth, “The lack of human trace evidence at the scene and the bodies ... you suggested a protective suit of some kind. Could this person be a crime scene investigator or someone from the Laboratory Division?”

“I think that’s quite possible. But Owen in there,” he said and indicated towards the TV with a sharp nod, “is convinced it’s someone close to you.”

“Well, it’s someone who knew I knew Karen; how far back did you go with acquaintances?”

“College. She pulled the plug on that.” Caine glowered at the screen and growled, “Preconceived ideas. The woman has no damn clue what she’s doing!”

No wonder she was being so nice. I felt as though she was gunning for my brother as the Son of Shakespeare killer. I blinked twice and witnessed my career go up in smoke.

Mac’s hand rested on my arm. I watched his fingers tracing the cast. “In Ellie’s High School yearbook I found a comment by someone; this is a long shot but we have nothing to lose ... This kid wrote, 'one day you'll notice me'."

"Ellie, you have anything to add?"

"Nope, I hardly remember him, his name was Tommy." Something else bugged me. "The DNA sample from under my nails ... where the hell is it?"

Caine replied, "Quantico."

"Owen said she'd run our entire division against that sample ... and got nothing. Did she run mine?"

"Yes."

"Okay, well that should prove without a doubt that my assailant was not a blood relative of mine, so why is she still gunning for Aidan?" A moment of horrendous doubt froze my insides. "It did show no link, didn't it?"

"Yes, Ellie, whoever attacked you was not a relative."

Caine turned and looked at me, his eyes gave nothing away. "He's used so many people in his deception that we can't be sure the assailant who cut your throat was the killer at all."

The television screen grabbed our attention as Aidan spoke. "I have been spending a lot of time out in Mauryville over the last three months, which is why the cat is in the cattery."

"Why have you been in Mauryville?" Owen asked, as she leaned back in her chair.

"Working on a project with Holly Edwards."

"What project?"

"How is this relevant?"

I groaned and whispered, "Just answer her stupid

question."

"What project?" Owens voice hardened a little.

Aidan replied, "A book ... we've been putting together a book; it will make its way to shelves in Borders and Barnes and Noble next week. The launch is in Mauryville on this coming Saturday."

Oh, could that be the Holly's secret? Damn!

"Holly said something odd when I talked to her last, she had a secret ... I want to know what that book is about and why neither of them mentioned it to me. Is it a coincidence that the launch of this literary wonder, is on the same day as the dance at Taylor's barn?"

I didn't have to wait long for some answers. Aidan spoke again. "If you go back to my Dad's room, there is a small black plastic bag in his bedside cabinet. It's an advance copy of the book."

Owen made a phone call, we couldn't hear what she was saying, but it seemed reasonable she would be having someone go for the book.

She finished the call and turned back to Aidan, "Who else can verify your whereabouts over the last ten days?"

"The local police ... Mr. Parker who owns the apiary ... most of the townsfolk. We've all been involved in this project. We discussed postponing due to the current problems but after Ellie's house was wrecked it was decided to continue. We all thought that she and Mac could do with some cheering up."

Owen pursed her glossed-lips. "How nice of you all. Ellie is lucky to live in such a close community." Insincerity oozed from every pore.

The door opened, an agent entered carrying a black plastic bag which he handed to Owen. I was dying of curiosity, desperate to see the contents. Watching her open the bag and remove the book seemed to stall time. Even then, none of us could see any detail. With bated breath, I waited while she flipped through it. How dare she get to see our surprise before us?

Mac's hand tightened over mine as she read the front cover aloud, "'Eternity's Whisper, a collection of poetry by Cormac Connelly and Gabrielle Conway.'"

My stomach churned in response to what they'd done, a book of our poems. That's not anything I ever would have guessed. They were private. They belonged to Mac and me and were never intended for the public.

"Did Special Agent Conway give her permission for you to use her work?"

"No."

"Did Cormac Connelly give his permission for you to use his work?"

"No."

"How did you get the poems?"

"I copied a poem Ellie had on the wall of her office that Mac had written for her; I borrowed a disk she had containing over two-hundred poems and Holly copied it."

"You stole a disk from your sister." Owen's nails clicked together. "When was this?"

Aidan replied, "Three months ago. I took the disk, had it copied then returned it. We went through the poetry and chose pieces that reflected how their relationship had grown. I borrowed another disk about six weeks ago, with some of their newer work on it. We copied that too, I returned it."

All I wanted to do was get my hands on that book. Mac stood up. He paced a few feet. There wasn't enough room for his customary pacing. I watched him and waited for whatever epiphany would emerge.

"Book," he said almost to himself and came to a stop.

Caine looked up.

"Book," Mac said with more conviction.

"What book? That one?" Caine asked.

"No. Ellie's yearbook from high school."

Caine twitched. "We seem to have taken a quantum leap here. Care to explain?"

"In her year book was a comment, 'One day you will notice.' It was signed Tommy."

"You mentioned it about ten minutes ago; where are you going with this?"

"The Unsub may be someone who knew Ellie from High School."

Caine pressed his fingertips together, his eyes narrowed, his lip twitched as he looked over at me. "Tommy who?"

"Vander something, I think. It was a long time ago. He didn't make an impression then; how the hell am I supposed to remember him now?" I just hoped we weren't grasping for straws.

"Vanderguard," Mac replied. "I looked him up in the

year book."

Kurt tapped something into a laptop resting on his knee. "No record of anyone named Vanderguard working for the Bureau."

Caine reached for a phone book sitting on the floor by his chair, he flipped through pages. "There are nine listings. Any clue on his parents names?"

"No."

"Kurt, see what else you can find." Caine was thinking. It appeared to be painful.

Kurt obliged. "I've run that name through our complete database, we have nada. No civilian ever attached to the Bureau has gone by the name Vanderguard, nor has there been any agent by that name. But I did find three generations of Vanderguard who were all police officers in Richmond City and all highly decorated; damn, he's from one hell of an impressive family."

"An impressive family can lead to impressive psychological problems. Them there are big shoes to fill." Caine picked up his phone and began making calls, He moved as far from our position as he could while Kurt carried on searching for references to Vanderguard.

"This name isn't getting me anything recent, he appears to have dropped out of sight after leaving College."

"Social security number?" Caine muttered while he waited for someone to answer the phone on his fifth call.

"I'm running a search through the Department of Motor Vehicles, if he held a driver's license I may be able to get his social security number from that."

I leaned back into the sofa. The interview hadn't progressed much. Caine yakked incessantly on the phone. Kurt's fingers tapped against the case of his laptop as he waited. Mac plonked himself next to me.

He whispered in my ear, "I think he's the guy."

"I hope he's the guy, otherwise Owen the Superbitch will do her best to get Aidan charged." For the first time since the mess began, I started to feel like we were close to getting this sonofabitch.

Caine held the phone to his shoulder. "Got his grandmother on the line."

Kurt said, "I got something, his social security number is registered to a Charles Boyd. He changed his name." I sat up straighter and listened. "I'm running the new name through our database."

Caine disconnected the call. "He changed his name a year after leaving college. Grandma says he took a scientific research position." He twitched. "Out in Quantico."

"I got him!" Kurt announced. There was a definite smile to his voice, "He went from lab research to crime scene investigation and specialized in serology; so far he's had an undistinguished career although has had several promotions. He did six months in the technology division."

My heart caught in my throat. "Where is he assigned?"

"He's on active duty, working the Son of Shakespeare case."

"Jesus!" Caine bellowed. He snatched up his phone and made another call. "Find out where Charles Boyd is right now. He's a crime scene investigator for the Bureau. Have him bought to me, now."

Caine made another call. I listened to his controlled voice.

"It's Grafton. All evidence from the Son of Shakespeare case is to be re-tested by an independent lab. I'll have the paperwork for you by morning. I want everyone working on any forensics and crime scene investigation from that case to be stood down, pending a full division inquiry."

On his next breath he said, "Provide me with a list of everyone who has handled any evidence. I want to see the chain of custody A-sap."

Curiosity chewed away at me. "Hey, Kurt, can you pull up a pic of this guy?"

"Sure." He pulled up his identity picture and turned the laptop to face us.

If I hadn't seen the picture of the creep who went into my mother's room, I wouldn't have recognized him. But I had and it was him.

"He's the guy in the cam pic from Mom's room."

Mac chewed his lip. "In the year book he was dark haired and wore thick glasses. Looks like Vanderguard reinvented himself as well as changing his name."

I looked at the picture of a blond male, no glasses and not hideous looking. Even knowing what he looked like I couldn't recall seeing him anywhere except on the hospital security cameras.

"How tall is he?" Mac asked.

"Six feet two, medium build with blue eyes, according

to this."

Caine made yet another call. "We have a lead on a possible suspect."

I watched the television screen and saw Owen talking on her phone. It took me a few minutes to realize Caine had called her. If she kept frowning like that, she'd need some serious Botox.

She put the phone on the desk and I waited for her to tell Aidan he could go. She didn't, she told him she had a few more questions.

"Where were you when your mother was killed?"

Aidan stuttered, "Wh-wh-what are you talking about?"

You evil troll-bitch from hell! That was unnecessary, he doesn't know yet. I felt a sharp pain as though something jabbed my head.

I scrambled to my feet and flung open the door.

Words flew across the room at Owen, "Fuck you and the horse you rode in on!"

I strode across the floor area between us, stopping twelve inches from her face.

"Special Agent Conway!"

"What?" I snarled.

Her cultured, smooth voice came back at me. "I would hate to see your record marred by an outburst like that."

Did nothing ruffle her perfectly-groomed feathers? Lee stood and made his way to Aidan.

"Not as much as I hate to see an investigation warped to fit your own preconceived ideas." Troll-bitch from hell.

"What are you talking about?" Her hand flapped sideways.

From the corner of my eye I saw Kurt closing in on me. I flashed him a warning glance. He stopped.

"We have a legitimate suspect, Aidan is not him."

"That maybe so, but I haven't finished speaking with your brother."

"Oh, yes, you have. You want to talk to him again, go through his lawyer."

I could see Aidan. He looked stunned, as if someone had smacked him with a sledgehammer.

"You had no right to mention our mother. No fucking right!"

Kurt's hand landed on my arm. I ignored him and looked at Lee. "Get him out of here!"

She had no right!

Owen spoke, "Lee, you'll do no such thing. I am not done."

I glared at her and hissed, "You are done. Aidan is going back to our father's room. You can sit here and wait for the real suspect to be bought in."

Lee motioned Aidan to his feet. "Sorry, ma'am, but unless you are prepared to charge Aidan he can walk when ever he feels like it. He is under no obligation to answer any questions."

My eyes landed on Lee's solemn face.

Lee said, "Looks to me like Aidan has had enough."

My vision blurred as I fought unshed tears. Don't cry! Kurt's grip tightened on my arm, he pressed me into a chair and whispered, "As your doctor I am advising you to be still and calm down."

I'm okay.

I heard Mac's voice behind me, he was speaking to Aidan in low, calm tones. I wondered where Caine was. He would have a full-blown fit over the whole, 'fuck you and the horse you rode in on' outburst. I was a little surprised that his hand hadn't grasped me warmly by the neck as soon as the words burst from my mouth.

She had no right to mention Mom. What was that bitch thinking?

Aidan's voice broke through. When I looked up, he was standing by Owen and had the book in his hand. He placed it back into the black plastic bag. Clutching the book to him protectively, he said with struggled calm, "If you get run over by a car, it shouldn't be listed as an accident."

Owen bristled. "Did you just threaten me?"

"No. If it was a threat I would have said 'When!'"

Owen nodded. "I am very sorry about your mother," she said with as much sincerity as a rattlesnake.

Aidan shrugged and turned away. As he neared me I saw a small smile on his lips. He whispered, "Ding dong the bitch is dead." I blinked, unsure if I had heard that or not. He touched my shoulder and said, "The poems, they're really good. The world needs more poetry."

"That wasn't your decision to make."

"I know. I'm sorry and I'm sorry she ruined it."

"Aidan, don't tell Dad; we'll tell him after his surgery tomorrow, when he's stronger."

"Okay." He smiled. Everything Mom stole from him was in that smile: His lost childhood and lost innocence.

"Go with Lee, everything's going to be fine."

How many times had I said that to him? Too many to count. Normally I followed it by saying, 'I'll take care of it Aidan, don't worry.' It's what big sisters do. It's part of my job description.

"Are you coming?"

"Soon."

Lee placed a meaty paw on Aidan's shoulder, "Come on bud, let's get you to your Dad."

Mac sat down next to me. "Caine is still on the phone. You okay?"

"Yep, I'm okay." My head is going to explode in tiny messy pieces and cover Owen's tasteful suit, and bits of brain matter will lodge in her perfect red hair. But apart from that, I am okay.

"Liar," he whispered with a smile.

I smiled back and with my voice just above a whisper replied, "We have no motive. I don't like our chances of a confession from this guy, he's too clever for that and without a motive, we're fucked."

Mac hugged me hard. "Have a bit of faith. We've got a sample of his handwriting from your yearbook."

I grimaced. "Writing bad poetry isn't yet a federal crime."

Although I often thought it should be; we've read some bad poetry over the years that would even make the Son of Shakespeare cringe. Thinking of poetry caused a well of sadness as I remembered the friends from our poetry room who'd died.

"What about leaving bad poems stuck to dead bodies?"

"Unless we can prove he was the one who did the killing." A smile crept in. "Although this could be a case of serial bad poetry. If it's serial it should come within the DeltA-Team perimeters, therefore making it federal."

Mac grinned. "Let's hope his computer will turn up some irrefutable evidence."

Kurt moved, turning in his seat towards us, "If Boyd is responsible there will be something, no matter how good he is." His voice dropped even lower, "It's been my experience that people who kill, as he supposedly has, tend to be quite proud of their achievements. Some even document each death to relive it later."

"You think he'd store something like that on his computer?"

"Hell, no, but he may store it in cyber space. We will find it, if it exists."

"I might know where to look," Mac said chewing his lip, "Got a laptop?"

"I'll fetch it." Kurt hurried back to the annexed room. He returned seconds later.

"Caine's looking grim."

I smiled. "How could you tell?"

Kurt grinned. "Same way you can. Years of experience."

Mac tapped away on the computer. We watched as he accessed our Cobwebs group site and started reading his way through screeds of information by members. Using owner privilege, we could access private areas of the site used by individual members. Many kept online journals; some were public, others weren't.

He typed in Addict_man. We waited as Mac scrolled through screens and screens of poems. I had almost forgotten Owen was still in the room, until her fingernails clicked annoyingly from the far end of the table.

She spoke somewhat reticently, "May I ask what you are all doing?"

Kurt replied in a smooth tone, "Looking for something. We'll let you know if we find it."

"What was the name linked to the photos on this site, the ones with the key loggers embedded?" Mac asked.

"Poetman," I replied.

"Ah, yes." Mac typed again. "Poetman has a journal. The first entry is seven months ago. There are links in here to other websites. Let's go see what they're about." Mac brought up the first web page; it was to a secure site and we didn't have the password. "Kurt, can you get us in?" He pushed the laptop past me to Kurt's outstretched hand.

"This could take a long while, but it's worth a shot." He opened another program and set it running.

"How long?" I asked.

"From minutes to hours – depending on the encryption."

"And then?"

"Hopefully, we'll have either a password or a way to

bypass the security features."

"We need another laptop." Mac looked at Lee's which was still sitting open on the table in front of his empty chair.

Owen looked over, "Go ahead if you need it use it."

Mac retrieved the laptop just as Lee walked in, "Do you mind?" he asked.

"Nope, you go right ahead." Lee pulled a chair over and sat with us, "Sam is coming up."

Mac grinned. "Did I really call him Mr. T?"

"Yeah, you really did," Lee and I replied together. Kurt frowned as if he'd missed something.

"So what are we doing?"

"Kurt is running a program to hack his way into a site we think may contain a journal written by the Unsub, and I am reading the other information he left on what used to be our group site."

"This Boyd fella, right?"

"Yeah." Mac looked as if he was going to say something else then stopped, he was frowning at the screen, "What do you suppose this means? It's part of a thread but it's been cut and pasted into his own notes ... 'I don't need to pretend I have a superpower, I am invisible always have been. The original invisible man. One day she will notice me.'"

"Sounds like we could be on the right track," I said sliding down in the chair and wondering if anyone was ever going to offer us coffee.

Caine strode into the room speaking, "I have two

agents from the Richmond office talking to Grandma Vanderguard now. I got a call back from them saying Boyd has stayed at his grandmother's and there is a computer in his bedroom. Grandma was very helpful and let them nosy about a bit; they saw a journal on his dressing table. He lived with Grandma during High School, didn't get on with his father." He twitched.

Caine's phone rang. He frowned at the display. "Check this out Ellie. This is a picture on Grandma's mantelpiece."

He passed me the phone. You gotta love technology and pxt capable phones. I couldn't quite believe what I was seeing. It didn't matter how hard I squinted at the small screen, it still made zero sense. "What the fuck?"

"That's a picture of Boyd and his girlfriend." Caine's twitch was the most dramatic I had ever seen. He was doing his own special version of an all-out delighted grin.

"That's me!" I said. At that point, Mac grabbed the phone from me to look then passed it to Kurt and Lee.

"Yeah," Caine replied. "It was on display. We don't need a warrant to see displayed photographs. What's even better is Grandma has loaned the photograph to us and I had someone pick up your yearbook, Ellie. We have compared the handwriting with several of the poems found on the bodies. We have a positive match even though that sample was twelve years old."

They sure weren't mucking around! Gone are the days when investigations take forever. The computer age made everything more accessible and easier. "Did Richmond field office do the analysis?"

"They did. The samples will be sent to the Questioned Documents Lab tomorrow for confirmation, but we have a match."

"I doubt they'll turn down a warrant request now. I have a call into the District Attorney. She is talking to a judge as we speak."

"Do you get the feeling this guy never expected to be caught?"

"If Mac hadn't seen your year book we wouldn't even have him as a suspect. I doubt he ever considered he'd be caught." Caine's phone rang. He answered it as he walked away from us and paced by the far wall, then made his way back to us. "Ellie, did you ever date Charles Boyd?"

"No."

He turned his attention back to the call. I still couldn't believe this moron had a photograph of me on his grandma's mantle. His girlfriend? Not in this lifetime!

Mac, Lee, and Kurt found the picture amusing. I was less amused, more disgusted and creeped out. He told his Grandma I was his girlfriend. Freak!

Caine's phone rang yet again, when he'd finished he sat down next to Owen; they conversed then he made an announcement.

"The warrant has arrived on the scene, complete with the District Attorney who will be staying for the search. All evidence will be brought here accompanied by the DA."

Owen nodded. Caine continued, "Boyd still hasn't been

located but we believe he may still be in the hospital."

I didn't want him still in the building. "Dad?"

"We have FBI and military police guarding your father. Sam has briefed Mac's Dad. He has also been armed."

"Can we move Dad?"

"We're looking into it, Ellie, waiting on a doctor's report to see if he's stable enough, if so we can use military medivac to fly him to Langley Air force Base"

"Does Dad know?"

"He knows we would like to move him for security reasons. He is reluctant and would like to discuss it with you."

He would be reluctant. He would be worried about Aidan and me, and then there was Mom. He had no idea about his wife.

Owen sat up straighter in her chair; her shoulders almost touched Caine's. "If you would like to go to your father, Ellie, I can have Kurt and Lee provide escort for you. We have a wheelchair available."

Escort me? It's not as if Mac would let me go anywhere without him. There's not going to be a wheelchair.

"Thanks, but that's not necessary. I can manage." Nothing and nobody would get past Mac. I didn't need anyone else running interference.

Caine shook his head. Owen pursed her lips. She wasn't so perfect after all. I noticed her lipstick had worn off in patches.

Caine's mouth became a no-nonsense straight line. His jaw squared as he choked out his favorite phrase, "Not in this lifetime!"

I almost smiled but suppressed the urge.

"You and Mac are in danger. You will not be going anywhere alone until this prick is sitting in front of me in handcuffs." He almost cut me with his sharp glance.

Uh huh, no telling how many times he could photograph me without my knowledge. My skin crawled as it dawned on me just how much he had invaded my privacy and how deluded he was. I'm okay. We'll all be okay.

Kurt interrupted, "It's done. I got in to this site. He kept a detailed diary. Looks like after each kill he wrote up his notes. And he's been sharing the details with other freaks on the site."

"Is there anything identifying him as Charles Boyd?" Caine asked tapping his fingers on the tabletop.

"No. Let's hope his own computer will show us a link; there is no way anyone but the Unsub could know these details. His record-keeping is meticulous, right down to the exact position of the bodies when discovered," Kurt said. "He knew Roy Matheson was DEA before he killed him. There are photographs on here."

"Photographs?" Caine sounded interested.

The thought of more pictures made me shudder.

"Before and after shots, the first pictures are of Karen Midlow. They're all dated: I'm downloading everything." Kurt leaned back, away from the screen he'd been hunched over. "I found photographs of Special Agent Kilby, there is a description of where his body is and an address."

“Where?” Caine asked, with his phone poised ready to issue retrieval instructions.

“Boyd left Agent Kilby in a public toilet two blocks away from a McDonald’s drive-thru. Looks like he dumped him in a hurry, he mentioned he didn’t write a poem or display him properly.”

Caine issued the instructions to the team who were conducting a scene investigation at the drive-thru we’d used.

I stood up and stretched, working some of the tension from my muscles. I was beginning to feel like a taut spring. A massage would be wonderful. Coffee would be superb.

“Anything about Karen in that journal? In particular why he held onto her so long before dumping her?”

Kurt scrolled for a few minutes. “Midlow is the key. She was the first kill. If we can understand why she was killed then the rest will fall into place.” He looked across the room at me. “He’s uploading to this journal within minutes of these acts. It’s possible he was in a car not far from those dumpsters writing his sick little entry and posting it to the web from his car.”

“He was watching?”

“I think so. Or at least for a little bit, he describes the look on your face as you climbed out of the dumpster. He also says he kept her body at his grandmother’s in the garden shed; she was inside an old wooden chest. Looks like it was lined with heavy black plastic. I found more pictures.”

"There was heavy plastic in the dumpster. Why did he dump her when he did?"

"This guy is so proud of himself, he wrote everything down. He followed Aidan to the Salvation Army store, which gave him the idea of dumping Karen. He'd set up Aidan, knew you would want to see what he dropped off and all he had to do was remove the boxes Aidan left then place the body."

"And to think I overlooked this scheming killer at High School. What was I thinking?"

The thought of a cigarette was now heavenly. I leaned against a wall and stretched some more. I felt eyes on me. It was unnerving. Mac, Kurt, and Lee were watching me.

"What?"

"You all right?" Mac's smooth voice stirred all manner of feelings inside me.

"I'm okay. Just getting a touch antsy is all."

Mac walked towards me. I felt my temperature rise as he neared. My back was against the wall. Mac's hands rested on either side of my head as he whispered, "You sure?"

My voice croaked as I replied, "I'm okay."

Kurt coughed.

"What?" I could see him from the corner of my eye. It's one thing to be watching me but why is he grinning like a fool?

"You two are so into each other." His smile resounded in his voice. "Get a room."

I dragged my eyes from Mac's and glowered at Kurt.

"Get back to work and tell my why Karen Midlow was his first!"

Kurt grinned and said, "I'm working on it. Let's get some coffee in here."

Finally, something I wanted to hear!

"I'll go on down to the cafeteria and get us some coffee, anyone want anything else?"

Caine spoke, "Just call down and get Sam to bring it all back." I heard an inflection in his voice that suggested he didn't want any of us leaving the room.

"Good plan." Lee punched in Sam's number.

"Sandwiches, Lee ... roast beef would be good," Mac said. He hadn't moved and I could feel my skin burning.

Lee's eyes rolled skyward as he fielded what I suspected were complaints from Sam. After a short discussion Lee told us Sam would be coming up with coffee and sandwiches.

We didn't have long to wait, Sam enlisted the help of an orderly and arrived in record time bearing trays of coffee and sandwiches. He stayed for a few minutes before excusing himself but not before speaking to Mac. I overheard three words that made me smile. "Five card stud."

I chuckled to myself. Our fathers were fleecing Sam. Bet they did more poker playing and drinking than they ever did fishing and hunting on their weekends away.

Chapter Thirty

Ring Of Fire

I looked at the date on the screen of my phone. Our days all had blurred into one. It was Wednesday, five o'clock in the morning. I drained my coffee cup and observed Mac puzzling over something. He spoke to Caine, "Walk me through this, will you?"

"What exactly?" Caine pulled a chair out and sat opposite us.

"What do these lab people do?"

I silenced my tongue before it could comment and share my latest insane notion triggered by Mac's question. I let the whole lab people thing settle. I refused my mind's efforts to conjure up yellow Labradors in white coats. They retrieved evidence and dropped it at Caine's feet. Refuse I did, conjure I most certainly did. Tails wagged frantically and drool dripped, as they anticipated a doggy treat. Stop it dammit!

"They do what we ask them to do," Caine replied.

Mac grinned. "This Boyd person is a lab technician, yes?"

I wished he'd stop saying Lab. I wished I didn't think such odd things.

"Yes." Caine used his patient training voice.

"So his role is what?"

"The role of lab personnel is a supporting role, but an

important part of the investigation process. We investigate crimes, we find evidence, and it's then documented, photographed and sent to the lab for testing," Caine paused for breath then continued his explanation, "For example, very basically ... we may find a handgun we think was used in a crime and have a bullet from a body we think came from that gun so both are sent to the ballistics lab. We ask if the bullet was fired by this particular weapon, and they tell us."

"Okay."

"They don't concern themselves with whose gun it is, that's our job; they just tell us if there's a match. We investigate the crime, they support the investigation or not as the case may be."

"What's their role in this case?"

"Same as always, the field investigators take evidence at the direction of the scene commander which is then taken to the lab. The lab tells us if it's relevant and hopefully can offer us a narrower field of inquiry, or suggest an avenue from the discoveries they have made, or confirm what we suspect happened," Caine said.

"Boyd was in the field this time, yes?"

"Yeah."

"I don't remember seeing him."

"Why would you? They don't take statements. They come in and do their jobs. They're the guys and gals on their hands and knees with a pair of tweezers, cotton swabs and a spray bottle of luminol."

I watched Mac; his facial expressions fascinated me

and I knew, once he started chewing his bottom lip, he was in serious thought mode.

He stopped chewing his lip. “Question.”

“Go ahead.”

“When Ellie was attacked at my home ... was Boyd at that scene also?”

I knew where he was going with this. If Boyd was the one who attacked me, he would have had very fresh deep scratches somewhere obvious, possibly his face or neck. Someone may have noticed.

Caine pulled a laptop closer and typed, he brought up a list of everyone at that scene. “He’s not on this list. One sec.” He typed again then paused, his eyes narrowed to small slits. “He was on call and unable to be reached. He was spoken to some hours later and produced a medical certificate stating that he was receiving attention for an injury at the time of the call.”

“Don’t suppose it says what type of injury?” Now I was interested and pleased the whole dog scenario had stopped.

“No.”

“And there was no reason to investigate that further?”

“None whatsoever; he was part of a forensic team put together for this case and had zero connection to you, as far as we knew.”

“How many crime scenes did he attend?” Curiosity began to choose my questions for me, with about as much finesse as a wolf going after a fresh blood.

Caine typed again, he leaned back, and stared at the

screen, “Information isn’t available.”

“Why the hell not?”

He gave me a long cold look. “I don’t know. What do I look like – the help desk?”

“No, that would be Mac.” It occurred to me that it had been eerily quiet in the printer phone call department since we’d left Fairfax. I should block more numbers.

Kurt was taking a break from reading; it was Lee’s turn to see first-hand how Boyd’s sick mind worked.

Lee grumbled something from our end of the table. Caine, who speaks fluent grumble, answered him, “Just give me a brief synopsis.”

Mac and I listened in silence as Lee cleared his throat then began, “I found a documented reason why he wanted Mac and Ellie together. It was here inside this delightful online journal.” Lee paused before sharing, “‘Once everyone else is disposed of’– his words – ‘Ellie and Mac will have cemented their relationship. Aidan will be arrested, as no other suspect could have known so much about Ellie.’ He rambles on a bit here then this ... ‘Once faced with multiple murder charges, my forensic evidence will help secure those convictions and ultimately he will end up on death row. Ellie, devastated by his guilt, will leave the Bureau.’ Boyd writes that six months after Aidan’s incarceration he plans to kill Mac. The next section is headed ‘The final blow. Ellie will be alone, destroyed. I shall swoop in.’ He says here he plans to kill her slowly over time. His last comment in this thing is ‘Do you see me now, bitch?’”

"Sick fuck!" Mac growled.

"Why?" I still don't get it, why is he doing this.

Mac rolled his eyes at me. "Why is he a sick fuck?"

I grinned and adopted a condescending tone, "You're so pretty."

Mac chuckled. "You are such a smartass."

"It's all part of my intrinsic charm." I was trying not to laugh at Mac. "So why is he doing this?"

Owen's lilting voice carried across the room, "I have a theory on that, Ellie."

I had forgotten Owen was there again; it's amazing what you can block out when you want to. I was all ears. Executive Assistant Director Owen had a theory! Someone should record this for posterity.

Mac's hand landed on my thigh, he applied slight pressure and whispered, "Listen and be nice." His tone implied that was a difficult thing for me to do.

For a split second, I wondered if my thoughts had somehow escaped from my mouth. Caine wasn't glaring at me so they couldn't have.

"I've been doing some digging while we waited," Owen said.

Gosh, hope she didn't chip a nail or get dirt on her hands. Mac's fingers squeezed my thigh again. Maybe Mac could hear my thoughts.

"I found some information from your senior year in High School. I have spoken to several of your teachers and your old Principal. I also have your school records, Vanderguard's and Karen Brown's."

Oh great! I took a breath and was about to make comment when Mac's hand applied more warning pressure. Ancient history revisited; yes, this is how I want to spend time. It wasn't fun the first time around. I doubt its going to be a blast this time either.

"And?"

"There was a complaint against Tommy Vanderguard made by Karen Brown."

I searched my difficult and uncooperative memory banks but couldn't recall it.

"What about?"

"Stalking. He had been following you and Karen."

Ohhh that!

"And that's it? He seems to have perfected his stalking technique since our school days."

"There's more. Every prize you took senior year, he came second."

I shrugged. I didn't know that. Why would I care? High School was only a means to an end. The end was escape from home.

"This I found interesting, you won the senior literary prize with a piece entitled an Ode to a Tree. He came second with prose entitled Shakespeare's Odyssey."

That was mildly interesting. Owen continued; she didn't seem to mind that I had no comment to make, "What was your grade point average, Ellie?"

"You know what it was, you have my records. I don't see the relevance."

"SAT score?"

"Again you have the records and I believe there is copy of my SAT scores in there."

Why was she doing this?

"Yes, I do know, but I don't know how many colleges you were accepted into. Let me hazard a guess: Every single one you applied to?"

I still don't see any relevance; she's right, but this is not pertinent to the murder investigation. "Where is this going?"

"After reading your school record, I see a very driven student. I see a student who didn't see what or who was around her, but focused on an end goal."

"How is that a bad thing?" I did have the feeling that this was going to be a bad thing. My perfect scores that I earned provided my way out. I did well and achieving is wrong?

She continued, "Some kids are bullied. Children of all ages can be viciously cruel. For some, it's name-calling and taunting. Others are beaten and then there are those kids who are ignored. Invisible kids, nobody sees them, no one cares. They don't exist, it doesn't matter how hard they work or how well they do. Someone is always beating them out of that one chance to shine, and back they go again to invisibility."

"So?" I never bullied anyone, ever. I never bullied anyone.

"Vanderguard was an invisible kid."

"So?" My mind flipped. "What are you saying? That he's a victim. I don't fuc'n think so!" Mac's fingers dug into my leg reminding me to pull my head in. "Sorry. I just don't see why we should provide a multiple murderer with victim status."

Mac's hand relaxed so I thought I was on the right track.

Owen looked me in the eye and asked, "Were you ever teased or bullied?"

"Yes, I was."

Courtesy of my mother I was one of those kids that went to school battered and bruised, often excused from sports by a note from my mother. Someone might have seen the bruises. She rarely marked my face, so I was lucky. Mac was one of those kids too.

I lowered my gaze to the table, composed myself somewhat, then dragged my eyes back up to meet Owen, "I was bullied and teased, and it wasn't fun. But I sure as hell didn't use my childhood as an excuse for my life."

"It's just a theory, Ellie. He seems to be after revenge and intent on extracting it from you. He perceives you as the enemy. How could he shine when you were always better? He couldn't even stand in reflected light because not only did you always win but you never saw him."

"It's an interesting theory. But as an adult he is not a victim, he made a conscious decision to carry out a plan that involved the brutal murders of innocent people. I'm not a big fan of the 'poor little me theory' at the best of times. There is no excuse for what he did."

"I'm not excusing it, Ellie. I am showing you a possible motive."

"Thank you."

"By the way, I wasn't in any way implying you were to blame for this. He has issues and fixated on you as the cause, sometimes its easier to blame than accept responsibility for our own shortcomings."

Issues? Imagine that!

"But I did ignore him."

She smiled. "For what it's worth I don't believe for one minute you intentionally ignored him."

She was doing it again, being nice. It was unnerving.

The niceness continued, "I think it would be best for you and your family if you rejoined them now."

"Excuse me?"

I couldn't decide if her smile was serene or condescending as she elaborated on her original thought. "Ellie, you have been through a lot. You need rest."

I was sure that I was hearing things. Things that sounded like Owen gave a shit. I must be sicker than I thought. A door opened behind us.

A large shadow fell over me followed by a voice that I knew, "Conway, you should be in bed."

I squinted into the deep shadow. "Sam?"

"Who'd you think it was, Mr T?" he said, with a huge gleaming grin, followed by a hearty chuckle.

Owen coughed politely. Once she had my attention she said, "Ellie, please go."

Something in her voice stopped my argument in its infancy. "Okay."

Kurt pushed his chair back and joined us at the door.

"I'm coming too." He looked towards the door. "Wheelchair?"

"Quit with the wheelchair comments! I can walk."

"You should be in a wheelchair," he replied.

"I'm not an invalid!'

Mac shook his head at Kurt, who joined us by the door.

"Miss Contrary here can argue till you're blue in the face," Mac said.

"If I said she can walk and didn't offer a wheelchair, you think she'd want one?" Kurt asked, looking over me at Mac.

"I think you're playing with fire," Mac replied then dropped his voice. "But you're right."

"I'm right here! And walking. Get over it," I responded, leaving no room for discussion. In that that instant, I proved to myself just how contrary I really was. I knew a wheelchair was smart; I knew I needed one. Yet with the offer made I clamored about it being unnecessary. Why can't I just take the easy way, just fucking once?

Sam nodded, understated as always, as he led the way.

Chapter Thirty-One

Ten Days

Dad rested. Aidan prowled the room. Bob sat in a chair close to Dad's bedside. I was relieved to see them all. My bed was still in the room and looked inviting. An empty chair was near my bed. The black plastic bag sitting on the bedside cabinet beside Dad reminded me we hadn't yet viewed this famed book. With much self-control I ignored it and sat up on my bed. Mac sat in the chair next to me. We exchanged smiles with Bob. Sam and Kurt were outside the door talking to two other agents and the military guards. The door remained closed so we couldn't hear their conversation, just the hum of their voices. It was early morning in a hospital.

"Any news?" Bob asked.

"They haven't got him yet, as far as we know," Mac replied. "It's looking like this Boyd guy is the Unsub."

Sam stepped into the room and beckoned to me. I slid off the bed and joined him outside the door.

"What?"

He handed me a cell phone, "It's Lee."

I smiled and answered the call, "What do you need?"

"I found the email account he was possibly running disposable addresses from, give me a likely password."

Without hesitation I replied, "Claude Rains."

"Damn, girl, that was quick, any other choices?"

"H.G. Wells."

I waited listening to him type then he said, "You sweetheart! Claude Rains it is. Thanks, Ellie."

"No problem. Do you yet know why Midlow was first?"

"She made the initial complaint against him in high school; seems he holds grudges. Most particularly, he held grudges against you and Karen Midlow. He didn't want her found first in case you made a connection."

I handed the phone back to Sam. He gave me a big grin. "How'd you get that password so quick?"

"Back in 1933 Claude Rains was *The Invisible Man.*" Maybe my head isn't full of useless information after all.

I went back into the room. Mac eyes wore an inquisitive expression. "Okay?"

"Yes. I'm just going to lie back on these pillows and wait for the news of Boyd's capture."

I could see no reason why I shouldn't lie down for a bit, Aidan was no longer a prime suspect. Everyone was looking for Boyd.

We were all safe. My head landed on the pillow. Mac sat on a chair next to the bed. Dad slept on. My eyes closed as I listened to the soft ping of the heart monitor and the low, hushed voices of Bob, Mac and Aidan.

Flames danced in the grate, they twisted around, and flickered at the last pieces of the old walnut tree. Coils of smoke rose from the orange and yellow flames, disappearing up the chimney. What's it like to be smoke? Visible in the fireplace and yet once outside it blended into the night. It blends into the mist of the night but the smell of woodsmoke lingers in the air. Smell is the most memorable of all sense. The fire warmed the room. Mom always liked an open fire. After the fire burned down she absolutely had to polish the next day because she said fires caused too much dust. I think she enjoyed the smell of furniture polish and the shine of gleaming wood.

Watching the flames from the comfort of the sofa I wondered why there was a fire in a hospital room, it didn't seem smart considering there was oxygen in use. I became aware of my fingers playing with the satin edging of a red blanket. The smell of the burning walnut grew ever stronger. In the corner of the room, I glimpsed white. It materialized into a larger white object as my eyes accustomed to the intrusion. A hospital bed, someone was in the bed. Fascinating, a hospital bed was in my parents' living room. I moved the red blanket aside and stood up cautiously. Unsure of why I was laying on the sofa to start with, and just in case I was ill, I decided I should move carefully. All seemed okay. When I reached the side of the bed I saw Mom, asleep. There was a familiar scent; as I stepped closer it vanished, when I stepped back it was there. I inhaled, what was the scent? I had smelled it before, a cologne maybe. I knew that smell. Where was it from?

A new voice in the room caused my hand to reach down to where Mac sat before my eyes opened properly. I felt for his holster. My fingers made contact with a recognizable shape, released the strap and tugged his gun free. Some skills were good to have, picking-pockets was not much different from swiping a gun.

I pulled my arm back obscuring the gun with my body.

I could see the new person: A man wearing a male nurse's uniform. He was maybe two feet from me I was looking at his back as he reached for the tubing of Dad's IV. Mac was closer to him than I was, but judging by the angle of Mac's head, he was asleep sitting up.

I could smell the scent. I looked over and saw Bob and Aidan in deep conversation, neither of them were watching the nurse or me. I sat up. My head reeled and keeping my hand steady was difficult.

"Stop. Turn around." At least my voice was strong. He didn't move. "Turn around."

Bob was now watching: His gun lay in his lap. Mac woke with a start, stood up from the chair, and blocked the nurse's exit.

The man turned and smiled. "Sorry to startle you, I was checking Mr. Conway's fluid."

I barked a little more than I had intended. "Step away from him."

"I'm a nurse!"

"Just do it. I'm a bitch with a gun and a headache."

He moved two paces left. I was now on his right and Mac still blocked his exit. "Place both hands on the bed."

"You're going to search me?"

"Is there anything sharp in your pockets or on your person?"

"I'm a nurse; of course there is."

"Remove all sharp objects and place them on the bed."

Mac and I made clear eye contact. A split second later I heard the door open and Bob's voice as he called the military police into the room.

The scent was stronger as the man removed scissors from his top pocket. "Anything else?"

"No."

I didn't believe him. I wasn't keen on searching him, but I did it anyway. I removed a roll of tape, a wallet, and a set of keys. From his trouser pocket, I gingerly removed a full syringe. It was firmly capped. "Care to explain this?"

"My next patient needs that."

I bet.

"Is it common practice to carry a loaded syringe in your trouser pocket?"

He shook his head. "I will get into serious trouble for that."

Mac took the wallet and removed the contents. No identification and three hundred dollars in cash.

"Where's your identification?" Mac scrutinized the man's face.

"I must've dropped it."

Didn't he just have all the answers? He wasn't even perspiring.

"We haven't seen you before." I glanced at Aidan for confirmation that he hadn't seen this man before either; he affirmed.

"My shift started half an hour ago."

"Name?"

"Jack Griffin."

A cog whirred inside my head. Jack Griffin. I knew that name. "The invisible man."

Claude Rains played Jack Griffin.

He smiled and there he was. Now he matched the picture I had seen. I grabbed hold of his right wrist and twisted it behind his back. One of the military police officers handed a pair of disposable cuffs to me. I pulled his other arm behind him and closed the cuffs. "Charles Boyd you are being detained pending the arrival of the FBI."

The two MP's stepped closer, one pulled Boyd out of the way and stood him by the far wall. The other assumed a position in front of the bed containing the contents of Boyd's pockets.

Mac hit a button on his cell phone. A few seconds later he said, "Caine, We have Charles Boyd in custody."

He looked at me. "He's on his way."

I smiled hoping to disguise the shakiness I felt.

"Ellie?" I didn't turn to the voice, for whatever reason I couldn't take my eyes off Boyd. I half expected him to evaporate into a smoky mist if I looked away.

"Yeah, Dad."

"Thank you."

"No problem."

I heard pounding feet in the corridor coming closer and louder with every footfall. The noise halted. I imagined Caine, Kurt, Lee and Sam all straightening their suits, smoothing their ruffled feathers, as they prepared to enter the room, cool calm and collected.

Boyd's eyes hit the door then back to me; he spoke, even his voice was non-descript. "Can I ask how you knew?"

"The one thing you didn't mask ... your cologne."

ABOUT THE AUTHOR

Cat Connor is a prolific crime thriller author hailing from New Zealand. Her expertise in the genre is reflected in her engaging and suspenseful narratives, which have garnered a loyal following. Her work is known for its intricate plots, dynamic characters, and relentless pace, keeping readers on the edge of their seats until the very end. She has authored multiple books, including the popular "Byte" series, which follows the exploits of an FBI unit that investigates serial crime.

Cat's passion for crime and espionage is evident in her writing, as she strives to create a world that is both authentic and thrilling. Her meticulous attention to detail and extensive research have won her critical acclaim and accolades from readers and peers alike. In addition to writing, Cat enjoys speaking on topics related to writing and publishing. Her talks are known for their candidness, humour, and practical advice. With her unique blend of talent, expertise, and passion, Cat Connor has established herself as one of the most exciting and accomplished authors in the crime thriller genre.

Her other passions include music, reading, tequila, red wine, coffee, and chocolate. When she's not writing she can be found binge watching TV shows and spending time with her much adored animals; Diesel the mastador, Patrick the tuxedo cat, Dallas the tortie Birman, and Jimmy the thug.

You can follow and contact Cat at the following places:

Website: www.catconnor.com
Twitter: @catconnor
Facebook: @cat.connor
Instagram: @catconnorauthor
Bluesky: @catconnor.bsky.social
Threads: @catconnorauthor

We hope you enjoyed Killerbyte by Cat Connor. Please turn the page for a preview of another exciting Ellie Conway story: Terrorbyte.

TERRORBYTE

Chapter One
If That's What It Takes

"Are you sure this is the alleyway?" I stared down the dreary lane, hoping Lee would say no.

The whole place reeked of urine and discarded syringes. With a sense of foreboding, I pulled my badge from my pocket and hung it around my neck by the lanyard. My eyes flicked up and down the close walls of the alley, looking for cameras. I spotted a bracket that may have once held a camera. How handy.

A heavy bulletproof vest hung from my arm. Begrudgingly, I pulled it on. They were uncomfortable and I preferred not to wear one unless absolutely necessary. Lee already had his on. They were definitely better suited to male bodies.

"This is the one she said," he replied, and slung his badge over his head. Lee didn't seem in any hurry to venture in.

"This is exactly how I imagined my Saturday morning would be," I said with a wry grin.

"Yep, me too. Life is good."

"Where's the nearest camera?" I asked.

"The bank, beside the alleyway. They have two cameras located on an outside wall, both covering the street."

"If we don't find anything we'll go visit the bank. We might get lucky with their footage."

Lee nodded. I was tempted to abandon the alley in favor of the bank right off.

I pulled the hair tie from my ponytail, scraped my hair back off my face and retied it higher and tighter. I felt a prickling sensation in the pit of my stomach. Adrenaline surged.

"Ready to rock?"

"Right with you, Ellie."

I stepped into the deep shade of the brick buildings that surrounded the alley, took a breath of cool air and decided it might be a pleasant place to spend an hour. A blast of strong urine odor hit the back of my throat and I changed my mind.

Lee flipped out his notebook and scanned a few pages. "The girl, Rose Van den Berg, said she looked back and saw a blue door with chipped peeling paint."

The door nearest me was a rusty red so I continued walking. Lee caught up in two strides and fell into step. The next door was a faded green showing patches of pink undercoat. We glanced at each other and moved on, noting two large dumpsters against the opposite wall just past the green door. At the end of the shadow-shrouded alley were two more dumpsters. I took an unfortunately large breath – stale, foul air caught in my throat, making me choke. I coughed into my elbow, trying to limit the noise and not hack up a lung.

I looked left: a blank brick wall rose up blocking out

the sky. No windows or doors broke the monotonous wall. I kicked at discarded fast-food wrappers tangling around my boots.

"There it is." Lee said. His notebook was gone, in its place a Glock 22.

We were about ten feet from the door. Above our heads were small frosted louver windows. I counted three windows. The door appeared to have an opaque glass panel at the top, but on closer inspection, it was dirt that obscured the glass. I removed my gun from my hip holster: it was time to see if this was the place the girl remembered. The place she said she was held captive and the last place she saw her older sister.

We approached the door with caution. If the shit hit the fan there was no cover. We'd be in the open until we reached the dumpsters.

Lee knocked. We both stood to the hinge side of the door, against the grimy brick.

Inside, someone shouted. The words were unintelligible. Maybe it wasn't English.

Lee knocked again.

Another voice called out.

Again, I couldn't understand the words.

I shook my head at Lee.

He reached over and knocked again, this time he followed up with a deep bellow, "FBI. Open the door."

Noise erupted. Yelling. Shuffling. Panic.

It is peculiar how some people react to us. You'd think the bad guys would learn to control their outbursts and better disguise their guilt. But not so much. Few people we come across are pleased to have us knock on their door.

Lee kicked the door in and stepped inside. I followed. Two men sat calmly at a filthy table. Not a sign of the panic we'd heard.

"FBI. Who else is here?"

They shook their heads. Language flew from the older man's lips as he gestured wildly with nicotine-stained fingers. Some things are universal.

"English?" I asked.

They shook their heads.

I had no idea what language they were speaking. I took clues from their appearance: swarthy, lined and leathery skin, dark eyes, dark curly hair. Mediterranean maybe. Greek possibly.

I lifted my radio from my belt and called in our back-up. Sam and a few other agents, in a concealed position out of the alleyway, were waiting for my call. Lee cuffed the two men and sat them back-to-back in the middle of the room on the rickety chairs.

He showed them the photo of Rose.

"Seen her?" he asked.

One man flinched; the other stared with cold dark eyes. Somewhere in the back, I could hear movement.

"Leave them," I hissed. "Let's do it."

I opened the inner door. A long hallway stretched away from us with a bare light bulb hanging from a wire. It gave off enough light to see four doors in the hall. We stood for a moment, listening.

"To the right," Lee said. "Could be Albanian." He cocked his head back towards the other room.

I nodded. I'd considered Greek, so I was geographically close.

I lifted my radio off my belt once more and updated the situation; our backup had already rolled into the alley. A smile flickered across Lee's face as he heard Sam's voice in the room behind us. It gave me a sense of security knowing he was there; it was probably the same for Lee.

Lee and I moved fast yet silently. The inner hallway was filled with hot sticky air, the kind of air that hurt to breathe. We located the door from where the noise seemed to be coming. We looked at each other from separate sides of the doorway. I held up two fingers. He nodded.

Lee turned the handle. It wasn't locked.

A scream bounced off the walls. Lee shoved the door open. In front of us, another swarthy man held a blonde girl against him, one hand clamped on her forehead, his free hand holding a knife to her throat. The blade pressed into the white flesh of her neck. Tears slid down her face. A trickle of red ran down her neck.

I trained my weapon on his head. Lee looked for a body shot, through the hostage if necessary. The girl looked like Rose.

"FBI," I said in a clear voice. "Drop the knife."

"No," he replied and shook his head.

Whatever.

"Have it your way," Lee snarled.

The girl sobbed. The man's grip tightened.

My palms were sweaty. He pressed the knife harder against her. I pulled the trigger. It seemed to take forever for the bullet to leave the chamber and hit the mark. A hole appeared in his forehead; his expression didn't change. He fell very slowly. Lee grabbed the girl and lifted her clear. He took her straight out of the room and handed her to a waiting agent and was back within seconds.

I stepped forward, kicked the knife away from the body and checked for a pulse. It seemed pointless as a pool of red grew quickly around his head and threatened my boots.

I rifled through the pockets of the dead man. No wallet, no identity information, not even a driver's license. Being close to him was unpleasant. I felt myself gag as his body odor and the smell from the pooling blood mingled into a cloying stench.

"Nothing," I said to Lee. "This fucker hasn't showered for a month. I can't believe the air in the alley is preferable to being near him."

Another voice sounded behind Lee. "You okay in there, Ellie?" It was Sam.

"Yep." I pulled my phone and snapped a picture of the man. "Search the rest of this place and call in the forensics team. Is there an ambulance for the girl?"

"Called already, she's with the paramedics now. We're

already searching," Sam replied.

Lee checked his cell phone then spoke to me, "Caine wants to see you, Ellie."

"He text you?"

"Yeah."

"Imagine that?"

Caine had been adamant for the last few years that he wouldn't be texting any of us, ever. In his words, he preferred to call and hear our delightful voices. And here he was texting. The old dog was learning new tricks and life was twisting on the weird scale. I was happy to leave the rapidly building stench coming from the dearly departed. My body craved oxygen, even the urine-filtered air of the alleyway would suffice for now.

I strode through the door, leaving Lee with Sam. They headed off to help with the search. Caine was waiting in the outer room by the alley door. We stood just inside the doorway.

"That kid, she's the sister of Rose Van den Berg. They're Dutch nationals, both reported missing six months ago," Caine said.

"From where?"

"They went missing in Johannesburg."

I sensed a backstory worthy of taking a few minutes to hear. "I'm listening," I said.

"They were traveling with their grandfather from the Netherlands to Johannesburg. At O.R Tambo International airport, immigration officials questioned the grandfather, saying they believed he was trafficking the girls. He produced their travel documents and assured the officials they were his grandchildren. Yet he was told he would have to go to the police station. The girls were not allowed to accompany him but he was guaranteed that customs officials would watch them. He never saw them again."

"Clever."

"When he arrived home, empty-handed, police in the Netherlands told him he was not the first person to fall victim to this particular scam."

"Interpol?"

"That's where we got the information."

We walked out to the ambulance.

"You're okay?" Caine asked.

I removed my vest, rotated my shoulders, working out the tension from the adrenaline that had flooded my body before and during the takedown.

I nodded. A wave of relief hit me, knowing we'd reunited the sisters and they were alive. Alive is good. Sometimes it's not all bad news.

"What condition is the body in?"

"You're going to need to use prints to identify the perp," I replied.

"That bad?" He raised an eyebrow.

I grinned. "Nah, he had no identification on him. My bullet hit him right in the middle of the forehead. Plenty of face left for family to view, if he has any here."

"We don't negotiate." His tone conveyed no room for what-ifs. "These idiots need to learn that and learn it well. Was the kid in immediate danger?"

We stopped in front of the ambulance, where Caine could see the girl receiving medical attention for a small neck wound. She'd need one or two stitches. I could see a Hudson mask on the gurney next to her and wished I could reach in and borrow it. Clean, cool oxygen would rid my lungs of the foul air I'd breathed.

"Yes, she was," I replied. I angled my body away from the scene in the ambulance.

He nodded. "Then it was the right call."

"How the hell did they end up in Washington?" I had questions.

"I'm hoping the girls can tell us."

"How'd the first kid escape?" The first two men we came across in the rooms weren't exactly spring chickens, and probably wouldn't be running after anyone. But the knife guy – the putrid smelling man – I knew he wouldn't let his meal tickets escape without a fight.

"She was left alone for a few minutes and discovered the door unlocked," Caine replied. "That indicates carelessness, and lack of experience in managing teenage kidnap victims, to me."

"An unlocked door? That was one lucky break and one feisty kid."

"Yes," Caine replied.

"Are we handling this?" It didn't seem like a case for Delta A.

"No, I'm passing it over to another team."

It was what I expected. We had dedicated teams that

specialized in finding lost kids and dealt with trafficking. A joint task force with ICE sprang to mind. I was immensely pleased to be out of that loop. I'd come across a particularly offensive Immigration and Customs Enforcement agent during another case. I certainly didn't want to repeat the experience. It begged the question of why we were called out in the first place.

"And we received the call – why?"

"I thought it might have been something else."

I shot him a questioning look. "Like?"

"We've got an ongoing case." He proceeded to explain. "Delta B team is working on a case involving an Albanian crime syndicate. So far, five dead: all with ties to the Albanians. When the kid described how she and her sister were taken and gave a description of the men that held them, the perps sounded Albanian to me."

The penny poised but didn't drop. Albanians were linked to human trafficking in both the United Kingdom and Belgium but, as far as I knew, here in the United States they were involved in drugs and general thuggery.

"Have the Albanians spread their human trafficking wings to include South Africa and here?" I asked.

"Not as far as we can tell. Everything we've seen so far suggests that this is an anomaly," Caine replied. He seemed certain, yet there was something ticking away under the surface. I could feel it.

My left eyebrow rose. "And, is this connected to Delta B's case?"

Caine's mouth twitched. "Different Albanians, but

might be good for some information."

"I take it we're the only team working in Northern Virginia?"

We may all be Delta, but we were often separate teams. Caine was Delta's Special Agent in Charge. He moved between us, helping whichever team needed him. Sometimes we all worked together but mostly the nine of us made up three teams to give better coverage.

"Yes, B is in New Jersey. All the murder victims were found in Long Beach." The sides of his mouth twitched so violently he almost smiled. "C is offering assistance down in Georgia where some market gardener dug up a few bodies."

I checked my watch. I really needed to get going. "I'll write my report then head home," I said.

"We'll all see you tonight," Caine said. "How's Mac coping with the fuss?"

I smiled. "Badly."

"He's probably made the connection between speeches and microphones," Caine said with a massive upper lip spasm.

"I'm sure he has." There was no stopping the smile on my face. Caine twitched his lips into a frightening grimace. "I don't know that we've helped him any by razzing him about the things he said while under the influence."

"I think you'll find it wasn't 'we'," Caine replied, pointing at me, then himself.

"No, it wasn't you," I agreed.

It was me, Sam and Lee. Mostly me. Memories of Mac

spaced out on Ketamine, courtesy of the Son of Shakespeare, were never far away. Memories of Mac and his rainbow people amused me on a daily basis; in the main, I kept them to myself.

"Wipe that grin off your face, Ellie. It's hard enough for him to move past calling Sam 'Mr. T' as it is."

Then I saw it. Suppressed amusement. He did find it funny.

"See you tonight," I said.

"Let me know if you need a persuasive escort," Caine said. His voice dropped to barely a whisper. "I'll have Mr. T and his pal, General Lee, pick him up."

I imagined Mac handcuffed and escorted to dinner. It was amusing but possibly necessary.

"Will do."

9MM PRESS

www.ingramcontent.com/pod-product-compliance
Lightning Source LLC
LaVergne TN
LVHW041054080826
845145LV00007B/1565
* 9 7 8 1 7 3 8 6 2 1 9 6 5 *